ASK A POLICEMAN

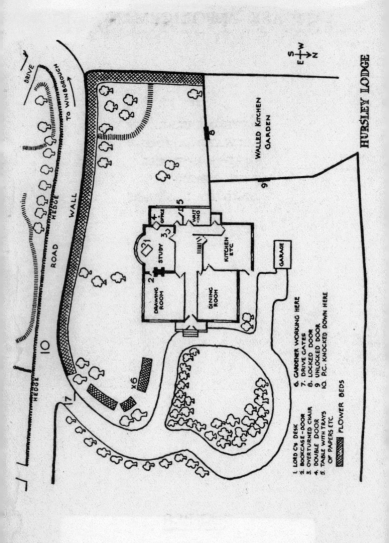

HURSLEY LODGE

DRIVE

To WINBOROUGH

ROAD HEDGE

WALL

HEDGE

10

7

WALLED KITCHEN GARDEN

8

9

GARAGE

KITCHEN ETC

DINING ROOM

DRAWING ROOM

STUDY

2

1

3

5

OFFICE

WAIT-ING

×6

N
E
S
W

1. LORD C'N DESK
2. BOOKCASE + DOOR
3. OVERTURNED CHAIR
4. DOUBLE DOOR
5. TABLE WITH TRAYS OF PAPERS ETC.
6. GARDENER WORKING HERE
7. DRIVE GATES
8. LOCKED DOOR
9. UNLOCKED DOOR
10. P.C. KNOCKED DOWN HERE

▨ FLOWER BEDS

ASK A POLICEMAN

BY

ANTHONY BERKELEY

MILWARD KENNEDY

GLADYS MITCHELL

JOHN RHODE

DOROTHY L. SAYERS

&

HELEN SIMPSON

HARPER

An imprint of HarperCollins*Publishers*
77–85 Fulham Palace Road
Hammersmith, London W6 8JB
www.harpercollins.co.uk

This 80th anniversary edition published in 2013

1

First published in Great Britain by
Arthur Barker Ltd 1933

ISBN 978-0-00-746863-8

Printed and bound in Great Britain by
Clays Ltd, St Ives plc

Find out more about HarperCollins and the environment at
www.harpercollins.co.uk/green

FOREWORD

ASK A DETECTIVE WRITER

By Martin Edwards

Ask a Policeman, first published in 1933, was the fourth in a sequence of collaborative mysteries produced in quick succession by members of the Detection Club. The Club was set up three years before this book was written, as an elite and rather secretive social network of leading detective novelists. It continues to flourish to this day, although current members include prominent thriller and espionage writers as well as specialists in the whodunit.

Ask a Policeman followed two radio serials, *Behind the Screen* and *The Scoop*, and a full-length detective novel, *The Floating Admiral*. These collective ventures generated enough revenue for the Club to rent premises in Soho, where, as Dorothy L. Sayers put it, members convened "chiefly for the purpose of eating dinners together and of talking illimitable shop."

In the early Thirties, detective fiction was hugely popular, and many writers treated the detective story as a game in which they pitted their wits against their readers'. It was supposed to be important to "play fair". Father Ronald Knox, a founder member of the Club, went so far as to devise a jokey Decalogue of ten commandments for the genre ("not more than one secret room or passage is allowable", for instance)—which he and his colleagues were happy to break whenever it suited them.

Anthony Berkeley, who organized the dinner meetings that led to the foundation of the Club, and Dorothy L. Sayers, a towering presence in its ranks, headed a group of talented crime writers who became increasingly determined to explore criminal psychology and write novels of literary merit. Yet they too relished the intellectual exercise of creating elaborate puzzles.

Writing a round-robin mystery presents a variety of challenges for any team of authors, and Club members had to decide how to top the success of *The Floating Admiral*. Their answer was to come up with a fresh concept—they would write a story in which they exchanged detectives with each other. This gimmick afforded contributors the chance to poke fun at the genre, and at the quirks of their colleagues' most famous sleuths. But transforming the idea into a readable story was bound to prove complex, with each contributor in turn needing plenty of space to develop the narrative in a distinctive way. This explains why, although 13 members provided ingredients for the mix in *The Floating Admiral*, just half a dozen created *Ask a Policeman*.

The original dust jacket blurb captured the gleeful spirit of the enterprise:

"Here is something delightfully new in 'thrills'—a story which combines the interest of detection with the fun of parody. A problem is propounded; ingenious, and, for the solvers, malicious, and in itself a parody of a thousand and one detective stories. A great newspaper proprietor dies in his study, and suspicion falls upon an Archbishop, a Secretary, a Police Commissioner, and the Chief Whip of the political party in power. There is, too, a Mysterious Lady. What, then, can the Home Secretary do but call in the Amateur Experts? There are four of them; each takes a hand and each produces a different solution."

The industrious and prolific John Rhode set the scene in a long introductory section. Rhode was the main pen-name of Cecil John Street (1884-1965), a former army officer who had won the Military Cross. His most famous detective was Dr. Lancelot Priestley, a rather severe intellectual who featured in a long line of novels but is absent here. Rhode was an efficient plot-builder, and created the perfect victim, a tyrannical media mogul whom every other character in the story seemed to have a possible motive to kill. In keeping with the fashion of the time, a plan of the scene of the crime was included.

The story was introduced by an exchange of letters between Rhode and Milward Kennedy. Kennedy (1894-1968) also concealed his identity under several pseudonyms—his real name was Milward Rodon Kennedy Burge. He worked in Military Intelligence during the First World War, and was awarded the *Croix de Guerre* prior to taking up a career in diplomacy. Like Anthony Berkeley, he wanted to push out the boundaries of the detective story, and several of his books experiment with the form. None of his characters, however, appeared in more than two books, and the absence of a series detective may help to explain why his fame did not last. To Kennedy fell the unenviable task of tying up the loose ends of the story, and one of the in-jokes of this book is that he gave the job of making sense of the case that had taxed Lord Peter Wimsey and others to a character who was, like himself, a civil servant. Another is his tongue-in-cheek admission to breaking the "Rules to which my fellow members of the Detection Club always, and I on all occasions but this, make it a point of honour to adhere".

Once Rhode had set the scene, the baton passed to Helen Simpson. Born in Sydney in 1897, she was both gifted and charismatic; Sayers, a close friend, said after Simpson's untimely death from cancer in 1940, "I have never met anybody who equalled her in vivid personality and in the intense interest she brought into her contacts with people and things." Simpson tried her hand at poetry and plays before collaborating with Clemence Dane on *Enter Sir John*, which introduced Sir John Samaurez, the actor-manager of the Sheridan Theatre. Sir John sets about clearing the name of a young actress who has been charged with murder, and makes such a success of the task that, by the time *Ask a Policeman* appeared, the two of them are husband and wife. *Enter Sir John* was turned into a film by Alfred Hitchcock called *Murder!* Simpson co-wrote two more books with Dane, as well as producing several solo novels, including *Under Capricorn*, which later became another Hitchcock movie. Turning to politics, Simpson was adopted as Liberal Parliamentary Candidate for the Isle of Wight before the cruel intervention of the disease that killed her. The energy, wit and skill with which, in this book, she tackles her portrayal of Gladys Mitchell's detective, Mrs. Bradley, seem typical of how she approached everything in her life.

Gladys Mitchell had been elected to membership of the Club shortly before this book was written. She too admired Simpson, describing her in an interview with B.A. Pike as "brilliant, witty, charming and highly intellectual"; she even allowed Simpson to bestow a second forename, Adela, upon her detective. Mitchell (1901-1983), combined writing with a career as a schoolteacher; she introduced Mrs. Bradley in a convention-defying mystery called *Speedy Death*, and continued to write about her for more than half a century. Her books often contain bizarre elements, but she attracted a devoted band of readers, including Philip Larkin, who called her "the Great Gladys". Mrs. Bradley, a psychiatrist and consultant psychologist to the Home Office, has the looks of a "sinister pterodactyl", but when *The Mrs. Bradley Mysteries* aired on BBC Television in 1998-9, she was played by Diana Rigg, a casting decision so eccentric as to be worthy of Mitchell herself.

Anthony Berkeley was one of crime fiction's leading innovators. His real name was Anthony Berkeley Cox (1893-1971), and he wrote a good many humorous articles for magazines before introducing Roger Sheringham in *The Layton Court Mystery*, which was at first published anonymously. Writing as Francis Iles, he produced groundbreaking—and deeply cynical—novels about crime, notably *Malice Aforethought* and *Before the Fact*; the latter was filmed by Hitchcock as *Suspicion*. The Sheringham mysteries often feature puzzles with ingenious multiple solutions; the most dazzling example, *The Poisoned Chocolates Case*, is name-checked by Sayers in this book. Berkeley liked to explore dilemmas about justice, and was intrigued by the idea of the fallible sleuth. So in his work, murderers sometimes escape unpunished, Sheringham does not always come up with the right solution to the mystery, and tricky plot devices are allied to a sharp, ironic wit. To take on the job of writing about Sayers' hero Lord Peter required some courage, as she was a formidable woman, held in awe by many of her Detection Club colleagues. But Berkeley rose to the challenge, and he captured Wimsey brilliantly, in a chapter that offers one of the finest of all Golden Age parodies as well as a clever solution to the problem Rhode had posed. Gladys Mitchell—who liked Berkeley rather more than Sayers—recalled in her old age that "Anthony's manipulation of Lord Peter Wimsey caused the massive lady anything but pleasure", but although in later years, these two strong, and often intimidating personalities came increasingly into conflict, it is hard to believe that Sayers failed to appreciate the flair displayed in Berkeley's contribution to *Ask a Policeman*.

At the time this book was written, Sayers was taking the detective story in a new direction. Wimsey had started out as little more than a caricature, albeit a caricature portrayed with affectionate humour. In *Whose Body?*, published in 1923, we are told that his "long amiable face looked as if it had generated spontaneously from his top hat, as white maggots breed from Gorgonzola". But once he met and fell in love with Harriet Vane, a detective novelist convicted of murder (was Sir John Samaurez' first case the inspiration for this idea?), he grew as a character. Sayers' depiction of his relationship with Harriet set the pattern for succeeding generations of crime writers, who preferred to create serious and believable protagonists with lives that change as the years pass, rather than 'supermen' detectives in the mould of Sherlock Holmes. Sayers (1893-1957) was self-consciously intellectual, and in her only non-series novel, *The Documents in the Case*, co-written with Robert Eustace, musings on the nature of life were integral to the plot. Sayers was dissatisfied with the end product, but her very attempt at such an ambitious undertaking showed that the genre had much more to offer than glorified crossword puzzles. In her chapter for *Ask a Policeman*, Sayers renders Sheringham effectively, with a neat joke when he overhears two employees of the late Lord Comstock being rude about him, and if the solution she puts forward is not quite as compelling as Berkeley's, perhaps that underlines her increasing focus on characterisation as opposed to mere puzzle-making.

After the start of the Second World War, however, she turned her attention away from crime writing, focusing on the translation of Dante, and writing about religious subjects. Similarly, Berkeley and Kennedy began to concentrate on reviewing rather than producing novels. But all three of them remained associated with the Detection Club, with Sayers holding the office of President from 1948 until her death.

Agatha Christie, who had participated in the first three Detection Club collaborations, sat this one out. However, it is a real pleasure to be able to include here a delightful essay she wrote about her fellow practitioners—the first time it has appeared in volume form. She wrote it in 1945, at the request of the Ministry of Information, for publication in a Russian magazine. Presumably because she was confident that none of her peers in the Detection Club would come across her comments, she was quite candid.

So it is interesting to see that Christie disapproved of Wimsey's transformation into a "handsome hero", and damned Rhode's prose style with faint praise as "straightforward", as well as to note her admiration for Anthony Berkeley's ability to provide first class entertainment. But she also made it clear that the writers she mentioned were those at the top of their profession. Today, though, not only are the books of H.C. Bailey, Rhode, Kennedy and many of their contemporaries forgotten by everyone except a small band of enthusiasts, surprisingly little is known about most of the Detection Club members themselves. I was honoured to be appointed as the first archivist of the Club— although the fact that the official archives are more or less non-existent is somehow typical of this unusual and mysterious institution. Its members—not just the usual suspects in Christie and Sayers, but also A.A. Milne and Baroness

Orczy, who in addition to their detective stories were the creators respectively of Winnie-the-Pooh and the Scarlet Pimpernel—played a much more significant part in developing popular culture in the twentieth century than has so far been recognized. Frustratingly, no minutes of meetings appear to have survived, and some of the reminiscences of early members are classics of unreliable narration. So the challenge of discovering more about the early days of the Club, and the lives of its members, is almost as fascinating as many of those Golden Age puzzles

Ask a Policeman is, when all is said and done, a period piece. Kennedy's solution does not really "play fair" with the reader, but the book is laden with charm as well as humour, and its reappearance is as welcome as it is overdue. Howard Haycraft, a noted American historian of the genre, hailed this book as "a matchless *tour de force*", and its success prompted plenty of other writers to parody the classic detective story. But few of them achieved such enjoyable results as the six members of the Detection Club who combined to create this lively entertainment.

PREFACE

DETECTIVE WRITERS IN ENGLAND

By Agatha Christie

What kind of people read detective stories and why? Invariably, I think, the busy people, the workers of the world. Highly placed men in the scientific world, even if they read nothing else, seem to have time for a detective story; perhaps because a detective story is complete relaxation, an escape from the realism of everyday life. It has, too, the tonic value of a puzzle—a challenge to the ingenuity. It sharpens your wits—makes you mentally alert. To follow a detective story closely you need concentration. To spot the criminal needs acumen and good reasoning powers. It has also a sporting interest and is much less expensive than betting on horses or gambling at cards! Its ethical background is usually sound. Very very rarely is the criminal the hero of the book! Society unites to hunt him down, and the reader can have all the fun of the chase without moving from a comfortable armchair.

Before speaking of present day English writers, I must first pay tribute to Conan Doyle, the pioneer of detective writing, with his two great creations Sherlock Holmes and Watson—Watson perhaps the greater creation of the two. Holmes after all has his properties, his violin, his dressing gown, his cocaine etc., whereas Watson has just himself—lovable, obtuse, faithful, maddening, guaranteed to be always wrong, and perpetually in a state of admiration! How badly we all need a Watson in our lives!

Most detective writing since then has been modelled roughly on the same structure. The detective is the "central character". But there has come to be something too artificial about a "private investigator". The essence of a detective story is that it shall be "natural" in its setting and characters. My own Hercule Poirot is often somewhat of an embarrassment to me—not in himself, but in the calling of his life. Would anyone go and "consult" him? One feels not. So, more and more, his entry into a murder drama has to be fortuitous. My Miss Marple is more happily placed—an elderly gossipy lady in a small village, who pokes her nose into all that does or does not concern her, and draws deductions based on years of experience of human nature.

At the present day, I should call Margery Allingham one of the foremost writers of detective fiction. Not only does she write excellent English, but her drawing of character is masterly and she has wonderful power in creating atmosphere. You can *feel* the sinister influences behind the scenes, and her characters live on in your memory long after you have put the book away: the grim autocrat Mrs. Faraday of *Police at the Funeral*; the kindly and lovable "belle" in *Death of a Ghost*; Jimmy Sutane, the sad faced dancer with the twinkling feet. They are unusual but real personalities, vividly interesting. And through the books moves "Mr. Campion", apparently vacuous, actually keenly acute, and with him the faithful Lugg (in whom, alas, I never can quite believe!) The pleasant negative inconsequence of Campion makes a dramatic contrast with the undercurrent of suspicion and fear that grows to a climax—particularly is this so in *Flowers for the Judge*. Sometimes, one feels, Margery Allingham is inclined to subordinate plot to characters. She is so interested in them that the *dénouement* of the crime sometimes comes rather flatly as inevitable, rather than as a surprising bombshell.

Dorothy Sayers, alas, has wearied of the detective story and has turned her attention elsewhere. We all regret it for she was such an exceptionally good detective story writer and a delightfully witty one. Her earlier books *Whose Body?*, *Unnatural Death* and *The Unpleasantness at the Bellona Club* are decidedly her best, having greater simplicity and more "punch" to them. Also her detective "Lord Peter Wimsey", whose face was originally piquantly described as "emerging from his top hat like a maggot emerging from a gorgonzola cheese", became through the course of years merely a "handsome hero", and admirers of his early prowess can hardly forgive his attachment to, and lengthy courtship of, a tiresome young woman called Harriet. One had hoped that, once married to her, he would resume his old form, but Lord Peter remains an example of a good man spoilt.

Not so Mr. Fortune, H.C. Bailey's great creation. Reggie Fortune is always the same, and marriage to a discreet and charming wife has left his incisive character untouched. The stories stand or fall by Mr. Fortune. It is not the cases themselves but Mr. Fortune's handling of them wherein lies the fascination. For Mr. Fortune is, undeniably, a great man. Now to label a man a great man and then write about him and *show* him to be a great man is a supreme literary feat! A noted surgeon and consultant to the Home Office, Reggie Fortune's handling of his problems is like a surgical operation. Where all is apparently straightforward, he feels, probes, notes some tiny fact that a complacent police official has swept aside, and then he cuts down to the heart of the trouble. His method is the method of the knife, ruthless and incisive. His rudeness to the wretched Lomas

(Assistant Commissioner of Police) is unbelievable—and leads one to speculate whether one day worm Lomas will turn and murder Mr. Fortune!

H.C. Bailey's longer books are not so satisfactory as his shorter stories. All the characters are inclined to speak a special Baileyesque language of their own—a clear clipped jargon. This is effective in short doses as the atmosphere of the operating theatre. But the atmosphere of an operating theatre is essentially artificial—created deliberately for specific purposes. It cannot be prolonged into a picture of daily life. Some of the best of the Fortune stories show the deduction of a whole malignant growth from one small isolated incident. For instance, the discovery of a couple of withered leaves in a woman's handbag, recognized by Mr. Fortune as Arctic Willow, cause him to inquire into an apparently satisfactory case of suicide.

Fat, lazy, incredibly greedy (his delight in cream and jam for tea make tantalizing reading in war days!), underneath Fortune's smiling exterior there is cold steel. Reggie Fortune is for Justice—merciless and inexorable justice. His pity and indignation are aroused by the victims—in execution he is as ruthless as his own knife.

John Dickson Carr (or Carter Dickson, for they are one and the same) is a master magician. I believe that only those who write detective stories themselves can really appreciate his marvellous sleight of hand. For that is what it is—he is the supreme conjurer, the King of the Art of Misdirection. Each of his books is a brilliant, fantastic, quite impossible conjuring trick.

"You watch my hands, ladies and gentlemen, you watch my sleeves, the hat is empty, nothing anywhere—Hey presto! A Rabbit!" He has, too, the gift of story telling, once you begin a book of his, you simply cannot put it down. As each chapter draws to a close, you see ahead a reasonable explanation, then, like Alice through the Looking Glass's path, it seems to shake itself, and off it goes in a twist of fresh bewilderment. His characterization is not particularly good, his people talk in a way quite unlike life, his events are fantastic. It is all stagey—set behind footlights—but what a performance!

Carr's penchant is for the impossible situation. He starts with that—either with the familiar "closed room", or "closed circle" or with, as in the "*Arabian Nights Mystery*", a setting of pure fantasy, with a set of people behaving apparently like lunatics. Then with a shake of the kaleidoscope you get the reason of it, all is quite normal—and then fresh impossibilities, fresh rationalisations. For some people, the twists of the plot may be too complicated. He can certainly be accused of occasionally loading the dice, but that can be forgiven for the brilliance with which it is done. The clues to the truth are so slight as to be almost unfair: one little sentence slipped into the middle of a tense situation; a mention of a car radiator on p. 30 that does not agree with the same car's radiator on p. 180. Do you notice it? Of course not! Your eyes are riveted on a suspicious circumstance which you think only you have spotted. Misdirection, again.

A crowd of people are assembled round a dinner table in *The Red Widow Murders*. There is a sinister room in the house, nailed up for many years. Anyone who stays in it alone is found dead. A man goes in, locks himself in while the others wait outside. Every quarter of an hour they call to him and he replies—but when the door is opened the man is dead, in a room with locked shutters and no secret ways in or out—and, what is more, that man has been dead *for over an hour*. The impossible has happened! You never noticed a little descriptive phrase about the man at dinner;

pale, nervous, *eating nothing but soup* ... Your clue was there, in those four words.

Dickson Carr's detective is the beer drinking Dr. Fell, Carter Dickson's sleuth is Sir Henry Merrivale, the "old man", a former chief of Military Intelligence. I much prefer him of the two—but it is the actual unfolding of the story that is the real strength of Dickson Carr's genius. He is a male Scheherazade—and certainly no cruel Empress could order his execution until she had heard the next instalment!

Ngaio Marsh is another deservedly popular detective writer. Her style is amusing and her characterizations excellent. *Surfeit of Lampreys* was a delightful book, though perhaps one so enjoyed the Lamprey family that one rather forgot about the murder. *Death in Ecstasy* is a very clever picture of a little coterie of worshippers in a "New Religion" adroitly put over by the infamous Father Garnett. *Artists in Crime* is a good story of murder amongst a collection of painters. Both the atmosphere and the people are first rate.

Then there is the master of alibis, Freeman Wills Crofts. Inspector French is a kindly painstaking man who accomplishes his results by sheer hard work. If you like *alibis*, then you will enjoy the efforts of Inspector French. *The Cask*, one of his earliest books, is a model of its kind. A cask arrives at a business firm in London and is found to contain the body of a young woman. From there on you trace the cask back to its sender and forward again—there seems no loop hole, no possible opportunity for the cask to have been opened and the body substituted for the original piece of statuary. Nevertheless, there *is* a flaw and at last, slowly worried out, the truth emerges.

There are many other good detective writers—space forbids the mention of all of them. There is Michael Innes, a brilliant and witty writer. There is straightforward John

Rhode with Dr. Priestley in charge. There is Gladys Mitch-ell with her fascinating Mrs. Bradley, ugly as a toad and armed with the latest up-to-date theories of psychology. And Austin Freeman's books remain interesting examples of scientific methods of crime deduction.

I have chosen out for fullest description those writers whom I myself admire most and consider at the top of their profession. No collection would be complete without the mention of Anthony Berkeley, founder of the Detective Club, although he has, alas, been silent for many years. But what delightful books he has written. Detection and crime at its wittiest—all his stories are amusing, intriguing, and he is a master of the final twist, the surprise *dénouement*. Roger Sheridan, the slightly fatuous novelist, is his detective, though Roger is not always allowed to shine. He remains always the gifted amateur—hit or miss—but whichever way it is, the entertainment is first class.

And now, perhaps, a few words about myself. Since I have been writing detective stories for a quarter of a century and have some forty-odd novels to my credit, I may lay claim at least to being an industrious craftsman. A more aristocratic title was given to me by an American paper which dubbed me the "Duchess of Death".

I have enjoyed writing detective stories, and I think the austerity and stern discipline that goes to making a 'tight' detective plot is good for one's thought processes. It is the kind of writing that does not permit loose or slipshod think-ing. It all has to dovetail, to fit in as part of a carefully con-structed whole. You must have your blueprint first, and it needs really constructive thinking to make a workmanlike job of it.

Naturally one's methods alter. I have become more inter-ested as the years go on in the preliminaries of crime—the interplay of character upon character, the deep smouldering resentments and dissatisfactions that do not always come to the surface but which may suddenly explode into violence. I have written light-hearted murder stories, and serious crime stories, and technical extravaganzas like *Ten Little Niggers* [*And Then There Were None*]. I have laid a crime story in Ancient Egypt, and a murder play on a modern Nile steamer. I have had the conventional Body in the Library, and Bodies in Aeroplanes, and on Boats and in Trans-European Trains. Hercule Poirot has made quite a place for himself in the world and is regarded perhaps with more affection by outsiders than by his own creator! I would give one piece of advice to young detective writers. Be very careful what central character you create—you may have him with you for a very long time!

CONTENTS

PART I

PART II

PART III

INTRODUCTION TO PART I

(a)

" DEAR JOHN RHODE,

" People ask me, when they find out (let me be honest, ' when I tell them ') that I write detective stories, ' Oh, *how* do you begin ? Do you think of a Murder and then work it out, or do you think of a Solution and do it backwards ? ' I suppose the question is inevitable ; I have never discovered the answer.

" At the moment I'm in a peculiar position : I've thought of a title—' Ask a Policeman.' That ought to suggest a nice murder, surely ? You know, with Cabinet Ministers, and Papal Nuncios, and Libraries, and all the rest of it.

" But the queer thing is, the title does nothing of the sort—to me : how does it strike you ?

" Yours ever,

" MILWARD KENNEDY."

(b)

" DEAR MILWARD KENNEDY,

" Yes, I know. I have never answered the question myself. I have come to the conclusion that writing detective stories is just like any other vice. The deed is done without one's having any clear knowledge of the temptation which led up to it. But I must confess

I

that I usually start with something more comprehensive than a title.

" I suppose your veiled suggestion is that I supply a plot to fit your title. But, honestly, to my simple mind ' Ask a Policeman ' suggests the pawning of a watch—or are you too young to remember the old song ?—rather than your galaxy of celebrities. Besides, I have never met a Papal Nuncio. I shouldn't know what to say to him if I did. But I have seen an Archbishop—in the distance. And once I used to hold awestruck conversations with a Cabinet Minister, whose powers of invective I have always admired.

" So here is your plot. As you will see, you have a choice of many Policemen to interrogate as to its solution.

" Yours,

" JOHN RHODE."

PART I

DEATH AT HURSLEY LODGE

By John Rhode

It was impossible to tell, from the Home Secretary's expression, exactly how the news had affected him. He was a big, heavy man, who looked much more like a country farmer than a Minister of the Crown. *Punch* was fond of caricaturing him in breeches and gaiters, with a pitchfork over his shoulder. You might have expected his position in the Cabinet to have been Minister of Agriculture.

But those who knew Sir Philip Brackenthorpe were well aware that a very keen brain was at work beneath his rather bucolic exterior. And that that brain was particularly active at this precise moment the Commissioner of Metropolitan Police had no doubt. The two were alone together in Sir Philip's private room at the Home Office. Through the open windows came the muffled roar of the traffic in Whitehall, the only sound to break the silence which had followed the Commissioner's terse statement.

" Comstock ! " exclaimed Sir Philip at last, " The man lived on sensation, and it is only fitting that his death should provide the greatest sensation of all. Yes, you're quite right, Hampton. I shall have to have all the facts at first hand. This business is bound to come up when the Cabinet meets to-morrow. Who have you got there ? "

" Rather a crowd, I'm afraid, sir," replied Sir Henry Hampton, " I don't know whether you'll care to see them all——"

" I'll see anybody who's got anything relevant to say about the affair. But, mind, I want evidence, and not speculation. But, before we start, I should like to see Littleton, since he'll be primarily responsible for the investigations. He came here with you, of course ? "

Hampton's tall, gaunt frame imperceptibly stiffened. The question had been asked a good deal earlier than he had anticipated. It was devilish awkward, for Sir Philip was not the sort of person who could be put off with evasions. " Littleton was not in his office when the message came through to Scotland Yard just now, I'm sorry to say," he replied simply.

No use going into details, thought Hampton. Littleton, the Assistant Commissioner in charge of the Criminal Investigation Department, might be expected to return at any minute now. He would find a message telling him to come at once to the Home Office. And then, as Hampton reflected grimly, he could tell his own story. And, if the amazing rumour which had reached the Commissioner as to his whereabouts was true, his story might prove particularly interesting.

Sir Philip must have guessed that Hampton was withholding something from him. " You are responsible for your own Department," he said, with a touch of severity. " You will naturally give Littleton such instructions as you consider necessary. But I want to impress upon you that the death of a man like Comstock is not an everyday event. It will require, shall we say, special methods of investigation. And that for many reasons, which I need scarcely point out to you."

From the far-away expression of his eyes, it seemed that Sir Philip was mentally addressing a larger and more important audience. Hampton wondered idly whether it was the Cabinet or the House of Commons that he was thinking of. The murder—if it was murder—of a man like Lord Comstock was an event of world-wide importance. The newspapers controlled by the million-aire journalist exerted an influence out of all proportion to their real value. Inspired by Comstock himself, they claimed at frequent intervals to be the real arbiters of the nation's destiny at home and abroad. Govern-ments might come and go, each with its own considered policy. The Comstock Press patronized, ignored, or attacked them, as suited Lord Comstock's whim at the moment. His policy was fixed and invariable.

This may seem an astounding statement to those who remember how swiftly and how frequently the *Daily Bugle* changed its editorial opinions. But Lord Com-stock's policy was not concerned with the welfare of the State, or of anyone else but himself, for that matter. It was devoted with unswerving purpose to one single aim, the increase in value of his advertisement pages. The surest way to do this was to increase circulation, to bamboozle the public into buying the organs of the Comstock Press. And nobody knew better than Lord Comstock that the surest way of luring the public was by a stunt, the more extravagant the better.

Stunts therefore followed one another with bewildering rapidity. Of those running at the moment, two had attracted special attention. To be successful, stunts must attack something or somebody, preferably so well established that it or he has become part of the ordinary person's accepted scheme of things. Lord Comstock had selected Christianity as the first object of his attack.

But he was far too able a journalist merely to attack. His assault upon Christianity had nothing in common with the iconoclasm of the Bolshevists. Christianity must be abandoned, not because it was a menace to Socialism, but because the Christian civilization had manifestly failed. The economic slough of despond had demonstrated that, clearly enough. Christianity had swept away the conception of the Platonic Republic, with its single and logical solutions of all problems which could beset the Commonwealth. " Back to Paganism ! " was the slogan, and the *Daily Bugle* devoted many columns daily to proving that by this means alone the existing economic depression could be finally cured.

One antagonist at a time, even so formidable an antagonist as Christianity, could not satisfy the restless spirit of Lord Comstock. He sought another and found it in the Metropolitan Police, his choice being influenced mainly by the implicit faith which that institution most justly inspired. Scotland Yard was the principal object of the invective of the Comstock Press. It was inefficient, ill-conducted, and corrupt. It must be reformed, root and branch. The crime experts of the Comstock Press, men who knew how to use their brains, were worth the whole of the C.I.D. and its elaborate machinery, which imposed so heavy and useless a burden upon the tax-payer.

Now and then it happened that a crime was committed, and no arrest followed. This was the opportunity of the Comstock Press. Without the slightest regard for the merits of the case, and safe in the knowledge that a Government Department cannot reply, the *Daily Bugle*, and its evening contemporary, the *Evening Clarion*, unloosed a flood of vituperation upon the C.I.D., from the Assistant Commissioner himself to his humblest subordinate. And the most recent instance of this—the echoes of the storm were still rumbling—was vividly in the Home Secretary's mind as he sat thoughtfully drawing elaborate geometrical patterns upon his blotting paper.

In fact, the shadow of Lord Comstock lay heavily on both men, as they sat in the oppressive warmth of the June afternoon. It was as though his invisible presence lurked in the corner of the room, masterful, contemptuous, poisoning the air with the taint of falsehood. That at that very moment he lay dead in his own country retreat, Hursley Lodge, was a fact so incredible that it required time for its realization. Hence, perhaps, the silence which had once more fallen upon the room.

It was broken by Sir Philip. "Did you know the man personally?" he asked abruptly, without taking his eyes from the figures he was tracing.

"I've seen him often enough, and spoken to him once or twice;" replied the Commissioner; "but I can't say that I knew him."

"I knew him," said Sir Philip slowly. From his manner it seemed as though he were more interested in his designs than in his subject. "At least, I knew as much about him as he cared for anyone to know. It wasn't difficult. He had only one topic of conversation. With men, at least. I've been given to understand that his conversation with women was apt to be more intimate. And that was himself."

With infinite care he drew a line joining two triangles apex to apex. He contemplated the result with evident satisfaction, then looked up, and continued more briskly. " He loved to talk about himself and his achievements, up to a point. You can guess the sort of thing. The contrast between what he was and what he became. You couldn't help admiring the fellow as you listened, however much you disliked him. He was an able man in his own way, Hampton, there's no getting away from that. An able man, and a strong man, with that innate ruthlessness which makes for success. You know how he started life, of course ? "

" Pretty low down in the social scale, from all I've heard," replied the Commissioner.

" His father worked in a mill somewhere up north. A very decent and respectable chap, I believe. Quite a different type from Comstock. Saved and scraped with only one object in view, to make a gentleman out of that scapegrace son of his. It's a mercy he never lived to know how completely his efforts failed. Anyhow, he sent the lad to Blackminster Grammar School. Lord knows what sort of a figure he must have cut when he first went there. But he was head of the school before he left."

" No lack of brains, even then, apparently," remarked the Commissioner.

" No lack of brains, or of determination. But then comes a gap. Comstock disappears from sight—conversationally, I mean—after that. Nobody has ever heard him mention the intervening years. The rungs of the ladder are hidden from us. He reappears in a blaze of glory as Lord Comstock, reputed millionaire, and owner of heaven knows how many disreputable rags. Ambitious, too. Life's work not yet accomplished, and all that sort of thing. And now you say he's lying dead at that country place of his, Hursley Lodge. I've never seen it. Male visitors were not made welcome there, I've always understood."

"Welcome or not, there were quite a crowd of them there this morning," remarked the Commissioner grimly. "Only quite a small house, too."

Sir Philip nodded. His reminiscent mood passed suddenly. "All right, bring them in," he said. "Your own people first. The police, I mean. This chap who was called in first. I'll leave you to get the story out of them."

The Commissioner opened the door which led into the Private Secretary's room beyond. He looked round sharply, hoping to see the truculent figure of the Assistant Commissioner among the group which stood there, nervous and ill at ease. A frown expressed his disappointment. He beckoned sharply to three men, standing by. In single file they followed him into Sir Philip's presence.

Hampton introduced them curtly. "Chief Constable Shawford, Superintendent Churchill, sir. Both of the Yard. This is Superintendent Easton, of the local police." Sir Philip glanced at the men in turn, nodded at each but said nothing beyond a curt "sit down," addressed to them all in general. They obeyed—the lower the rank, the greater the distance maintained from the Home Secretary. The Commissioner at first occupied a large arm-chair touching the desk, but as the interview went on he ceased to have a regular station—he would sit one minute, stand the next, lean on the big desk, and almost promise (so it seemed to the inexperienced Easton) to whisk away the Home Secretary and occupy *his* chair.

2

Sir Philip, picking up his pencil again, drew with more deliberation than skill, a large circle upon his blotting-paper.

" Easton's district includes Hursley Lodge, sir," the Commissioner began, without further preface. " He was at the police-station when a call was received that Lord Comstock had been found dead in his study. This was at 1.7 this afternoon."

Sir Philip glanced at the clock on his desk. It was then 2.35 p.m.

" He drove at once to Hursley Lodge, and was received by Lord Comstock's secretary, Mr. Mills, who took him straight up to the study. His story will be more easy to follow, sir, if you keep this plan in front of you."

He placed a neatly-drawn diagram on the desk, and Sir Philip studied it curiously. " Where did this come from ? " he asked.

" Easton brought it with him from Hursley Lodge, sir," replied the Commissioner, with a touch of impatience. He was anxious to get on with the facts.

Sir Philip looked up, and for the first time Easton appeared to him as an individual. He was tall, with a soldierly moustache and bearing, but obviously unnerved by the distinguished company in which he found himself ; the Home Secretary's glance had somehow brought him to his feet, and under his gaze he shifted from one foot to the other, and with difficulty suppressed an almost irresistible inclination to salute.

" Pretty smart of you to get hold of a plan like this, Easton," said Sir Philip encouragingly. " Where did you find it ? "

" Mr. Mills gave it to me, sir—the secretary," replied Easton. Something in Sir Philip's manner seemed to have put him quite at his ease. During the rest of the interview he addressed himself to him exclusively, as though some mysterious bond of sympathy had been established between them. He even took a couple of paces towards the Home Secretary's desk.

" Mr. Mills gave it to you, did he ? " said the Home Secretary. " Where did he get it from ? People don't as a rule have plans of their houses ready to hand like that."

" It's a rough tracing of a plan of the drains, really, sir," Easton explained gravely, " with the drains left out and a few other things put in. Mr. Mills told me that a new system of drainage had recently been put in at Hursley Lodge, and the builder left a plan behind in case any alterations were required."

" I see. Very well, Easton. Tell me what you found when you got into the study."

" It was a large room, sir, with a big bow-window on the south side. The frames were of the casement type, and were all wide open. There was very little furniture in the room, sir. A row of bookcases round the walls, and half a dozen chairs standing in front of them. One of them had been overturned, and was lying close inside the door leading into the hall. There were two other doors, sir. One led into the drawing-room, and was disguised as a bookcase. The bookcase swung open with the door, if you understand me, sir."

Sir Philip nodded. " And the third door ? " he asked.

" That was a double door, sir, leading into the room which Mr. Mills used, and which he called the office. At the farther end of the room was a heavy desk, standing close to the window. Behind this desk, and between it and the window, lay the body of Lord Comstock. His lordship lay on his right side, with his knees drawn up towards his chin. I could see at once that he was dead, sir."

" And did you discover as promptly what had killed him ? "

" There was a very small bullet-wound in his left temple, sir. So small that I thought at first it was a stab with some round weapon like a thick hat-pin."

" What made you alter your opinion, Easton ? "

" When I looked on the desk, sir, I found this," replied Easton simply. He put his hand in his pocket, and produced something wrapped carefully in a handkerchief. He opened this out, and disclosed a miniature revolver, which he laid on the edge of the Home Secretary's desk. At the sight of it, Chief Constable Shawford made a sound as though about to speak. But a sharp glance from the Commissioner silenced him before he could utter anything articulate.

Sir Philip looked at it curiously. " Vicious little toy ! " he exclaimed. " And you think this is what killed Lord Comstock, do you, Easton ? "

" I think so, sir. One chamber has been discharged, and that quite recently, by the look of the fouling. But, as far as I have been able to make out, sir, there are no finger-marks."

The Commissioner rose and stepped to the desk. " You had better take charge of this, Shawford," he said. " The sooner it is examined by the experts the better."

He was about to pick up the pistol, when Sir Philip waved him aside. " No, let it stay there for the present," he said. " Now, let's get this clear, Easton. You say that Lord Comstock was lying on the floor, and that the pistol was on the desk. Did it occur to you that Lord Comstock might have shot himself ? "

" It did occur to me, sir. But if he had been sitting in his chair at the time, I don't see how the pistol could have fallen to where I found it. It was on the other side of the desk, sir."

" When you found it, perhaps. But other people must have entered the room before you reached the house. Several other people, I dare say ? "

It was the Commissioner who replied. He was evidently anxious to atone for his slight *faux pas* over the pistol. " Two at least, Sir Philip. Comstock's secretary and his butler. They are waiting in the next room. Shall I bring them in ? "

" All in good time," said Sir Philip. " I expect that Easton has more to tell us yet. I should like more light on the point of whether Comstock could have shot himself. There are no finger-prints to be seen on the pistol. The inference is that whoever handled it last wore gloves or else it has been wiped over. Was it as hot in the study at Hursley Lodge as it is in here ? "

" It was certainly very warm, sir."

" I expect it was. It's one of the hottest June days I remember. I say, Hampton, would you mind putting one of those candlesticks on my desk ? "

He nodded towards the mantelpiece, on which stood a pair of silver candlesticks. The Commissioner walked up to the nearest one, picked it up, and laid it down beside the pistol.

" Thank you, Hampton. Now, Chief Constable, will you look at that candlestick and tell me if you can see any finger-prints on it ? "

Shawford gingerly picked up the candlestick and

breathed on it. " They are very plainly visible where Sir
Henry Hampton touched it, sir," he said solemnly.

" That settles the point, I think," said Sir Philip
briskly. " If anybody had touched the pistol with their
naked hands this morning they must have left finger-
marks upon it. Comstock would not be wearing gloves
indoors. We can leave it at that for the present. Now,
Easton, what did you do after you had looked round
the study ? "

" The first thing I did, sir, was to telephone to my
Chief. I thought he would want to know at once what
had happened. When I had done that, sir, I asked Mr.
Mills to send for the doctor who usually attended his
lordship."

" By his Chief, Easton means the Chief Constable of
Southshire, sir," the Commissioner put in. " Colonel
Graham. He rang me up about half-past one, and
repeated what Easton had told him. He wanted the
Yard to take charge immediately. I thought it best
that you should hear all the circumstances at once, and
I therefore put a call through to Hursley Lodge. Easton
answered it, and I told him to come here as quickly as
he could, bringing with him all available witnesses."

Sir Philip nodded. " Sit down over there in the corner,
Easton," he said. " You've done very well. Ah, wait !
one point—when did you reach Hursley Lodge ? 1.15 ?
Right. Now you can produce your witnesses, Hampton.
One at a time, of course."

The Commissioner went to the door, and beckoned.
" This is Mr. Mills, Lord Comstock's secretary, sir," he
announced.

A young man, somewhere near the thirty mark,
entered the room. He was elegantly, a little too elegantly,

dressed, his coat cut to suggest a slimmer waist than in fact he possessed. His hair was curly and shone with an odorous ointment. His narrow eyes roamed round the room, his expression a mixture of alarm, bravado, and surprise, and settled finally upon the inexpressive countenance of the Home Secretary.

" Sit down, Mr. Mills," said Sir Philip briskly. " I want to hear what you can tell us about Comstock's death. I saw him in London not many days ago. How long had he been down at Hursley Lodge ? "

Mills moistened his lips. It seemed as if he spoke only by a great effort. " Only since the day before yesterday, sir," he replied.

" Had he any particular reason for leaving London just now ? "

" Not to my knowledge, sir. He often went down to Hursley Lodge for a few days at a time. He could work there without being interrupted, or he could, as a rule, sir."

" Did you always accompany him on these occasons ? "

An unpleasantly sly look came into Mills' eyes at this. " Not always, sir. But on this occasion he told me to come, as he would probably want me."

" I see. Now please tell me, in your own words, exactly what happened this morning."

Again Mills moistened his red lips. He hesitated, and seemed at a loss where to begin. Then all at once he seemed to make up his mind, and spoke rapidly in a harsh and monotonous voice.

" Lord Comstock came into the dining-room as I was finishing breakfast, sir. I did not expect him so early, as at Hursley Lodge he rarely appeared before half-past nine. Nine was just striking as he came in. He asked me why I wasn't at work, and without waiting for my answer told me that he would be in his study all the morning, and that he wasn't on any account to be disturbed. I suppose that he was anxious to think over the policy of the newspapers."

" By which you mean the ' Back to Paganism ' movement, and the attack on the police, I suppose ? " the Commissioner inquired.

" It was probably the latter, Sir Henry. He had that cause very much at heart ! Yesterday he was very much upset when he learnt that Mr. Littleton had refused to give the crime expert of the *Daily Bugle* certain information in connection with the Little Cadbury case. He said that the police were deliberately practising a policy of obstruction, entirely contrary to the interests of justice."

Sir Philip glanced at the Commissioner. " Do you know anything of this ? " he asked.

Hampton shook his head, but Shawford cleared his throat apologetically. " I beg your pardon, sir, but I think I know of the incident to which Mr. Mills refers. Mr. Littleton had given orders that no information was to be given to the press for the present. The case concerns the body of a girl who was found murdered in a wood near Little Cadbury, sir. We have a clue, which is being followed up, but we can only succeed if complete secrecy is maintained."

" I see. You're probably right, Mills. Comstock was no doubt looking for a stick with which to beat Scotland Yard. He gave orders that he was not to be disturbed, you say. Was there anything unusual in this ? "

" Nothing at all, sir. It was the rule that Lord Comstock never saw anybody at Hursley Lodge unless he sent for them. He would occasionally ring up one of his editors on the private line to Fort Comstock, and tell him to come down at once. But he very rarely had any other visitors, at least when I was with him. I was all the more surprised when I was told that there was somebody to see him this morning."

"One moment, Mills. Where were you when Lord Comstock entered his study?"

"In the office, sir, which communicates with it by double doors."

"And you were there when you were told that somebody wished to see Comstock. What did you do?"

"Just after half-past eleven Farrant, the butler, came into the office, sir. I had already told him that Lord Comstock would see nobody. But he said that His Grace the Archbishop of the Midlands had called, and insisted upon seeing his Lordship. Farrant told me that he had shown His Grace into the drawing-room. I hurried in there at once, sir. The Archbishop told me that he was one of his oldest friends. If I may say so, sir, this seemed to me very extraordinary, knowing Lord Comstock's aversion to the Church."

Sir Philip smiled. "The Archbishop of the Midlands!" he exclaimed softly. "The Most Reverend William Anselm Pettifer, D.D. Archbishops never lie, you may be sure of that. And in this case Doctor Pettifer was manifestly speaking the truth. He was certainly one of Comstock's earliest friends. Not that they can have seen much of one another recently. Rather curious, that, eh, Hampton?"

"I'm afraid that I don't quite follow," replied the Commissioner, with a puzzled expression.

" Don't you remember that Doctor Pettifer was for many years Headmaster of Blackminster Grammar School ? He only left there when he became Bishop of Bournemouth. He must have known Comstock as a boy, of course. Go on, Mr. Mills, what did Lord Comstock say when you told him that the Archbishop had called to see him ? "

" He—er—he indulged in some very bad language, sir. I went into the study through the door leading from the drawing-room, being careful to shut it behind me, of course. Lord Comstock asked me what the devil I meant by coming in without being called for, and I replied that the Archbishop was waiting. He was very much annoyed, sir ; in fact I may say that he was furious. I should not like to repeat the actual words he used, sir."

" I think that we had better hear them," said Sir Philip. " I doubt if even Comstock's language could shock the present company."

" Well, sir, he said that it was a piece of damned impertinence on the part of the bloody old hypocrite to intrude upon him like that. He spoke so loud, sir, that I am afraid that he must have been audible in the drawing-room. And then he told me to tell His Grace to clear out of the house and get back to his own job of preaching poppy-cock. He was in a very violent mood, sir."

" So it appears," said Sir Philip. " I presume that you did not deliver his message verbatim to the Archbishop ? "

" I was not given the opportunity of delivering the message at all, sir. While Lord Comstock was still speaking, the door opened, and His Grace walked in. I thought it best to leave them alone together, sir, so I retired to my office."

"Then you do not know what passed at the interview between your employer and the Archbishop? Their conversation can hardly have been of a most cordial nature on both sides, as the newspapers would say."

"I had the impression that it was not, sir. Owing to the thick wall and the double door between the office and the study, I could only hear the sound of voices, raised apparently in altercation. I fancied once or twice that I distinguished the word 'clap-trap' uttered by Lord Comstock, but that was all, sir. The interview had lasted for a quarter of an hour or more, when Farrant entered the office to announce a second visitor."

"It seems to have been your busy day, Mr. Mills. Who was this second visitor?"

Mills hesitated for a moment, as though he were not sure how his answer would be received. "Sir Charles Hope-Fairweather, sir," he replied uneasily.

Sir Philip, who had never abandoned his pencil, drew an elaborate curve before he made any comment upon this. Then he glanced at the Commissioner. "Comstock's visiting list is more varied than I imagined. Did you know that he and Hope-Fairweather were on speaking terms? No, of course you wouldn't. You're a policeman, not a politician. But it seems odd to me that the Chief Government Whip should have business with a man who devoted columns daily to denouncing the policy of that Government."

"I might point out, sir, that he devoted fully as much space to denouncing the Faith of which the Archbishop of the Midlands is a distinguished champion," replied the Commissioner meaningly.

" Yes, but the Chief Whip ! I can't think what Hope-Fairweather was about. The Prime Minister will ask him some very pertinent questions, I expect, when he hears of this." Sir Philip turned sharply upon Mills. " How long had Comstock known Sir Charles Hope-Fairweather ? " he asked.

" I—I was not aware that they were acquainted, sir," replied Mills, with a return to his original awkward manner.

" You were not aware that they were acquainted ? " repeated Sir Philip impressively. " Then you have no knowledge of any previous interview having taken place, or of correspondence having passed between them ? "

" I have no knowledge of anything of the kind, sir. But Lord Comstock may have met Sir Charles Hope-Fairweather socially."

" I should be very much surprised to hear that the two had ever met in public," remarked Sir Philip. " However, Hope-Fairweather himself can enlighten us on that point."

He picked up the telephone on his desk, and spoke to his private secretary. " That you, Anderson ? Ring up the Whips' Office, and get hold of Hope-Fairweather, will you ? Give him my compliments and ask him if he can make it convenient to come and see me in half an hour from now. Thanks."

Sir Philip pushed the instrument aside, and turned once more to Mills. " Comstock being still engaged upon theological discussion with the Archbishop, how did you dispose of this second visitor ? " he asked.

" Farrant had told me that Sir Charles Hope-Fairweather was in the hall, sir. I went there, and found him waiting impatiently. He had not taken off a light coat that he was wearing, and he had a pair of driving gloves on his hands. He told me that he had driven from London in a great hurry, and that he positively must see Lord Comstock on the most urgent business.

" I explained to him that Lord Comstock was extremely busy, and had given most definite instructions that he could see nobody. But Sir Charles refused to accept my statement. He insisted, very excitedly, that I should inform Lord Comstock of his visit. When I hesitated, he threatened to walk in and announce himself."

" He knew his way about the house, then ? " asked Sir Philip sharply.

" I think not, sir. But from the hall there was no doubt which room Lord Comstock occupied, since his voice was clearly audible. In order to save any unpleasantness, sir, I promised to inform Lord Comstock as soon as he was disengaged. Meanwhile, I asked Sir Charles to come into the waiting-room, which is a small room opening into my office."

Sir Philip glanced at the plan. " You mean the room with one door opening into the office and another into the hall ? "

" Yes, sir. I then went into my office, shutting the door between the two rooms. I could still hear Lord Comstock's voice faintly through the wall, so that I knew that His Grace could not have left. After a few minutes it occurred to me that I had better tell Farrant to admit nobody else to the house. I was afraid that Lord Comstock might resort to violence if his orders were further disobeyed. I therefore went into the hall for this purpose. There, to my astonishment, I found Sir Charles Hope-Fairweather."

" Unable to resist the temptation to listen to the highly-edifying conversation between Comstock and the Archbishop, perhaps ? " suggested Sir Philip.

" I don't know, I'm sure, sir. Before I could say anything, Sir Charles told me that he had just come out of the waiting-room because he wanted to take a message to his car that he might be kept longer than he had expected. I said that I would see that the message was conveyed, and waited till I saw Sir Charles re-enter the waiting-room.

" I then went to the front door, and looked out into the drive, expecting to see Sir Charles' chauffeur with the car. But there was no car in sight. I did not like to be absent from my office too long, in case Lord Comstock should summon me. I therefore came back into the hall, intending to call Farrant, and give him the message to the chauffeur and instruct him as to refusing admission to any further visitors. But at that very moment a car drove up; I imagined that it must be Sir Charles' car. But the driver got out and confronted me, and I saw at once that he was not a chauffeur."

" What, a third visitor ! " exclaimed Sir Philip incredulously. " I begin to have some sympathy with Comstock. It is outrageous that a man's privacy should be invaded like this. And who was it, this time ? "

Mills' eyes wandered furtively from the Home Secretary to the Commissioner. " It was the Assistant Commissioner of Police, Mr. Littleton, sir," he replied.

Sir Philip's busy pencil stopped abruptly. The atmosphere of the room suddenly became tense as though a threat of thunder had overshadowed the bright afternoon. For several moments there was silence, and then the Home Secretary spoke in a curiously quieter tone.

" You knew this, Hampton," he said, as though stating a very ordinary fact.

" Far from knowing it for certain, sir, I had only heard a suggestion that Littleton might have gone to Hursley Lodge," replied the Commissioner, firmly enough, with a glance in the direction of Chief Constable Shawford.

Sir Philip seemed to divine the direction of that glance, though he did not appear to intercept it. " Perhaps Littleton confided his intention to one of his subordinates," he said icily.

There was a pause before Shawford summoned up the courage to speak. He was conscious that the Commissioner's eye was upon him, and, between that and the awe which he felt in the august presence of the Home Secretary, his manner was deplorably nervous.

" The Assistant Commissioner was speaking to me first thing this morning, sir," he said. " He was talking about the Little Cadbury case. I mean, sir, about the crime expert of the *Daily Bugle*. He was very heated about it, sir, and said it was intolerable."

Sir Philip looked up blandly. " Intolerable ? Of course it is intolerable that a poor girl should be murdered in a lonely wood, and that her assailant should escape from justice."

" It is, indeed, sir," agreed Shawford, positively squirming in his chair. " But that isn't exactly what the Assistant Commissioner meant at the moment, sir. His meaning, so far as I could follow it, was that it was intolerable that the Yard should be dictated to by irresponsible journalists."

" He had evidently taken Comstock's criticisms to heart. Well ? "

The sharp monosyllable increased Shawford's distress.

" I can't say for certain what happened, sir. But the Assistant Commissioner went on to say that it would have to be stopped. He said that if the Government hadn't got the pluck to stand up to Lord Comstock, he had a very good mind to go and have a few words with him himself. And as I left the room he rang for his car to be sent round, sir. He didn't tell me where he was going."

" He may have thought that he had said enough for you to infer that for yourself," remarked Sir Philip sardonically. " Why those in charge of Departments should habitually attempt to mystify me upon matters within their jurisdiction has always been an insoluble puzzle to me."

" I had no intention——" began the Commissioner sharply, but Sir Philip silenced him with a gesture. " Later, Hampton, later," he said. " Mr. Mills has not yet completed his story. You hardly expected a visit from the Assistant Commissioner, I suppose, Mr. Mills ? "

" For a moment, sir, I was quite at a loss. I endeavoured to explain to Mr. Littleton that Lord Comstock already had two visitors, and could not possibly receive any more. But he refused to listen to me, sir. He deliberately pushed past me into the hall, saying that police officers were not on the same footing as ordinary callers. I did not like to ask him if he was in possession of a warrant, sir."

Sir Philip smiled slightly. " It's a pity you didn't," he said. " The situation that would have ensued would probably have added interest to so strenuous a morning. So, in spite of all your precautions, a third element of unrest was introduced into the peaceful household ! It must have taxed your ingenuity to dispose of Littleton ! "

" I had the greatest possible difficulty in dissuading Mr. Littleton from going straight into the study, sir. He overheard Lord Comstock's voice, as Sir Charles must have done previously. He asked me who he had got with him, and I replied that it was a visitor who had an appointment. On that Mr. Littleton said that he would wait till the fellow came out, and then go in."

" Littleton is a most determined person," said Sir Philip gravely. " Did he carry out his threat ? "

" I couldn't say, sir, for I had not the opportunity of speaking to Mr. Littleton again."

Something in Mills' voice caused the Home Secretary to glance at him sharply. " Go on," he said, in an encouraging tone.

" I saw that it was no use attempting to argue with Mr. Littleton in his present frame of mind, sir. I therefore suggested to him that if he insisted upon waiting, it would be more comfortable for him to do so in the drawing-room. He allowed me to show him in there, sir."

" Why the drawing-room rather than the waiting-room ? " Sir Philip asked.

" Well, sir, Sir Charles Hope-Fairweather was in there," replied Mills hesitatingly. " And Sir Charles had given me the impression that he did not wish his visit to be generally known."

" That I can easily understand," remarked Sir Philip grimly. " I admire your handling of the situation, Mr. Mills. Comstock's comments upon it should have been worth hearing. His habitual method of expression lent itself admirably to lurid description. As I understand it, the position was now this. The Archbishop was closeted with Comstock in the study, presumably

3

endeavouring to snatch him as a brand from the burning.
Hope-Fairweather had at last settled down in the
waiting-room, and Littleton had consented to be interned
in the drawing-room. You, as stage-manager, returned
to your office to await events, I suppose ? "

" I did, sir. It was striking the hour by the clock on
my desk as I entered. I remained there for a few
minutes. I was very apprehensive as to what Lord
Comstock would say when he heard that two fresh
visitors had been admitted, and I was wondering how
best to put the matter before him. And then I remembered that I had not yet taken Sir Charles' message to
his chauffeur, nor had I seen Farrant. I was about to
leave my office for the purpose when I distinctly heard
a dull crash from the direction of the study."

" A crash, eh ? " said Sir Philip, glancing almost in-
voluntarily at the pistol on his desk. " This sounds as
though it might interest you, Hampton."

" Could this crash you mention be described as a
report, Mr. Mills ? " asked the Commissioner quickly.

" It might have been. It was certainly a sharp sound.
But, as I have explained, the wall between the study and
the office is very thick, and sounds heard through it are
very deceptive. Although Lord Comstock was in the
habit of speaking very loudly at times, it was only rarely
that I was able to catch his actual words."

" Did you attach any significance to this crash at the
time ? "

" I did not. Lord Comstock, when he was roused, had
a habit of picking up, say, a chair and banging it down
on the floor, in order to emphasise his remarks. If I
thought about the sound at all, I attributed it to some
incident of this nature. I left the office, and went into

the hall. As I did so, the door of the study into the hall opened violently, and His Grace appeared. He slammed the door behind him, and seemed for some moments unaware of my presence. He strode towards the front door, and I heard him distinctly say, twice, ' The wages of sin.' "

" I overtook His Grace before he reached the front door, and asked him if he had a car waiting, or whether I should telephone for a taxi. But he seemed hardly to hear me. He shook his head, then walked rapidly down the drive towards the gate. I watched him until he passed out of sight, and then went back into the hall."

" The Archbishop's interview seems hardly to have been satisfactory," Sir Philip remarked. " But it is curious that he should have refused the offer of a taxi. He can hardly have proposed to walk all the way back to his Province. Ah, but wait a minute, though. Convocation is sitting at Lambeth Palace, isn't it ! I forgot that for the moment. That explains Dr. Pettifer's presence in the neighbourhood of London. How far is Hursley Lodge from the nearest station, Mr. Mills ? "

" About a mile, sir, and it is almost twenty minutes from there to London by train."

Sir Philip nodded. " No doubt the Archbishop is at Lambeth Palace by now. But, after his departure, you had the other two visitors to deal with. How did you proceed, Mr. Mills ? "

" I had come to the conclusion that it would be best to introduce them without previously mentioning their presence to Lord Comstock, sir. They would then at least have a chance of explaining their insistence. As I passed through the hall after seeing His Grace off, I opened the drawing-room door. My intention was to tell

Mr. Littleton that Lord Comstock was now disengaged,
and that I would take the risk of showing him into the
study. But then I remembered that Sir Charles Hope-
Fairweather had the first claim, and that possibly Lord
Comstock would be less displeased to see him than Mr.
Littleton."

" What made you think that, Mr. Mills ? " asked Sir
Philip quietly.

If he had expected to catch Mills out, he was disappointed. " It occurred to me, sir, that if Sir Charles
was a personal friend, Lord Comstock's refusal to see
visitors might not apply to him."

" Very well, you determined to give Hope-Fairweather
the preference. You fetched him from the waiting-room
and ushered him into the lion's den ? "

" Not exactly, sir. I had opened the door of the
drawing-room, but on thinking of Sir Charles I shut it
again, thankful that I was able to do so before Mr.
Littleton had time to interrogate me. I had not seen
him when I glanced into the room."

" One moment, Mr. Mills. I should like you to explain
that point a little more fully. As I understand you, you
opened the door, glanced in, and shut it hastily. Was
the whole of the room visible to you from where you
stood ? "

" Not the whole of it, sir. The half-open door hid the
wall between the drawing-room and the study from me.
If Mr. Littleton had been standing close to that wall, I
might not have seen him."

The Commissioner glanced at Sir Philip, who nodded,
almost imperceptibly. Then he addressed Mills sharply.
" At the moment when you opened the door, you would
have been surprised to find the room empty. Any

suggestion that that was the case would have impressed itself upon you. Yet you shut the door again without making further investigations ? "

" I did. As I have explained, I was anxious to see Sir Charles before Mr. Littleton. I was still in the hall, when I heard a second crash, not dissimilar from the first. For a moment I thought it came from the study, and the thought flashed through my mind that Mr. Littleton, overhearing the departure of His Grace, might have carried out his threat, and entered the study un-announced through the door between that room and the drawing-room."

The Commissioner interrupted him, this time without ceremony. " But that door is concealed by a bookcase, is it not ? " he asked.

" On the study side, yes. The drawing-room is panelled, and the door is so arranged as to form one of the panels. It has no handle, but a concealed fastening, operated by sliding part of the framework of the panel."

" In fact, a stranger would not perceive that it was a door at all ? "

" Not at first sight, perhaps. But very little investiga-tion would show him that the panel could be opened."

Sir Philip began to show signs of impatience. " That, surely, is a matter which can be decided on the spot," he said. " Please continue your narrative, Mr. Mills. Did you proceed to investigate the cause of this second crash ? "

" I ran into my office, sir, and there, to my astonish-ment, found Sir Charles Hope-Fairweather. He was bending down and picking up a litter of papers which lay on the floor. The door leading into the waiting-room was open. Sir Charles, who appeared to be very much embarrassed, explained to me that he had entered the office to tell me that he could wait no longer. As he did so, he had stepped on a mat which had slipped beneath him on the polished floor. To save himself from falling he had clutched at a table which stood just inside the door, and on which was a wooden tray containing papers. This, however, had failed to save him, and he had fallen, dragging the table and tray down with him."

" Would this have accounted for the crash you heard ? " inquired the Commissioner.

" It might have done so. In fact, it seemed to me at the time a likely explanation of the crash."

" You said just now that Sir Charles was wearing gloves when he entered the house. Was he still doing so ? "

" Yes, he was. I noticed that as I dusted him down after his fall. A minute or two later, I escorted him through the hall to the front door, and immediately hurried back to the drawing-room."

" Littleton's turn had come, certainly," remarked Sir Philip.

" That is what I thought, sir. My idea was to make one more effort to induce him to go away without seeing Lord Comstock, and if I failed, to introduce him. I walked into the drawing-room, to find it empty."

" Upon my word, your visitors seem to have wandered about the house as if it was their own ! " exclaimed Sir Philip. " There was no doubt this time that the room was really empty, I suppose ? Littleton wasn't hiding under the sofa ? You can never tell what a policeman may do, you know."

" The room was certainly empty, sir, and the concealed

door into the study was shut. I could only conclude that Mr. Littleton had passed through it into the study. He had certainly not left the house, for his car was still in the drive when I saw Sir Charles off at the front door."

"Where was Littleton's car standing?" asked Sir Philip, glancing at the plan.

"A few yards south of the front door, sir. Almost immediately in front of the dining-room window. I went to the east window of the drawing-room, and looked out to see if the car was still there, and found that it was. A plot of grass, with a clump of tall beeches growing in it, hides the farther sweep of the drive from the windows of the house, sir. As I looked out I saw a big saloon car come out from behind it, and head for the gate. I recognized the driver as Sir Charles Hope-Fairweather, by the colour of his coat.

"A moment later, sir, I saw Mr. Littleton. He appeared round the north-east corner of the house, running as hard as he could across the lawn towards the front door. He jumped into his car, swung round the trees, and set off towards the gate at a reckless speed."

"But this is most extraordinary, Mr. Mills. Where did you imagine that Littleton had come from?"

It seemed that Mills had prepared an answer to this question. At all events, his reply was ready enough. "I imagined that he must have left the house by the front door, and gone round on to the lawn, while I was helping Sir Charles to brush his clothes, sir. As soon as I had lost sight of Mr. Littleton's car, I went back to my office."

"You did not go into the study?" asked the Commissioner quickly.

*That would be north of the front door.
* north-west, according to the map

" There was no reason to do so. Sir Charles and Mr. Littleton had gone, and I had no desire to disturb Lord Comstock unnecessarily. I certainly expected him to ring for me and inquire what Mr. Littleton had been doing on the lawn, since I thought he must infallibly have seen him. But, since he did not do so, I resumed my work."

" Which had suffered considerable interruption," Sir Philip remarked. " What time was it by then ? "

" I glanced at the clock as I sat down, sir. It was then twenty-two minutes past twelve. I did not move from my chair again until about five minutes past one, when Farrant flung open the doors leaning into the study, and shouted to me to come in."

" Ah, yes, the butler," said Sir Philip thoughtfully. " Have you got him outside, Hampton ? If so, he had better come in."

The Commissioner went to the Private Secretary's room and came out followed by an elderly man with a melancholy, almost morose, expression. It struck Sir Philip that Comstock had not been very fortunate in his choice of subordinates. Mills, in spite of his apparent candour, had not impressed him. There was a shifty look in his eyes that the Home Secretary did not quite like. And as for Farrant—well, there was nothing against him yet. But then, from all accounts, no self-respecting person would remain in Comstock's household any longer than he could help. Sir Philip caught the Commissioner's eye, and nodded slightly.

" Now, Farrant," said the latter briskly, " I understand that you were the first to discover Lord Comstock's death. How did this come about ? "

" Punctually at one o'clock, sir, I came to inform his

Lordship that lunch was on the table. I opened the study door, sir——"

" How did you reach the study, Farrant ? " the Commissioner interrupted.

" I entered the hall by the service door from the kitchen, under the stairs, sir. The door of the study is nearly opposite. I opened this door, sir, and the first thing I saw was his Lordship lying on the floor by the window, with his chair half on top of him, sir. I ran up to him, thinking he had fallen over in a fit or something, sir. And then as soon as I looked at him and saw his head, I knew that he had been shot dead. And then I ran to the waiting-room and called Mr. Mills."

" You knew that he had been shot dead, did you ? And how did you know that ? "

The sharp question seemed to confuse Farrant. " Why, sir, there was the wound, and the blood round it. And his Lordship was lying in a way he wouldn't have been if he hadn't been dead."

" Yes, dead with a wound in his head, Farrant. But why *shot* dead ? "

Farrant's eyes strayed to the pistol, in full view on the Home Secretary's desk. " I knew there was a pistol in the room, sir," he replied confidently.

" Oh, you knew that, did you ? When did you first see it there ? "

Farrant glanced towards the chair in which Mills was sitting. " I saw it there yesterday evening, sir. I took the opportunity of tidying up the study then, since his Lordship had gone out to dinner."

The Commissioner turned his attention to Mills. " Do you know where Lord Comstock dined last night ? " he asked.

" I don't. Certainly not at Hursley Lodge. He went out with the chauffeur in the car about seven, and did not come back till midnight. He was not in the habit of informing me of his movements unless for some definite purpose."

" You appear to have examined Lord Comstock's body fairly closely, Farrant ? "

" I bent down to pick him up, sir, before I realized that he was dead."

" Did you disturb it at all ? "

" I moved the chair a bit to one side, sir, and I may have shifted the body slightly, but not so that one would notice it. And I dare say I pushed in the drawer an inch or two, so that I could get round to His Lordship."

" What drawer was this, Farrant ? "

" One of the drawers of the desk, sir, that was pulled nearly right out."

The Commissioner looked at Easton. " You said nothing of this drawer being open in your report, Superintendent," he said accusingly.

" When I entered the room, sir, all the drawers in the desk were shut, sir," replied Easton positively.

" Well, having disturbed everything, you thought it time to call Mr. Mills," continued the Commissioner. " Are you quite sure that you touched nothing else first ? "

" Perfectly sure, sir," Farrant replied.

" Was the drawer that Farrant mentions open when you came on the scene, Mr. Mills ? "

" I did not notice it at the moment. I was too much concerned with Lord Comstock's condition. I could see at a glance that he was dead. I immediately sent Farrant to the telephone in the hall, with orders to ring up the police-station."

" In the hall ! Is there no telephone in the study, then ? "

" An extension. The main instrument is in the hall."

" The extension would have served the purpose equally well, I should have thought. Had you any reason for getting Farrant out of the room ? "

" Well, yes, I had. I had noticed by then that one of the drawers of the desk was slightly open, and I knew it to be the one in which Lord Comstock kept documents of a highly confidential nature. Upon Farrant leaving the room, I opened the drawer wide, and found the documents it contained lying in great disorder. I looked them over rapidly, and then shut the drawer."

" Have you any reason to suppose that any of the documents it should have contained were missing ? "

" I do not know what documents it contained. But all those I found, though highly confidential, had passed through my hands at one time or another. But I have my own reasons for believing that it had contained something of an even more confidential nature."

" I should like to hear those reasons, Mr. Mills."

" I may be wrong. But, when I entered the study earlier in the morning to announce the arrival of His Grace, that drawer was wide open and Lord Comstock was bending over it. As soon as he heard me, he slammed it violently. I certainly got the impression, at the time, that there was something in it that he did not wish me to see. Something particularly private, other than the documents which had passed through my hands already, I mean."

" Then, if your suspicions are correct, it would appear

that those documents have been stolen," said the Commissioner weightily. " That is, unless Lord Comstock himself removed them and placed them elsewhere. This incident of the drawer may prove to be of some importance. You appear to have been somewhat over-zealous, Mr. Mills. You should have left the drawer as you found it. Did you touch anything else in the study before the arrival of the police ? "

Mills shook his head. " Nothing whatever," he replied sullenly.

At this Farrant, who had been listening attentively to the conversation, coughed decorously. " Excuse me, gentlemen," he said. " But I think Mr. Mills has forgotten the telephone ? "

The Commissioner turned upon him. " What do you mean, Farrant ? What telephone ? "

" The private telephone, sir. Mr. Mills was using it when I came back from the hall."

To Sir Philip, who had been a silent spectator of the scene, it had been apparent from the first that there was no love lost between the secretary and the butler. His pencil moved more deliberately than ever as he awaited developments.

" Oh, so there is a private telephone," said the Commissioner. " Where does it lead to ? "

It was Mills who answered him. " Fort Comstock. Naturally it was my duty to ring up the chief editor, and inform him of Lord Comstock's death. That was hardly touching anything in the study, in the sense you mean."

" Did you speak to anybody at Fort Comstock besides the chief editor ? "

Mills hesitated. " Well, yes," he replied defiantly. " I spoke to the crime expert of the *Daily Bugle*, and gave him a short account of the events of this morning.

This statement fell like a bomb among the Scotland Yard contingent. Audible mutters came from the corner where Shawford and Churchill were sitting together, and it was only by an obvious effort that the Commissioner restrained himself. He contented himself with a glance at Sir Philip, on whose lips something very like a smile was visible. Then he turned to Farrant. " You overheard this conversation ? " he asked sharply.

" A bit of it, sir. I wondered why Mr. Mills should take so much trouble to tell his Lordship's people and nobody else."

" What do you mean by that ? "

" Well, sir, Mr. Mills had been given notice by his Lordship," replied Farrant malevolently. " I heard his Lordship tell him so at lunch yesterday. Something about selling information to rival newspapers, it was, sir."

" Is this a fact, Mr. Mills ? " the Commissioner asked.

" It is certainly a fact that Lord Comstock threatened me with dismissal at lunch yesterday. He had just seen something in one of the rival papers which he believed to be known only to himself. He accused me of having sold this information for my own benefit. But I did not treat his outburst seriously. Similar incidents have occurred before."

The Commissioner shrugged his shoulders. He had a feeling that the inquiry was straying from its proper course. In order to bring it back to realities he turned to Easton. " You made certain investigations outside the house, I believe ? " he asked curtly.

" Yes, sir. I thought it possible that Lord Comstock

might have been shot by somebody from outside the house, through the open windows of the study. As you can see by the plan, sir, there are no doors leading from the house directly on to the lawn. The back doors lead out of the house on the opposite side. Anyone wishing to reach the lawn would have to pass through two gates, one leading into the kitchen garden, the other from the kitchen garden to the lawn. Alternatively, he would have to climb the wall at the south-eastern corner of the house. That is, of course, sir, if he did not pass round the front of the house."

The Commissioner, who had been looking over Sir Philip's shoulder at the plan on the desk, nodded. " Yes, I see ; go ahead, Easton."

" Well, sir, there were no marks on the flower-beds below this wall, and no sign of anyone having climbed it. It is seven feet high, and would be difficult to climb in any case, without assistance. The gate between the kitchen garden and the lawn was locked. It is a heavy wrought-iron affair, and I was informed that only two keys to this exist. One was produced by the gardener to whom I spoke. The other I found upon Lord Comstock's desk."

Sir Philip looked up. " It doesn't look as if anybody had reached the lawn from that direction, does it, Easton ? " he remarked pleasantly. " And yet we have heard of somebody "—there was a significant emphasis upon this word—" of somebody who appeared upon the lawn. He must have come round by the front of the house, I suppose ? "

" I think not, sir," replied Easton, glancing at the Commissioner. " The gardener——"

" Oh, the gardener has something to say, has he ?

Have you got him outside, Hampton ? Bring him in, if so. We'll hear his story from his own lips."

So the gardener, an incongruous figure in that solemn room, was introduced. But his evidence tended to make things still more obscure. He had been working all the morning at the flower-beds beside the drive. Two or three motors had passed him, but he hadn't taken any heed of them. He hadn't expected his Lordship down that week, and he was late with the bedding-out. His Lordship had given him a proper dressing-down because there wasn't a good show of flowers. He was too busy to take much notice of motor cars and such.

" But you would have noticed if anybody had walked on to the lawn, I suppose ? " asked the Commissioner impatiently.

" I couldn't very well help noticing the lady when she stopped and watched what I was doing. She didn't say nothing, though, and I couldn't say who she was. I don't mind that I ever saw her before."

Sir Philip looked up and caught the Commissioner's eye. The fact that there was a lady in the case was a further complication. And it was very curious that neither Mills nor the butler had mentioned her presence. But the Commissioner was alert enough to display no surprise.

" Oh yes, the lady, of course," he said rather vaguely. " Do you remember what time it was when you saw her ? "

" Can't say that I do, sir. I'd left my watch in my coat pocket in the potting-shed. But it was a fair time before Mr. Scotney came out just afore one to call me."

" Mr. Scotney ? " the Commissioner asked. " Who's he ? "

" Why, the chauffeur, to be sure, sir. He always gives me a call just afore one when I'm working round the front. And I saw the lady long before then."

The Commissioner curbed his impatience. " Can't you give me some idea of how long before ? " he asked.

" Might have been one hour, might have been three. A man don't take much heed o' time when he's bedding-out. 'Tis a dull job, that is, and precious little praise at the end of it from his Lordship."

" The lady walked on to the lawn, you say. Did you see where she came from ? "

" Why, where would she come from ? Not out of the house, that's sure. Must have come in through the drive gate, I suppose. In one of they motors, most like. I didn't give it a thought. And she hadn't been on the lawn many minutes before she comes back again, quicker than she went."

" How far on to the lawn did she go ? "

" Bless you, sir, I can't tell you that. I had more to do than watch the visitors what come to the house. Besides, his Lordship wouldn't thank me to be too curious of any lady that might come to see him. Them as is shortsighted gets on best in some situations."

" Well, if you didn't see how far she went, you can tell what became of her, I suppose ? "

" Aye, I can do that, sir, for I saw her again a few minutes later. A motor drove out through the gate, and she was sitting beside the gentleman who was driving it. That was before I saw the other gentleman, of course."

" Before you saw which other gentleman ? " asked the Commissioner angrily.

" Why, him that came running round the corner of

the house across the lawn, to be sure, sir. I thought he was trying to catch up the lady. He had a motor, too, for I see him jump into it and go off after the car with the lady and the other gentleman in it."

" Oh, you saw that, did you ? Did you see anybody else whatever on the lawn this morning ? "

" Not a soul, sir. 'Twasn't usual for anybody to go that way in the morning."

" Did you leave your bedding-out to go to the kitchen garden at all ? "

" Not this morning, sir. I hadn't any occasion to, since I'd brought in the vegetables for the house afore nine o'clock."

" When did you last unlock the gate leading from the kitchen garden to the lawn ? "

" Not since the day before yesterday, sir, when I was mowing the lawn and carried the grass through that way to the marrow bed."

The Commissioner glanced at Sir Philip, who shook his head. At a sign from the former, Shawford led the gardener to the door, motioned him through, and shut it behind him. Then the Commissioner turned to Mills, " Who was this lady ? " he asked sharply.

Mills shrugged his shoulders. " I really can't say," he replied. " I never saw her, and this is the first I've heard of her. But, since she apparently went away with Sir Charles Hope-Fairweather, it seems reasonable to suppose that she came with him."

Apparently Farrant had not seen her either. As he was speaking, the telephone on Sir Philip's desk buzzed discreetly. The Home Secretary picked up the instrument and put the receiver to his ear. " Thanks, Anderson," he said. Then, to the Commissioner,

4

" Hope-Fairweather is here. We'd better have him in, I think." He returned to the telephone. " Show him in, will you, Anderson," he said.

The door opened, and Sir Charles entered the room. He was a tall man, exquisitely dressed, and with an impressive presence. But this was lost upon the group in the Home Secretary's room. By a common impulse each member of it turned his eyes upon the newcomer's hands. He still wore a glove upon his left hand, in which he held the second glove, withdrawn from his right.

He had clearly expected to find the Home Secretary alone. As he glanced round the room and saw its un-accustomed occupants, he came to an abrupt standstill. He glanced first at the Commissioner, who averted his eyes, and then at Sir Philip, who nodded towards a chair. " Sit down, Hope-Fairweather," said the latter brusquely. " I've got a question or two to ask you. You went to see Comstock this morning, I believe ? "

Sir Charles' eyes lighted up suddenly, whether with fear or astonishment it was impossible to say. He glanced round the room once more, and for the first time recognised Mills. His handsome face grew very red. " Yes, Sir Philip, I went to see him," he replied. " On a purely personal matter, of course. But, as his secretary will tell you, I was unfortunately compelled to leave the house without getting a word with him."

" A purely personal matter, you say ? Am I to under-stand that you and Comstock were on cordial terms ? This seems very curious for a man in your position."

Again that queer look came into the Chief Whip's eyes. " The terms we were on were anything but cordial," he replied. " In fact——" But he checked himself hurriedly.

" Yet you took the trouble to go to Hursley Lodge to see him," persisted Sir Philip. " Had you a previous appointment ? "

The Chief Whip shook his head violently. " Most certainly not," he replied. " I drove over merely on chance. I had something to say to Comstock which could only be mentioned at a personal interview. But, as I have said, I was unsuccessful. I had no opportunity for entering his presence."

" You were not able to penetrate into the study ? "

" I was not. Somebody else was in there all the time. I could hear Comstock's voice talking angrily off and on all the time I was there."

" From what Mr. Mills has told us, you seem to have been rather restless during your visit. You asked him to convey a message to your chauffeur that you might be detained, I believe."

" To my chauffeur ! " exclaimed Sir Charles. " Certainly not, I had no chauffeur with me. I was driving the car myself. I may have told the secretary—ah, yes, quite so, Mr. Mills—that I was going out to take a message to my car, when I happened to meet him in the hall."

" Somebody was waiting for you in the car, then ? " asked Sir Philip quietly.

Once more the Chief Whip grew very red. " Yes, a friend of mine," he replied in a tone of forced unconcern.

Sir Philip nodded. " Ah, I see. A lady, was it not ? "

The Chief Whip glanced swiftly round the room, as though trying to discover who could have revealed this fact. " Yes, it was a lady," he replied slowly. " Since she was not in any way concerned with my visit to Hursley Lodge, there is no necessity to mention her

name. I asked her to wait in the car while I went in to
see Comstock, telling her I should not be longer than a
few minutes. She knew nothing whatever of the matter
which I wished to discuss with him."

" You left in a considerable hurry, didn't you ? "

" I did. I had a luncheon appointment in town, and
I had already waited so long—till past mid-day—that I
was in danger of being late. Besides, my presence didn't
seem particularly welcome. I noticed that Mr. Mills
seemed very anxious to get rid of me."

Sir Philip was about to reply, when for the second
time the house telephone buzzed. With an impatient
gesture he picked up the instrument. " What is it now,
Anderson ? " he asked. " Oh, is he ? Very well, I'll
tell Hampton." He turned to the Commissioner.
" Littleton's on the phone, asking to speak to you," he
said. " Better have a word with him in Anderson's
room."

The Commissioner fairly rushed to the door, and, once
in the outer room, almost snatched the receiver from the
private secretary's hands. " Hullo ! " he exclaimed.
" Hullo ! Damn it, we've been cut off ! Yes, yes !
Hampton speaking. Is that you, Littleton ? Where are
you ? Where have you been all this time ? "

" I'm at Winborough." Littleton's voice replied.
" I say, I've had a devil of a time You've heard by now
that that swine Comstock's been murdered, I suppose ? "

" Heard it ! I've heard of nothing else for the last
hour and a half. What I want to know is, how the devil
you were mixed up in it. What in Heaven's name took
you to Hursley Lodge of all places this morning ?
Comstock's secretary, Mills, has told us all about it."

" Has he ? I shall want a few words with Mills when

I see him. What did I go to Hursley Lodge for ? Why, to see Comstock, of course. I had an idea that I could put a stop to that anti-police stunt of his. You've seen what his blessed rag says about the Little Cadbury case ? "

" Yes, yes," replied the Commissioner impatiently. " Get on, man, I can't stop talking to you here. We are holding a conference in the Home Secretary's room."

" Oh, that's it, is it ? Well, I'll give you the facts as briefly as I can. I knew of a way in which pressure could be brought upon Comstock. I happen to have come across a pretty sticky piece of work. There's a woman in it, of course. You'll hardly believe me when I tell you——"

" Not on the telephone. Never mind about that. What happened when you got there ? "

" A devil of a lot happened. I drove up, and found that young chap Mills at the door. Can't say that I was struck by the look of him. Wanted to keep me out, I fancy. But I soon put a stop to that nonsense. Told him that I meant to see Comstock, whatever he said. At last the fellow showed me into what looked like a drawing-room, and shut the door on me. And as soon as he'd gone, I heard voices from the next room. Comstock and somebody else having a devil of a row, I could tell that.

" I looked about the room a bit, and found that there was a dummy panel, forming a door, which must lead into the room where Comstock was kicking up all the rumpus. I didn't want to butt in, so I strolled across the room and looked out of the window on to a sort of lawn. There was nobody about outside as far as I could see but a gardener chap pottering about the flower beds."

"Did you see a car in the drive, besides the one you came in?" interrupted the Commissioner.

"Hullo! What do you know about that car? No, I didn't see it, that's the queer thing. Next thing was, I heard people moving about in the hall, and after a bit everything became quiet in Comstock's room. I waited for a bit, expecting that young chap Mills to come and show me in to see Comstock. But he didn't come, and I got a bit impatient. I meant to see Comstock, whether he and his secretary liked it or not. So I just opened that concealed door and looked in. I tell you, Hampton, it takes a lot to surprise me. But when I looked into that room I got the shock of my life."

"What did you see?" the Commissioner asked coldly.

"I saw Comstock lying in a heap in front of his desk with his chair on top of him. Of course, I went in then. Couldn't very well do anything else. Didn't take me long to see what had happened. Wound in the head, still bleeding. Chap dead all right, must have been killed instantaneously. And while I was looking at him, I heard a car drive off from somewhere in the drive. Fellow who killed Comstock, I concluded."

The Commissioner frowned. "Did you touch the body or anything in the room?" he asked.

"Hardly. Besides, I hadn't time. Just a chance I might catch that car, you see. I made for the open window, and jumped out. Lucky I didn't break my neck. It was a lot farther to the ground than I had bargained for. Crocked one knee a bit, as it was. However, I managed to run to my car, and set off after the chap I'd heard.

"Then a rotten thing happened. I swung out at the gate, going like hell, I'll admit, and before I knew where

I was I was into a constable riding a bicycle. The idiot was right over on the wrong side of his road, and I couldn't help myself. 'Pon my word, Hampton, I didn't know what to do. If I stopped to pick him up, I should lose all hope of catching the car I was after. But the fellow lay so darned still, with the bicycle twisted up like a Chinese puzzle, that I felt I couldn't leave him there. So I stopped the car, got out, and had a look at him. And then I saw that he was pretty badly injured. Only thing to do was to take him to hospital.

" I had noticed a hospital place on my way to Hursley Lodge. I picked the poor fellow up and hoisted him into the back of the car, and off I went. After all, Comstock was dead, and I couldn't do any more for him. But I might save this chap's life if I could get a doctor to him at once."

" A live dog being better than a dead lion," remarked the Commissioner. " Get on, man."

" Well, my luck was dead out. I suppose it was a couple of miles or so to the hospital. And I was just about half way there when I ran out of petrol. There'll be hell about that when I get back to the Yard. My orders are that my car is always to be filled up as soon as she's brought in. Of course, I was carrying a spare can, and I tipped that in. But the blessed autovac didn't seem to suck properly. I had to crank up the engine for a devil of a time before I could get any petrol to the carburetter."

" Yes, yes; never mind these details. You were delayed. What then ? "

" I got the poor devil to hospital, but there seemed to be nobody there but a fool of a woman. Matron, I suppose. Regular cottage hospital, more cottage than

hospital. Got the poor chap to bed. Rang up a doctor.
Out. Rang up another. Out. Matron woman warned
me that patient was in a very bad way. Getting desperate, when a doctor looked in. I was afraid the poor
chap was done for this time, but after a good wait doctor
came down and told me he had a fighting chance, lot
of ribs done in, and heaven knows what else. And then
I got him to have a look at my knee, which was devilish
painful and so stiff I could hardly move it. Altogether,
it was past a quarter to two before I got away from that
infernal hospital.

"It struck me then that I had never seen the number
of the car I'd been chasing. I drove back to Hursley
Lodge, thinking that someone about the place must
have noticed it. But at first I couldn't find anybody
with any sense in their heads. There was a local sergeant
in charge, chap like a bullock, with about as much
intelligence. He told me that the local superintendent,
Weston, or some such name, had been mucking about the
place. Destroyed every vestige of a clue, I expect. You
know what these local men are. And, if you please, he
trotted all the likely witnesses up to town. Did you
ever hear of such an ass ? "

"Superintendent Easton acted upon my instructions,"
the Commissioner remarked acidly.

"Sorry, I didn't know that. It looked to me as though
the local people were blundering, as usual. So I thought
I'd better do what I could to put things straight. I
went round to the garage, and there I found Comstock's
chauffeur, a very decent, sensible chap by the name of
Scotney.

"He had seen the other car, all right. It had been
standing in the drive for quite a long time. It's difficult

to explain, but the drive's got a sort of kink in it. Goes round in a circle, with a clump of trees in the middle——"

" Yes, I know all about that," the Commissioner interrupted. " The trees were between you and the car, so that you couldn't see it. What about this chauffeur ? "

" You seem to know the dickens of a lot, Hampton. The chauffeur ? Oh, most observant chap. He had noticed the number, all right. QZ7623. Came out with it pat. Hadn't ever seen the car before, he told me. Twenty horse Armstrong saloon, nearly new, painted blue. Very fine car, according to Scotney. And, would you believe it, the local chaps had never even asked him for the description !

" Well, I happened to remember that QZ are the registration letters of the borough of Winborough, not more than seven or eight miles away. So off I went, straight away, to see the licensing authorities there. Sleepy old place, and sleepy old people. Took me a devil of a time at the Town Hall to find the man I wanted. Then we looked up the records, and found that QZ7623 had been allotted to the parson, Canon Pritchard. Chap at the Town Hall told me that his parishioners had just presented him with an Austin Seven. I saw at once there was something wrong, but I went on to the vicarage. There was the Austin in the garage, where Mrs. Pritchard swore it had been all the morning. Couldn't see the vicar himself. Up in London, they told me, attending some sort of a conference of parsons."

" Convocation, of course. Well, what then ? "

" Well, it's clear that the car that was at Hursley Lodge is sailing under false colours. I got on the 'phone to the Yard, to give orders to stop any car with the number QZ7623. As soon as I got through they told me that you had been asking for me, and were now at the Home Office. So I put a call through, and here I am. Any orders ? "

The Commissioner hesitated. It was in his mind to tell Littleton his candid opinion of his behaviour. Jumping to conclusions like that ! Why the devil hadn't he stayed at Hursley Lodge like a rational being ? Only the presence of Anderson, the private secretary, restrained Compton from expressing his feelings.

" You don't seem to have been particularly successful in your search for the murderer," he said. " The best thing you can do now is to get back to the Yard as quickly as you can. You can give me fuller details then."

He put down the telephone, and returned thoughtfully to the Home Secretary's room. Sir Philip was still busy with his designs, which by now had almost completely covered his blotting paper. He looked up as the Commissioner came in. " Well, Hampton ? " he asked cheerfully. " Any news ? "

The Commissioner was not in the least anxious to repeat the conversation which he had had with his assistant. He felt quite incapable of making it sound convincing in Sir Philip's highly critical ears. Littleton had made a fool of himself, but there was no point in revealing this fact before an audience. Later, perhaps, he might have a chance of justifying himself privately. " Littleton told me nothing of importance that we do not know already," he replied evasively.

" Didn't he ? " said Sir Philip gently. " I confess that I had hoped that he would be able to solve the mystery.

It does not often happen that the officer in charge of the Criminal Investigation Department is actually on the spot when a murder is committed. Littleton's lack of information is disappointing. Most disappointing."

Rather an awkward silence fell upon the room. The Commissioner hastened to break it. He turned abruptly to Sir Charles. " What is the make and number of your car ? " he asked.

" It's a comparatively new Armstrong saloon, and the number is QX7623," replied Sir Charles without hesitation.

The Commissioner nodded. So that point was explained. The chauffeur had probably memorized the number wrongly. QZ instead of QX. An easy enough mistake to make. QX was one of the London letters. But he was still anxious to divert attention from Littleton's exploits. The pistol, lying on Sir Philip's desk, caught his eye, and he picked it up.

" You say that Lord Comstock kept this on his desk, Mr. Mills," he said. Do you know why he did so ? Had he any fear that he might be attacked ? "

Mills smiled rather contemptuously. " Lord Comstock frequently expressed himself as being afraid of nobody," he replied. " In any case, he would not have relied upon firearms to protect himself. One of his crime experts gave him that pistol, I believe. It was to form the basis of one of his criticisms of the methods of the police, or so I understand."

Hitherto, the pistol had been hidden from Churchill, seated at some distance from the desk. But as soon as the Commissioner picked it up, he could see it plainly. It was a small, vicious-looking weapon, not more than three inches over all. Churchill stared at it in amazement as Mills was speaking. Then he could no longer control himself. " Well, I'm blest if that isn't another of them ! " he exclaimed in what he may have believed to be a whisper.

But it seemed that Sir Philip had remarkably good ears. He looked up at once, and took in the situation at a glance. Churchill's remark had, for some reason, scandalized both the Commissioner and Shawford. They were frowning ominously, and the wretched superintendent looked as if he wished the floor to open and swallow him up. Another departmental secret, of course, thought Sir Philip.

" I think, Hampton, that we have heard all that the witnesses can tell us for the present," he said. " If you have no objection, we will talk this matter over together. But, in the absence of Littleton, I think that the Chief Constable and the Superintendent should remain."

Mills, Easton, and Farrant could, of course, be thus summarily dismissed ; it was not even a compliment that the Commissioner went with them to the next room. The Chief Whip needed different treatment ; and the Home Secretary was at pains to show his personal indebtedness for Sir Charles' visit before he handed him over to the experienced ministrations of Mr. Anderson.

The Commissioner, Shawford, and Churchill had time to await Sir Philip's return in silent apprehension, but not to concert any measures of mutual support. Sir Philip resumed his place and his pencil, and immediately destroyed Churchill's faint hope that his unfortunate remark has gone unnoticed.

" Now, Superintendent ! " he said sharply. " Perhaps you will tell us where you have seen a pistol like this before ? "

Churchill gulped, and ran his finger round between his collar and his neck. " I'm not sure about it, sir," he began desperately. " When Sir Henry Hampton held it up just now, I thought——"

" Let me have that pistol a moment, will you, Hampton ? " said Sir Phillip. " Thank you. Bring your chair close up to the desk, Superintendent. I should not like you to be mistaken. Examine the pistol closely. Now, have you ever seen one like it before or not ? "

Churchill knew from the tone of the Home Secretary's voice that he was not to be trifled with. He picked up the pistol gingerly, and laid it down again. " Yes, sir, I have seen one exactly like it," he replied. " I don't think that there are many in this country. The race-gangs are beginning to use them, sir. You can't see a pistol that size when it's held in the palm of the hand, and yet it's a deadly little weapon at its own short range, and quiet too—*sounds* most like a toy pistol. A week or two ago the Sussex police got hold of a chap at Lewes races, and he had one of these on him. That's how I came to see it, sir."

" Where did you see it, Superintendent ? "

" It was sent up to the Yard, sir, and Mr. Littleton called some of us into his room to show it to us."

" Oh, Mr. Littleton showed it to you, did he ? When was this ? "

" Yesterday morning, sir. Chief Constable Shawford was there at the time, sir."

" Did Littleton show you this interesting specimen, Hampton ? " asked Sir Philip.

" No, he didn't," replied the Commissioner brusquely. " He did mention to me, however, that he had been sent a pistol captured at Lewes races."

" What did Mr. Littleton do with the pistol after he had shown it to you, Superintendent ? "

" As far as I remember, sir, he put it down on his desk."

" He put it down on his desk. Nasty thing to have lying about, especially as it might have been loaded. Was it loaded, do you know ? "

" It was when I first saw it, sir. But Mr. Littleton unloaded it while I was in the room, sir."

" A wise precaution. Now, Chief Constable, you told us that you were in Mr. Littleton's room this morning discussing the Little Cadbury case, if I remember rightly. Did you see this pistol that the Superintendent talks about then ? "

Shawford cleared his throat. " Yes, sir. It was lying on Mr. Littleton's desk."

Sir Philip looked speculatively at the designs upon his blotting-paper. " I wonder if it is there now ? " he said gently. " I think, Hampton, that it would be as well if you rang up the Yard and asked them to look."

The Commissioner was about to leave the room, when Shawford spoke again. " I don't think it will be there now, sir," he said timidly.

" Don't you, Chief Constable ? And what makes you think that ? "

" Well, sir, while I was talking to Mr. Littleton this morning, he picked it up and put it in his pocket. He said something about taking it round to a gunsmith for expert opinion, sir."

Sir Philip sighed, and leaned back in his chair. " It is extraordinary how difficult it is to elucidate the truth," he said wearily. " I might surely have been told this fact without the necessity for cross-examination. I begin to feel that Comstock's attack on the police was not without some justification. I shall expect you, Hampton, to take some action in regard to this want of frankness."

Fortunately for the Commissioner, his reply was interrupted by the buzzing of the house telephone. Sir Philip picked up the instrument and listened. " Yes, certainly, Anderson," he said. " A special edition, you say ? Oh, I know how they got hold of it. The enterprising Mr. Mills gave them the information over the private telephone from Hursley Lodge. Yes, bring it in, by all means."

Anderson came in, bearing a special edition of the *Evening Clarion*, which he handed to Sir Philip. Across the whole width of the front page were the glaring headlines :

MURDER OF LORD COMSTOCK.
WHAT DO THE POLICE KNOW ?

Sir Philip glanced through the heavily-leaded letter-press. It contained a vivid account of the events of the morning, obviously derived from Mills' message. Following this was a special article by " Our well-known Crime Expert," who was obviously in his element.

" In spite of the fact that one of the Assistant Commissioners of Metropolitan Police, the official who is at the head of our ludicrously inefficient Criminal Investigation Department, was actually present at Hursley Lodge when the dastardly crime was committed, no arrest has yet been made. The British public, accustomed to repeated failures of a similar kind, may see nothing extraordinary in this. But we venture to ask the question, what was the Assistant Commissioner doing at Hursley Lodge ? We have authority for stating that his visit was not by appointment with Lord Comstock,

and that, in fact, his appearance was entirely unexpected.
This visit may have been made with perfectly innocent
intentions. But once more we call upon the Home
Secretary to insist upon a thorough investigation of the
circumstances, and that by some independent body.
The Criminal Investigation Department is clearly prejudiced, since its chief official must appear as an actor in
the drama. Only the most impartial investigation can
be relied upon to solve the mystery of this dastardly
outrage."

And so on, to the extent of a couple of columns or
more.

Sir Philip's expression did not betray his thoughts as
he handed the paper to the Commissioner. " Well,
Hampton, what do you make of that ? " he asked.

The Commissioner ran his eye through the article,
and frowned. " It seems that Comstock's stunts live
after him," he replied.

" Stunt or no stunt it seems to me that Littleton's
visit to Hursley Lodge will want a lot of explanation,"
said Sir Philip gravely. " As this fellow asks, what was
he doing there ? We know that he bitterly resented
Comstock's attack on Scotland Yard. Several other
details have been revealed, which place his actions in
none too favourable a light. And the grim fact remains
that Comstock has been murdered."

There was no mistaking the significance of the Home
Secretary's words. But the Commissioner, bitterly
annoyed as he was with Littleton's account of his actions,
was not prepared to acquiesce tamely in his guilt. Not
that he considered it impossible. Littleton was notori-
ously headstrong. It was certain that he and Comstock
could not have met, even for a moment, without a furious

altercation arising immediately. This would undoubtedly have led to personal violence if the characters of the two men were considered. Littleton would not have shot Comstock in cold blood. But if Comstock had threatened him with the pistol found on his desk——

No; the Commissioner's reluctance to admit the possibility of Littleton's guilt was not based upon conviction. It was due to his appreciation of the scandal which must ensue if such a thing were suggested. It might well be argued that if an Assistant Commissioner of Police were capable of murder, Comstock's attacks upon that force were fully justified. For the honour of the Department of which he had charge, it was essential that no breath of official suspicion should cloud for a moment the reputation of his subordinate.

" If you will forgive my saying so, sir, it is ridiculous to suppose that Littleton can have had anything to do with the crime," he said stiffly. " I am well aware that he is impulsive to a fault, and that he would go to almost any lengths to defend his colleagues from outside attack. But nobody who knew him well would believe for a moment that he would condescend to murder. Chief Constable Shawford, who for years has worked in close association with him, will bear me out in that."

" That I will, sir ! " exclaimed Shawford courageously. " I'd sooner suspect myself than Mr. Littleton."

" The *esprit de corps* displayed by the officers of your Department is really touching, Compton," Sir Philip remarked drily. " In vulgar parlance, they'd rather die than give one another away. I am not likely to forget the difficulty which I experienced in extracting the truth about the second pistol. If you insist that Littleton cannot be guilty, what alternative do you suggest ? "

5

" I would point out that Sir Charles Hope-Fairweather's replies to your questions were scarcely satisfactory," the Commissioner replied equally.

" Hope-Fairweather ! I'll admit that some politicians are hardly qualified to sit among the angels. But they do not as a rule indulge in personal murder. Besides, why in the world should Hope-Fairweather want to murder Comstock ? "

" There must be a good many people who, for various reasons, will rejoice at his death. He was the sort of man who makes private enemies as well as public ones. For instance, his dealings with women were notorious, and in some cases sufficiently scandalous. And Hope-Fairweather had a woman, whose name he refuses to divulge, with him when he went to Hursley Lodge."

" *Cherchez la femme*, eh ? You suggest that this woman supplied the motive, direct or indirect, for Comstock's murder ? "

" I suggest nothing at present. But I maintain that the identity of this woman calls for investigation. And I cannot overlook Hope-Fairweather's extraordinary behaviour while he was at Hursley Lodge, nor the fact that he was wearing gloves the whole time he was there."

" The evidence on these points is derived solely from a witness who is himself not wholly free from suspicion," said Sir Philip swiftly. " I shall require something very much more substantial before I can bring myself to believe in the guilt of the Chief Whip of my own party. You say it is ridiculous to suspect Littleton. I reply that it is infinitely more ridiculous to suspect Hope-Fairweather. If the police can produce no more plausible theory than this, I can understand the failures with which Comstock charged them. What have you to say on the subject, Chief Constable ? "

Shawford, thus suddenly appealed to, sat bolt upright in his chair. He was in a quandary. While anxious to shield Littleton at any cost, he did not dare, in the face of the Home Secretary's disapproval, support the Commissioner's opinion. He fell back upon a suggestion which seemed to him infinitely tactful.

" Mr. Mills, as you point out, sir, is a witness not wholly free from suspicion," he replied. "Lord Comstock seems to have treated him pretty badly, by his own account. And there's that matter of his having been given notice. His explanation of what Farrant said about that doesn't sound very convincing to me, sir."

Sir Philip nodded. " I did not care very much for Mills' manner. The impression I derived from his statement was that he was withholding at least part of the truth. What do you think about it, Hampton ? "

" I think that Shawford is talking nonsense," the Commissioner replied angrily. He was annoyed that the Chief Constable had not endorsed his suggestion. " Farrant is no more worthy of belief than Mills. He may have trumped up that story about Comstock giving his secretary notice to screen himself. It would be just as reasonable to suppose that he shot Comstock himself. If Mills wanted to murder his employer, he had plenty of opportunity for doing so. Would he have been likely to choose a time when the house was beseiged by visitors, including the Assistant Commissioner of Police ? I think we can safely disregard such an absurd suggestion."

" It would appear that all theories as to the identity of

Comstock's murderer must be equally absurd," Sir Philip remarked. " But perhaps Superintendent Churchill has formed some opinion ? "

Churchill, who had hoped to be overlooked, flushed crimson. He had formed an opinion, but he would infinitely have preferred to have been allowed to keep it to himself, at least for the present. After all, only one of the visitors to Hursley Lodge had been admitted to Lord Comstock's presence, and the evidence of a serious altercation having taken place between them was beyond dispute. Moreover, Churchill had been brought up to the narrowest and most fanatical religious views. In his childhood he had been taught that all ecclesiastical dignitaries were servants of the Scarlet Woman, and, since he had probably never met one of them, the influence of this teaching was still strong.

And yet he hesitated, not at all certain of how his suggestion would be received. It was not until Sir Philip had thrown him a word of rather impatient encouragement—" Come along, Superintendent, let us hear what you have to say ! "—that he could bring himself to speak. And then he was surprised at the confident tone of his own voice. " None of the witnesses admits having seen Lord Comstock alive after the departure of His Grace the Archbishop, sir."

The Commissioner looked at the wretched Churchill as though he suspected him of having taken leave of his senses. He did not even deign to make any comment. The Archbishop, Comstock's old headmaster ! Words failed him to express his contempt of such an idea.

But Sir Philip had taken up his pencil once more. " There is more than one example in history of a criminal Archbishop," he said reminiscently. " But recently the type seems to have gone out of fashion. However, I suppose that none of us here have any experience of what an angry Archbishop is capable. He might consider himself to be the instrument of the justice of Heaven. I don't know."

The Commissioner frowned. He was anxious to get back to Scotland Yard and have a heart-to-heart talk with Littleton. "If I may say so, I do not think that guess-work will help us much, sir," he ventured. "Until we have had an opportunity for further investigation——"

But Sir Philip interrupted him. "That's just it, Hampton. Who is going to conduct this investigation ? "

The Commissioner stared at him. "The officers of the Criminal Investigation Department, I presume," he replied stiffly.

"With Littleton at their head ? " Sir Philip asked. "No, that won't do, Hampton. You're prejudiced, of course, but you must admit that there is something in what this journalist fellow says. It is essentially a bad principle to entrust the conduct of an investigation to one of the parties interested."

The Commissioner shrugged his shoulders. " I should not be inclined to pay much attention to the ravings of the Comstock Press," he replied contemptuously.

" You do not seem to understand that we must take care not to justify those ravings, as you call them. In any case, I must insist that Littleton be suspended until the mystery of Comstock's murder is solved."

The Commissioner hesitated for a moment, then bowed his head in assent. After all, no great harm could come of this. It would keep Littleton out of further mischief. He had certainly not distinguished himself so far. His subordinates were quite capable of carrying on without his direction.

"Very well. That point is settled," Sir Philip continued. "Now, I think we might go a step farther. Comstock and his gang have always maintained that the police are inefficient, and that outside experts, given the necessary facilities, could succeed where they have failed. Comstock himself is now the victim of murder. It seems to me that it would be no more than poetic justice to put his own principles into operation in order to discover the criminal."

"I will give instructions that representatives of the Press shall be given such information of the progress of the investigation as seems expedient," said the Commissioner.

Sir Philip shook his head. "That won't do, Hampton," he replied. "In this case, public opinion must be satisfied that the police are hiding nothing. Comstock's campaign has produced a deeper impression than you are ready to admit. My instructions are these. Your department must hold its hand—make sure that the inquest does not go beyond evidence of identity, and then adjourns *sine die*, but that's all. Instead of you, the outside experts are to be called in, allowed forty-eight hours to make their reports, and, without any reserve whatever, given all the information in your possession to help them to do so. There must be no suggestion of the concealment of the smallest detail. This is the only way to restore the reputation of the police, already compromised by Littleton's actions."

The Commissioner, astounded by this speech, would have raised objections. But Sir Philip gave him no opportunity to speak. "No, Hampton, that is my last word," he continued. " I have myself had evidence this afternoon of a certain lack of frankness among members of your department. If the public were to get the impression that the police were capable of shielding suspects because of the positions which they occupy, the results would be disastrous. I shall be glad if you will see that my instructions are carried out without delay. And here," he concluded, " is a list of the experts with whom I propose to get in touch at once."

The Commissioner took the list, hoping to find in it an opening for a renewed protest. Instead, he found himself gaping at a neat time-table, and particularly at its last phrase :

9 a.m.	Comstock at breakfast.
11.35 a.m. (say).	C. interviews Archbishop.
11.50 or 55 a.m.	Fairweather arrives.
By 12 noon.	Littleton also there.
	H.-Fairweather in waiting-room.
At noon.	Mills in Office.
	Littleton in waiting-room.
	Comstock and Archbishop in argument.
12.22 p.m.	Mills returns to work in the Office, all the visitors having departed.
1.5 p.m.	Butler calls Mills from Office.
1.7 p.m.	Police informed.
1.15 p.m.	Easton arrives.
1.30 p.m.	C.I.D. informed by Chief Constable.
2.30 p.m.	Home Secretary takes personal charge.

" But—do you mean, Sir Philip, that you personally . . . ? "

" What ?—Oh, *that's* not the list. Those are my notes. This will come up in the House, you know. Here's the

list I meant. If I add to it, I'll tell Anderson to let you
know. That is perfectly clear, I hope ? " He recovered
the time-table.

The Commissioner bowed. Further argument, he
knew, was useless. He shepherded Shawford and
Churchill from the room, and returned to Scotland Yard,
taking with him the pistol which had been found by
Superintendent Easton.

Littleton had not yet returned from Winborough, but
the Commissioner found a lengthy medical report await-
ing him. He read it through, and made a note of the
principal points contained in it.

The examining surgeon reported that, from the
appearance and temperature of the body, Comstock
must have been dead for certainly more than one and
probably two hours when examined at 2.15 p.m. Death,
therefore, must have taken place before 1.15 p.m.
(" helpful," snorted the Commissioner) and probably
before 12.15 p.m.

From the nature of the wound, death must have been
practically instantaneous, The cause of death was
penetration of the brain by a bullet, which had entered
the head by the left temple. No traces of burning or
of powder blackening could be found in the neighbourhood of the wound.

The course of the bullet had been slightly upward.
That is to say, it had been found at a spot slightly higher
in the head than the point of entry. It had been
extracted, and was of very small calibre, ·15 inch, as
far as could be judged. Owing to slight flattening, however, it was impossible to measure the calibre exactly.
The marks of the rifling, however, could still be detected
near the base.

The bullet itself, wrapped up in tissue paper and enclosed in a pill-box, accompanied the report. The Commissioner unfolded it and looked at it closely. It was certainly flattened at the head, but the base appeared to have retained its original dimensions.

He took the pistol from his pocket and inserted the base of the bullet into the muzzle. It fitted exactly.

INTRODUCTION TO PART II

"DEAR JOHN RHODE,

"You do indeed know how to take a hint! This is a superb Problem, with all the recognised ingredients—save only our old friend the "blunt instrument," of which I should have reminded you.

"Yet I am not much farther forward, for I cannot imagine what the solution of your problem can be. However, there is, as you have shown, a friendly readiness amongst the members of the Detection Club to help the weaker brethren, so I have written to one or two of our friends to ask them to tell me what, in the opinion of their Sleuths, the solution is.

"By the way, my earlier letter to you rather suggested that *I* had thought of the title 'Ask a Policeman.' Actually, Arthur Barker suggested it to me, but an author is naturally reluctant to give any credit to a publisher.

"Yours ever,
"MILWARD KENNEDY."

"*P.S.*—I find that I have made an awkward blunder. By a clerical error I have mixed up the sleuths. I have asked Dorothy L. Sayers for Mr. Sheringham's views, Anthony Berkeley for Lord Peter's; I have applied to Helen Simpson for Mrs. Bradley's aid, and to Gladys Mitchell for Sir John's. Never mind; let us see what happens."

PART II

CHAPTER I

MRS. BRADLEY'S DILEMMA

BY HELEN SIMPSON

(1)

MRS. BRADLEY was the perfect guest. Even relatives-in-law, those touchy, difficult, and chary hosts, continually requested her to stay, were disappointed when she refused, and frolicked about her like puppies unleashed when she spared them a week in the summer. This similitude might hardly apply to the stately gambols of Lady Selina Lestrange, who weighed fifteen stone, and seldom moved far save under haulage ; but the moral effect of Mrs. Bradley's visits may be thus, not inadequately, represented. The lure on the present occasion had been horticultural and psychological.

" Really, Adela dear, I want to consult you about Sally. She seems to be growing quite morbid, won't go about, meets a most impossible person secretly, and has been getting, I find, all sorts of dreadful medical books from the London Library. I wrote to them and stopped it, of course. She is behaving very badly to that nice Dick Paradine, you knew his father, and of course *I* have *no* influence, but I believe the child really respects

your opinion. Our borders are exquisite, it seems hard
to realize that with all this taxation we may have to
cut down the outdoors staff, and next year it will be a
wilderness. So do come——"

- Thus Lady Selina, at her none too extensive wits' end;
to which Mrs. Bradley crisply replied :

" I should like to see your garden, and will come, if I
may, next Monday. Sally, I imagine, needs something
to do rather than someone to marry."

The result of this interchange was Mrs. Bradley's
arrival in time to drink tea under an immemorial elm on
the Lestrange's lawn, and, with a bright, black eye alert
for wasps, to listen to her sister-in-law's moan.

"——and she won't be civil, except to this awful young
man, and she huddles herself up all day in her room. It's
morbid, and if there's anything I dread—it's bad enough
having Ferdinand always in the papers."

" To say nothing of me," supplemented Mrs. Bradley
with a gleam.

" Darling, I know you never actually seek notoriety.
But I mean, all this obsession with crime ! I do think
Ferdinand might sometimes find someone respectable to
defend."

That famous criminal lawyer's mother gave a loud
cackle of laughter that set off Lady Selina's parrot, who
had been brought out for an airing in the June sun.

" Ha, ha, ha," observed the parrot shrilly. " Give us a
kiss, give us a drop o' beer. Smack ! "

To this Mrs. Bradley's cackle played second, and the
duet brought a figure to one of the second floor windows
of the distant house. Mrs. Bradley's sharp eyes noted
it at once ; noted, too, an odd appearance about the
mouth, as of a thin dark moustache. " Pencil," pro-

claimed her thoughts, while her remarkable voice responded in the negative to her hostess's question concerning more tea.

"Delicious, but no more. Your garden's divine. I simply must walk about."

"Shall I come with you?" Lady Selina's fond gaze was on the strawberries, of which she had already consumed two platefuls.

"Stay where you are," commanded Mrs. Bradley. "Goodness, I've known you more than seven years."

"I thought that was poking fires."

"Gardens too," responded Mrs. Bradley firmly, who detested a personally-conducted tour as intensely as she favoured a solitary stroll. Her objection was sustained by the parrot, who exclaimed with hospitable heartiness:

"Give 'er air, give us a drop o' beer, hullo, hullo, she's my sweetie!"

Mrs. Bradley thus encouraged set off on her tour, keeping well within the field of vision of the second floor window, slowly ranging, surveying flowers with almost professional deliberation. She had worked round to that side of the garden where rhododendrons, past their prime but still heavy with bloom, made an impermeable screen, when she heard the expected voice.

"What are you doing, Aunt Adela, snooping about?"

"I am snooping, Sally, if that nondescript word means exploring, your mother's garden." She eyed swiftly, piercingly, the slim young figure before her. "And what about you?"

"Mummy's asked you to talk to me, hasn't she?" asked Sally with no preliminary sparring.

"She did," admitted Mrs. Bradley, unconcerned, "but I shan't need to."

"Oh!" Sally was momentarily dashed.

"When," pursued Mrs. Bradley, "I hear of a girl who shuts herself up in her room, and gets in medical books, and snubs her admirer, I don't jump to the concluson that she's going to murder him. I assume at once that she is writing a detective novel."

Sarah stared a moment, and gave vent to an expletive which wrinkled Mrs. Bradley's eyes with distaste.

"Blast! And I didn't want Mummy to know!"

"So you shut yourself up, and don't go out, and won't be civil, and generally behave in a way calculated to drive her to frenzy."

"Don't go out! Where is there to go? You don't know how dull it is here."

"Dull, with his lordship of Common-Stock at your back door?"

"He's an old toad. He's vile to everybody. Teddy Mills told me——"

She halted. "Oh, well, I don't suppose it matters. Teddy's leaving the old brute, anyway. But he said sometimes he feels like strangling him. He uses money like a bludgeon, and publicity like poison-gas."

"A quotation from your book, I presume," said Mrs. Bradley, "or from Mr. Edward Mills?"

"As a matter of fact," Sally answered, with an innocent air, "I thought it would be rather fun to make my murderer someone like Lord Comstock."

"Never embark on a jargon you don't know. Landed gentry are more in your line, and journalese is one of the more difficult languages."

"Oh, Teddy helps with that."

"H'm!" Mrs. Bradley cleared her throat with emphasis, and lifted one yellowish claw covered with admirable but equally yellowish diamonds. "Edward is forbidden fruit; Edward takes your fancy. Edward's employer is unsympathetic. Your mother also is unsympathetic. Don't interrupt me. Comstock keeps Edward's nose to the grindstone and makes his life a burden generally. It is difficult for you to meet Edward often; whose fault? The employer's, naturally. You therefore start a novel, in which you avenge yourself on the employer by proxy, and with impunity. The name for this process is wish-fulfilment. Two centuries back people stuck pins into wax figures with the same idea."

Sally, who had begun by looking angry, now had subsided to something like reluctant awe.

" I say, Aunt Adela, that's most awfully good. Grand sleuthing——"

" Is it correct? "

" Pretty well. I mean, Teddy's fearfully good-looking, and good at things, and that old animal won't ever let him off the chain. And then Mummy's always ramming Dickie Paradine down my throat."

" Do you want me to speak to your mother about it? "

" Oh no, please," said the girl in a great hurry. " You see, there wouldn't be much money, and of course he's frightfully young and so am I really, if you come to think of it."

Mrs. Bradley came to think of Sally's seventeen years, and found them surprising in combination with this very reasonable attitude.

" The question of marriage hasn't arisen, then? "

" No. Why should it? Why should one start off being all stuffy? Marriage is like cold cocoa, nourishing but nauseous."

Mrs. Bradley surrounded this last remark with

6

quotation marks, labelled it "Edward Mills, Esq.,"
and passed on.

"I think I shall have to meet this young man."

"Mummy won't have him here. Mummy's mad-
deningly county, sometimes. I mean, Teddy's meeting
Cabinet Ministers and people like that all day. He's
bound to get on."

"I see. Ambitious?"

"Oh yes, fearfully."

"Yet he is leaving this employment where he meets
such daily stepping-stones to ambition?"

The girl flushed.

"Teddys awfully sensitive. Why should he stay and
be treated like a pickpocket? Aunt Adela, swear you
won't say a word to Mummy about all this?"

"I'm your mother's friend, you know," Mrs. Bradley
reminded her.

"Yes, but you didn't play fair. I mean, you got it out
of me—I mean, it's Teddy's secret as well as mine. And
after all "—a touch, could it be of relief?—" he'll be
going away soon."

"We'll see," said Mrs. Bradley. Then, briskly, "Let
me help you with the book, at any rate. How far have
you got?"

"Only the first two chapters."

"Body on the floor, I suppose, in the study?"

"Yes. Shot. Lots of blood," Sally responded with
relish.

"Off with his head! So much for Comstock," pro-
claimed Mrs. Bradley grandly, her amazing voice lighting
up even so uninspired, so very blank a verse, into poetry.
Another voice, an excited and bubbling voice, but one
that knew its place, said at her shoulder :

" For you, madam. A note. Gentleman's waiting."

Mrs. Bradley was too much of her generation to give any outward sign of irritation or dismay. She did say, however, plaintively :

" Now, who can have found me here ? " as she opened the envelope. The note was long ; it covered two sheets, and when she had read it she paused a moment, weighing it in her hand with pursed lips, thinking. At last she asked of the waiting butler an unexpected question.

" What's the time ? "

It was six ; five o'clock by what the agricultural neighbourhood called God's time, and completely light. Her next question was to Sarah.

" Dear child, do you think your mother's ban on young men would extend to an Assistant Commissioner of Police ? "

And she handed the note, which Sarah conned.

" Heard in the village you'd just arrived. Look here, may I see you ? Sorry, but it's something really urgent, and I've got to get back to London at once. Please. A. L."

" Now what," pondered Mrs. Bradley, " can Alan Littleton's really urgent trouble be ? "

It was a rhetorical question, one, that is, which anticipates no answer ; but answered it was, and from an unexpected source.

" Pardon me, madam," said the voice of the salver-bearer, tremulous with that sweetest, supremest human joy, the joy of being first with the news. " Can the gentleman be referring to the murder of Lord Comstock ? " And, while they gaped : " Found in his study, miss. Shot through the 'ead. (Just 'ad the news from the grocer's boy, madam.) Shot right through the 'ead ;

blood "— the gleam in the salver-bearer's eye betrayed
him an amateur of crime—" blood everywhere."

(II)

The situation was more than usually unfair to Lady
Selina. Seated in a pleasant torpor, comfortably involved
in a patent garden chair from which no unaided exit
was possible, her contented gaze resting upon an empty
cream-jug, she was suddenly assailed by her daughter,
breaking the news that an Assistant Commissioner of
Police was on the premises, and that her neighbour,
whom she ignored while detesting, had been murdered
during the day. At first her reaction to the double news
was slow; the effect of the latter part, not unpleasant,
being cancelled out by the former statement, which
seemed to have more than a savour of the dreaded
morbidity. But that savour, like a clove of garlic artfully
used in cookery, rose gradually to appal and permeate
her whole mind. That the neighbour should meet a
thoroughly deserved end was nothing much ; that her
roof should harbour policemen was serious and unsettling,
and a matter that must at once be dealt with in person.

Her first recorded utterance was : " Bother Adela ! "

Her second : " Well, I suppose—but I cannot and
will not have him to sleep ! "

Her daughter, wrought to politeness and tact by this
new excitement, reassured her.

" He only wants to talk with Aunt Adela. And he
says he's probably not a policeman any more."

" Then why does he come here ? "

" Aunt Adela, Mummy, I told you. He's come about
the murder. It's frightfully important. Oh, Mummy,
don't go all Çadogan ! "

Thus Sally who, with tact, but at a great expenditure of self-restraint, kept apart herself, and fended off her indignant mother from the concentrated talk which was proceeding in the breakfast-room, and whose progress, through the windows, she could witness ; an impressive sight. Aunt Adela, shockingly and expensively dressed in her orange satin coat and skirt, sat bolt upright like a Buddha, only her quick black eyes moving. A dark lean man with a moustache gesticulated, standing. As she watched she saw him sketch a gesture, a very characteristic gesture, a sudden tugging at the lobe of the left ear by the right hand. He laughed as he did it. Sally did not laugh. For that was the way Teddy pulled his ear, and the very thought of Teddy, so sensitive, involved in this mess, turned her for a moment still as stone. When Alan Littleton came out to his car she was waiting by it.

" I meant to ask you—do you think I could have a word with Mr. Mills ? "

Littleton looked at her.

" He's at Winborough."

" Winborough ? Why ? "

" He's been—" he softened it—" asked to make a statement, I believe. But I can't give you any exact information. I'm here as a private individual, you know. Must be off up to London again at once."

" But what can Teddy know about it ? "

" The police have to question everyone. It doesn't mean they think he's done it. I'm sorry, I must be off now."

She watched the neat blue car with the recent dent in its mudguard disappear, spurting gravel as it went, and admired the Commissioner's handling, for the drive was tricky. As an individual, however, she had less admiration for Major Alan Littleton. He had been abrupt with her. He had mimicked Teddy and laughed. He had a dark lean kind of good looks for which the rather ambrosial head and well-covered person of the late Lord Comstock's secretary had given her a distaste. She wandered back into the hall, pondering. "Asked to make a statement." What did that mean ? Encountering Aunt Adela she referred the question to her.

"Probably," responded that lady, "that they're holding him on some sort of suspicion." The girl flinched. "My dear child, what else could you expect of local police ? Or Cabinet Ministers either ; imbecility unfortunately isn't confined to one class. They've suspended Alan, for instance, just because he happened to be there. And they're asking all the wrong questions, of all the wrong people. This isn't a crime that can be solved by measuring burnt matches and watching the clock. It isn't a premeditated crime at all. Therefore "— Mrs. Bradley suddenly knuckled her niece jocosely in the ribs—" therefore it wasn't Teddy, so try and look a little more cheerful."

"Of course it wasn't Teddy," said the girl resentfully ; and then, instinct demanding a backing of reason ; "Why wasn't it ? "

"Girl ! And you aspire to write stories about this sort of thing ! A house full of respectable, right honourable and right reverend people, to say nothing of others we know nothing about as yet, but who may be presumed to come within one or other of those categories ; the cook, the gardener, the unknown lady in Sir Charles' car—you haven't heard about that, of course ; a house where policemen go casually bicycling by ; a house swarming with visitors. And the confidential secretary, with all the twenty-four hours of the day to do his murder, chooses just that one, with eminent men popping in and out like cuckoos from clocks. Nonsense! The whole thing was a psychological explosion; the pistol, so to speak, was merely a symbol, merely the physical expression of a mental state. Whose? Well, we shall have to ask a few questions ourselves."

(III)

Mrs. Bradley began inquiries that night at dinner. It was easy enough, for despite Lady Selina's anguished glances, and steady leading of the conversation to the Women's Institute performance of *Box and Cox*, impending three weeks hence, her guests could not be induced to talk of anything but Lord Comstock's death. He had never been invited to her table in life—not that he would have come, though he knew to a sixpence the news value of a marquess's daughter; his notions of entertainment were quite other. Now, by reason of a small blue hole in his temple, he took possession of her mahogany, and lorded it over the excellent food, the candles, the tranquil roses. But this disregard of the hostess's wishes was understandable considering that one of the guests was none other than Canon Prichard, the Vicar of Winborough, he whose car had been aspersed by the Assistant Commissioner as that which fled so guiltily down Lord Comstock's drive.

"When the police inquired of me by telephone," said the Canon, to an attentive audience, "naturally I assured them that the car had never left the garage. I was in London all day—a most difficult session; Bishops' ideas nowadays are startlingly modern in some matters.

I walked to the station. I walked back from the station this evening. But when I went at seven-thirty into the garage, unlocking the door as usual——"

(" A padlock, Canon ? " from Mrs. Bradley.

" Quite an ordinary padlock, yes.) I went in, I inspected the car, which looked much as usual. I did not examine the speedometer. But—and this is a very curious coincidence ; quite providential, if one may use that word with reverence in connection with machinery. Just at the entrance to your drive, Lady Selina, by the lodge, my car coughed, and spluttered, and finally ceased to move."

Exclamations from the rapt throng.

" You will guess, probably sooner than I did, the true cause. I examined the tank by the aid of a handy little pocket rule which I make it a practice to keep among my tools. Empty ! The tank, which to my knowledge had held a gallon when I returned last night from a visit to Meauchamp, was empty."

This was sufficiently exciting and suspicious ; the entire table buzzed with conjecture. Mrs. Bradley, however, in royal blue and looking oddly like a travestied lizard, would attempt no guesses and volunteer no statements. She was most unsatisfactory, and the vicar had a reproachful eye for her, as for a parishioner spied drowsing in sermon-time. But at the duckling stage of the meal she leapt into public favour again.

" Beg pardon, madam," said the tremulous voice of that gratified crime-fancier, the butler, " Sir Ferdinand Lestrange on the 'phone."

Mrs. Bradley left the table to its buzzing, and sought the telephone in the hall.

" Well, Ferdinand ? "

" Look here, mother. Do you want to take a hand in this Comstock business ? "

" Dear child, I'm human, I hope."

" I've been talking to the Commissioner. He's going to give facilities to a chosen few——"

" Not newspapers ? "

" No, no ; amateurs ; Wimsey among others. I thought as you were down there already——"

" Of course. I'm greatly obliged to you, Ferdinand. Especially as, from what I hear, the police are going about the whole business in an entirely idiotic way. Suspending Alan Littleton, for instance."

" He was there, you know. With a similar weapon. They could hardly do anything else."

" Where are the two revolvers now ? " *pistols*

" The local fellows are holding them, I believe. No finger-prints on either. On the one he was killed with, none at all."

" The one he was killed with ? Dearest child, aren't you assuming a good deal ? "

" The one found by the body ; I apologize. The bullet has been extracted. By the way, one bullet only had been fired."

" Thank you, dear. I like my news crisp. Now, there are some people I would very much like to talk to. I've spoken with Alan ; but there are these two unfortunates who are being detained——"

" I'll get the Commissioner's office to telephone permission. Have you seen Comstock's *Clarion* this evening ? Black borders an inch thick, and a suggestion in the leader that he should be buried in the Abbey."

" I think that honour should be reserved for his murderer. Very much obliged, dear boy. Good-night."

(IV)

In the morning there was a pitched battle with Lady Selina.

" Adela, I will not have it. You are quite old enough——"

" Sixty-four, dear." A macaw-like screech.

" ——to judge for yourself, but I will not have my daughter mixing herself up in police-courts."

" Daddy was on the bench. He always said you saw simply masses of human nature like that. Why shouldn't I go in with Aunt Adela ? "

" I will not have you cheapening yourself by running after a young man whom I have always refused to have in the house, I'm thankful to say. Of course, you'll take no notice of me——"

" He's absolutely innocent, and I don't know what you call Christianity, letting people down when they need help most."

" Don't be irreverent, Sally. You must go out of the room if you can't speak properly. It is your aunt's fault for encouraging you. No, Adela, I will not listen, and much as I enjoy having you here, you know that I cannot have you encouraging Sally to be disobedient and wilful."

In short, Lady Selina was roused to the point, which occurred about once in five years, of putting her large and sensibly shod foot firmly down. Nothing could be done. Mrs. Bradley could do no less than withdraw her support from Sally, who unquestionably had displayed bad manners ; and a quarter-hour later set off in a car, leaving the protagonists to simmer down. With a sigh for the tactlessness of parents she saw, as she stepped into her vehicle, the younger combatant, in an old leaf-coloured skirt, slipping away in the direction of Comstock's house, and hoped, but without much confidence, that the child would keep out of mischief.

They held Assizes in Winborough, which was the county town, and there was accommodation in its gaol for every degree of prisoner. Her name and permit had preceded her ; and at eleven o'clock she found herself at last in the presence of Mr. Edward Kimberly Mills.

He was shaven and kempt, and less offensive than Mrs. Bradley had feared ; but he had already been a good deal questioned, and his manner with her was at first a trifle restive. But the third sentence broke it down.

" I don't usually deliver this sort of message, Mr. Mills ; but my niece, Sally Lestrange,. sends her love."

He steadied at that.

" Does she ? Has she told you——? "

" Not a great deal," said Mrs. Bradley, who, having paid her tribute to sentiment, was not prepared to let Mr. Mills drivel. " Now, you know, I'm only here to help. I dare say you've been so much questioned that you've got your story quite fixed in your mind by this time, but I want you to be flexible. Let us try a few relaxing exercises. For instance, what was the late Lord Comstock's manner to dependants ? "

Mr. Mills stared, smoothed his too-curly hair with a somewhat podgy hand, and replied :

" Rude, mostly."

" Ah ! Familiar, ever ? "

" Sometimes. But look here, I mean, don't get the idea it was Farrant shot him, you know."

" Farrant ? That's your fellow-detainee ? No, I

didn't suppose it. Did Lord Comstock ever have periods of intense depression ? "

" Funny you should ask that," returned Mr. Mills, with a touch of awe. " He was always up and down. Cursing the soul out of somebody, or else sitting tight with a face screwed up like a fried sole."

" Or a lost one," said Mrs. Bradley softly.

" Which ? Oh yes, I see. Bright of you spotting that. He was a bit of a genius, of course ; you expect ups and downs. But," said the young man again, with a gleam of alarm, " he didn't shoot himself, you know. I mean, he may have been depressed, but I'd take my oath he didn't do it."

" No," dubiously Mrs. Bradley agreed, " possibly not while he could get himself noticed in any other way. These inferiority complexes always prefer to make other people suffer."

" Inferiority ? But he was——"

" A blusterer ; I know. You've misapprehended the term as people do. Men conscious of inferiority are always trying to impose themselves on others, because they know that underneath they are cowards or cretins. Very occasionally they see themselves as they are ; then they go down in the dumps. I don't want to put the police type of question, but you must excuse just one. Is it true that you were under notice to leave Lord Comstock's service ? "

Mr. Mills shot her a look ; but the lizard's face was smiling in kind wrinkles, and the beautiful voice was persuasive.

" Well, as a matter of fact—but absolutely wrongly. I mean he'd got absolutely the wrong idea."

" What was the right idea ? "

" He thought I couldn't hold my tongue."

" But you can, of course."

" Of course. Only what I mean is, you've got to make it worth a fellow's while. I'd had one or two offers to sell information, you see ; nibbles. I turned them down, of course. But I told Comstock I'd had them, and I—well, I sort of suggested that I could have found a use for the money. Just a hint, you see. After all, there was the future to think of. Only instead of giving me a rise, he told me to get out," said the injured young man, " that was two days ago. Just the sort of thing he was always doing himself, too ; only he gets—got—away with it."

" I see." Mrs. Bradley pondered, and looked at him with unblinking lizard's eyes.

" Do you know, Mr. Mills, if you'll allow an old woman to comment, I don't think you're cut out for a career of piracy. It takes a good deal of strong, sterling, bumptiousness and a thick skin to succeed as a blackmailer."

" Look here," said the young man desperately, " I've had quite enough bullyragging. As much as I can stand. You're Sally's aunt and all that, but——"

" Sally's aunt," repeated Mrs. Bradley gently. " You haven't actually taken any money, have you, Mr. Mills ? From the nibblers, I mean ? "

Mr. Mills, his eyes intent and frightened, faced her and made no answer.

" Because if you had," went on Mrs. Bradley, as if musing, " of course that clears you from any suspicion of murder."

" Clears me ? " echoed the young man, and rather painfully cleared his own throat.

" Of course. Comstock was the goose that laid the

golden eggs ; he contrived the plans and—stunts, isn't
that the hideous word ?—that the nibblers paid you for.
It was to your direct advantage to keep Comstock alive,
and planning, and the nibblers well informed. Of course
you'll say "—Mr. Mills' mouth was opening, fish-like—
" that he had already found out and dismissed you. But
I imagine that, even so, you would not have lacked for
information. There are always impressionable typists,
and you with your remarkably good looks—you mustn't
really mind an old woman." Mr. Mills, crimsoning once
more, flinched as she dug him in the ribs with two bony
fingers. " So, you see, it might be as well to own up."

Mr. Edward Mills hesitated, gulped, and came out
suddenly with a request.

" I say, please, you won't tell Sally, will you ? The
typist, I mean. I can't think how you got hold of it,
there's absolutely nothing in it, only this girl—well,"
said Mr. Mills relinquishing all hope of an explanation in
words, and relying on Mrs. Bradley's intuition, " you
see how it is." He smoothed his too-curly hair, with just
the hint of a lady-killing smile.

" I do," said Mrs. Bradley. " I see how quite a number
of things are. You belong psychologically to a very large
class ; I won't bother you with the technical name. But
they all copy their neighbours, and do in Rome as Rome
does, and in the right environment they can remain
perfectly honest on a thousand a year."

She moved, with a gesture of farewell, to the door.

" But look here," said Mr. Mills, following, " I haven't
admitted anything. I'm not going to admit anything——"

" Oh," said Mrs. Bradley, with superb impatience,
" my dear good ostrich of a young man, good-bye ! "

p.33 Bishop.

(v)

The two revolvers were indeed in Superintendent
Easton's charge, and obedient to the wires pulled miles
away by Sir Ferdinand Lestrange they were produced,
with something of a tolerant and condescending smile.

"Ah," said Mrs. Bradley, peering down at the pair
through lorgnettes, "American make, I see ; ·15, or
thereabouts."

"Correct, ma'am," agreed the Superintendent, a trifle
surprised at this show of technical knowledge. "No
finger-prints on either."

"No," said Mrs. Bradley, "naturally. The butt's
rough. And as for the trigger, one doesn't pull with the
tip, whichever finger one uses. Personally, with a ·38—
but that's a good deal larger—I find I have more complete control pulling with the middle finger, and steadying
with the fore. However. Which was the revolver from
which the shot was fired ? "

The Superintendent scanned both butts, and handed
her the one to which a small red label was attached.

"That's the weapon. Fully loaded in all chambers, one
shell fired, finger-prints wiped clean, *and* barrel." Mrs.
Bradley almost jumped. "Yes, ma'am. Barrel clean
as a whistle."

"When's the post-mortem ? " Mrs. Bradley asked,
paying no attention. "And where's the bullet ? "

"Doctor's in there now." The Superintendent indicated the direction of the mortuary with a jerk of his
head. "Well, talk of angels, as they say."

For a neat grey gentleman had appeared in the doorway, smelling not disagreeably of disinfectant.

"That's over, Superintendent ! " he announced after

one single curious but gentlemanly glance at Mrs. Bradley, who, dressed as she was in peacock green, seemed the last person to be expected in a police-station.

" This is the bullet, ma'am," said the Superintendent cheerfully, producing a small wooden box from his pocket. " And Dr. Raglan might have heard us talking about him. Of course," he opened the sliding lid and eyed the greyish fragment, " this won't tell us much till they get the microscope to it."

It was a small bullet. The nose had mushroomed; but there was enough lead left, the stalk, as it were, of the mushroom, in its original shape, to display the characteristics by which each barrel sets its own stamp upon every bullet fired from it.

" Yes," said Mrs. Bradley slowly, " I suppose we must wait for the microscope. Who wields it ? You, Dr. Raglan ? " Her smile drew him into the conversation.

" I'm not an expert, I'm afraid. It's a very expert job, you know. Vital to be accurate."

" Browne and Kennedy ; yes, I realize that." She picked up the other revolver, broke it, and was squinting down the barrel and the chambers in turn. " And this is the weapon Major Littleton was carrying. Yes. You'll fire test bullets from both, of course ; and then compare the markings with this." She indicated the grey fragment.

" That's the ticket," said the Superintendent jovially. " Then we shall know for certain which gun it came out of."

" But not who fired the gun," said Mrs. Bradley very gently. " Well, gentlemen, I'm greatly obliged to you. Dr. Raglan," she paused, " is it possible that you attend the cottage hospital here ? "

" I am one of the surgeons, yes."

" The policeman who was so unfortunately run over, how is he ? "

" Not conscious yet. He's had a very nasty knock."

" Funny it should be the A.C."—the Superintendent corrected himself—" Major Littleton, that run him down. He's always one to be thoughtful for the men. And him working out a traffic scheme to bring down the number of road accidents, too ! Well, there's no saying the funny way things'll go," said the Superintendent, who was reckoned something of a philosopher in the town, " a waggonload of monkeys is nothing, you might say, to Fate. Anything more I can do for you, ma'am ? "

" You might let me know the result of the test with these."

She indicated the two revolvers.

" Right you are. Anything else you'd care to see now ? "

" One only. The Vicar's cook."

(VI)

From that interview, on which no stress need be laid, Mrs. Bradley emerged a trifle flushed ; but it was the flush of victory. Dr. Prichard, when he returned that evening, was given notice by the cook ; an event less cataclysmic than that lady supposed, since, unknown to her, the Vicar had for months been summoning courage to get rid of her. " Leaving to be married," was the cook's excuse, and conflicting conjectures were made as to the swain ; but the cook kept his name to herself, together with the fact that he was an unemployed garage

7

hand, now upon the dole. All this was later. It is some tribute to Mrs. Bradley's personality that on the day of their encounter the cook was left in tears, while no ripple disturbed the unblinking tranquillity of the other's saurian gaze.

Mr. Mills, the Superintendent, and the cook between them had taken some two and a half hours to interview ; highly-concentrated and intensive interviewing, which might have been expected to leave Mrs. Bradley exhausted. It did not, however. At the first newsagent's shop she stopped her car and bought an armful of papers ; one with a deep black border, Lord Comstock's own organ of opinion, the others paying their tribute of ebony headlines to that least picturesque of robber-barons. There were interviews with the highly-respected suspects. There were photographs—a rival paper had somehow secured one of the late peer at the age of four, sullen, in Fauntleroy velvet and curls, and one at the age of eighteen, still sullen, with a caption where, by some compositor's regrettable error, a superfluous " s " had crept in : THE MAN OF PROMISE(s). Mrs. Bradley read them all, holding the sheets with one hand, while with the other she wielded her lorgnettes. She read and re-read the tribute of the Archbishop and Sir Charles Hope-Fairweather.

" This has been a terrible shock to me," stated His Grace, " the more so that I had long known the late Lord Comstock and was indeed with him very shortly before the tragic occurrence which has robbed British journalism of "—Mrs. Bradley could imagine the Archbishop hesitating at this point, murmuring *de mortuis*, and non-committally plunging—" a virile figure. Our long acquaintance was not always unchequered with differences. His most recent campaign had indeed given me considerable pain, and I felt it my duty to endeavour to restrain him in what I felt to be a course of action unbefitting his strictly Church upbringing. His death so closely following upon this interview was a considerable shock. He might be described as the most robust influence in British journalism of recent years. It is now over a quarter of a century since as a boy he was committed to my charge, and I have no hesitation in saying that he regarded me as a true friend ; one who never flinched from the duty of recalling him when necessary to those Christian principles from which it is my belief that, in spite of recent aberrations, he had never in his heart of hearts departed. Modern England will mourn her strongest man."

" In fact," mused Mrs. Bradley, " exactly the same thing three times over. Let us see what Sir Charles has to say."

Sir Charles, despairing of being able to voice one single word of praise for what Lord Comstock was, went off into panegyrics of what he might have been. " A sportsmanlike effort," was Mrs. Bradley's verdict, " considering that Comstock had probably been blackmailing him " ; and she read the brief soldierly phrases with care.

" He had sound views on many political and Empire problems. That he was a man of immense energy cannot be denied. His patriotism was unquestioned. His potential influence for good can hardly be overestimated."

Thus Sir Charles, all public-school tradition, refraining from hitting a man when he was down, and no doubt, like the Archbishop, muttering the Latin tag to himself. He was brief, however ; for if one were to speak the truth, and yet record of such a person as Comstock nothing save good, there remained very little indeed to be said by any honest man.

There was a picture of Mr. Mills, taken at Cambridge, and looking a little too healthy, and jolly, and curly ; all these the camera recorded, together with the strange flightiness a face acquires from having small eyes set too wide apart. Lady Selina's consternation at the thought of having such a person inside her doors was, in face of this photograph, very easily explained. Mrs. Bradley was fond of her niece, and would have deplored as whole-heartedly as Lady Selina such an acquisition to the family. The family, however, if it displayed only a modicum of intelligence, was in no danger, and she explained as much at luncheon to a harassed mother whose only chick had not returned for food.

" My dear Selina, there's nothing between these two that you need worry about."

" But "—the hostess drew back, gave expert consideration to the food at her elbow, helped herself with discretion, yet amply—" but Adela, they've been meeting ! "

" Of course they have. You put obstacles in their way. An obstacle is something to be surmounted. If you'd only taken the trouble to put a few in the Paradine boy's path they'd be engaged by now."

" But, dear, what could I do ? I couldn't have that really dreadful young man here. I saw him—once." She shuddered. " No, no, Adela."

Mrs. Bradley, while mentally re-enacting the shudder, remained calm.

" Then don't have the Paradine boy here either. Forbid him the house."

" How can I possibly do that ? What excuse could I make ? "

" You might say," Mrs. Bradley considered, wickedly smiling, " you might say that you thought Sally was seeing too much of him."

" Darling Adela," said Lady Selina, sighing, and absently helping herself to more green peas, " things always look so simple to you."

" Do they ? " Mrs. Bradley's voice took a graver note. " I wish they did."

(VII)

But in the afternoon, about three, when Lady Selina was stertorously resting, a tap came at Mrs. Bradley's door. (She, too, " rested " after lunch ; she knew that the guest who neither rests nor writes letters puts too much strain upon a hostess.) To her call the door opened, revealing the small impish face of Sally Lestrange.

" Well, darling child," said Mrs. Bradley who was walking about the largest guest-room, clad in a magnificent Chinese coat covered with dragons, from whose voluminous sleeve the dark barrel of a revolver peeped. " I suppose you know your mother is, very rightly, most incensed."

" What on earth are you doing ? " responded Sally, who had caught sight of the revolver.

" Oh," said Mrs. Bradley, surprised, " that ! Just a theory. Quite untenable, unfortunately. Where have you been ? " She put down the small black weapon, tidying it into its leather case. " You oughtn't to stay away from meals, you know, without warning or cause."

" I've been snooping."

" Indeed ! And what have you discovered ? "

" A lot. I've been talking to the servants and the policemen. Briggs, the gardener, is our chauffeur's uncle. I know it sounds rather like the penknife of the gardener's boy, but he is. D'you know what he says ? He's absolutely certain that he saw a woman go round that way."

" Which way ? "

" Round to the—north, I suppose it would be ; the way the study window faces. And I don't believe he remembers her coming back. And do you know what I think she did ? Shot Lord Comstock—he was facing the window, wasn't he ?—and then just ducked round and hid in the sort of corner the study makes, jutting out. The office hasn't got a window on that side ; I rather particularly noticed it hadn't. So she waits there, and hears all these other people jumping out of windows —Major Littleton made a fearful mess of the turf—and then she just strolls round after all the cars have gone." Sally scribbled a rough plan with the best guest-room pen on the inviolate guest-room blotting-paper.

" Look, really, Aunt Adela. It's quite sound. Here's the place ; nobody could see her there. Nobody would be likely to come round that way——"

" The gardener ? "

" Why should he ? "

" To get to the kitchen garden."

" If he hadn't got his vegetables in by twelve o'clock he ought to be ashamed of himself," riposted Sarah virtuously, " and the cook would have his blood. As a matter of fact I asked her, and Lord Comstock likes very young peas, and they take ages to shell, so she'd got everything in that she wanted by eleven."

* by the map, it faces south

Mrs. Bradley clapped delicately with her small yellow hands.

" Excellent, Sally ! Nothing omitted except the most important thing."

" I didn't ! I snooped for hours, I never took my nose off the ground, there's absolutely nothing left out——"

" Except the motive."

Sally was dashed for the moment.

" Oh, the motive ! But then, when you've established how a thing was done, you can always think out a motive afterwards."

Mrs. Bradley laughed, her sudden screech.

" All very well for detective fiction, dear child, but detection fact runs quite the other way."

" It was a woman, all the same."

" How can you tell ? Don't please say you've found the usual shred of cloth on the garden wall."

" No, I didn't, but I found heel marks. Outside the study on the grass, just where someone would stand to look in. She must have been tall. The window-sill's round about five foot six from the ground. I measured it as well as I could." And with pride Sally produced a small and wizened dressmaker's tape-measure.

" May I ask how you were allowed to obtain all this information ? "

" I know most of the people round here," Sally answered innocently, " and pretty well all the policemen. I don't drive awfully well, that great car takes half a mile to turn in, so I'm always getting summoned. Well, cautioned and my number taken. Same thing. It's Walter Borthwick on duty up there now, and he's engaged to one of the girls at our lodge, so he just winked the other eye. He thought it probably was a woman, too."

" You shared your suspicions with him ? "

" Well, I thought I might as well give him something to think about. One idea lasts Walter quite a long time. What we couldn't make out was how she got away."

" Or how she happened to have a revolver identical with the one on the desk," said Mrs. Bradley a trifle tartly, but she was not as devastating as she might have been. This Sally, cheerful to the point of impudence, wildly investigating, more wildly arguing, was a Sally changed for the better. Mrs. Bradley had not much cared for the sulky adolescent of the day before, with her blighted love affair and her seclusion. It was remarkable that the girl had not as yet inquired for Mr. Mills ; remarkable, and comforting from a family point of view.

" How do you know it was one of those revolvers ? " Sally asked defiantly. " I suppose the police stuffed you up with that ; always taking things for granted. I wouldn't mind betting, Aunt Adela, here and now, that it was an absolutely different revolver ; not either of those at all."

" Two of a kind—coincidence. Three of a kind—a good deal the other side of improbable. I saw the bullet—unusual one ; it was quite certainly from a ·15. My dear child, find your motive, your state of mind. All these things—bullets, footprints—they all wait on that one fact. Don't bother with all these people's finger-prints ; try to follow the whorls and convolutions of their minds." Mrs. Bradley absently picked up the small gun in its leather sheath. " All the same, you've done remarkably well. Thanks, dear child."

Sally slipped away. At the door she turned.

" Half a crown to sixpence on that bullet, Aunt Adela ? "

" Done," responded Mrs. Bradley, in a voice like the dropping of stone into a well ; and was fingering her revolver again as the door closed.

(VIII)

Next morning, after a somewhat tropical breakfast of fruit and coffee, encouraged by the parrot with cries of " Give 'er a glass of beer, watch 'er put it down, hullo, smack ! " Mrs. Bradley was summoned to the telephone, Alan Littleton's voice came ghostly over the wires.

" Will you do something for me ? How are you, I suppose I ought to ask first."

" I'm well. No farther on, though. What is it you want ? "

" I've been worrying over that policeman, poor chap ; the one I ran down."

" Would you like me to go and see how he is ? "

" Bless you ! Just what I was going to ask. And, look here—find out how they are off for money, will you ? He'll draw his insurance and so on, but that ought to go to the hospital. All the cottage hospitals are going broke with accidents brought in and never paying. Just find out, if you can, how things are, and offer to help his wife. I feel badly about this."

" Why don't you come down and do it yourself, Alan ? And we can talk other matters over."

The ghostly voice laughed, briefly.

" Hardly be in good taste, would it ? I'm supposed to have had a hand in the business, you know. It was

intimated that I had better stay where the official eye
can find me if it wants. No country jaunts."

" On account of the revolver ? "

" And our personal feud, and opportunity, and half a
dozen other things—what's that ? "

For Mrs. Bradley had been murmuring, in the manner
of another eminent inquirer, Sir John Saumarez, a
quotation from Shakespeare about opportunity ; something to the effect that opportunity was the real culprit
in all matters of crime. Major Littleton, a person on
whom the point of quotations was blunted, save those
which derived from Army or Police Regulations, replied
without the reverence that better-educated persons
accord to such hallowed platitudes :

" Well, of course, if a man isn't there you can't plug
him." And he returned to his urgency about the
policeman.

" I'll do it this morning," said Mrs. Bradley. " Now
listen to me, Alan. Where are you speaking from ?
Your own flat ? You speak German, don't you ? Very
well." In a strong British accent Mrs. Bradley embarked
upon a series of questions in that tongue, in which Sir
Charles Hope-Fairweather figured literally as *die Peitsche*,
the Whip ; was there a woman in *die Peitsche's* car ?
What like ? What height ? The answers were hesitating.
There might have been. He certainly had seen a woman
in the waiting car before he went into the house. Where
was the car ? In the loop of the drive. He thought it
must have been a woman ; it had a red hat, anyhow.

" Did you see that hat in the car you chased down
the drive ? "

" I don't know. It was a saloon ; the blind at the
back was pulled down."

" Was there a chauffeur ? "

" No."

" Whose was the chauffeur you saw afterwards ? "

" Comstock's."

" He gave you the number of the car, didn't he ? "

" Yes. Wrong."

" You know, Alan, that might be very interesting."

" It made me look an absolute fool, if you call that interesting."

" Was he acquainted with the Canon's cook, do you know ? "

" I didn't happen to ask," replied the ghostly voice, heavy with irony. " There had been a rather sudden death, and an accident or so just before I spoke to him——"

" Now, my dear boy, don't be angry because I ask you a question and you don't happen to know the answer." Mrs. Bradley, under stress, had broken once more into English. " I'll find out myself, and let you know."

" Thanks," said the voice, still ironic, " it would bring a ray of sunshine into my life to know for certain that that ensanguined fool——"

" Alan, Alan ! "

" Was acquainted with the Canon's cook."

" Dear child, you're in a temper," said Mrs. Bradley calmly, " I think you'd better ring off now. Keep in touch with me, Alan."

" Right. See my policeman for me."

" I will," said Mrs. Bradley reassuringly, and did. Sally drove her in that car which had been the means of introduction to so many of the local force to the cottage hospital, where a pleasant matron gave them news

Nasty concussion, but hopeful. His wife was with him.

" Oh ! I wonder if I might speak to her ? " Mrs. Bradley asked, in tones that would have lured a dragon from its cave. The matron succumbed at once to the will of that strangely persuasive old lady in royal blue, and fetched in Mrs. Bartelmy, who stood miserably before them, her rid-rimmed blue eyes asking what the visitors could possibly want.

" How d'you do," said Mrs. Bradley, with her curiously-high, old-fashioned handshake, " and please sit down, won't you ? What an anxious time this is ! You must save yourself all you can."

" Yes'm." Mrs. Bartelmy sat, uncomfortably. Mrs. Bradley was a little overpowering, and it was Sally who set her at her ease.

" Your husband was so awfully kind to me once when I forgot my licence. And that time I ran into the sheep one market day. I mean, it might have been fearfully awkward for me, only he made everything all right. I'm so glad he's better."

Mrs. Bartelmy's eyes began to fill again, and she muttered something about Alf always trying to do 'is best.

" This smash is such disgustingly bad luck. We were rather wondering——" the girl glanced at Mrs. Bradley ; but before that lady could take up her cue, Mrs. Bartelmy had launched a torrent of words.

" Always on time, always out, even nights when there's plenty'd wait about in shelter, always worrying to be doing right. Why, when 'e come to this morning I was there ; and what's the first thing 'e says ? Not a word for me nor the children, nor where am I ? Nor anything what you'd expect. He opens his eyes, and sees me there, and 'e says, if these was my dying words they're gospel, 'e says, ' Annie, I was on my right side ! ' " Mrs. Bartelmy wept.

" When he was run into ? Was that what he meant ? Well, my dear Mrs. Bartlemy, this kind matron says that you haven't anything to fear for him, he's out of danger ; and now I'm just going to ask her to give you a tiny whiff of smelling salts so that you will be able to be brave again, and tell me a little about yourself and the children."

Mrs. Bartelmy sniffed, and whiffed ; heard what Mrs. Bradley had to say, accepted with more tears what Mrs. Bradley had to bestow, gave two heartfelt handshakes, and returned comforted to her Alf.

Mrs. Bradley went, musing, Sally at her side, out to the car.

" Which way," she demanded suddenly, " does Lord Comstock's house lie ? "

" I'll drive you past it."

Twenty minutes at speed down the green lanes brought them to a high red wall.

" This is it. I'll go slowly, shall I ? "

" Do, my dear."

They cruised along, and at the gate halted for Mrs. Bradley to get out. A large policeman on duty there eyed her, as did several otherwise unoccupied persons come to gaze upon the spot where the murder was committed. Mrs. Bradley accosted none of them, and made no attempt to enter ; but Sally at her side indicated the points of interest with all the fervour of a charabanc guide.

" Here we have the drive, you see how it goes. It's

about 150 yards to the house if you go direct, and about an extra 75 yards if you go round. That's where Sir Charles left his car : you can't see where Major Littleton left his, it's behind the trees. You can't see the bulge the study window makes, either, from here. Look here, Aunt Adela, wouldn't you like to go in ? Borthwick would let you."

" Orders, miss," said the large policeman ; but dubiously.

" Thank you," returned Mrs. Bradley pleasantly, " but I can see all I need from here."

" You can't see a thing. Those footprints ought to be grand still, there hasn't been any rain since——"

Mrs. Bradley turned and eyed her pupil and niece.

" What did I tell you ? "

" Yes, I know," admitted Sally, shuffling, " motive and all that. But it does seem silly to absolutely neglect the other things."

" We won't do that," returned Mrs. Bradley grimly. " Let us inspect the scene of the accident."

They moved to the other side of the road, a godsend to the unoccupied curious round the gate. The road was macadamized, its surface dust revealed no tyre tracks that could be identified. Sally, the omniscient, had obtained a few details about the affair during her previous day's snooping.

" There was some blood here," she said in a detached manner, pointing to a patch of grass at the roadside near the wall, " but I expect they've cleaned it up. There were flies, rather." She gave a little shudder which belied the detachment.

" Which way was our conscientious policeman riding ? To or from Winborough ? "

" Towards, I expect. He was going off duty. He was on his wrong side, you see, if the accident was here."

" So was Alan Littleton, in that case. They were both going the same way."

" Well, but——" Sarah hesitated. She held no brief for the A.C., but her own deductions were dear to her. " I know. This must be what happened. Bartelmy is riding somewhere about the middle of the road, Major Littleton comes haring out and bumps him on to his head and then drags him on to the grass just here." She indicated the stained patch, and turned, preening herself a little, to receive praise ; but her aunt, unimpressed, was surveying the opposite hedge with a bright eye cocked sideways.

" D'you cut your holly in these parts ? "

Sally read no Kipling ; she remembered nothing of " that sacred tree which no woodman touches without orders " ; but she had lived in the country all her life, and had an indignant answer ready.

" Of course not ; not in hedges. It isn't lucky."

" I see," said Mrs. Bradley gravely, examining a sturdy holly twig which had been broken short to the general hedge-level. " Then there's somebody hereabouts, a stranger probably, who's not superstitious."

(IX)

The matter of the cook's acquaintanceship with that chauffeur who had so annoyingly given Major Littleton the wrong number of a fleeing car was soon settled. It was done circuitously, to the accompaniment of helpless disapproval from Lady Selina, who, though she thought it her duty to see that her staff went to church and saw doctors, objected to intruding upon what she called their private lives.

" They have just as much right to their love-affairs," said Lady Selina, devouring asparagus with ladylike greed, " as we have." She looked round ; the butler was not in the room. " I mean, naturally, I don't allow the younger maids to have followers, and Strutt and Malkin are long past that age, and I never would have young menservants because it always makes trouble ; but apart from that I do think one ought not to interfere."

" My dear Selina," implored Mrs. Bradley, " calm yourself. I do not propose to throw any further grit into Canon Pritchard's domestic machine." She eyed Sally blandly ; Sally, that accomplished snooper, dear to servants and aware of all the relationships for miles around. The hint was taken, grinning ; Lord Comstock's chauffeur that day was to be Sally's job.

This was a relief to Mrs. Bradley, who privately considered her niece's cure not yet so complete that she could be allowed with any safety within the walls which harboured the unjustly accused Mr. Edward Mills. She issued further instructions, when Lady Selina was well out of earshot, by which her assistant was empowered to draw up a plan of Comstock's garden, drive, and the road beyond it. This settled, she went off alone to Winborough.

" Mills again ? " said the Superintendent. " Well, I suppose you can see him. I've got some news for you, after."

Mrs. Bradley declined the proffered privilege of a look at Mr. Mills. That unfortunate, she learnt, had been throwing his weight about, such as it was ; he was a nuisance, and the Superintendent, confidentially, did not agree that there was any need for his detention.

" A young fellow like that stand up to a bully like Comstock, and shoot him in front ? Not much," said Easton. " Why, the first thing he asked me to send out for was, what d'you think ? A solicitor ? No ! A bottle of brilliantine and some pills."

Mrs. Bradley agreed that Mr. Mills in the rôle of violent criminal was unconvincing, and brought the official back to his point of departure.

" Well, Superintendent ! And what is this treat you have in store for me ? "

" Ah ! Now you're asking."

He went to a drawer, unlocked it with precautions, and returned bearing an envelope strengthened with cardboard ; the kind of envelope in which photographs are despatched.

" It's about those guns," said he.

" Ah, yes," Mrs. Bradley was grave at once. " The tests. What news ? "

" Mighty funny news," returned the Superintendent. " News that turns the whole case upside down. Look." He spread before her, like a hand at poker, five photographs. Two of these were pictures of the mushroomed bullet, immensely magnified, showing the striations made by the revolver barrel. Numbers three and four were labelled : " Test bullets fired from ·15 red label."

" That was Comstock's own ? " she asked.

" Mills says so. Just you look at the marks. I've got a reading-glass here if you want."

But Mrs. Bradley waved it away, and used her lorgnettes. She spent two full minutes over the photographs

8

of the mushroomed bullet; two more over the photograph of " red label " ; then put both quietly down.

" It wasn't fired from that gun."

" No more it was. Try the other."

The other was the revolver which Alan Littleton had carried. She took up the picture and lifted her glasses —ten seconds later she dropped them with an exclamation.

" Eh ? " said Easton jovially. " Thought that'd get you. It did me. Couldn't believe my eyes for the moment. Not a mark the same; not the faintest resemblance. Didn't I say you could never be up to Fate ? Not if you were as clever as a wagon-load of monkeys with their tails burnt off. Now that means, as of course you understand, ma'am, that we've got to look for a third gun. More trouble for us, but it lets out Major Littleton, and I'm glad of it."

Mrs. Bradley was still staring down at the photographs, still tapping them with her lorgnettes, and her bright dark eyes were dull as pebbles. She came to herself with a start at the Assistant Commissioner's name.

" What's that ? Oh yes, Major Littleton. Obviously not from his gun, but a ·15 bullet all the same, Inspector. What, then, is the official explanation of the single spent shell in the revolver that was on the desk ? "

" Easy. Mr. Mills put us on to it. Wonder we overlooked it ; it's kept us barking up the wrong tree all this time. Why, it never was fired that day at all ! Mills says his employer used to pot at rabbits with it of an evening, from the window. Butler corroborates. Funny thing to do ; why, you'd only wound the animal, if you did hit one, with a toy like this——"

" Lord Comstock had no prejudice against inflicting

suffering," said Mrs. Bradley. "Yes? And so this probably was fired at another time altogether?"

"That's right. Then he might run a rag through the barrel next day and not notice the shell; this make doesn't throw 'em out, you know. So there we've been, from the Home Secretary down to your humble, all sweating our souls out (pardon me) over a bullet that's down a burrow this fortnight."

The Superintendent laughed with extreme heartiness at the idea of the Home Secretary and a whole assembly of other distinguished persons thus ironically employed. Mrs. Bradley, however, did not laugh. She was horribly white, and her small alert face seemed sunken into twenty new wrinkles all in a moment. The Inspector, with a quick glance at a subordinate who stood by, conjured up a glass of water for her, and proffered it firmly, with apologies for not having anything stronger. She sipped it civilly, set it down, rose, took adequate leave with thanks; but her gallant bearing had much ado to carry off the small stricken face atop.

"It's what I always say," said Easton to the subordinate after her departure, "you can't be up to women, try how you will. I've seen a woman tried for murder lend her handkerchief to the wardress when the judge put on the cap. And there's my own wife; if I broke my leg to-morrow, nothing'd be too good for me, and yet if I was to break a vase to-night she'd give me hell. You can't be up to 'em. Now, this Mrs. Bradley, she's a sensible woman and she knows which end of a gun the shot comes out of; and Major Littleton is a friend of hers. Yet you see!"

"The relief," opined the subordinate. "It makes you come weak at the knees."

" Weak in the head, you mean," rejoined his superior vaguely, but with intent to rebuke. " When you're my age, you'll get over trying to find a reason for anything a woman does. Get a move on."

(x)

After dinner, which was oddly silent, but also, a good excuse for the silence, remarkably succulent, Mrs. Bradley went off alone, wandering into the near-by wood. She had refused the company of Sally, and gently set aside the suggestion of Lady Selina that they should play a fiendish form of joint patience called " back-bite." Lady Selina was as sulky as an excellent meal's aftermath would permit, for she had not only been foiled in an attempt to ask Dick Paradine to dinner, but had actually been obliged to listen to a treacly commendation of Mr. Mills from her sister-in-law in her daughter's presence ; everything extolled, his curls, his innocence, his devotion. It was a little too much even for Sally, who, to Mrs. Bradley's encomium of his hands—which were fattish and hairy, a very weak point —replied uncomfortably that anyhow they were pretty strong, and changed the subject. Somehow Mr. Mills in captivity lost some of his charm, as do certain animals. Lady Selina had the wisdom to know that her sister-in-law's treatment of the affair was the right and effective one ; but it is always galling to see a stranger easily succeeding where reproaches from those who should be the rebel's nearest and dearest so lamentably fail. She did not interfere, therefore ; but she was in a temper, a fact appreciated both by her daughter and her guest. A glance from Mrs. Bradley, refusing escort on her

stroll, implored her fellow-sleuth's co-operation ; a word,
spoken low as the tray with coffee was taken jangling
up, secured it.

" Be good, please, child."

Followed a miracle. Sally of her own accord approached the baize-covered table, suggesting herself as
fellow-backbiter ; and on Lady Selina's reluctant but
acquiescent smile, Mrs. Bradley departed unquestioned
through an open French-window, towards the wood.
She had her great brocade work-bag slung upon her arm,
out of which, in the green seclusion of the trees, she
produced a small revolver, though not so small as those
in the hands of the police, a few brass-shod cartridges,
and the dark tubular cap of a silencer. With these she
went through various manœuvres, firing bullets into a
piece of ¾-inch plank which she set up against a tree
for the purpose. All her movements were business-like,
unhurried, and sure ; some of them, to an observer,
would have been puzzling. For when she had fired
three times she took from the brocade bag, inexhaustible
apparently as Mrs. Robinson's of the Swiss Family, a
small pair of scissors, the back of whose blades was
roughened to the semblance of a file. This, breaking
the revolver, she applied to some small part, a mysterious
performance no more than ten seconds long. A moment's
thought ; then she stooped, and did some other in-
explicable thing with a small ramrod and a handful of
earth ; loaded again and fired, with seeming carelessness
and extreme accuracy, until six bullet holes stood in a
neat row along her piece of wood, the bullets themselves
remaining embedded. Then she put all her paraphernalia
back into the magnificent bag, covered the collection
with hanks of coloured wools, and came strolling back

to the drawing-room as the gilt Cupid adorning Lady
Selina's mantelpiece struck ten times with a hammer on
his bell.

Mother and daughter were still bent over their cards.
They played for counters, yellow, red, and white, which
were gathered mostly under Lady Selina's hand ; that
lady was beaming.

" Unlucky at cards," said Mrs. Bradley to Sally. " I
must tell Mr. Mills."

" I'm lucky at sleuthing, anyhow," returned Sally,
reddening. " What about that half-crown ? "

" I don't know," said Mrs. Bradley, and her voice
suddenly was lifeless. " Perhaps you owe me sixpence."

" What ? Was it really another gun that shot him ? "

" Give 'er air, give 'er a glass of beer, that's right,
pop ! " The parrot, waking from his drowse upon the
perch, checked Sally's movement, and her mother's
remonstrances concerning the unsuitability of crime as
a drawing-room topic checked further speech. Mrs.
Bradley, looking ill, went out of the room and without
further explanation to bed. She had concluded her
investigations.

(XI)

From Mrs. Bradley's diary :

June 14th.

Sensation ! Somebody, whose public - spiritedness
cannot be too highly commended, has shot Lord Comstock in his own house. A. L., strangely enough on the
spot, and gave me full details. (Follow the circumstances
of the crime, so far as these were known at the time of
Major Littleton's message.)

It is impossible really to blame anyone, with the single exception of His Grace the Archbishop, who ought to have brought up the late C. better while he had his hands on him.

June 15th.

All still agog with the murder. Ferdinand has arranged for me to have facilities for inquiry. Bless the boy! Accordingly, to kill two birds with one stone, went to-day to interview E. Mills, who is detained on suspicion. Quite awful! Sally must have been out of her mind with boredom to have considered him for one moment. Her mother's fault, of course. He represented romance, though he has hands like suet puddings. A little judicious encouragement would have worked wonders. However.

M. is quite obviously not guilty. He is terrified, because he is playing a double game, and is afraid that this will come out and debar him from future employment. There is a good old Scots word, spunk, which means, I believe, tinder; he has none. No affront, no bullying could ever strike a spark out of him. An unpleasing specimen. May be safely left out of all calculations, even Sally's.

Saw the guns in question; also the bullet, but only a microscope would reveal anything there. Curious about the one empty shell, and the clean barrel. It looks rather as though somebody had intended to clean it completely and had been disturbed. But surely one would remove the shell first of all? Difficult.

Interviewed Vicar's cook. Red-headed, handsome, truculent; the sort that would bully a decent man to death, and work her hands to the bone for a waster.

Admits joy-ride with latter in Vicar's car, thus making a curious coincidence. (See trial of Frenchwoman who stated that the burglars who murdered her husband were dressed as stage Jews. Burglars disproved, but three costumes such as she described *had* been stolen from the Jewish Theatre that very night. The long arm of coincidence is really *endless* !) The chauffeur's statement, confusing numbers of the cars, pure malice probably. Had seen the Vicar's car out, and thought he would give the joy-riders a fright. Sally must inquire.

Disposed of two further suspects on way home in car. Sir Charles H.-F. could never, NEVER, shoot a quarry sitting. (C. may have been standing, but *morally* the analogy holds.) Sir Charles would not know what to do with a revolver. An elephant-rifle, 12-bore, or fists are his weapons. Possibly, if driven beyond endurance, a horsewhip. Nothing so unsportsmanlike as a revolver. (The bullet was fired from one, that is quite conclusive.)

H. G. the Archbishop, also discharged without a stain on character, except that noted under yesterday's date. Read his message to the press, and came to the conclusion (irresistible) that he could never have rested content with one shot, even if that had done the business. Tautologous by nature, as all ex-schoolmasters are. Could not have resisted repeating himself. Pistol would have been another matter. Revolver, and only one shot fired, puts him out of court. A relief. One does not like to think of the scandal, had it been otherwise.

Remains Farrant, the butler, A. L. (but not likely), and Person Unknown. Query, lady with Sir Charles ?

This theory supported by Sally's information. (Too enthusiastic, but probable.) Woman hid in blind corner beyond window. Difficulty of getting away. Bribe to gardener? Unlikely. If so, a tall woman. Worth considering. (Sally displaying common sense, glad to say.) Trouble here is to discover how woman could have come into possession of one of the weapons. Query, bullet may not belong to either? (Remember Sally bet 2s. 6d. to 6d. that it did not.)

Memo.—Sudden thought. How if spent cartridges had been transferred to C.'s gun from guilty weapon, with a view to making crime appear suicide? This illustrates a murderous device I have not so far seen used, but which I believe was begun here and interrupted. There was no blackening round C.'s wound; this a second shot (blank) fired from his own gun at close quarters would have supplied. (The noise of the shots would be negligible; the fatal shot was, in fact, either not heard at all, or not identified. A revolver-shot is nothing like the crash of a falling table, or a thumped fist. It is a short, sharp sound, more like the bursting of a tyre.) The assailant, having wiped the gun, would close the still warm fingers of the victim round it, and make off. Comstock's temperament a possible one for suicide, which would support the illusion.

Objection.—This would imply that the assailant concerned did not know that the bullets from two different guns can be identified. Therefore, no expert, and *not* A. L. Thank God. (Note for future use: even this objection does not apply to shot-guns. Small shot does not take the markings of the bore.)

June 16th.

Went to see injured policeman, at A. C.'s request. Not visible, but out of danger. Saw wife, who reported first coherent statement. " I was on my right side, Annie."

Not on left side of road?

Query, a reference to the accident ? Examined site of
collision. Blood on wrong side road, but broken holly
in the hedge (right side) with other damage, looked as
though a heavy body had fallen on it. Possibly the
bicycle ? But A. L. is confident P.C. was on wrong side
of road. Accident difficult to understand, even so. Road
visible for fifty yards down drive, and P.C. was *well
past*, going in same direction, when hit ; must have
been full in view, unless cycling at high rate of speed, for
at least three seconds. Alan an expert driver. A mere
detail, but worrying. He is always so concerned for the
men under him, and so censorious of drivers who cause
this sort of accident.

A visit to the police. Photographs shown me of the
original bullet and the tests. Marks on the murderous
bullet *do not coincide* with either of the two guns in
police possession. An idea sprang into my mind, but I
must prove it before I even commit it to paper. It was
a considerable shock to me, as I am afraid the Inspector
perceived. Horrible ! I felt quite sick all day.

June 17th.

I tested my conjecture last night ; afterwards with
my watchmaker's glass scrutinized the six bullets, and I
have my proof.

Reconstruction.—One must suppose that Alan Littleton
went through the book-concealed door immediately the
Archbishop left. I cannot exactly state the cause of
quarrel ; but C. was working to deprive Alan of his job,
and had, we know, a most bitter tongue. I imagine
that the shooting, though not premeditated, was deliberate, possibly in answer to some gesture of C.'s, pulling
his own gun from the drawer, where, according to Mills,

he usually kept it. Alan Littleton knows all about firearms ; I believe that the sham suicide plan (see entry
under June 15) occurred to him, and was halfway to
execution when a sound disturbed him. Query, Sir
Charles trying the door ? " Attempt but not deed
confounds us." He leapt out of the *study* window,
jumping well to the left according to the prints, which
come under the *drawing-room* window in Sally's plan.
His first argument would run like this :

" I must pretend to have found Comstock dead—
murdered, since I had not time to give the blackening
shot. This car is my excuse for getting away ; it may
be the murderer escaping. I must give chase."

But by the time he has got into his own car this
argument changes its complexion.

" If I overtake this car, I must challenge the driver.
That means revealing that Comstock is dead. But
possibly his body will not be found, if I leave things
alone, for another half-hour. I must play for time. I
must have an excuse for *not* overtaking this car."

The policeman, quietly bicycling by, supplies this
excuse. Alan Littleton deliberately drove into him
from behind, and concocted the story of his being on
the wrong side ; trusting (*a*) to the macadamized road
leaving no traces of the accident, (*b*) to the blood on the
wrong side where he laid the unfortunate man, (*c*) to
the concussion leaving only a confused memory of the
actual occurrence. Here he miscalculated, as Mrs.
Bartelmy's story clearly shows. It will be a danger
point for him, if the investigations should ever get on
the right line.

His story about the petrol is not true. The tank was
full as usual, but he needed an excuse for delay, and

therefore poured the petrol out of the tin when he came
to a secluded place. (He displayed powers of quick
thinking and resource, to say nothing of courage, through-
out the whole business.) This secluded place was probably a lane on the road to the hospital, which I noted
as being very suitable for such a purpose ; a sharp turn,
shielded by a high hedge and trees. I believe that a
search along the border here to try and discover where
the petrol was spilt would certainly reveal some traces,
either of dead grass or earth disturbed. He drove in
to this lane with Bartelmy unconscious beside him ;
who, however, might regain consciousness at any
moment. There was much to be done, and he must have
moved quickly. His immediate object was to deface
the inner barrel of the revolver in his pocket before
handing it over to the police, who would inevitably ask
for it. He did this by a simple method which I have
myself tried out, scratching the barrel thoroughly with
earth or sand. This process would take five minutes ; the
removal of every grain of sand possibly longer. He must
have filed the tip of the striking pin, which can be done
with a pocket file, or a thin rough stone. It is an
infallible way of changing a gun's personality, but only
a man with considerable knowledge of firearms would
have thought of it. He completed his task, and arrived
at the hospital at the hour he stated.

My case is clear, but it cannot ever be proved. The
bullet which killed Comstock was fired from a weapon
whose characteristics have been destroyed for ever.
But Alan Littleton is a man of probity and honour, and
if an innocent person is accused I have no doubt that he
will speak. Meanwhile, until then I shall hold my
tongue, and record it as my conviction that there are

occasions when killing is no murder. The late Lord C. is very much better dead.

Irony! After all my lectures to Sally, I have my crime complete, with footprints, bloodstains, and the rest of the detection-story paraphernalia all in its right place. The only thing lacking is the motive, into which I do not propose to inquire further. I am satisfied that, in spite of the revolver in Alan's pocket, the crime was not planned, and that the various emergencies were met with quick thinking as they arrived. I do not think this death will lie heavy upon A.'s conscience; but if Bartelmy dies, I believe the guilt of that will haunt him to the end of his days. Crimes, like sorrows, never go singly.

N.B.—To quiet suspicion, and encourage the third-gun theory, I had better pay Sally her half-crown.

CHAPTER II

SIR JOHN TAKES HIS CUE

By Gladys Mitchell

" *Helen*, to you our minds we will unfold."

" Stand, ho ! Who is there ?
—Friends to this ground
And liegemen to the *Dane*."

I

" In fair round belly with good capon lined . . .
Full of wise saws and modern instances."

" But people do not come to this theatre to see a play ;
they come to see Sir John Saumarez. I challenge you
to disprove what I say."

The silky, ecclesiastical voice, as exquisitely modulated
as Sir John's own, ceased suddenly. The whole company,
at table on the stage of Sir John's own theatre, drew in
a deep breath, but before Sir John or anyone else could
take up the gage the challenger continued, smoothly,
easily, and with that air of quiet authority which was
making Sir John's magnificent shoulders twitch irritably,
although his mouth retained its genial smile of host and
layman.

" The Sir John walk ; the Sir John voice ; the Sir
John manner ; those are what your audiences come for.

Nobody wants to see real acting nowadays. There *is* no real acting. You, Sir John, are not an actor ; you are simply—and intelligently !—a set of unvarying mannerisms to which you have accustomed your public, and for which they are prepared to pay with applause, flattery, and money."

" And what," asked Sir John, smiling at the wine in his glass, while the company, who were wondering, half in awe, half in pleasurable excitement, what further heresy the white-haired prelate in their midst was prepared to utter, " do you mean by *real* acting, my dear Pettifer ? "

The Archbishop of the Midlands refreshed himself with a sip of water, much as a public speaker will do when he feels he has made a point and wishes it to sink in.

" By real acting," he replied, dabbing his full lips with a snowy napkin, and, this time, addressing the whole table—for, as an ex-schoolmaster, he always took for granted the attention, if not the interest, of his audience —" I mean character acting. And by character acting " —the Cathedral at Bournemouth, where he had been Bishop for a number of years, was extremely high, and he had accustomed himself to a very slow delivery, unctuous and ripely articulated, eminently suited to the acoustics of the Bournemouth Cathedral, but exceptionally trying to his hearers in ordinary conversation— " I mean an absolute alteration of the tones of the actor's natural voice, and the adoption, by him, of a completely different personality. An actor should *live* his part—I have coached boys for Shakespearian productions at school, so I claim to know just a *very* little about the subject—he should *live* his part. Judged by this standard—this type of acting, if you will—judged,

I say, thus, what I call *real* acting is as defunct as the Dodo. We *have* no actors nowadays."

" The Dodo," Sir John observed, his eloquent shoulders deploring while they acknowledged the fact, " is more than defunct. It is extinct. We now prefer our monsters, hide, fin, and feather, a little less—monstrous. ' Legg'd like a man, and his fins like arms ! ' Unfashionable, nowadays, I fear. So Mr. Crummles, of revered memory, if he returned to the English stage."

Sir John, a little tired of being told that he could not act, that his mannerisms and not his art were what the public came to enjoy, drank, and replaced his glass ; his slender hand toyed with its slender stem. The prelate, too much the pedagogue to make an ideal guest, returned to the assault.

" Ah, Crummles, yes." His tolerant smile wiped Crummles out of the argument. " But, my dear fellow, I was referring to actors—to actors, not mountebanks. Now, I have seen you act several times—quite several times ; and it seemed to me that with your gifts—your —shall we say ?—very considerable gifts "—there was the hint of an unwifely grin about Martella's mouth as she caught her husband's eye—" you could break the tradition that an actor-manager is a kind of tailor's dummy, due occasionally for a change of clothing, but, in all essentials, eternally the same."

He drank water again. The man on Martella Saumarez's right said audibly :

" The old fool's tight."

Sir John still smiled. His mannerisms might possibly be a matter for argument. His charm was not.

" One does not disappoint one's public." He had a momentary vision, vivid as it was fleeting, of his faithful gallery, waiting in the rain for a first night, applauding until the last instant, while the stalls collected wraps and furs ; clapping when he appeared for less than an instant between car and stage-door. Sir John's gallery queue was nearly always divided by his zealous commissionaire into two long tails, with the clear passage-way to the stage-door between them ; and the stage-door was a good twenty yards from the gallery entrance.

" One panders to it," said His Grace drily. " Self-indulgence, my dear Sir John."

Sir John, who was hearing a longer sermon on a week-day in his own theatre than he was usually called upon to endure on a Sunday in church, looked resigned. Taking this for a sign of grace, the Archbishop continued : " I fear we live in a particularly self-indulgent age. One strolls where one should march ; one idles the precious time away when the trumpet is calling to labour and to war."

Sir John, who called himself a lazy man, and yet, even as he made the admission, experienced strange doubts as to the veracity of the description, shrugged negligently, while the company, his own company, who knew their Sir John and knew of his genius in escaping the conversation of moralists and bores, glanced at one another, marvelling. Their leader's character-acquiring eye summed up the Archbishop ; a pompous, self-opinionated man whose natural self was overlaid with the fatty tissue of schoolmaster and church dignitary combined. The original William Anselm Pettifer, Sir John decided, had been lost to history for some two dozen years at least. Replying to the Archbishop's concluding remarks, he answered smoothly :

" Your tradition of the Christian soldier militates

9

against mine of the strolling player. Yet our object is the same. We seek to entrap the unwary citizen. Make him listen to something that may make a better man of him." He smiled. " For you, a trumpet call. For me, the still small voice——"

" Yes, of the prompter," said the Archbishop, with unlooked-for felicity. Sir John led the laughter. Conversation became general following his Grace's happy quip, but, with determination and tact so nicely mingled that none realized what he had done, Sir John caught back the Archbishop into their own conversational backwater, and, after banalities, was able to observe :

" Back to our sheep, my dear Pettifer ? "

" By all means," said the Archbishop, delighted with himself. " You find them interesting ? "

" Absorbing," said Sir John. He had looked up and caught Martella's eye. His own was penitent. His wife interpreted his look ; resignedly, she accepted his unspoken declaration that the conversation was important. " Sufficiently important," said Sir John's expressive glance, " to keep us out of bed a little longer."

" Absorbing ? " The Archbishop repeated, lusciously, the word. His full lips savoured it. " Indeed ? "

" This question," said Sir John, " of what one's public wants."

Sir John's own public wanted whatever it pleased Sir John to give it. He ignored this fact. His was not the small mind that fears to be inconsistent.

" You assume," said the Archbishop, displaying an ability to grasp the point which caused Sir John a momentary surprise, " that you and I are actors. Both of us."

" I do. You have your public. You have your exits

and your entrances. You effect certain alterations in your costume during the course of the service. You have accustomed your congregation to a certain William Anselm Pettifer who, in point of fact, does not exist. You imagine him. You compel your vision upon people who ' sit under ' you. This character that you enact has certain turns of speech. He has mannerisms, inflections of the voice, attitudes—with what rich unction," Sir John continued lyrically, " does he make his genuflexions, chant responses, and deliver the magnificent ' curtain lines ' of the Absolution ! ' "

" With unction," said the Archbishop, " but sincerely. That's the difference."

" I, also, am sincere," Sir John declared. " But my point is this. Admit you have a public to whom you have given a certain definite impression of yourself. The picture is sincere. That I admit. But it is not a picture of the whole man, nor necessarily of the whole Archbishop. Give them a different view-point—only one. What would their reaction be, I wonder ? "

" Apply the question to yourself," his Grace said blandly. " I believe that you and I are more, not less, ourselves, when we are—acting. Oh, I admit your argument. I see the force of it. I take my little brief authority and use it towards what good I may. You in this theatre, I in my cathedral, hold sway over men's hearts and minds. On our respective platforms we are more than human. In our appointed spheres we are a little lower than the angels. Outside them, you, at least, are a man as other men are."

He smiled and ruminated.

" True, true." Thus Sir John, complacently convinced that this was only half the truth. He, at least, was not as other men. The Marxian doctrine of the essential equality of man would have been the last item of belief in the creed of Sir John Saumarez. This was not vanity, but the result of wide-eyed experience, both of his own powers and of his world.

" And outside the cathedral you regard yourself as something *less* than a man ? " he said.

The Archbishop permitted himself to smile. He lingered lovingly upon a devastating reply, but lingered half a second too long, for young Peter Varley, Sir John's juvenile lead, coming, as he fancied, to the rescue of his chief, to whom he owed something more than to relieve him of the conversation of a bore, boldly inquired his Grace's views on greyhound racing. His Grace, who purposed giving them to the daily press in the immediate future, and had no objection whatever in trying them on the dog to find out how they sounded, surrendered gracefully to Peter's crisp-haired youthful charm, and gave them at some length and with enviable assurance.

Sir John waited patiently, and then, having regained his principal guest's attention, said, without warning:

" I mean, my dear Pettifer, suppose for instance that you had murdered Comstock this morning, what would be the reaction of your congregation ? Would they regard you as the popular hero ?—as the twentieth century champion of the Church ?—as a neo-Georgian Crusader, ridding the world of an infidel dog ?—or how ? "

His Grace appeared perplexed.

" You know, I was there at Comstock's house this morning," he observed.

" My dear Archbishop ! You really must forgive me ! I have no excuse ! Positively no excuse ! " Sir John's distress was evident. No one would have guessed that, in addition to the information he had garnered from the evening papers with their staring headlines, the Home Secretary had sent him all the details of Lord Comstock's death, Lord Comstock's household, and Lord Comstock's visitors which the police had been able to obtain.

The Archbishop, waving plump white hands, besought him not to distress himself, especially upon so interesting and happy an occasion.

The occasion was the " last-night " supper on the stage of Sir John's own theatre—the Sheridan—at the end of a seventeen months' run. Sir John, who had not taken a single day's holiday during that time, had promised himself at least two months' rest, except for the inevitable rehearsals of the new play which he was producing in the autumn. Meanwhile it was June, and the long run was over. The usual floral tributes for Martella and the *ingénue*, the laurel wreath for Sir John, the " last-night " enthusiasm of the loyal gallery, and the speeches of thanks, had preceded the supper. The supper itself was almost over, and the darkened auditorium on the other side of the curtain held only the ghosts of by-gone playgoers. The clock in Martella's dressing-room, whither she repaired the moment the guests had been speeded on their way, showed ten minutes past one. The end of a long run always left her feeling stale, flat, and unprofitable, and on the morrow they were due, she and Johnny, at a vicarage garden party. Absurd, thought Martella, rebelliously. It was ridiculous of Johnny ! And to have asked that insufferable old idiot of an archbishop to the supper !

Her husband's voice without said quietly :

" I say, Martella, may I come in ? "

" Of course." She opened the door. Sir John assisted her with her wrap and walked with her to the stage-door. It took a little time to respond to the farewells, but at last they were left alone.

" What's the matter, Johnny ? " Martella said.

" Nothing. But—would you mind going home alone, Martella ? I can't come just yet. I won't be very long."

He knew how tired she was ; how near to tears ; realized, with tenderness, exactly how she felt at the end of the long run. His voice was very gentle.

When, hat in hand, Sir John had watched the tail-light of the car disappear at the first turning, he became aware that His Grace the Archbishop of the Midlands was standing just behind him on the pavement.

" Ah, Pettifer," he said superbly. The Archbishop, as nearly as was possible to so self-possessed a man, seemed ill at ease.

" Ah, Saumarez," he said. " A pleasant night, is it not ? I was wondering—one does not sleep these hot nights unless one has one's stroll after dinner—or, as in this case, supper. And I have not thanked you for your hospitality, my dear fellow. A charming occasion, charming ; and, to me, of course, unique—quite. Yes, thank you a thousand times. Shall we—ah—walk a little of the way ? "

" There is nothing," Sir John said—sighing to himself, for he had supposed that they would sit and talk, in which case he could have handled the conversation so as to keep his promise to Martella ; if they began to walk there was no telling how long they might be— " nothing I should enjoy better. The Comstock case, of course ? "

There were, he realized, several more tactful openings

leading up to the same point, but time was fleeting and very precious.

"The Comstock case." The Archbishop fell into step, and they moved off down the deserted street. "Most tiresome and unpleasant ; and dreadful, of course. Most dreadful. Such a promising fellow. An old pupil of mine, you know. A clever lad. A clever, promising lad. I was with him, as I told you, almost immediately before his death."

There was silence, except for the echoing of their foot-steps ; a silence which Sir John was resolved not to break. His patience was rewarded in a few moments.

"And so—you won't misunderstand me, my dear Saumarez—the whole thing is both upsetting and exceedingly embarrassing for me."

"Quite," said Sir John.

"I have interviewed everybody who can possibly matter," his Grace went on, "but the fact remains that while the time of death is so extraordinarily vague, my position in the matter is, to say the least, unsatisfactory in the extreme. So unsatisfactory is it, that, if I did not fully realize how utterly impossible it is that I should be implicated in the affair, I should be very seriously perturbed. Very seriously perturbed indeed, Saumarez."

There was another long pause. Sir John, who apprehended perfectly whither these preliminary remarks were tending, wished that the Archbishop would come to the point and let him go home to bed. It took his Grace another five hundred yards to do so. Sir John took advantage of his companion's preoccupation to lead the way towards his own flat in Berkeley Square, so that when the conversation terminated he would be within measurable distance of his beauty sleep.

" You have heard some of the details, I take it ? " his Grace went on, at last.

" I have read the evening papers," said Sir John cautiously. It was the truth, but not the whole truth. However, it sufficed.

" I was wondering——" His Grace coughed, uncertain how to proceed, and they traversed another two hundred yards. The great feature of a square, Sir John reflected, is that one can walk round and round it, exercising body and brain without appreciably increasing the distance between oneself and one's front door. " I understand that on occasion you interest yourself in a little detective work."

Sir John permitted the remark its full meed of silence. Then :

" The occasions are rare," he said, " and my interest in them is always guided by my interest in, shall we say, the protagonists in the drama."

" Surely. Sure—ly." The Archbishop, delighted to have launched the subject so satisfactorily, began to purr. " And your interests, no doubt, my dear John——"

Sir John noted the nominative of address, and smiled wickedly into the darkness.

" Are with the right and against might, mob law, any kind of a frame-up, and so on." Thus Johnny Simmonds on his own naïf beliefs in innocence and justice.

" Quite, quite. Well, my dear fellow, it is criminal, quite criminal, to keep you out of your bed any longer, but I am sure I can rely on you. *Noblesse oblige*, you know ! Any information I can give you—you have only to ask. I would that I could shed upon the unhappy affair all the light it needs ! Poor Comstock ! Such a promising fellow. I am sad—sad."

Sir John stopped dead in his tracks.

" And what do you suppose I can do ? " he inquired.

" My *dear* John ! " The Archbishop's tone was benign. It was almost princely. Sir John, recognizing a fellow artist, chuckled inwardly. The man was as much a *poseur* as he was himself ; as vain ; as great an egoist. " I place myself entirely in your hands. I do not dictate. I implore. Believe me, I am not thinking only of myself. I am a shepherd of souls, you know." He smiled his bland, ecclesiastical smile. He was usually caricatured as a cherub. " I am a doorkeeper in the house of the Lord. For that very reason I went to see poor Comstock. You know, of course, how he received me."

" You had no means of finding out beforehand what your reception would be ? " Sir John inquired.

" My dear fellow, I did not risk attempting to make an appointment with him. I knew he would not see me."

" Guilty conscience ? " inquired Sir John.

" Partly, I think. I used to teach him once. Blackminster Grammar School, you know."

Sir John did know ; had spent precious hours that very afternoon in finding out all he could about the school. It amounted to very little. The Archbishop seemed to have made a successful headmaster. Scholarships had been won. The O.T.C. flourished. The games record had been sound.

" What effect would Comstock's policy have had, I wonder," mused Sir John aloud, " upon the general public ? Comstock the Apostate. . . . What influence would he acquire ? "

The Archbishop shrugged.

"He did his soul harm, not the church."

"You realize," Sir John said slowly, "that you are supposed to have had a motive for the murder?"

"Of course! Of course! How, otherwise, should I presume to encroach upon your time like this?"

"You know——" Sir John began. They were standing beneath the street lamp which was nearest to Sir John's front door. He knew by the light at the front of the house that Martella was still waiting up for him. The Archbishop waved the plump white hand of the *pontiff*.

"I know the worst there is to know," he said. Sir John recognized the curtain line. He was also annoyed at being interrupted. He let the curtain fall.

"Good-night," he said, and went in to Martella. She had sent her maid to bed long since. Her husband took her by the elbow and conducted her into the bedroom.

"You go to bed," he said. "I won't be long."

She was about to protest, but, knowing the futility of doing so, gave in. Sir John, having prepared himself for bed, retired to the study.

Well-disciplined in her double capacity of wife and leading-lady to Sir John Saumarez, Martella shrugged one shapely shoulder, glanced sadly at the empty twin-bed beside her own, looked at the bedroom clock and then switched off the light.

In the study Sir John was frowning over the Home Secretary's letter. A sheaf of newspapers lay on the floor beside his desk. The topmost of them displayed in thick black type the caption:

MURDER OF LORD COMSTOCK:
ASTOUNDING DISCLOSURES.

Sir John folded the Home Secretary's letter and glanced with distaste at the pile of newspapers. He rose, gave an elaborate yawn, stretched his arms wide so that the magnificent Chinese dragon across his magnificent shoulders stretched also and was revealed in all its Oriental glory, let his arms fall to his sides, and went over to a gramophone cabinet in the corner. One of the biggest gramophone companies in the world had recently persuaded Sir John to make half a dozen records for them of famous speeches from Shakespeare. It was not one of his own records, however, that Sir John selected from the cabinet and placed upon the gramophone. A harsh, resonant, arresting voice said firmly :

" And *I* tell you this ; I, Comstock. Our civilization is doomed. Doomed ? It's dead ! "

Abruptly Sir John curtailed the remainder of Lord Comstock's speech at the Albert Hall on the subject of the Sunday Amusements (Greater Facilities) Bill, and replaced the record with great care. Then he closed down the gramophone and went into the bedroom. Martella, reclining against pillows banked like cumulus cloud, was reading her bed-book. In the soft light Sir John's pyjamas, proudly-hued as the peacock, shimmered in all their silken glory as he removed his dressing-gown and climbed into bed. Martella laid aside the book.

" Tired, Johnny ? " Sir John cocked an eye at her.

" You are, I expect," he said.

" Tell me," she said, interpreting his need. She switched out the light. Sir John's bed creaked as he flung himself on to his side.

" Comstock," he said. " A scoundrel. A wicked devil, if ever there was one."

" And you've been asked to find out who killed him," said Martella, into the darkness.

" And why should I ? " said Sir John irritably. " It's nothing to do with me."

" Well, don't bother then," said his wife. " You're tired. You want a holiday. It doesn't matter in the least who did it. If they hang the wrong person, it's still nothing to do with you."

" You're an irritating devil, Martella," said her husband, not for the first time during their married life. " In addition, you possess the gift of second sight. How did you know ? "

" Good-night, Johnny," said Martella. " You'd better go and see him in the morning."

There was a considerable interval of silence. Then Sir John coughed very gently.

" It's all right. I'm awake," Martella said resignedly.

" Look here, Martella," said Sir John, " when we get to that garden party to-morrow you might collect our hostess and get her away from me, will you ? "

" All right," she said. " Who's going to be there, Johnny ? "

" I'm not sure. It is a shot in the dark. I cast my bread upon the waters," said Sir John magnificently.

" You realize, don't you," said Martella, speaking slowly, " that there must have been a cook ? No, don't jump up and down in bed, darling. It's bad for the springs."

" Forty-eight hours ! " Sir John said tragically.

" Oh, I could round up the cook," said his wife. " There might also be a wife belonging to the gardener, mightn't there ? You know, the gardener who saw the mysterious lady."

" Who has been telling you the details ? " asked Sir John.

" Oh, they are in all the evening papers, darling," said Martella innocently. " You must let me have the Rolls to-morrow morning. I think you had better have the cook brought to the garden party—it is certain to be admission by ticket—vicarage garden parties always are."

" I could go over and see the gardener's wife at Hursley Lodge. It is eight miles by road from Winborough Vicarage. But if Littleton did it——" began Sir John.

" Alan Littleton ? He couldn't ! " Martella's voice was confident. " I've known him for donkey's years."

" Proof positive," murmured her husband.

" Don't be beastly, Johnny. Sometimes I believe you've got a cynical outlook. Alan *couldn't* have done it."

" On temperament," mused Sir John, his eyes beginning to close in spite of his efforts to remain alert and clear-headed, " Alan is by far the most likely person to have done it.

" No," said Martella drowsily. " I don't believe it."

II

" Depress'd he is already ; and deposed
'Tis doubt he will be."

Sir John's vapour bath fulfilled a double purpose, one-half of which was to allow him a period of seclusion in the early morning during which he could think over the occupations of the day and its problems. Accordingly, on the morning following that upon which Lord Comstock had met his death, the knight, enclosed to the neck, considered the day. It overflowed with things to be done and bristled with problems.

" . . . as a personal favour to me," the Home Secretary's letter had said. The sentence tickled Sir John's sense of dramatic irony. The smile on his flushed handsome face appeared but for a moment, however, and then faded, and he frowned. By the early morning post—he had been downstairs in his dressing-gown to look over his correspondence—had come another letter, containing the same request as that made by Sir Philip Brackenthorpe, the Home Secretary, and by His Grace the Archbishop of the Midlands, but couched in somewhat different terms from those in which the Archbishop, verbally, and the Home Secretary, in writing, had seen fit to express themselves.

" For God's sake, Johnny, find out who did it, or I can see myself in jug," the impetuous Assistant Commissioner of Police (temporarily suspended) had inscribed on a sheet of notepaper ; and the sheet upon which he had expressed his anguish of soul had been so hastily torn from a writing-pad that at least one-seventh of its total surface area had never got as far as the envelope, but remained adhering to the parent block, mute witness to the Assistant Commissioner's state of mind.

A further sentence in the Home Secretary's admirably-worded letter, as well as a portion of the police dossier of Comstock's death, had revealed the damaging fact that the Assistant Commissioner, who looked like having to resign his office on the strength of it, was in the extremely delicate position of having been on the premises—actually inside the house, it appeared—when the murder of Lord Comstock was committed.

Martella was breakfasting in bed, so, the appointed

time for slimming-cum-meditation being over, Sir John went into the pleasant morning-room and breakfasted in solitary state. After breakfast he went into the bedroom and acquainted his wife with the fact that he was going out, but added that he would return to a very early lunch.

" How early, darling ? " asked Martella. Lady Saumarez, even more attractive at thirty than she had been during her early twenties, was beautiful at any hour of the twenty-four which constitute a day. She did not look the least so in bed, leaning back against the propped-up pillows.

" Say twelve," he replied. " We can't be late for that garden-party. I must be there. There's certain to be gossip, and if we can lay hands on the cook you promised me——"

" Johnny," said Martella, " you know you'll hate it. And after all, why should you trouble ? Alan is certain to be all right. You don't know who did it, and you don't care ! Why should they use your brains ? Let the police do their own work."

" The trouble is," Sir John said slowly, " that although in a sense I don't care, I do know, Martella. But proof ! Proof ! " sighed Sir John. " I may do innocence an injustice unless I prove myself either right or wrong."

He left her, and called for the car. Sir John leaving his London house was usually an impressive spectacle, but this morning, except for the butler, who opened the door of the house, and the chauffeur, who opened the door of the car, there was no one to see him off. His secretary had been given a holiday ; his valet had been waved away and instructed to have suitable raiment in readiness, for Sir John proposed to attend a garden-party that afternoon. No last-minute commands had to be issued ; no odds-and-ends were needed to be carried out to the car. A seventeen-months' run was over. Sir John was not prepared to produce his new play before October at the earliest ; and, masterful yet suave, had put off indefinitely the signing of a new film contract. He paused a moment at the top of the flight of stone steps which led from his front door to the street, unconsciously posing against the background of the house. Then gracefully, and enjoying to the full his own appreciation of his own grace, he descended the steps and entered the waiting car. In deference to Martella's suggestion that she should use the Rolls, Sir John had commanded his second car to be brought. He dismissed the chauffeur and drove himself.

The Assistant Commissioner was at home.

" And likely to be, until this hellish mess is cleared up ! " he snorted. " I suppose you can't see daylight yet, Johnny ? "

" So much," replied Sir John, " that my eyes are dazzled."

" Case of can't see the wood for trees, if you ask me," said Littleton, scowling at the tip of his cigarette before he tapped off the ash. " Likewise, too many cooks spoil the broth. Likewise—oh, hell, what's the good of talking ! I suppose you know the police have been shoved right out of it ? "

" For forty-eight hours, I understand," Sir John replied equably.

" Right out of it ! " Littleton went on, without noticing his visitor's remark. " My own department, mind you, not allowed to do me a ha'porth of good. ' The Home Secretary takes charge ! ' Tchah ! "

There was a long silence. Sir John smoked placidly, supine in a long chair. His eyelids drooped. There were some of his most ardent admirers who declared that never had he appeared to greater advantage than in the part of Sir Percy Blakeney, the immortal Scarlet Pimpernel. It was a nice point. He was permitting his mind to dwell on it when the impetuous Littleton broke out again :

" Of course, any one of us could have done it. That's as clear as mud. But the devil of it is that only one of us did. You've heard the evidence, I suppose ? Lovely, isn't it ? The Assistant Commissioner of the C.I.D., the Archbishop of the Midlands, and the Chief Whip of the Central Party, all about equally involved ! Oh, we're sitting pretty, all of us ! "

" ' Sweet are the uses of adversity.' And the weight of the circumstantial evidence goes very slightly against the Archbishop," murmured Sir John.

" Oh, you think that, do you ? " Littleton sat bolt upright in his chair. " Do you know that the shot went in so clean that it drilled the neatest little hole in Comstock's head you ever saw ? And it wasn't fired particularly close, you know. There was no powder blackening on the head, and no traces of burning in the neighbourhood of the wound. It was a perfect shot, man ! Death instantaneous ! Course of the bullet slightly upwards, and all that sort of thing. Are you telling me that an Archbishop fired a shot like that ? "

" Queer, though," said Sir John, " how nobody seems to have seen Comstock alive after the Archbishop left him."

" Queer be damned ! The murderer saw him alive ! And that gets us back to where we started from ! There

10

simply isn't another bally jumping-off place at all. I'm
a policeman ; therefore, to most of the bone-heads that
make up the great mass of the British public, I'm hardly
likely to be a murderer. The Archbishop is a churchman,
and murder is a sin. That lets him out. As for Hope-
Fairweather, he'll be lucky if it doesn't ruin his career,
getting mixed up in a business like this. If he's jugged,
I expect he'll pray to be hanged. Personally, I'd like to
pin it on that secretary bird. A nasty growth, that one."

" Surely," Sir John said mildly, " the secretary could
have picked a better time. House full of people, all unexpected visitors ; a possibility that others might arrive.
It isn't credible."

" Well, but, isn't it ? " Major Alan Littleton stood
astride the hearthrug, and looked down upon Sir John's
limp elegance reclining in the long and well-sprung chair.
" Could he have picked a better time ? " he asked.
" Damn-all he could ! There's no more evidence against
him at this moment than against the three of us ! Less,
in fact. Each one of us—Pettifer, Hope-Fairweather,
and I—has a thundering great hefty motive that sticks
out a mile. What motive has Mills ? None, so far as
anybody knows. If you ask me, that bird's worked it
jolly well if he did commit the murder."

" He was under notice of dismissal," said Sir John.
He was not arguing with the vehement Assistant Commissioner so much as letting him talk and listening to
what he had to say.

" Yes," snorted Major Alan Littleton, " but would
Comstock dare to dismiss a man who knew as much as
Mills did ? Of course he wouldn't. No, no, Johnny !
So far as anybody knows at present Mills had no motive
for killing Comstock, and my view is that he took advan-

tage of the presence of all three of us to get away with the
murder. He would know we all had a grudge against
Comstock, and he would know what the grudge was. He
is a clever fellow, used to taking all sorts of risks, I should
say, and having to be ready to act on the spur of the
moment with nothing but his mother-wit to help him."

" You are not suggesting that he arranged the time
when you, Hope-Fairweather, and the Archbishop were
to visit Hursley Lodge ? " inquired Sir John. The
Assistant Commissioner reluctantly shook his head.

" So far as I'm concerned that isn't so," he said. "I
really did go down on the spur of the moment and without
a word to anybody. I had got hold of some information
which I hoped would give Comstock the hell of a jerk,
and I rushed down to Hursley Lodge to put it across
him and call him off his anti-police stunt. Honest,
Johnny, what was your opinion of the swine ? "

Sir John rose.

" ' I come to bury Cæsar, not to praise him.' " He
walked to the door.

" You're not going ? " Littleton said. Sir John
inclined his head.

" Forty-eight hours. Twenty of them gone," he said,
and made a perfect exit.

(III)

> " And praise we may afford,
>   To any lady that subdues a lord."

To say that Canon Pritchard had persuaded his wife
to fix the Annual Garden Party for a date when he knew
very well he would be attending Convocation would be
an overstatement. The fact, as noted by the recording
angel, was that after the date of the Annual Garden

Party had been fixed, the Vicar discovered that it coincided with Convocation, a discovery which he kept strictly to himself until it was too late to do anything about it.

He was not sorry to have an excuse for absenting himself from the revels. Attendance at any garden party was not in itself his idea of spending a thoroughly enjoyable afternoon, and, even if it had been, he might have been forgiven for considering that a garden party given not for the benefit of the guests but for the benefit of the Church fund hardly came under the heading of an entertainment ; for the Vicarage Garden Party held in June was like the Church Bazaar held in November ; its *raison d'être*, purely and simply, was to rook the wealthiest or most generous of the parishioners—the adjectives were not, of course, synonymous—of the greatest amount of money in the shortest possible time.

According to Mrs. Pritchard—but it was against the Canon's better nature to agree with her in the matter— the parishioners were exceedingly fortunate in being invited to enjoy themselves in such charming surroundings as those of the garden attached to their vicar's residence. The garden comprised a lawn, some shrubs, a pond, a paddock, and a small orchard, for the vicarage was situated almost on the outskirts of the sleepy old town. Beyond the orchard was a little stream, and on the other side of the stream flat water-meadows, broken by clumps of willow, led to the railway line whose steep green embankment cut short the view southwards. If enough stall-holders and side-show enthusiasts could be gathered together, it was the custom of Mrs. Pritchard to cause or permit her garden party to overflow into the water-meadows (which were nice and dry in the middle of the summer), by means of a small plank bridge. On this particular occasion—although it made no difference to anybody but Sir John Saumarez—she had arranged to have the greater tea tent there, and also one of the fortune-teller's booths. There were always two fortune-tellers. One read hands and the other the cards. There was also Mrs. Band, who helped in the tea-tent and read tea-cups, but she was never allowed to charge more than twopence, owing to the fact that the tea was made in an urn and so hardly any tea-leaves were available. The Vicar's wife liked people to have value for their money if it was at all possible. Usually it was not possible, and so her conscience was quite clear.

The sadness which the Vicar's absence might have caused in any other year was entirely eclipsed on this occasion by the fact that the famous London actor-manager, Sir John Saumarez, and the famous London actress, his wife, had promised to be present ; had asked if they might come, in fact ; and were actually upon the scene of action just after two o'clock. It seemed as though the fame of the Vicarage Annual Garden Party— (tickets of admission one and sixpence before the day, two shillings on the day, right of admission strictly reserved)—had gone abroad even unto the uttermost ends of the earth. The rank and fashion of Winborough —for Winborough society still maintained most of the charming features of Cranford—spent a busy morning discussing what to wear, and a busy noon getting ready to wear it. There was not the slightest doubt in anybody's mind as to whether it was desirable to meet an actor-manager and his wife. Happily, the vexed question of the social significance of stage celebrities has now been settled once and for all, at least as far as the present generation is concerned. To meet Sir John was becoming the life-ambition of all Canon Pritchard's female parishioners, most of whom spent valuable time in inventing suitable phrases with which to describe the overwhelming occasion to all those of their acquaintance who had not met Sir John, were not likely to meet Sir John, and were going to pass the rest of their lives, if Canon Pritchard's female parishioners were worth their salt and knew anything about themselves and their friends, in rueing the fact that not to them had been accorded the privilege of having met Sir John, and that therefore they must hide their diminished heads on all social occasions for years to come.

Sir John himself possessed to perfection the politeness of princes in that, being inwardly bored and irritated, he remained outwardly urbane and charming ; and in that, wanting nothing so much as to get away from the great cloud of witnesses who were preparing to go home and brag to their nearest and dearest that they had actually conversed with Sir John, he yet found the exact quip, the perfect repartee, the unerring remark for each. Yet while smiling-eyed, gardenia in button-hole, he gave of his best, all the while he was watching and waiting for one whom he felt certain would appear. His hostess, scattering the throng of young and old maids as though she were shooing poultry, took him apart almost at the beginning of the proceedings, and besought him to sell autographs. She pressed fountain-pen and loose-leaved notebook upon him, set him upon a garden chair, dragged a wicker table towards him, and left him high and dry, like Matthew at the receipt of custom, with strict instructions to get what he could, but on no account to take less than a shilling a time. Sir John permitted his shoulders to indicate that he yielded to the situation. Martella's grin, as Mrs. Pritchard carried her off to sell button-holes to the male portion of the parish, he ignored ; he only hoped she would be able to produce the promised cook at a suitable moment, and that the cook herself might have something helpful to confide to him.

When his hostess and his wife were out of sight he rose, and with the assistance of a little girl who seemed disposed to spend the entire afternoon in leaning over his shoulder and breathing heavily into his right ear, moved chair and table nearer the garden gate. Fortunately for his purpose, there was only one entrance into the vicarage grounds, and Sir John, salesman of autographs at not less than one shilling a time, was not as tremendously sought after as Sir John, private lion warranted to roar nicely and not to bite, had been ; and so, as the crowd melted away, he was able to keep one eye on the autograph hunters and the other on the gate. He worked off a dozen or more autographs, and the little girl, coming, apparently, to the conclusion that the performance, although interesting, was not going to vary, removed herself from his vicinity. So did all the people who either could not or would not afford a shilling, and Sir John, caressing his ear with a silk handkerchief, began to feel that the Vicar's wife, despite herself, had done him a good turn. The June day was warm. At the back of Sir John's chair stood a tall tree, young, but clothed with all its dark green summer leaves. Sir John removed his hat and laid it, after a preliminary survey of the surface, on the little table ; perceived at a little distance a deck-chair, inviting and untenanted. With a hunted glance, to make certain he was not detected in his lapse from duty, he drew it beneath the shade of the tree and in less than three minutes he was reclining in it with his eyes closed.

His satellite approached him.

" Mrs. Pritchard said I was to make all the people come to you and buy an autograph. I don't think any more want to come. Can I go and play now ? "

"Surely," breathed Sir John. "An ice? Lemonade?"

The maiden accepted half a crown with some alacrity and darted off. In a few moments she was back again.

" Thanks. Here's the change. Ice-cream fourpence. It was a brick. Lemonade threepence. I had the home-made. I'd rather have had fizzy, but it was fivepence."

She pressed one and elevenpence, all in coppers, into the knight's reluctant hand.

" And the pretty one—she's your wife, isn't she ?—said where do you want the cook put, because she's found her."

Sir John dashed sleep aside, and, incidentally, one and elevenpence in coppers on the ground. They grovelled for them.

" Finding's keepings," Sir John exclaimed, managing to find twopence halfpenny by leaning over the side of the chair. And then, " I'll come," he said, preparing to rise from its depths.

" No. She said not. She said you're safer where you are."

Sir John, chuckling inwardly at Martella's elliptically expressed warning, relaxed again.

" I'll bring the cook. She's fat. She'll want a chair. Your wife said she'll give you a quarter of an hour—and I think that's all."

" It would be," said Sir John, but he said it to the

empty air. He glanced at his watch. Twenty-five
minutes to four. Experience told him that the refreshment tent would be comparatively empty for another
quarter of an hour at least.

The cook appeared, a balloon of a woman, short of
breath, perspiring, and obviously impressed by Sir
John's sartorial magnificence.

A nice cup o' tea ? Nothing she couldn't do with
better, thanking you kindly, sir. And she always did
say that tea slaked the thirst better'n all these cooling
drinks, so-called.

The big marquee, in charge of one of the daughters
Pritchard, was dark and cool. Sir John chose a table,
steered his companion to it, called for tea, fruit salad
and cream, bread, butter, and cakes, mortified his
shrinking interior for the sake of establishing an *entente
cordiale* ; and got his story.

" We all knowed he was a wrong one. But there !
Nothing to do half the year or more, and me with a
widowed sister and her two boys. Both at the County
School and doing well. It wasn't for me to say his P's
and Q's for him. Too old to take any harm, what with
not being his style, too, and all. So I stopped. Too
quiet for some, but there ! I likes a quiet life, I do,
having buried two husbands and one at sea."

Sir John, also at sea, nodded, afraid to interrupt the
flow.

" So that very morning, funny enough, two magpies
flew acrost the kitchen garden. ' Means something,' I
said to George Briggs, ' though what,' I said, ' who can
tell ? ' Anyway, Mr. Farrant orders the lunch, same as
usual, and him never to eat again, poor man, which I
can't help but shed a tear," said the cook, producing,

largely for Sir John's benefit, a black-bordered handkerchief, and wiping her eyes, "wrong one though he was. But there! What are lords for, if not to do the things we're all too poor to afford ? "

This piece of philosophy appeared to give her considerable food for thought.

" Farrant ordered the lunch," Sir John reminded her, after a tactful interval of silence and the shuddering consumption of a small piece of tinned pineapple. Recalled, not so much to the thread of her narrative as to her duties as a guest, the cook scraped up the last vestiges of cream from her plate, stretched forth a be-ringed hand to the cakes, and then observed :

" Ah, Mr. Farrant. I never *took* to that man. Friendly as you please we was, but reely to say *trust* him, no, that I never couldn't. But find out things ! There's nothing that man didn't know. All the ladies, *and* their names, *and* where they come from. And that's not all.

" ' 'Is Grace is in there,' Farrant says to me, ' going for 'is lordship 'ammer and tongs. You come and listen to 'em,' he says. So I did, under the stairs, there being a door there from the kitchen, and not having to put the cutlets on for another half an hour, and the vegetables done and covered up against cooking 'em. My word ! You should 'ave 'eard it ! Not words, mind you, I didn't hear. At least," the virtuous woman amended, pursing her lips, " I *did* hear one or two, from his lordship, has I should be very sorry to repeat, even on oath, which I suppose it's got to come to."

Sir John inclined his head.

" One fears so. Yes." He introduced a portion of tinned apricot into his mouth and swallowed it heroically.

" Have some more cream, sir," said the cook. " Wholesome cream is, I always say."

With inward misgivings and a sigh for the reactions of his waistline to this heresy, Sir John accepted the lavish spoonful which she dolloped on to his plate from her own teaspoon. His smile and his thanks, however, were minted from the finest gold of courtesy. The cook beamed.

" So you didn't really hear anything of what was said ? " Sir John suggested. The cook bridled.

" Who said I didn't ? I could have heard plenty, if I'd wished. But ladies don't wish. Brought there to hear the row I was, and hear the row I did. And awful was his lordship's fearful words," said the cook, feeling, apparently, that nothing but blank verse could do justice to the subject of his lordship's language. ' Guts of a flea,' he says. And ' blasted hypocrisy.' And ' whited sepulchres. That's out of your own book of clap-trap barley sugar,' he says. And all like that. Abuse. Just vulgar. Though he *was* a lord, he'd raised hisself from dirt, as well we knew. And dirty does that dirty is," said the cook, inspired. " No class. That's what it come to. But the Archbishop, poor old man, I couldn't hear a word of him except his voice, and then when his lordship knocked his swivel chair over, me hating violence, which my first husband used to throw the flat irons about in his rage——"

" You think Lord Comstock's chair was knocked over ? "

" As who shouldn't ? Who done the dusting in that room ? Why, me. Can't you see a butler doing dusting ? It was the swivel chair at his lordship's desk that went over, of that I'm certain."

Sir John produced the police plan of Comstock's study.
On it was clearly marked an overturned chair. But it
was the chair near the door. He showed it to the cook.

" That chair may or may not have been overturned
when the police turned up," said she, " but if I was on
oath, which surely is what it's got to come to, the chair
I heard crash was his lordship's swivel chair. A woman
gets to know furniture, sir, you know. Besides, the
sound wasn't by the door."

> " 'Tis far off ;
>   And rather like a dream than an assurance,"

Sir John said under his breath.

" A dream ? " said the cook. " Ah, and in a dream I
thought I was when no less than that police officer turned
up all unexpected. It was Mr. Farrant told me, else
never should I have guessed he was anything to do with
the police. All spruced up as nice as ninepence and in
a suit like everybody else, and looking quite the gentleman. ' He's in the drawing-room,' says Mr. Farrant,
' hoping to get into his lordship. Breach of promise at
last, I'll warrant you,' says Mr. Farrant to me, ' and him
with a warrant in his pocket, I shouldn't wonder. Well,
he'll have to wait till Sir Charles has had his do, warrant
or no warrant, I'll bet,' he says."

" Sir Charles ? "

" And the spit and image of his picture in the papers,"
said the cook excitedly. " He was in the waiting-room
while all the to-do was going on. The police officer
gentleman came afterwards. Sir Charles I *was* not quite
surprised to see. Some funny fish being fried in politics,
Sir John."

Sir John indicated gracefully his appreciation of the
point.

" I think so. Yes, I think so. Alas ! Poor Yorick."

" Not having heard him so referred to, but always as Sir Charles," the oracle replied. " However, there we was, and me nearly jumping out of my skin when they said his lordship was dead. ' *All* of 'em seen him and *nobody* done it ? ' I says to Mr. Mills, which is too much like something on the pictures to altogether take my fancy, present company accepted," said the cook magnificently.

" Thank you, indeed. Thank you," said Sir John, acknowledging the tribute.

" No. Say those gals what they like of Adolphe Menjou," the cook continued—" me taking no stock in Ronald Coleman as too tall and with that spoilt look —your sideface makes my 'eart go all of a leap, which is not," she concluded archly, " as it ought to be. But there ! we all go girlish at the films, you know, Sir John, and no harm done that I knows on."

(IV)

" What's to do ?
—A piece of work that will make sick men whole."

" I had to come," said the voice. " I inquired at your house. They said you were here. Dear Sir John——"

Dear Sir John rose.

" Ah, Miss Hope-Fairweather," he said. He glanced round cautiously. Their portion of the garden was deserted except for the small girl who had found a swing and was now engaged in seeing whether it was possible to kick the roof of the summer-house. Sir John smiled and beckoned. With a jolt that threatened to dislocate every limb, she dropped to earth.

" Would it be possible for you to find Mrs. Pritchard and give her these," he said, handing her the loose-leaved notebook and the pen. The child considered him.

" What shall I say you've done with the autograph money ? "

Sir John raised his eyebrows in mock seriousness.

" Do I understand that you are questioning my good faith ? " he asked. He gave the money he had made, having first considerably augmented it. The little girl counted it carefully, vouchsafed him an approving smile, said, " Thirteen pounds twelve. Righto," and trotted off.

" Shall we walk ? " Sir John suggested, steering Miss Hope-Fairweather across the lawn and past a meagre shrubbery.

" You don't seem at all surprised to see me," the lady said. She was young and charming and, it was obvious, a prey to considerable anxiety. Sir John considered her.

" I'm not easily surprised," he said. As a matter of fact, he had expected her. " I hoped to pick up information here. Gossip. You know these county towns."

She said she did.

" But there ! " his rueful smile was eloquent. " Once I was coerced into collecting money, people fled from me. My shadow frightened them. The place wherein I was became a desert."

In spite of anxiety, she laughed at that.

" I don't believe there is much information to pick up," she said. " Poor Brother Charles is in despair. He feels—I don't mean to be ungrateful, Sir John !—but he does rather feel that it is madness on the part of the Home Secretary to keep the police out of the case for two whole days. He says that every possible clue will

be cold and dead by that time. I came to see whether I
could be of any help. I know all that happened. I
know "—she floundered, but recovered—" I know someone else went with him, and, as he can't appear in the
affair—— Oh, it is unfortunate! He is so brilliant—
his career—everything ! "

Sir John, his eyes upon the unweeded gravel path,
managed to convey by the expression on his flawless
countenance, presented profile-wise to her, his entire
agreement that the whole affair, from start to finish, had
been one vast " misfortune." Greek tragedy, this death
of Comstock, invented by the gods who kill us for their
sport, Sir John's face said ; his hands, with a gesture of
helplessness, bore witness to it ; while his shoulders,
expressive always, deplored the sense of humour of the
gods.

Martella, beautifully gowned, exquisitely cool in spite
of the warmth of the day and her efforts on behalf of
the church fund, manifested herself apparently from the
depths of the shrubbery. Sir John, who knew her in-
herent dislike of spiders and most of the forms of animal
and insect life which haunt the shady places, realized
that this could not actually be so. She came up to them,
a hunted expression in her eyes.

" My dear, they've just begun the Country Dancing.
Listen ; you can hear the music."

They all three listened. The strains of a solitary
violin, wailing like a lost soul which had found its way
into the vicarage garden and could not remember how
to get out again, came to their ears on a rising cadence
and then faded away.

" Mrs. Pritchard is singing the instructions and
dancing, and pushing all those who don't know how to

do it, and calling out, ' B music again, please,' until I couldn't bear it," Lady Saumarez explained, exhibiting a distressing tendency to giggle. " It seemed a splendid chance to slip away. You could get over to Hursley Lodge now, Johnny, if you wanted to go. We shan't be missed for an hour at least. Mrs. Pritchard is in her element. Oh, and she has changed into her Girl Guide uniform."

In three seconds they had sneaked out at the vicarage gate and were in the car. Very gently Sir John let in the clutch.

A constable was on guard at the gates of Hursley Lodge, and another kept the door. Sir John, slowing the car to a decorous five miles an hour, produced the Home Secretary's pass, received the official salute, passed on, took the left-hand bend of the drive, and pulled up exactly opposite the steps. The Home Secretary's pass having been duly scrutinized and saluted again, Sir John followed Miss Hope-Fairweather and Martella into the house.

" What do you expect to find ? " Martella whispered. The stillness—the queer hush of death which hung over the place—was unnerving.

" I have not the faintest idea," Sir John replied, also in a whisper.

" I wonder which is the study ? "

He again produced the plan of the house which had been supplied to him, and copies of the police photographs of the room where the murder of Lord Comstock had occurred, and in they went. The big desk stood in the bay window, with the light entering to the right of any person who sat at it. The revolving chair backed the light, and anyone sitting in it was facing the concealed door in the bookcase. This concealed door Sir John opened, and through the opening entered the drawing-room. He soon returned to the study, however, sat at the desk, and, after telling the two women what he was going to do, he pushed over the revolving chair. Then he inspected the overturned chair near the hall door, entered the office through the double doors, and then rejoined Miss Hope-Fairweather and Martella in the hall. To his wife's inquiring look he vouchsafed a most eloquent shrug of the shoulders.

" Come into the garden," he said. But when they were out on the drive and had thrice circumnavigated the clump of trees, he was still silent and so obviously preoccupied that his companions did not interrupt the flow of his thoughts. At last he said to Miss Hope-Fairweather :

" What does Sir Charles make of the secretary, Mills ? "

She shook her head.

" I don't believe Charles has seen him since. Mills is being detained at Winborough, isn't he ? Won't you—could you find time to go and see Charles, Sir John ? Or you could have him to see you, if you wished, I suppose, couldn't you ? "

" I can't see that Mills would gain anything," said Sir John, almost in a stage aside. " It would be killing the goose that laid the golden eggs."

Miss Hope-Fairweather clutched his arm.

" But if you found that Mills *would* benefit by Lord Comstock's death——" she said. She caught her breath, and added bravely, " But I *can't* believe that Mills would have been able to seize his opportunity when all those people were in the house. Imagine it ! The Archbishop, the Assistant Commissioner of Police, and my

II

brother were all either in the study or in a room next-door to it. How could Mills have stood the slightest chance of committing the murder and remaining un-detected?"

"But that," Sir John said quietly, "would apply to everybody. Don't worry about Sir Charles. It is a pity that he went at all. But it can't be helped."

"Oh, I know Charles behaved like a fool," said Sir Charles's next-of-kin. "But it was only his sense of duty! [He's so enthusiastic. He never has spared himself. Whether he did it or not—but, of course, he didn't—it will ruin him!"

"Of course, Sir Charles has behaved recklessly. He was stupid. A hopeless blunder, this, which he will find it difficult to retrieve." Sir John, pretending to be un-aware of two indignant faces, halted, produced a cigarette, fitted it into a holder, lighted it, all with maddening elegance and precision. Miss Hope-Fairweather kicked the gravel with a pointed, patent toe-cap, the threatened tears averted. Sir John winked solemnly at Martella and resumed his stride. He could bear almost anything but tears.

"This gardener," said Sir John, changing the tempo briskly. He went up to the front door and made dis-creet inquiry. The constable, who was a local man, indicated the way to the gardener's cottage.

"I think——" Sir John said, hesitating, and glancing at his wife.

"Not in these shoes," his wife said promptly, inter-preting the unspoken request. "We'll sit in the car until you come."

So Sir John, clothed like the lily of the field, from beautiful hat to lavender gloves and the most perfect shoes in the world, set off alone. The cottage was not difficult to find. He passed between banks of blazing colour up to a rose-arched open door whereon he tapped.

"Briggs, sir? Yes, please, sir. He's having his sleep."

"I know," Sir John sighed profoundly, or appeared to, at the disturbance he was causing. "I know. It's quite too bad. But important. Really important," said Sir John. He was invited in. One chair was dusted to receive the knight; another to receive his hat and gloves.

"Thank you. Thank you."

Briggs was called.

"George! George! A gentleman to see you. Ay, and put your collar on. No, it *isn't* one of they newspaper fellows, neither. 'Tis a gentleman, I tell 'ee. Brush your hair. Well, put on dickey, then, but do you hurry yourself, not to keep company waiting."

"Well, George?" Sir John smiled, man to man. "Don't throw me out. I know you've been vastly bothered. But murders, George, don't happen every day."

George grunted; seated himself; grinned.

"No offence, sir."

"None," Sir John agreed, most cordially.

"Only badgered ain't the word. Swarm of bees, more like. All day yesterday, and all this morning. 'Tell you?' I says. 'Well, what *can* I tell you?'

"'Tell us about the lady,' says one.

"'Give us your own views,' says t'other.

"'What about Sir Charles?' says t'other.

"'Who killed Comstock?' says the silliest fool of the whole lot. Him I give a look to. 'Not me,' I says. 'But not for want of wishing, neither,' I says."

Sir John produced his card; held it between two slender fingers. George wiped his large hands on his thighs and took the card by the smallest possible corner; gazed at it. Suddenly he called:

" Emmie ! "

" Ah ? "

" Come you in here." She came. " Take a read of that, my gal. We've been to your theayter. Ah, and seen you act, my lord," he said, addressing the knight with awe, and conferring on him a title which had the merit of being æsthetically correct.

" Beautiful it was. Right beautiful," sighed Emmie. " Lovely you looked, Sir John, you in your crown. A dook you was. And when you forgave her all, I could ha' cried me eyes out."

" Did, too, nearly," said her husband, grinning. " Used up your own handkercher, ah, and mine as well."

" But you must come again," Sir John said cheerfully. He took the card and scribbled on the back. " Any date after the end of September. Send this to the box office and they'll give you seats. Dress circle you would like, I think."

After that, it seemed, they would tell him anything. George told the tale, which was earnestly edited by Emmie. It was no different, however, from the version which had been given to Sir John in the Home Secretary's letter. Sir John forbore to cross-question, and, as soon as it was possible to do so, took his leave. Before he reached the garden gate, however, George came trotting after him.

" There *was* one thing," he said. " Mebbe nout, but I'll tell 'ee. Mr. Mills is a dead shot wi' a rook rifle. Ah,

a proper O.T.C. I calls him. All bombast and no belly,
if you take me, sir."

Sir John walked on. The most interesting point
which had emerged, both during the interview in the
Home Secretary's private room at the Home Office and
in the present instance, was George Briggs' personal
dislike of his late employer. Sir John had hoped to
eliminate suspects. To find himself adding to their
number was, to say the least of it, disheartening. But
behind his disappointment another feeling struggled.
Sir John racked his brain, for the feeling was one of
enlightenment on a hitherto obscure point. Yet, for the
moment, the point itself, no longer obscure, nevertheless
had become elusive. It eluded him for seven miles out
of the eight that lay between Hursley Lodge and the
vicarage. As the outskirts of Winborough came into
view, however—a church tower stood up out of a flat
green field—he suddenly accelerated, and the car tore
over the last few hundred yards. Sir John said urgently :

" We shall have to get away, Martella. How long do
you think it will take you to find our hostess, and make
our farewells ? "

Martella was saved from the necessity of replying,
for Mrs. Pritchard, perspiring and ready to overwhelm
Sir John with thanks for the autograph money, was
bearing down upon them. Sir John was graceful, charming, modest ; his leave-taking was unexceptionable.
His hostess, still in her Girl Guide uniform, a modern
Boadicea surrounded by her daughters, stood in the
gateway waving her valedictions until the car was out
of sight. Miss Hope-Fairweather had driven away in
her own car. Martella was taken home. Sir John sat
back in the car and possessed his soul in patience during

a traffic jam. Once he looked at his watch. The time was twenty minutes past six. At twenty-six minutes past six he was at the Home Secretary's private house.

" The pistol ? Certainly you can borrow it. We've the two of them, you know," Sir Philip said. " Want to see the bullet that came out of Comstock's head ? You don't ? Oh, all right. Any news ? "

" Plenty," replied Sir John, " but not for broadcasting." He noted that Sir Philip looked harassed and pale.

Sir Charles was pleased to see Sir John ; or said he was. He referred to the murder of Comstock as the devil of a mess, and invited Sir John to dine with him at his club. Sir John smiled ; shook his head ; said he had come to badger Sir Charles ; deprecated the fact that he was a nuisance. But had Sir Charles really worn his gloves all the time he had been at Comstock's house ? Sir Charles, who gave his questioner a fleeting but none the less a distinct impression that he had expected to be asked a far more awkward question, flushed slightly and replied that really he was damned if he knew.

" I was impatient, you know, Saumarez, at being kept waiting. I particularly wished my interview with Comstock to be secret. It would have been most damaging to me in my public capacity if it had got about that I was visiting Comstock privately like that ! In fact, it hasn't done me a bit of good, apart from the fact that the silly ass got himself murdered like that. You take me ? Devilish awkward. And when I'm impatient, I fidget with things. Gloves, for instance : Take 'em off, put 'em on—any old thing. Just fidgety, you know. But how much I had 'em on—or off——"

" Marksman ? " said Sir John.

" Eh ? What's that, my dear chap ? "

" Do any shooting ? "

" Oh, shooting ? Well, of course, when I get the chance. Oh, I take you ! Forgotten for the moment that Comstock was—ah—shot. Oh yes, I'm pretty deadly on my day. Enjoy it, you know. Scotland. Don't care for shooting over English moors. Tame. Devilish tame. And for fellahs who are going to hit a beater, Scotland is less expensive. Fellahs up there are so hardy. Scarcely notice a few pellets in the leg, or whatnot."

He laughed. Sir John joined him. They drank whisky, and parted on the best of terms. For some reason—possibly, Sir John reflected, because he did not know of it—Sir Charles had made no mention of his sister's visit to the vicarage garden.

" For a man whose career is ruined——" mused Sir John.

The Archbishop of the Midlands was staying at the Neo-Hydro Hotel in Piccadilly. So handy, he explained, for Lambeth Palace. Sir John looked at the luxuriously appointed room and, rather cautiously, agreed.

" But you come on business ! " the Archbishop exclaimed. " Tell me all, my dear fellow. You have solved our little problem ? " He, too, seemed jauntier than the circumstances appeared to justify.

Sir John came to the point abruptly.

" Why ' the wages of sin,' I wonder. What were you thinking about ? "

" Poor Comstock," replied the prelate, without hesitation. He set his finger-tips together and nodded. " Comstock."

" A prophecy, of course," Sir John remarked.

" It would appear so. Yes. Striking, that. I spoke in metaphor. I was very much disturbed. But— prophecy, yes. Poor fellow. Poor misguided fellow."

> " But yesterday the word of Cæsar might
> Have stood against the world,"

murmured Sir John.

" Yes, yes. How true. Very true. A power in the land. Poor Comstock. Against the law, against the Church—and yet he had a soul to save. A brilliant boy, determined, brave, ambitious boy. Do you know, Saumarez, the boy that was Comstock—before he became Comstock, you know—had almost endless potentialities. A remarkable boy. And, to finish your own quotation—

> ' now lies he there,
> And none so poor to do him reverence.' "

They brooded. Then Sir John said suddenly :

" If you are interested in acting, come to my house to-morrow. Ten o'clock, say. An informal occasion, but not without interest, if you wish to prove your point."

" What point, my dear fellow ? "

" That there are no actors nowadays," Sir John said, with his charming smile.

" At ten to-morrow ? But how very pleasant. I shall enjoy it above all things ! "

" That," said Sir John, " is excellent."

(v)

> " What, a play toward ! I'll be an auditor ;
> An actor too, perhaps, if I see cause."

The most imposing piece of furniture in the room was a magnificent wireless receiving-set. It was at the side

of the room between the door and the fireplace, and, on
the opposite side to it, chairs were arranged as though
for an audience to watch private theatricals. Beside the
receiving-set was a revolving chair of the kind used in
business offices.

" But what are you going to do, Johnny ? " asked his
wife, surveying the transformed drawing-room not with
amazement, for she had learned the uselessness of ever
being surprised at Sir John's doings, but with a certain
amount of resigned displeasure. " I thought, after that
awful affair yesterday afternoon, that we might spend a
quiet day."

" That reminds me," said her husband. " I wish you
would go back to bed. You don't mind, do you ? This
is a joke—of a kind. You wouldn't be interested. It
will last less than an hour."

Martella said again, " Why need you bother ? "

" You answered that yourself yesterday," he reminded
her. " I'd rather you went, Martella. Please. I shan't
be very long." His eyes were smiling, but his chin was
purposeful.

She gave in, knowing well enough that he anticipated
danger ; she was conscious, too, that she would be in
his way ; would take some part of his mind from his
task if she insisted on remaining.

A quarter of an hour later the audience, consisting of
Sir Charles Hope-Fairweather, the Assistant Commissioner, the Archbishop of the Midlands, the editor of
the *Daily Broadcast*, the editors of Lord Comstock's own
Daily Bugle and *Evening Clarion*, a couple of dramatic
critics, and a distinguished dramatist, had assembled and
were seated. The chief protagonists in the drama looked
profoundly uncomfortable. The other guests were agog.

"What's Johnny up to now?" said one of the dramatic critics to the editor of the *Daily Broadcast*. The editor looked omniscient, but felt curious. The dramatist smiled slightly. He seemed less excited than the others. An unconscionably late session in this same room on the preceding night—Sir John had let his visitor out of the house at twelve-thirty and had gone to bed himself at five to four, word-perfect, but un-utterably weary—had sapped his appetite for sensation.

A manservant entered and began to draw heavy curtains across the windows, excluding every vestige of light. An electric switch clicked somewhere, and a dull glow appeared on the ceiling high above the audience's heads. Sir John remained invisible, but his voice came across the room, masterful, suave, and soothing:

"Gentlemen, an experiment. Something new in broadcast plays. Scene, the interior of the late Lord Comstock's study at Hursley Lodge. Time 11.35 a.m. on the day before yesterday."

There was a disconcerted rustling among the audience. The Archbishop of the Midlands was heard to make inarticulate sounds. There was a moment's silence. Then, from the direction of the wireless receiving-set, an arresting voice, harsh and resonant, said angrily:

"And to what, sir, am I indebted for this pleasure?"

The editor of the *Evening Clarion*, cursed with the imagination of a film-fan, swore under his breath in a scared manner. His more experienced colleague grunted and half-laughed. But both were silenced by the second voice, smooth, ecclesiastical, and cool:

"Ah, Comstock, forgive me if I interrupt your work——"

Then the voice of Sir John Saumarez broke the spell.

" Gentlemen, the conversation you are going to hear is not the conversation which did actually and indeed take place between the late Lord Comstock and his Grace the Archbishop of the Midlands on that fatal day."

Sir John permitted the rubber stamp remark to emerge unchallenged by his critical faculty.

" What are we going to hear ? " It was the voice of the dramatist asking a pre-arranged question. Sir John replied courteously :

" Pardon me. That will be for you all to say when you have heard it."

There was a long pause, while the peculiar ticking of the wireless set, indicative of the fact that the broad-casting station was active but that the programme was held up for the moment, tautened the nerves of the susceptible and imaginative editor of the *Evening Clarion*. He was about to whisper a remark to his colleague of the *Daily Bugle* for the sake of breaking the tension when the ticking noise ceased abruptly, and the an-nouncer's voice said winningly :

" Hallo, everybody. This is the Daventry National Programme. We are going to broadcast an imaginary dialogue between the late Lord Comstock, who was murdered by an unknown assailant at his country residence, Hursley Lodge, probably between the hours of noon and one-fifteen p.m. on the day before yesterday, and the Most Reverend William Anselm Pettifer, D.D., Archbishop of the Midlands. This dialogue is the first of a series of talks between great men in differing walks of life, putting the points of view of each before the public. Our aim—the aim of the B.B.C.—is to give you an opportunity of hearing arguments in favour of and against such varying modes of living as those of an

Archbishop of the English Church and a peer who made most of his fortune out of " stunt " attacks on that Church and, indeed, on all the forces of law and order, through the medium of privately owned but very widely circulated newspapers."

There was another pause, of shorter duration this time, and then the two sentences which had preceded Sir John Saumarez's last remark were repeated, and were followed straight away by the promised Imaginary Conversation.

" And to what, sir, am I indebted for this visit ? "

" Ah, Comstock, forgive me if I interrupt your work. You received my letter, I think ? "

" Letter ?   I received no letter.   And I'm busy."

" You received no letter ?   Then, my dear fellow, a thousand pardons for coming upon you so unceremoniously.   You must forgive me, Comstock, but, believe me, it is for your own sake that I have come.   May I sit down ?   Over here by the door ?   Admirable."   The silky voice faded.   There was a slight pause before Lord Comstock's harsh tones came over again.

" Say what you've come to say, sir, if you please.   I really am extremely pushed for time."

" Of course, of course, my dear fellow," the Archbishop's voice said soothingly.   " I will come to the point at once.   Comstock, for your own sake, stop printing your newspaper attacks on the Church."

" I am not attacking the Church.   Why the devil don't you read intelligently ? "   The grating tones caused the rough words to sound positively belligerent.

" My good boy——"   The silky tones took on the exasperated note of flouted authority.

" And I'm not your good boy !   I was your good boy at school, but I'm nobody's good boy now."   Lord

Comstock's voice was rising to a yell. " All this blasted clap-trap about good boys—I'm free of you, I tell you, free ! " The word echoed through the room, a triumph of barbarianism. " And I tell you, too, I'll have all your churches in ruins about your ears before I've finished with you ! It's not the Church that I'm attacking ! It's the whole foundation of the Church, Christianity itself——"

" Comstock, beware of what you say ! " There was a cutting edge to the warning words. The schoolmaster was reaching for his cane. " There is such blasphemy as, even to-day, in this material age, God punishes. I am no prophet to bring fire from heaven ! I am a weak old man, unworthy, even in mine own sight, but this I swear. The wages of sin is *death* ! *Death*, Comstock ! And you, boy, are unfit to die ! " The headmaster had eclipsed the archbishop for the moment. Comstock, an angry boy, raged furiously. " I am not a boy ! Clap-trap ! Clap-trap ! I'm not afraid of death ! Death is nothing ! That's why I'm not afraid of it ! Get out of here, you damned old hypocrite ! You whited sepulchre ! And that's out of your own book of clap-trap barley sugar ! When I was a kid I had to listen to all that sort of poppycock ! But I'm damned if I'll listen any longer ! " There was a crash, as of a table being thumped.

" Yes, you will listen, Comstock. Shall I tell you something ? " The voice was smooth again. It had regained its gentleness, like steel re-sheathed in velvet.

" Get farther away then ! " Comstock was petulant. " I can't breath with you standing over me like a blessed Solomon Eagle ! Why the devil don't you sit down ! If you've got anything to say, say it, man ! You don't seem to have the guts of a flea ! "

" What are you afraid of, Comstock ? " the gentle voice, surcharged with tenderness, inquired.

" I'm not afraid ! What the hell have I got to be afraid of ? But I want air, man, air ! " It was the voice of a man fighting Fate.

" There is little enough air in the grave, Comstock. But I will sit down if you wish it, my boy. Listen, Comstock ! " Persuasion and irony were so nicely blent in the voice of the Archbishop as to be almost indistinguishable.

" I don't *want* to listen, I tell you ! Shut up and get out of here ! I'll ring the bell and have you chucked out, dammit ! "

" Listen, Comstock." The soft voice was inexorable. " ' When I was a child I spake as a child, I understood as a child, I thought as a child. But when I became a man I put away childish things.' You remember, Comstock ? I know it was in your last term that I preached a sermon in the big school hall, with that as my text. You do remember, Comstock ? "

" Oh, clap-trap ! Twaddle ! Poppycock ! " It was the shout of a boy shouting down his own fears of the dark. The audience stirred uncomfortably.

" I think not, my boy. You see, my dear Comstock, you never have put away childish things. Have you ever watched a little tiny boy with a hammer, Comstock? No, you wouldn't, because your adventures do not lead you into lovingly watching children at their play."

" You old swine ! Shut up ! Mind your own business, and be damned ! " The voice was hoarse now, rough with hate, indescribably coarsened.

" A little boy with a hammer wants to smash things,

Comstock. You want to smash things, too. Poor little boy, Comstock ! Poor destructive little boy ! But a grown man, conscious of his manhood, also uses a hammer to subdue things to his will. It helps him, Comstock, to mend and make——"

" Like a schoolmaster uses a cane, eh, Doctor ? " The sneering voice was ugly.

" As you will, Comstock, as you will. The loveliest and most prolific plants require the stoutest canes, Comstock. Your gardener, I am sure, would bear me out in that."

" The lazy hound ! No flowers on show ! Well, practically none ! He got the rough side of my tongue, confound him ! "

" Don't change the subject, Comstock."

" Who's changing the subject, Pettifer ! "

" You are, my dear fellow. It is usually a sign of fear, I believe."

" Fear ! Tchah ! I don't believe I know the meaning of the word ! "

" Unfortunate boy ! "

" Oh, to hell with you and your ' boys.' I am not a boy, I tell you ! And I'll smash you ! You and your Church ! You and your religion ! And your twaddle ! And your superstition ! And your damned idol-worship ! You shan't lead the people by the nose ! You shan't promise them heaven ! You shan't threaten them with hell ! I've got the tabs on you ! You're done for ! Germany's gone Nudist already ! England——"

" What signifies the Nudist Movement, Comstock ? Adam and Eve, the first Nudists, fell from grace by putting on clothing, not by taking it off." The voice was amusedly tolerant, as of untutored wit.

" Oh, you can laugh ! You can jest ! Nero fiddled while Rome burned, didn't he ? "

" Perhaps the wisest thing he could do under the circumstances, Comstock."

" At any rate, ' Back to Paganism ' is my slogan, Doctor. The thought of it makes me better-tempered already ! Christianity is outworn ! It's dead ! We want a creed with good red blood in it ! "

" Blasphemer ! Pause ! Think ! " The voice had changed. " I beseech you, Comstock, in the name of your own brilliant boyhood ; in the name of the sacrifices your dear father made for you, so that you should become, as he said to me, a gentleman. Dear Comstock, pause and consider. With your gifts you could right wrongs, Comstock. With your wealth you could do great kindness, Comstock. With your personality, your grit, your magnetism, you could affect great numbers of your fellow-creatures, and for good, not evil. I beseech you, hear me——"

" I won't hear you ! *Damn* it, sit down, man ! Don't come hovering here ! Get away from the table ! Leave that gun alone ! Don't meddle with my things ! And leave me alone ! You needn't think that poppycock gets anywhere with me ! It doesn't, I tell you ; it doesn't ! "

" Comstock, do you ever read Rudyard Kipling ? "

" Get out of here ! "

" There is a story about schoolboys—you were a schoolboy once—and about a very brave headmaster. Once *I* was a headmaster. You remember, Comstock ? "

" I remember a prating old fool ! "

" This headmaster saved a boy's life, Comstock——"

" Oh, dry up with your ' Comstock, Comstock ' ! I know my own name, don't I ? "

" I don't know, Comstock, I'm sure. You see, we haven't used your *own* name yet, have we ? "

" Given me by my godfathers and my godmother and all that bunkum, I suppose ? "

" No. I meant your father's name. The name he kept respectable and respected, Comstock. Not a *purchased* name—for services rendered, Comstock."

" Damn you, shut up ! I'll not be insulted in my own house ! "

" This headmaster, Comstock, saved a boy's life by sucking diphtheria infection out of his throat through a tube."

" More fool he ! "

" You think so, Comstock ? I'm going to be a bigger fool than that ! "

" You can't be a bigger fool than to risk your life ! "

" Oh yes. Quite easily. You can risk your soul, Comstock."

" I don't believe in souls ! "

" Nevertheless, you have one, and so have I. And I am going to risk mine to save yours, Comstock. Yes, I'm going farther off. . . . Yes, get up, Comstock. . . . Ah, the chair's going over. . . . Now, Comstock. . . ."

There was the crash of a falling chair, and, at the same instant, the flash of a discharged revolver, but no sound of a shot. Several of the audience leapt to their feet. At the same time the lights went up, and Sir John Saumarez, smiling but jaded, blinked in the sudden glare, and said, deprecatingly :

" A poor thing, gentlemen. But mine own."

" Good God, Johnny ! That was never *you* imitating those two voices," exclaimed the more important of the dramatic critics. Sir John, looking white and tired, bowed his acknowledgment of the compliment.

In the second row, the Archbishop of the Midlands blinked. Everybody elaborately avoided looking at him. He rose, and walked out to Sir John. The audience, conscious that the most dramatic moment was at hand and had not yet been staged, looked curious yet uncomfortable, as though the play was over and they were eavesdropping upon a dressing-room scene more tense than the play but no business of theirs.

The Archbishop linked his arm in that of Sir John. Magnificently master of himself, especially when his old eyes grew accustomed to the light, he said :

" Dear John, I am in your hands. I can only say, my dear fellow, that I wish to God I had conducted myself one-half as well. As a matter of fact, I lost my temper at the interview. Lost it completely. Poor Comstock ! But you've proved your point magnificently."

The audience was filing out. Nobody was speaking ; but, decorously, as though in the presence of death, three editors, two dramatic critics, a Chief Whip (dazed), an Assistant Commissioner (temporarily suspended and softly swearing), and a famous dramatist (shaking his head as though over some dubious course of action), made irreproachable *exeunt* through the high door of Sir John's drawing-room and were shown out into the street by an impeccable manservant. Once away from the precincts they broke into a conversation more excited by far than that which was going on in the room they had lately left.

" I found that you had started a branch of the O.T.C. at Blackminster," Sir John was saying. " And, of course, the dramatic instinct is strongly implanted in you ; fostered by your vocation."

" Johnny ! " Martella called.

" Just coming," Sir John replied. " Pardon me. I won't be more than "—he was meticulous in such matters—" five minutes."

He glanced at the open door and then at His Grace. It might be said by those who did not know him that he winked. Then he went out to his wife.

" Johnny, you *can't* ! "

Sir John affected to consider the point. Then he said : " You're a wonderful woman, Martella."

" Am I ? " She smiled at him.

" And you're right. Utterly right." He remained pensive for a moment. Then the front door slammed. " I appreciate your point." He paused. The footlights glared. The curtain prepared to descend. " And I believe," said Sir John, still pensive, " that the Archbishop has appreciated mine."

He walked to the window. The ecclesiastical gaiters were almost out of sight.

CHAPTER III

LORD PETER'S PRIVY COUNSEL

By ANTHONY BERKELEY

Note.—I was fortunate enough to induce Lord Peter Wimsey to add one or two footnotes to the narrative supplied by Mr. Anthony Berkeley.—M. K.

(I)

" WELL, the secretary, Mills, had orders not to disturb him, but——"

" My dear Charles," interrupted the young [1] man with the monocle peevishly, " I do wish you wouldn't do this. I keep telling you it's no good. Never tell thy love, but let concealment, like a worm i' the bud, feed on thy damask cheek. We are not interested."

" I've never known you not interested in a case of murder before," grumbled Detective Chief-Inspector Parker.

" But this isn't murder. Dash it, Charles, you can't look on the wiping out of a thing like Comstock as murder. If you really want to know, I'm jolly glad somebody's shot him at last. It ought to have been done years ago. The man was a public nuisance. Well,

---

[1] An elastic adjective. I was born in 1890 and wore a dear little sailor suit in the year of the Diamond Jubilee. *Eheu*, alas ! how fast the dam *fugaces*, to quote the Austin Freeman.—P.W.

requiescat, I suppose, *in pace*. Good-night, sweet merchant-prince, and flights of angels sing thee to thy rest. But here's to the man who put you to sleep." And the young [1] man with the monocle drained his glass of Chevalier Montrachet 1915 in one regrettable gulp.

" Don't you understand, Peter, that it's your plain duty to take the case up ? " pursued Parker doggedly.

" It isn't your plain duty to eat caviare if you don't really like it, you know," said the young man with the monocle kindly.

" I don't mind it," said Detective Chief-Inspector Parker.

Lord Peter Wimsey looked pained, but heroically refrained from speech. He did, however, nod towards the waiter.

The waiter contrived to remove the Chief-Inspector's caviare, and, almost in the same gesture, present for Lord Peter's inspection a dish of *sole bonne femme*. Wimsey adjusted his monocle, but his examination was only perfunctory. At the *Bon Bourgeois* one can trust the *sole bonne femme*.

" Clear the old palate with an olive, Charles," Wimsey suggested, pushing the little plate across to his companion as the waiter served the fish and took away the half-bottle of Montrachet. " Who knows ? It might clear your mind as well of such distressin' subjects as dead millionaires. Too many dead millionaires spoil a dinner, don't you think ? *De mortuis nil nisi bonum*, no doubt, but at a dinner-table to omit even the *bonum* is a sound working rule before the savoury. Oh no, we never mention them, their names are never heard. Do have an olive."

[1] See footnote, p. 172.

"Why are you so anxious for me to have an olive?" asked Parker suspiciously.

"I'm only trying to do you a good turn, dear old thing," said Lord Peter plaintively. "I want to get this morbid taste of corpses out of your mouth. We're going on to something really rather special in the matter of hocks in a minute, and you can't judge wine if your mind is on other flavours."

Parker grunted.

Wimsey consumed a couple of mouthfuls of the sole with an air of close attention, before his expression relaxed.

"You know, Charles, just to show you what sort of a man Comstock was, I'll tell you that with my own eyes I once saw him grab a piece of preserved ginger after dinner and shove it into his beastly mouth just before taking his first sip of a '63 port. Preserved ginger! Did I say the man was a public nuisance? He was a private one, and that's a whole lot worse. Shooting's a jolly sight too peaceful an end for a man who could do a thing like that."

"You knew Comstock, then?" Parker inquired.

"One meets all sorts nowadays," said Lord Peter with resignation. "And that's quite enough of Comstock for this evening. I don't want to spoil my digestion entirely. Let Comstock and his kind take wing, 'tis not of them I'm going to sing."

"Don't be an ass, Peter," Parker said severely. "You know perfectly well you're going to take this case up. Considering what the H.S. said, you can't very well do anything else. Anyhow, I've been told off to give you the facts first and guide your faltering footsteps afterwards, and I'm jolly well going to do it. But I'll hold up the facts till the savoury, if you like."

" My lord, I will inflame thy noble liver," groaned Wimsey. " Very well, have it your own way. But I warn you, there isn't going to be a savoury, so I don't quite know what you'll do about that. No, don't tell me. I prefer not to know."

A dish of *tripes à la mode de Caen* succeeded the sole. The hock was good, and Wimsey found himself becoming mellowed. Parker strictly observed the ban against murder and sudden death, but Wimsey himself introduced a reference to the Little Cadbury case.

" The clue of that rusty file petered out this afternoon ? Of course it did. I warned Churchill he was on the wrong lines with that ironmonger's assistant. You tell him from me to look into the butcher's alibi. It's not nearly so cast-iron as you people think. Churchill will be making a mucker of the case if he isn't careful. And has he asked the dustman yet what he found in the bin outside the cottage the next morning ? Yes, of course he hedged, but Churchill could get it out of him if he threatened to apply to the council for a permit to search the refuse-dump. No, I know it wouldn't be on the dump ; but that would show the man that Churchill *knows*. Anyhow, he ought to try it."

Over the dessert Parker was allowed at last to proceed with his exposition without interruption. It was the evening of Lord Comstock's murder, and so far only a short account of the facts had been made public. Even the recital in the *Clarion*, though not lacking in length, had been more of a howl for vengeance than a statement of fact.

As the story went on, Wimsey threw off more and more of the pretence of indifference with which he had begun to listen. The fact that three such notable hounds

on Comstock's trail had been in at the death, struck him
as particularly piquant. When Parker explained how
the Archbishop had pushed his way out of the study,
muttering frenziedly about " the wages of sin," Wimsey
grew quite excited.

" Oh, bosh, the worthy bishop said, and bumped him
off as in the picture. Only, unfortunately, in this case
there isn't a picture. Charles, this is beginning to grow
on me. I hadn't realized all the possibilities. I knew,
of course, that those three were there, but I hadn't
gathered that it was probably one of them who did the
'orrible deed. Even the good old *Clarion* didn't go so
far as to hint that. At the moment my money's on the
Archbish.[1] Very ominous, that line of patter of his ;
very ominous indeed. And why not ? No doubt he
looked on Comstock as a direct emissary of the Antichrist. And if good Bishop Odo could batter in the heads
of the enemies of the Church with a thumping great club
in 1066, why shouldn't a modern prelate poop 'em off
equally with a gent.'s natty racing pistol ? Echo answers
why ? Tell me some more, Charles."

Parker told him more.

" Do you know," said Wimsey, when the story had at
last been brought up to 2.30 p.m. that same afternoon,
and a great many questions asked and answered, and

[1] I cannot account for my having used this vulgar abbrevia-
tion, unless it was the result of studying the Comstock Press,
which swarms with American journalese and has a regrettable
habit of referring to royal personages and female tennis stars
by their Christian names, without indication of rank or civil
status. But I seem to have been talking at random. I know
many Church of England prelates, and nothing could be farther
from their truly established minds than a serious belief in
Antichrist.—P. W.

more than one glass of a wholly admirable old brandy consumed—"do you know, Charles, I believe you were right all the time. I have that sensation of internal gloating which has never let me down yet. By the pricking of my thumbs, something jolly well worth investigation this way comes. The fever is upon me, said the Lady of Shalott."

" Of course I knew you'd want to get your nose into it," said Mr. Parker complacently.

" And you are right, and I am right, and all is right as right can be. Anyhow, I'll take these notes of yours back with me now and study them till pearly dawn ; and I must say it's very nice and considerate of your people, Charles, to have got out such a full dossier already. Then to-morrow morning I'll get busy. I think," Wimsey said meditatively, " I'll begin with the Archbishop. I don't know why, but the Archbishop does attract me strangely. Do you really think he could have done it, Charles, at his time of life ? Oh, wild Archbish, thou breath of autumn's being! Anyhow, I believe my mother knows him pretty well, so I'll see what can be done. And with Hope-Fairweather too, of course, for that matter."

" Yes, and don't forget the Major," said Parker, in a voice of such concentrated sarcasm that a waiter came hurrying across in alarm, under the impression that there had been a mistake in the bill.

" No," Wimsey said gravely. " No, I won't forget Major Littleton."

Parker raised his eyebrows, and then evidently thought better of what he had been going to say. Instead he asked, conventionally : " And how do you propose to tackle His Grace ? "

Wimsey reflected.

" I will leer upon him as a' comes by ; and (if, Charles, you happen to be near) do but mark the countenance he will give me. Enough, said he, throwing back the ear-flaps of the deer-stalker and disclosing the well-known lantern jaws. I'm Hawkshaw, the detective, and I have my methods."

(II)

Lord Peter emerged from the bathroom, wrapped in magenta silk, and called for Bunter.

" My lord ? "

" Bunter, what do you advise in the matter of suitings for a call on an Archbishop whom one suspects of having committed a murder ? "

" I regret, my lord, to have seen no recent fashions designed to impress homicidal Archbishops. I would suggest, my lord, any suit which your lordship considers might be said to combine an air of holiness with a certain flavour of the man of action."

" I don't fancy," said Wimsey thoughtfully, " that I possess any suit that could be said to produce quite that effect."

" Then may I advise, my lord, the pale grey willow-pussy with the mauve pin-stripe ? That should convey a delicate hint of half-mourning which would not be out of place ; and if worn with a subdued amethyst tie and socks, I think should convey to His Grace that note of cautious sympathy and understanding which I take it your lordship would wish to imply in view of the object of His Grace's onslaught."

" With a soft hat, of course."

"A soft hat, my lord, undoubtedly. A bowler would introduce quite the wrong note."

"And, I fancy, no stick."

"Subject to your lordship's better judgment, I should like to point out that by tensing the muscles of the hand on a stick, a highly eloquent whitening of the knuckles may be produced. This might perhaps serve your lordship more usefully at certain moments than words, which in the circumstances can hardly fail to be difficult."

"Bunter," said Wimsey, "you're always right."

"It is kind of your lordship to make the observation. Breakfast is ready at any moment your lordship pleases."

"Early bacon, early bacon," said Wimsey with enthusiasm.

An hour later, having breakfasted, dressed, and smoked a thoughtful cigarette, he summoned from her fastness in a neighbouring garage his Daimler Twin-Six (called "Mrs. Merdle" on account of that lady's notable aversion from row) and turned her long black nose in the direction of the Dowager Duchess of Denver's town house.

The Dowager Duchess greeted her son with her usual vague affection.

"How early you are, Peter! But then I suppose you're working on this dreadful affair of the Comstock person. Such an odd title to choose, though really not so odd when one remembers what he looks like; but I don't suppose he chose it for that, because people so seldom know what they look like, do they? I remember so well that your Uncle Adolphus always reminded me of a seal, even when he was quite young; but I don't expect he ever knew he looked like one, because of course

I never mentioned it to him, people are so touchy about that sort of thing."

Lord Peter tucked his arm through that of the Duchess. " Well, what do I look like, Mater ? It might be useful to know, in case I ever want a nice original disguise."

" You, dear ? I know when you were a baby I used to think you were rather like a dormouse ; but now you're much more like a crane, aren't you ? Or, aren't you ? " added the Duchess uneasily.

" I expect I am, if you say so," Wimsey laughed. " Anyhow, Mater, you're perfectly right. I am working on the Comstock case, and I want you to give me a line to the Archbishop, or ring him up and tell him I'm coming. I don't know him, you see, and what with Convocation and this and that, there might be some difficulty in getting admitted to the presence. I just want to ask him a question or two."

" Yes, dear, of course I will," agreed the Duchess, sitting down at once at her writing-table. " But don't ask him why he did it, because he'll feel bound to deny it, and then, of course, his conscience will worry him afterwards. So inconvenient, I always think, being a clergyman and unable to tell lies ; I suppose they have to be at home to every caller. Dear me, poor Willy (the Archbishop, you know, dear, though I never can get used to the idea of Willy being an Archbishop, he used to use hair-oil so very freely when he was a boy), one can't help sympathizing with him, I feel, remembering the Comstock person, though I suppose murder always is murder really, even when done with a very small pistol, and after all so medieval for a bishop, though I remember now Willy always was old-fashioned. Do you think they'll hang him, dear ? I do hope not, because really I don't think one should hang Archbishops, almost sacrilegious in a way, and in any case most disrespectful to the Church; but then I suppose he'd be a martyr, and we haven't had a martyr for a very long time now. Here's your note, dear. Must you go already ? Well, do be as nice as you can to poor Willy, and don't accuse him of anything too plainly, because he certainly wouldn't like that at all, having been a headmaster and all that kind of thing before they made him a bishop, and you know how headmasters get. Good-bye, dear. Come and see me again soon."

Wimsey kissed his mother affectionately, and turned Mrs. Merdle's rakish black lines and polished copper twin-exhausts towards Lambeth Palace.

(III)

" And except for the fact that he thinks he *may* have bumped into something on his way out of the study," said Lord Peter resentfully, " I got nothing out of the old sharpshooter that we don't know already."

" That would account for the overturned chair by the door, of course," nodded Parker.

" And the first crash," Wimsey said sharply.

" Yes, perhaps."

" Yes, certainly. My dear Charles, you haven't seriously been considering those two crashes as anything but mere crashes, have you ? You haven't been thinking that anyone could possibly describe the tiny little crack of a pistol like that as a ' crash ' ? Charles Parker and Scotland Yard, lend me your ears; I come to poop off Cæsar, not to bomb him."

" His Grace didn't by any chance admit to you that he'd done it, I suppose ? " asked Parker, disregarding this side issue.

" His Grace did not. And I omitted to ask him. To tell the truth, Charles, I realized as soon as I saw the old boy that the good old tradition of militant Bishops isn't by any means extinct. I had the dickens of a job to find a plausible excuse for asking him questions ; I simply hadn't got the nerve to say I was working for the police—quite officially and all that, for once. I can tell you, when he shot his eyes out at me from under their thickets I wobbled in front of him like any mere prebendary. I wouldn't have been a bit surprised at any minute if he'd picked me up by the scruff of the neck, put me across his knee, and given me six of the juiciest—and I believe I should have let him ! I wonder," said Wimsey, " if that's just what happened to Comstock, and Comstock shot himself after it in sheer shame. Oh, death, where is thy sting-a-ling-a-ling now, you know. Have some more spuds. Bunter chips rather a marvellous spud, doesn't he ? "

Parker helped himself, and agreed that Bunter chipped an impeccable potato.

" I must say," remarked Wimsey, doing the same, " that a proper bloody steak is a relief now and then. One does get a bit tired of restaurant meals."

" Yes," said Parker, who had no chance of doing so. " Well, failing the Archbishop, what are you going to do this afternoon, Peter ? You've only got till to-morrow evening, you know."

" By to-morrow evening Brackenthorpe shall have the miscreant, manacled and fettered ; I swear it on my honour as a sleuth. This afternoon ? Well, I thought we might run down and visit what the newspapers call the scene of the crime. But before we go, I'd like you to throw your eye over a few notes I made last night. You may find something illuminatin' in 'em, for I'm blessed if I can."

When lunch was over, the two men moved into the adjoining room. The day was warm and sunny, and the deep windows stood open to Piccadilly. Streaming in, the sun lit up with a mellow glow the rich old calf bindings of the books which lined the walls, and danced on the rosewood case of the grand piano that stood open on one side of the room. Two or three bowls of vivid crimson roses added a brighter note in shaded corners. Wimsey waved his guest into one of the two deep arm-chairs, and himself perched on an arm of the enormous Chesterfield, loaded with cushions. Bunter put down the coffee-tray on an exquisite little Sheraton table near the Chesterfield, and retired with the noiseless, gliding tread of the man-servant who really knows his job.

Wimsey poured out the coffee, and then dropped a little sheaf of papers on Parker's knee.

" I fancy those make things a bit clearer," he said, " but otherwise I don't seem to have done much good. The most interesting thing's the time-table. It shows something that I hadn't realized before I made it out, and that is, that there were no less than seven minutes between the Archbishop's exit and Littleton's discovery of the body. That is, if we can rely on Littleton's account ; there's corroborative evidence for the Archbishop. So there is quite a chance, you see, that somebody else did it and not the old boy at all."

" We hadn't made up our minds about His Grace,"

The Butler discovered it and told Littleton
(1pm)

said Parker, studying the time-table in question. " Yes, this seems pretty accurate."

" Of course it's accurate," said Wimsey, with some indignation. " Dash it all, Charles, you ought to know me better than that by now. I only wish you were always equally so. Accuracy ! The very word is like a bell, to toll me back from thee to my sole self, Charles."

The time-table was as follows :

11.35 a.m.	Comstock interviews Archbishop.
11.50 ,,	Farrant announces Hope-Fairweather.
11.55 ,,	Mills finds Hope-Fairweather in hall.
11.58 ,,	Littleton arrives.
12 noon.	Littleton in drawing-room, looking out of window on to lawn.
,,	Hope-Fairweather in waiting-room.
,,	Archbishop in study with Comstock.
,,	Mills in office.
,,	Comstock undoubtedly alive.
12.8 p.m.	First crash, in study.
12.9 ,,	Archbishop comes out.
12.12 ,,	Mills opens drawing-room door.
12.13 ,,	Second crash.
,, ,,	Mills runs into office and finds H.-F.
12.16 ,,	Littleton goes into study. Comstock dead.
12.17 ,,	Mills escorts H.-F. to front door.
12.18 ,,	Mills says drawing-room empty, door into study shut.
12.19 ,,	Hope-Fairweather starts up his car.
,, ,,	Littleton still in study.
12.20 ,,	Hope-Fairweather's car disappears.
,, ,,	Littleton running across lawn.
12.22 ,,	Mills resumes work.

1.00 Farrant Head Comstock dead
1.05 Mills sees body

" All that is assumin' that each of those four is telling the truth, of course," said Wimsey, flicking through the pages of the official police report. " One of them probably isn't, so we've got to allow for that. But it's interestin', that interval of seven minutes, isn't it ? And possibly illuminatin'."

" Yes," Parker agreed. " I'll admit I hadn't realized it was so long."

Wimsey was still turning carelessly through the police dossier of the case. Suddenly he stiffened.

" Hullo ! what's this ? Ha ! do mine eyes deceive me, or is this Banquo's ghost ? Funny, isn't it, Charles, how one can look and look at a thing and never see it at all ? "

" What have you seen now ? "

" Why, that we've been wasting our time on the Archbish. He was a phantom of delight when first he gleamed upon my sight, Charles, but unfortunately he was only a lovely apparition sent to be a moment's ornament. In other words, Innocence hath privilege in him to dignify Archbishop's laughing eyes. Those seven minutes let him out. Litteton says that when he found the body, the wound was still bleeding. No wound of that nature would be bleedin' at least seven whole minutes after it had been inflicted."

" Well, that's one of our four out of the way," Wimsey resumed. " I wonder if we can eliminate any of the others ? Turn, Charles, to the page headed ' Corroborations.' That's rather illuminatin', too, don't you think ? "

Parker nodded.

" Take Mills, for instance. At 12.10 p.m. he was still with the Archbish ; from 12.13–12.16 p.m. he was with Hope-Fairweather. That only leaves him two minutes, 12.11–12.12 p.m., without an alibi. Hope-Fairweather

13

similarly gets his alibi from Mills for 12.13–12.16 p.m.;
he's got only the three minutes 12.10–12.12 p.m. un-
corroborated. Well, I suppose either of them could have
put his head round the study door and had a pot at
Comstock in those times, but the trouble is that in either
case that puts Comstock's death at not later than 12.12
p.m. Would the wound have been bleedin' when Littleton found him at 12.16 p.m.? I'm pretty sure it
wouldn't. And since the butler, you tell me, gets an
alibi for all that time from the cook. . . ." Wimsey
paused.

" Yes ? " said Parker.

" Well, it's pretty beastly, but you see what I mean."

" Major Littleton ? " said Parker, without expression.

Wimsey nodded. " There's no gettin' away from it,
he's the most likely. He's the only one, you see, whose
statement isn't corroborated by anyone else at all. And
there was always that convenient door between him and
the study. Mind you, I don't think we need give too
much importance to Mills' statement about opening the
drawing-room door at 12.12 p.m. and fancying afterwards that the room was empty. If Littleton had been
in the study then, Mills would certainly have heard the
voices ; because it's pretty well out of the question that
Littleton would have walked into the study and taken
a pot at Comstock without saying a single word. And
in any case, if Littleton's speaking the truth that the
wound was bleeding at 12.16 p.m., it's almost certain
that the shot must have been fired not much before
12.14 p.m. Deuced fine margins we've got to work in.
But you see the trouble, Charles, and we can't shut our
eyes to it. If Comstock was killed between 12.14 p.m.
and 12.16 p.m., as it seems most likely that he was, neither

Mills nor Hope-Fairweather could have done it. And what's more, they were probably too occupied with each other just then to hear anything that might have been goin' on in the study."

" I'd as soon believe I'd done it myself," said Parker, unconvinced.

" No doubt," Wimsey said bitterly. " Nevertheless, that's what we're up against."

There was a silence, full of things unsaid.

Then Parker said slowly : " If Major Littleton had shot Comstock, the markings on the bullet would correspond with those of the pistol which he handed over yesterday to Easton. They don't."

" No. And they don't correspond with Comstock's own pistol either. I think we can take it that Comstock was not shot with either of those pistols. Outside a detective-story, there's not much chance of faking a bullet's markings. No, there's a third pistol, which isn't in the local police-station at this moment. And Charles, I don't want to over-emphasize, but who really is the most likely person to have that third specimen of a rather rare type of pistol in his possession, just in the ordinary course of routine ? "

" There's no evidence at all that the Major had two of those pistols," Parker said quickly.

" No," Wimsey agreed. " That's about the one bright spot on an uncommonly murky horizon."

" After all, you haven't proved anything more than opportunity, and we knew all about that."

" Opportunity, and motive ; and a nasty powerful combination they are. Dash it all, Charles, you needn't glower at me like that. I don't want to prove that Littleton shot Comstock. I hope to goodness he didn't.

But at present you must admit that he's the likeliest of the four."

" Hope-Fairweather kept his gloves on all the time he was in the house," Parker said sullenly. " Why the hell did he want to do that ? "

" Perhaps his hands were cold," Wimsey said flippantly.

" He hadn't even taken them off when Mills found him picking up the papers in the office."

" That cock won't fight. If he had his gloves on, as you're implyin', for the purpose of leaving no finger-prints on the pistol, he'd naturally slip them off the moment they'd served their purpose. He wouldn't want to call attention to them, you see. The fact that he didn't strikes me as a pretty big point in his favour."

" There was a discharged shell in the pistol on Comstock's desk."

" Yes, and the barrel was clean. If you're suggesting that Hope-Fairweather had time to shoot Comstock, *and* search that drawer, *and* clean the barrel of the pistol all in those three minutes, then I tell you straight, Charles, the thing's an impossibility. And the same for Mills. Besides, in any case it doesn't apply, because Comstock wasn't shot with that pistol. We don't know how that shell got discharged, but I'll lay you a pony to a dollar that it wasn't done by Comstock's murderer. No, if we want to clear Littleton we've got to look a bit farther afield. For instance, didn't it strike you how very pat that chauffeur came out with the number of Hope-Fairweather's car ? A most observant bloke, that chauffeur, don't you think ? "

" Why shouldn't he ? It was in his own line."

" You think he not only notices but remembers

afterwards the number of every car that comes up his employer's drive ? Well, perhaps he does. All I can say is that in his place I shouldn't, and my eyes work pretty well automatically."

"We're not overlooking the chauffeur," said Parker.

"I should jolly well hope you're not. If you want to get Littleton out of this mess you can't afford to overlook anyone. But Mills and Hope-Fairweather. . . . Well, I don't know, but I've got a sort of feelin' that they're out of the case now. One can't get round those alibis, you know, unless the two of them are accomplices, and I don't quite see that. No, *exeunt* Mills and Hope-Fairweather, I rather fancy, through gap in time-table, all talking, all singing, all dancing, laughing ha-ha, chaffing ha-ha, nectar quaffing ha-ha-ha. Anyhow, I'm sick of personalities. Let's take one long last fond look at the facts. No harm in getting things as clear as we can before we pop down there. Find the page headed ' Facts ' in that little lot. I pulled 'em out like plums from the duff of your people's report. (What is duff, by the way ? It sounds quite disgustin'.) With infinite tact he pulled out each fact, and said what a good boy am I. These are the real bones of the case, and any merry little theory we produce has to cover all of them. Read 'em out, Charles, there's a good chap."

Parker began to read :

" FACTS

" Body between desk and window ; chair half on top of it.

" Bullet wound in *left* temple.

" No powder marks round wound.

" Wound still bleeding at 12.16 p.m.

" Pistol, one chamber discharged but barrel clean, lying on desk, far side from chair and window.

" No finger-marks on pistol.

" Pistol of uncommon type ; not many in this country.

" Pistol was in study previous evening. (But where ? Ask butler.)

" Study windows all open.

" Overturned chair by door into hall. (Probably by Archbish.)

" One drawer of desk pulled nearly right out ; documents in disorder ; Mills thinks one or more missing.

" Way on to lawn from kitchen-garden almost impossible.

" Lady stopped and watched gardener, sauntered on to lawn, and then came back ' quicker than she went.' "

" Thank you, Charles," Wimsey said politely. " The tuneful voice was heard from high, arise, ye more than dead ! It's funny about that lady, by the way, isn't it ? "

Parker looked up sharply. " It was Easton's very first idea that Comstock had been shot by someone outside the house."

" No, I didn't mean that. I meant that although Littleton says in his report that he stood by the drawing-room window looking out into the garden, he apparently never saw the lady at all ; and yet she must have been in full sight of the drawing-room windows for at least two or three minutes. I wonder how it was Littleton never saw her."

" He saw the gardener."

" Yes, but he could have seen him from the drive, couldn't he ? Well, well, there seem to be a good many questions in this case that want answering. I wonder, for instance, where Comstock dined the previous evening. Nobody seems to know that."

" The chauffeur might, if you think it's important."

" It's my belief that chauffeur knows a whole lot of things, but whether he'll part with them or not is another matter. Well, shall we be moving ? Mrs. Merdle's all ready and waiting."

Parker groaned apprehensively, but rose.

" There's one thing," said Wimsey, as they went downstairs, " that I should very much like to ask Hope-Fairweather, but I'm afraid it would only be waste of time."

" What's that ? "

" Oh, nothing,' said Wimsey.

Parker, however, recognized the tune the other was humming. It was " Who's Your Lady Friend ? "

(IV)

Mrs. Merdle covered the eighteen miles to Hursley Lodge in twenty-nine minutes, which, allowing for the traffic in London, as Wimsey pointed out, was not bad. From Parker's comments as he clambered out, it might have been gathered that he did not agree. Parker seemed to think it had been nothing but bad.

Wimsey rang the door-bell with a hurt expression.

" My dear Charles, I am not a bad driver, as you seem to think. On the contrary, I'm an astonishingly good one. We're still alive, aren't we ? What more do you want ? "

The door was opened by Farrant, the butler. Parker asked for Mills, and the two were shown into the drawing-room, a long, low room with pleasantly big windows overlooking the garden on one side of the house and the drive in front. Wimsey drifted from one to the other, and then shook his head.

" It's a pity that Littleton didn't notice the lady, you know, Charles. Who knows ? He might have seen something quite interesting. It's a pity he overlooked her, don't you think ? "

Parker grunted. He might have added something more, but the possibility of further retort was cut short by the secretary's entrance.

Wimsey recognized Mills instantly from the police description. The plump hands, the too-great readiness to smile, the general air of complacent toadyism, at once indicated his type. Parker, who had not seen him before, displayed his credentials and asked to see Farrant.

." Not a very nice young man," Wimsey said, when Mills had smiled himself away in search of the butler. " And capable, I rather fancy, under provocation, of turning quite a nasty young man. I wouldn't put it past him for a moment of inserting a piece of lead in his employer's anatomy. And yet I don't think he did."

" I'm not so sure. By the way, is there anyone else you want to see besides Farrant ? "

" Not a soul," Wimsey said blithely. " I don't think we're likely to learn anything more from the gardener ; and as for Mills, the only way to get things out of that young man is to frighten them out, and unfortunately we haven't got anything yet to frighten him with. No, so far as I'm concerned, Farrant—Farrant is the boy. In fact, and not to put too fine a point on it, he is my sunshine and only joy. I've got the glimmering of an idea about Farrant."

Before Parker could ask what the idea might be, Farrant anounced himself.

Parker addressed him more peremptorily than usual.

"Now, Farrant, I'm from Scotland Yard, as you know, and this is Lord Peter Wimsey. We want to ask you a few questions about this business."

Farrant bowed sombrely.

Parker began to put him through an examination on the points already covered in the police report, filling in the time till Wimsey should indicate the direction of his own idea regarding the butler.

Wimsey, however, seemed to have lost interest in the proceedings. Indeed he was becoming rather patently bored. He lounged by the window with his hands in his pockets, and did not even trouble to stifle a slight yawn. The butler's practised glance had already wandered from Parker's blue-serge suit, cut rather for utility than elegance, to Wimsey's Savile Row figure, but his expression had not shown what he thought of the contrast. It was, however, noticeable that whereas only Parker was putting the questions, Farrant's answers appeared to be directed rather to the Savile Row silhouette than to Oxford Street's serge.

At last Wimsey took his hands out of his pockets, and stretched slightly.

"I say, Charles," he said peevishly, 'can't we throw an eye over the jolly old study? Eh? That's what you promised me, you know. You said we could have a look at the study."

Parker took his cue promptly. "Yes, of course," he

said, in a humouring kind of voice. " Farrant, take us to the study."

Farrant swung back a section of the bookcase and stood aside for the others to precede him.

" Ah," said Wimsey, in a pleased voice, " the concealed doorway, eh ? Jolly ingenious. All right, carry on, Charles."

Parker and Farrant passed through into the study. Wimsey, however, did not follow immediately, and when Parker looked round the concealed door was again closed. He resumed his questioning of Farrant, and in a minute or two Wimsey appeared.

" The jolly old door swung to," he said, " and I couldn't find the catch. So this is the scene of the 'orrible crime, is it ? Chair still reversed, as on discovery of body. Well, well, gives you quite a nasty feeling, doesn't it, Charles ? But I suppose you're used to all this kind of thing. Well, well." He teetered round the room with an air of well-bred vacuity.

" Carry on, Charles," he added. " Don't mind me, if you want to get on with your questions, you know. By Jove, I suppose this is the very desk where the revolver was found, what ? Most excitin'."

The slight wink which accompanied these words showed Parker what was wanted of him. He began to question Farrant about the pistol and his discovery of it the previous evening.

Farrant could not undertake to say how the pistol had come into Lord Comstock's possession ; no doubt Mr. Mills might have information on that point. Yes, the evening before the crime was the first time he had seen it. Yes, it had been lying on the desk then.

" *On* the desk ? " said Parker sharply. " What was it doing *on* the desk ? "

" I couldn't say, sir, I'm sure."

" You're certain you didn't see it in one of the drawers ? "

" Quite certain, sir," Farrant replied imperturbably.

" Um," said Parker. " And what did you do with it ? "

" I gave it a bit of a wipe over, sir, and left it where it was."

" You left it——"

" Did it make much of a noise when you pooped it off, Farrant ? " inquired Wimsey pleasantly.

Farrant looked a little shaken. " S—sir ? " he stammered.

" When you pooped it off that evening and chipped the picture rail over there," Wimsey said, in a voice of amiable interest. " Did it make much of a row ? "

" N—no, my lord." Farrant was still showing signs of distress, but he had recovered himself sufficiently to give the other his correct rank. " Hardly any, my lord," he added, with the air of one who, having taken the plunge, does not find the water quite so cold as he had expected.

" Just a sort of sharp crack, not much louder than a dry twig snapping ? "

" Very little louder, my lord."

Wimsey turned to Parker with a look of childish triumph. " There you are, Charles, you see. I told you the noise of that pistol couldn't possibly be described as a crash. That's a jolly interestin' bit of evidence, Farrant. Thanks frightfully for tellin' me."

Parker turned a sternly official countenance upon the butler. " Why have you said nothing of this before ? "

" I don't expect anyone asked him," Wimsey chipped in. " Did they, Farrant ? No, I thought not. Well, suppose you tell us now what happened and how you came to poop the thing off. Did a corner of the duster catch in the trigger ? "

" That is precisely what happened, my lord," Farrant said, with a look of relief. " The pistol was lying on the desk, and I picked it up to slip it into the top drawer, not thinking that a thing like that ought to be left about, when I noticed there was some oil on it. I just went to give it a rub over with the duster, and the next thing I knew was that it had gone off and there was plaster flying in that corner over there. It was careless of me, my lord, because I know how to handle a pistol· Anyhow, I cleaned the fouling out of the barrel to stop it sweating, but I couldn't reload it because there didn't seem to be any ammunition ; so I just left it as it was, with the empty shell in."

" Of course you did," Wimsey nodded approval. " And jolly sensible too. There you are, you see, Charles ; nothing of the least importance after all. By the way, Farrant, can't you tell us something about this paper that's supposed to have disappeared out of the drawer you found open ? I know, of course, that you would never have opened any of Lord Comstock's private drawers, but you might have seen at some time quite by accident what was in 'em. I expect you've got some kind of an idea what paper it is that's missing, eh ? "

Farrant's face had, however, taken on its usual morose expression. " I fancy, my lord," he said, smoothly enough, " that there is no paper missing."

" What ? But Mills said there was."

" Mr. Mills thought at one time that there might be,"

Farrant corrected respectfully, "but I fancy that he thinks now that he was mistaken."

"Oh, he does, does he?" said Wimsey thoughtfully. "Well, in that case there doesn't appear to be much more that you can tell us?"

Farrant performed a slight bow. "I have already informed the police of all I know in connection with the crime."

"I see. Then we needn't keep you any longer. Nothing else you want to ask Farrant, Charles? All right then, Farrant."

Farrant withdrew.

"That was clever of you, Peter," said Parker.

"Oh, I don't know. I just had a hunch that that chap was keeping something up his sleeve, and it struck me there might have been some funny business about the pistol. It was a shot in the dark, of course, but it came off. So now we know how the shell of that pistol came to be empty, why there were no finger-prints, and that Comstock's edition of the pistol had nothing to do with his death. What we don't know is the part that Farrant took in the Mystery of the Missing Document."

"You think he knows something about that?"

"He's certainly got ideas. Didn't you see how his eyes veiled over like a snake's as soon as I introduced the topic? That's a slippery customer, Charles, and I advise you to keep tabs on him." Wimsey was standing in the bow-window, facing the room. He turned round and looked out into the garden, and then began twisting his head and body at different angles.

"Some new kind of physical jerks?" asked Parker.

"If you were anything of a sleuth at all, Charles, you'd see that I'm trying to work out the angle from which the shot was fired. It was the left temple, you see, which complicates matters. Curse this window ! Why couldn't it have been a nice flat one, instead of this three-sided affair. It gives us too many angles altogether."

" You think the shot was fired from outside, then ? "

" I do. I've already proved to you, if only you'd been listening, that it's extremely unlikely that any of the people inside the house fired it. Remains, the outside. And the windows were all open, don't forget. I wish to goodness they hadn't been. Let's see now. He must have been standing up, mustn't he ? If he'd been sitting down, he'd just have slumped back in his chair, not tumbled on to the ground and brought the chair on top of him. So I should say he was standing with his body towards the window, or more or less towards the window, and his head turned to the right. Or he might have been standing like this, looking out of the right of the window and presenting his other temple to an assassin firing through the left of the window. Does that give us anything ? Nothing at all, so far as I can see. Oh, hollow, hollow, all delight. Well, I'm going to have a nice quiet stroll round the garden while you get hold of Mills and ask him why the blazes he's changed his mind about the missing document. He won't tell you, but ask him."

In the garden Wimsey sauntered round with apparent aimlessness. He paced across the lawn, had a look at the wall which divided the grounds from the road, examined the wall that separated the lawn from the kitchen garden and rattled the locked gate in it, strolled round the drive, and finally made his way to the garage.

The chauffeur was there, washing the car, and appropriate reflections occurred to Wimsey regarding the unimportance of human life and the immutability of small jobs.

"That a nice-looking bus," he remarked, glancing over the Phantom Rolls with an expert eye.

The chauffeur, a tall man in dark green breeches and gaiters, straightened himself and passed his forearm over his face to wipe the perspiration away. Evidently he was too used now to being interviewed by complete strangers even to start when one addressed him unexpectedly from behind.

"Ah," he agreed. "Beauty, eh? Never given a minute's trouble since we got her."

For a few minutes they discussed the more notable points of the car's excellence. Then Wimsey gently drew the conversation on to Comstock's death. Chatting easily, he took care to win the other's friendliness before he put the question for which he had sought him out. At last he began to lead up to it.

"By the way, Scotney, I expect the police have asked you where you drove Lord Comstock the evening before, I suppose for dinner?"

"No, sir; not the police. They haven't asked me anything, not since yesterday afternoon. Another gentleman did, though, this morning."

Wimsey wondered which of his fellow-sleuths had forestalled him. "Yes, and you said . . . ?"

"I drove Lord Comstock to Maggioli's restaurant, in Dean Street. He told me to come back at eleven, and I drove him home."

"I see." Wimsey knew Maggioli's quite well. The food there is famous. So are its private rooms. "Oh, and one other thing, Scotney." As if casually he brought out his important question. "Major Littleton, the

Assistant Commissioner, you know, told me how bright
you'd been over the number of that car that was waiting
in the drive. Deuced smart piece of work. You're
evidently an observant fellow. You'd recognize the lady
in it if you saw her again, I expect ? " At the last
moment Wimsey had framed his question differently, and
not asked merely if the chauffeur had seen the lady at
all. One never knows, and a chauffeur may be chivalrous ; the amended wording would not put so great a
strain on any possible chivalry accruing to Scotney.

Possibly Wimsey's caution had been unnecessary, for
the chauffeur replied without hesitation. " I'd know her
all right. A chap doesn't forget a proper good-looker
like her in a hurry."

To pass on to the lady's description was easy.

She was exceptionally tall, it seemed, and slim, and
not so much pretty as real handsome ; no, not so young ;
about thirty-five, Scotney opined, but it was a job to
tell nowadays, and that was a fact. What was she
wearing ? Well, she had a red hat on, of that Scotney
was sure, and some sort of a dress—might have been blue
or might have been black. Was she dark or fair ? Well,
there you had Scotney, but probably darkish, well, not
fair, anyway ; but they don't show much hair under their
hats nowadays, do they ? And reely, Scotney wouldn't
like to say one way or the other.

" Thanks very much," said Wimsey, and rewarded
Mr. Scotney in the recognized manner.

As he was turning away, he put one more question.
" By the way, how did you come to remember the car's
number ? You must see a lot of cars in a day."

" I make a habit of it," returned Mr. Scotney with
pride. " Lord Comstock didn't like me driving too fast,

and when a fellow overtakes you at a corner or does the dirty on you some other way, Lord Comstock always liked to report him to the next A.A. man, and he used to blow hell out of me if I hadn't got his number pat ; so I made the habit of remembering the number of any car I notice. It comes easy after a bit, quite automatic."

"Ah," said Wimsey, as if a doubt had been resolved, and took his departure.

Parker was waiting for him on the steps of the house.

"Finished here ? " he asked gloomily.

Wimsey nodded. "Why weep ye by the tide, laddie, why weep ye by the tide ? I told you Mr. Mills would defeat you. It doesn't matter. The important thing was that Mr. Mills should be made just a little worried by being asked that particular question."

"If he was," said Parker, shoe-horning himself into Mrs. Merdle, " he certainly didn't show it. Mills, Farrant, Hope-Fairweather—we seem to be going round in circles."

Wimsey pressed the self-starter. "Meaning that the murderer isn't among them ? Nay, my fair coz, oh, wish not one man more. For *she* was there. . . ."

"Who was there ? "

"My hope, my joy, my own dear Genevieve. Which way do we go for Winborough, right or left ? "

"Right. What are we going to Winborough for ? "

"To visit a sick. I thought it would be a nice friendly act to ask after that constable whom Littleton ran down so brutally. It was just about here that the deed was done, wasn't it ? "

They had turned out of the drive gates, and Wimsey brought Mrs. Merdle to a halt at the side of the road, while he looked carefully up and down the road.

14

" What are you looking for here ? " Parker asked.

" He hunted high, he hunted low, he also hunted round about him. Gore, Charles. Spot where the body was found marked by gore. But there's no gore, so that doesn't help us." Wimsey got out of the car and walked slowly up the road and back again.

" Are you seriously looking for blood ? " asked Parker, as he climbed back again into the driving-seat.

" Well, not seriously, perhaps. But I should have liked to see where the accident happened. I'm blest if I can understand, you see, why that bobby was on his wrong side of the road."

" These country police," said Parker, with correct scorn.

Wimsey drove on.

In Winborough it was learnt that the unfortunate constable was still unconscious. Wimsey asked to be notified as soon as the man was fit to be interviewed.

Superintendent Easton was not at the station. A by-election was in progress, and he was busy with the Chief Constable. The two examined the pistols and the other exhibits with a proper show of interest, but seemed to learn nothing from them.

" I suppose, though," Wimsey remarked, as they drove back again towards London, " that it's inevitable that the bullet was fired from a pistol of that type ? I'm not much of a whale on firearms. There couldn't be any other kind of weapon that would fire a bullet of that size ? "

" Hardly a rifle," Parker said doubtfully. " It's a lot smaller than a ·22, you see. I can ask our expert, if you like."

" Yes, you might. I don't suppose there's anything

in the idea, but I'm puzzled how to account for another of these little pistols being at Hursley Lodge that day, when you tell me there probably aren't more than a dozen of 'em in England altogether. In fact, there are quite a lot of things that puzzle me in this case. I think I'll give up sleuthin' and buy a farm. Alas, what boots it with uncessant care to tend the homely, slighted sleuther's trade and strictly meditate the thankless corpse ? Were it not jolly well better done, Charles, as others use, to sport with Amaryllis in the shade ? Upon my soul, sometimes I think it were. Exit Hawkshaw the detective through concealed trap-door ; enter Corydon, singing and dancing and covered with straw. Poetry."

The way back to London took them again past Hursley Lodge. To Parker's surprise Wimsey once more insisted on stopping the car, this time against the boundary wall of the Lodge, and mounting on the seat, peered long and earnestly across the lawn at the house.

" I want to have one more look at those angles," he explained. " One last fond look, and then farewell. One gets rather a good view from here. Oh, for the eye, for the eye of a bird. Not that a bird's eye is really needed. Funny thing about plans, isn't it ? They never prepare you for what a place really looks like. Now I'd taken it for granted that the lawn here was about a hundred feet across, and it's not much more than thirty. The plan told me that, of course, but I hearkened not to its pleading. Whisper and I shan't hear ; that's the motto for plans. Well, well." He climbed down again, fitted his long form neatly into the narrow seat, and slipped in the gear.

From Hursley Lodge to Piccadilly Wimsey spoke only

once. Between two trams on the outskirts of Mitcham he lifted both hands from the wheel in a gesture of triumph, and exclaimed :

" I've got it ! "

Parker shudderingly averted his eyes from the imminent death that was bearing down upon him. " Got what ? "

" Whom Mills reminds me of," said Wimsey, grasping the wheel again just in time to curvet away from the bows of the approaching tram. " William Palmer, the poisoner."

(v)

" The question is," said Wimsey moodily " is a woman justified in shooting her blackmailer, or is she not ? "

He was sitting in Miss Katherine Climpson's little drawing-room. Having stowed Mrs. Merdle away and sent Parker about his business, he had put through two telephone calls, and one of them had been to Miss Climpson to ask whether he might come and drink a late cup of tea at her flat, a proposal which had received an enthusiastic assent.

"Personally," he added, " I hold that she is. Strongly."

Miss Climpson helped herself to another piece of wafer-thin bread and butter before replying. The long gold chain round her neck, hung with an assortment of small ornaments, jangled in unison with the numerous bangles which encircled her thin, lace-covered wrists.

" Well, really that is a very *difficult* problem, isn't it ? " she said, sitting very upright in her chair. " We are taught quite clearly that murder is *wicked*, but then blackmailing is wicked too. *Outrageously* wicked.

Really, Lord Peter, as you know I am not a *violent* woman, but when I hear, as I sometimes do, of the *misery* that has been caused by blackmailers, it makes my blood positively *boil*. Even I," said Miss Climpson, her sallow face growing a little pink, " feel that I could do simply *anything* to them. But whether one *ought* to shoot them or not—well, don't you think that *depends* ? "

" Yes, I do. But supposing it is a case where she ought to shoot him, and supposing some interfering busybody of an amateur sleuth finds out that she did shoot him, and supposing she'll get away with it if he holds his tongue and get hanged if he doesn't. . . . Oh, hell. I beg your pardon."

" Not at *all*," said Miss Climpson with energy. " I always think it *quite* right for a man to swear occasionally, when he feels it warranted. It is a male *prerogative*. So long as he keeps within *reasonable* bounds, of course, and I know, Lord Peter, you would always do *that*. I remember an uncle of mine would invariably ejaculate ' *Assouan !* ' when he was deeply moved, which as you know is the largest *dam* in the world, or was then, and he was a *dean*."

" Where the dean clucks, there cluck I," said Wimsey, with a ghastly smile.

" And I am afraid, dear Lord Peter," said Miss Climpson, the ornaments on her gold chain clinking agitatedly, " that you are deeply moved too. Do please let me give you another cup of *tea*. Tea is really *so* soothing in times of mental stress. At least, I know *I* always find it so, though men, I know, pretend to despise it ; but I'm afraid I haven't any whisky. Don't you think," said Miss Climpson all in a rush, " that you had better tell me all about it ? A trouble shared, they

say, is a trouble *halved*. But not, of course, if you think
it inadvisable ; because you mustn't think . . ."

" I think," said Wimsey, taking his cup of tea, " that
you're a darling, Miss Climpson ; and I am going to tell
you all about it. My theory, you see, is that she shot
him from the near side of the window while his head
was turned towards the farther side of the room—the
door, we'll say, of Mills's office. She could have done
it quite safely. The gardener had his back turned, and
the pistol made no more noise than a breaking stick,
which is quite the kind of noise one would expect to
hear in a garden."

" Did you ask the gardener if he heard a stick break
after the lady had gone past him ? " asked Miss
Climpson acutely.

" No, I did not," Wimsey answered, with a kind of
restrained violence. " Because I don't want to know
if the gardener heard a noise like that or not. This is
only a theory, remember. I can't prove it, and I don't
want to prove it. But the devil of it is that I've already
proved to Parker, or as near as dash it, that the shot
must have come from outside the house, because of the
times ; and it doesn't need a man from Scotland Yard to
work out, from the upward direction of the wound and
the height above ground of the window (Littleton himself called it a goodish drop), that the firing-point might
have been pretty close to the window. And it certainly
doesn't take Scotland Yard to know," Wimsey concluded
bitterly, " that the only person pretty close to the window
just then was Hope-Fairweather's girl friend."

Miss Climpson nodded her iron-grey head. " I see.
Poor thing ! How dreadful she must have felt to do such
a terrible thing. But Lord Peter, let us look on the

bright side, as my dear father used to say. Perhaps she didn't do it. We don't *know*, you see; do we? And I always think it is so much better not to be quite certain of the truth about anything really dreadful. Where *ignorance* is *bliss*, you know. But, of course, in this case it isn't bliss, is it? " added Miss Climpson rather lamely, with a glance at Wimsey's anything but blissful face.

" I shall drop out of the case," Wimsey said savagely. " I don't care a hang about the Home Secretary, or anyone else. It's the only decent thing to do."

" You're quite certain it was *blackmail*, then? " asked Miss Climpson, a little timidly.

Wimsey told her about the missing document.

" And the joke is," he said, brightening a little, " that Mills and Farrant each think the other's got it. They're both of them hedging on their stories now, because there's a partnership in the air to pool the paper and split results; but each of them still believes the other's got it."

" And who has got it? " Miss Climpson asked.

" Hope-Fairweather, of course," said Wimsey.

Miss Climpson buttered a second scone with deliberation. " Then do you know what I should do? I should go to Sir Charles Hope-Fairweather and have a talk with *him*."

" Miss Climpson," said Wimsey with enthusiasm, " doesn't it ever give you a pain in the head, a kind of swelling pain, being always right? "

(VI)

The idea of seeking an interview with Sir Charles had, of course, been in Wimsey's mind already. He had put it aside, because he had no wish to drag out of that unfortunate man a truth which he would much prefer to leave unconfirmed. Now he saw that things could not be left quite as they were. The best thing would be to see Sir Charles, drop a hint or two about what he knew, and at the same time mention his decision to retire from the case, and then drop another hint or two about what he might do were he in Sir Charles's place. For Wimsey not only had every sympathy with Sir Charles, he had every sympathy, too, with the lady whom he had referred to as Sir Charles's girl friend. If people will go a-blackmailing, and in a particularly dirty way, they must be prepared to be shot ; and Wimsey was not going to lift a finger against their executioners. On that point his determination was now firm.

Wimsey had not been quite so open with Miss Climpson as to be indiscreet. He had told her very little more than what she was bound to learn shortly from the newspapers. Not for a moment had he let her guess that the name of Sir Charles's girl friend was perfectly well-known to him, as indeed was the lady herself.

Already, on the chauffeur's description, he had had his suspicions ; the second of the two telephone calls which he had put through on reaching his flat, had confirmed them. It had been to Maggioli's restaurant. Maggioli's had the reputation of being extremely discreet. But discretion does not always pay, and a successful restaurant proprietor is not he who knows how to be discreet, but he who knows when not to be discreet. Maggioli was a very successful restaurant-proprietor. He knew all about Lord Peter Wimsey ; and he had not the least hesitation in informing his lordship, in the strictest confidence, that the lady with whom Lord Comstock had dined, in a private room, the night before his death, was Mrs. Arbuthnot. And Mrs. Arbuthnot was not only Sir Charles Hope-Fairweather's niece, but she was the sister-in-law of Freddie Arbuthnot ; and if the other had not settled it, that did.

Wimsey saw Sir Charles late that evening, when he got back from the House. He had been waiting in the big library in Eaton Place for over an hour, and with every minute he disliked more the interview ahead of him. But Miss Climpson had been perfectly right. It was one of those things which have to be done.

Sir Charles came in just before midnight. He looked tired, and Wimsey thought the lines on his face more deeply incised than when he had seen him last. Quite obviously he was not too pleased to see his visitor.

" Ah, Wimsey. You want to see me ? Not been waiting long, I hope. You've got a drink ? It's about this Comstock business, I suppose."

Wimsey nodded. " 'Fraid so, Sir Charles. Sorry to bother you, and all that."

" Oh, I'm getting used to it," said Sir Charles, mixing himself a drink and dropping into a chair. " I'd better not be so unofficial as to say straight out that this is a fool idea of Brackenthorpe's, calling the police off and all you other chaps on, but if it isn't, I'd like to know what a fool idea is. All right, get on with your questions."

" I haven't come to ask any questions, Sir Charles," Wimsey said softly. " Ask, and it shall be answered unto you. I don't want to be answered."

Sir Charles lifted his eybrows. " Eh ? Don't get you, I'm afraid."

" I'm retiring from the case."

" Oh ! "

There was a grim little silence. Wimsey sipped his drink and stared straight ahead of him.

Sir Charles said quietly :

" Care to explain why ? "

" I don't think I need, need I ? We'll say, if you like, that I prefer not to find out the truth."

" Ah ! "

" But it's probable, you know," Wimsey said gently, that someone else may. Dashed probable. And what I've really come for is to say that if there's anything I can do. . . ."

" Ah," said Sir Charles again, unhelpfully.

There was another little silence. Wimsey was determined not to break it. He had said all he meant to say, and more quickly than he had expected ; and if the other wanted to leave it at that, Wimsey was quite ready to do the same.

" Am I to gather," asked Sir Charles with some care, " that you consider the world well rid of Comstock ? "

" What I have found out," Wimsey answered, with no less care, " makes me rather anxious not to find out any more."

Sir Charles took a sip of his whisky-and-soda. " You think I shot the fellow ? " he asked, in a more conversational tone.

" Oh no, I don't. On the contrary, I'm pretty sure you didn't."

" Then why all this hush-hush business ? "

Wimsey laughed. " Sorry if I've been turning melodramatic. Enter Wimsey, the Masked Bandit, disguised as a sleuth ; fly, all is discovered. No, but seriously, sir, and without trying to butt in, I do hope that document's safely destroyed."

" What document ? "

" The letter, or whatever it was, that you nicked out of the drawer in Comstock's desk. A pretty smart piece of work, Sir Charles, if you don't mind me sayin' so."

" Ah," observed Sir Charles again, and lit a cigar rather elaborately.

" You trying to pump me ? " he asked, when the cigar was drawing nicely.

" No. I told you, I'd retired from the case."

" Have you got any idea as to who shot Comstock ? I'd rather like to hear it, if you have. Because, I can tell you, it beats me."

" Ah," said Wimsey.

Sir Charles glanced at him sharply. " Don't believe that, eh ? "

" It doesn't matter what one believes, does it ? " Wimsey said evasively. " The point is, I don't know."

Sir Charles shifted his position in his chair. " Look here, Wimsey, we're talking at cross-purposes. You've evidently got some notion in your head, and I'm pretty sure it's a wrong one. Anyhow, is this pow-wow official or not ? "

" If you mean, will anything you spill to me now go any farther, it won't. But take my advice, sir, and don't spill it."

" No," said Sir Charles ; " I think I will. I'm going to tell you something I deliberately kept back from Brackenthorpe ; and I kept it back because I doubted very much whether he'd believe it, and in any case I didn't see that it would help matters. The truth is, young feller, that I'm in a bit of an awkward position. I know that, of course ; and I'm going to tell you this because it's a case of who is not for me is against me, and you

seem to be busy informing me that you're among the
pros. Anyhow, I'm going to let you in on what I actually
saw happen ; and if you can make anything of it, go
ahead and do so—so long, of course, as you don't give me
away."

"I won't give you away," Wimsey promised gravely,
"or Mrs. Arbuthnot. I thought," he added, "that you'd
better know that I know that."

"I was afraid it would come out," said Sir Charles
equably ; but the sudden tightening of his fingers on
the cigar showed what his voice was so careful to conceal.

"So far as I know, that piece of information is
exclusive to me," Wimsey soothed him.

"Ah ! Well, let's hope it remains so. Betty's had
trouble enough already without getting mixed up in this
business," Sir Charles pronounced.

Wimsey raised his eyebrows ever so slightly, but did
not speak.

"Anyhow, here's what's happened. I went down
there that morning to get those letters out of Comstock,
by hook or by crook. I needn't go into details, but
Comstock was about as low as they make 'em where
women were concerned. And he'd got hold of these
letters of—of someone whose name we needn't bother
about. She'd come here late the night before and told
me the whole rotten story. She was pretty well desperate ;
just been having dinner with him, and he'd put things
to her. Well, I knew there was no time to waste, so
down I went the next morning. She insisted on coming
too. I knew where the letters were ; I think he'd told
her, or she'd seen 'em ; and I was quite ready to knock
the fellow out, if I could, to get them.

"Well, then, there was that trouble about seeing him

at all. I tried to get rid of that secretary chap with a message to the car, but it didn't come off—luckily, as it happened. Then, when I heard the Archbishop being shown out, I thought I'd better nip in and tackle Comstock before Mills could get busy again. I remembered the lie of the rooms at Hursley Lodge well enough to know that I could get into Comstock's study without showing myself in the hall, so I waited till the voices died away, and then went through.

"Comstock was standing by the window. He turned round when I came in from the office and looked a bit surprised, but said 'hullo' civilly enough. I went straight to the point—told him he was a blackguard, and that I wanted those letters. He began sneering, and I was just on the point of going for him when suddenly he crumpled up without a word, and sort of slithered *via* the chair to the floor, upsetting it on top of him. I thought he'd had a stroke, and to tell you the truth I didn't care what he'd had, because it had given me the chance to get those letters. The drawer was actually open, and the packet was lying on the top. I simply grabbed it, had a quick look out into the garden to make sure that no one had seen me through the window, and beat it back to the secretary's office. I was trying to get through to the waiting-room, but my sleeve caught a tray of papers and crashed it on to the floor. While I was picking them up, the fellow came in. Luckily I must have pulled the study door to behind me. You know the rest. But I can tell you, Wimsey, when I heard in Brackenthorpe's room that Comstock had been shot, it gave me a nasty moment. I simply hadn't the faintest idea."

"Well, I'm dashed!" said Wimsey. "You know, Sir

Charles, that's an uncommonly interestin' story." He was trying to pick out the vital facts. One in particular stood out. " You say you looked out into the garden within a few seconds of Comstock's crumpling up. Who was there ? "

" No one ! That's the astonishing thing. Comstock must have been shot from the garden. Everything goes to prove that. It was the left temple, wasn't it ? Well, that fits ; he was standing sideways on to the window, facing me ; his left temple was towards the garden. But I'll swear that when I looked out there was nobody within sight except the gardener, and Betty just crossing the drive."

" Mrs. Arbuthnot was just crossing the drive ? " Wimsey repeated innocently. " I wonder if she saw or heard anyone."

" No. I've asked her. She says she'd just walked on to the lawn, feeling anxious, and then decided that she had better not be seen, got in a bit of a panic and hurried back to the car. She swears, too, that there was nobody else in the garden. But she has got a vague notion that she might have heard a subdued crack as she was stepping on to the drive, because she remembers looking back at the gardener under the impression that he'd broken a rake or something."

" She was going away from the house when you saw her ? "

" Oh yes."

" Ah," said Wimsey. If Betty Arbuthnot had been crossing the drive fifteen seconds after Comstock had been shot, with the gardener between her and the house, then it was quite impossible that Betty Arbuthnot could have fired the shot.. Of course Sir Charles might be shielding her, but on the whole Wimsey thought he was speaking the truth. " Here be mysteries," he said.

" I'll tell you what I think, Wimsey. It wasn't any of the people who are known to have been in and around the place that morning, who shot Comstock. The crime was carefully planned, and the murderer was hiding somewhere in the garden. He's left no clue, nobody's got the least idea who he was, and he won't be found. And I for one shan't be sorry if he isn't."

" On the whole," said Wimsey, " I'm inclined to agree with you."

He asked the other a few more questions, but could elicit nothing more that looked helpful. Now that his first theory seemed to be disproved, his investigating instincts were once more roused. He had told Sir Charles that he was retiring from the case, and so he would, officially ; but perhaps unofficially he might still retain a paternal interest in it.

" It's lucky," he remarked, " that you were so quick off the mark, isn't it ? Otherwise, as things turned out, you'd have lost those letters. *Bis rapit qui cito rapit.*"

" Well, as a matter of fact it was on my way. I was going to Winborough that morning in any case. The by-election, you know. There was a big lunch-hour meeting that day, with Brackenthorpe speaking, and a lunch afterwards. I only had to start a bit earlier. The only trouble was putting Brackenthorpe off. His chauffeur was laid up and he wanted me to drive him down. Brackenthorpe hates driving himself. However, I managed to get out of it."

" And lucky you did," Wimsey said, rising. " Well, Sir Charles, I can promise you none of this will go any farther, and thanks frightfully for marks of confidence and all that in telling me. I agree with you that the chap who shot Comstock was too cunning. I don't think they'll get him. No, I won't have another drink, thanks."

It was past one o'clock when Wimsey got home, but Bunter appeared in the little hall almost before the latch-key had ceased to turn in the lock.

" Bunter," Wimsey said severely, " I keep telling you not to wait up for me when I'm late, but you will do it. Why won't you obey me, Bunter ? It makes things frightfully awkward for me, you know. Especially this evening, when every prospect pleases, and only Bunter's vile."

" May I inquire, my lord, whether you have solved the Comstock mystery ? "

" Don't talk like the title of a detective story, Bunter. No, not to say solved it. I had a theory, but it's just died on me, I'm glad to say."

" Indeed, my lord ? "

" Yes, it was a nasty little theory. I never liked it. Nor did Miss Climpson. Have you got a Miss Climpson, Bunter, to take all your troubles to ? You should have. What lasting joys that man attend, Bunter, who hath a polished female friend."

" So I have always understood, my lord," said Bunter, mixing a whisky-and-soda from the tray which stood ready on the Sheraton table.

Wimsey settled himself comfortably on the couch. " Well, it may interest you to hear that I've proved that Comstock wasn't shot from the house, and he wasn't shot from the garden. Therefore there's only one place he could have been shot from, and that is the road. You've studied the plan of the place? Then you'll have realized, as I didn't, that it's barely thirty feet from the house to the road. I stopped the car there this afternoon and had a peep over the wall. If I was a good shot with a revolver, which I'm not, I could have picked off anyone standing in the study window as easy as falling off a log. What do you think of that ? "

" I must admit, my lord, that it is a possibility which had already occurred to me after a perusal of the plan."

" It would have," Wimsey said bitterly. " I have to go down there and run about with my nose to the ground, of course, to see anything so obvious ; but you're like one of those Austrian professors of criminology, who solve everything without moving out of their studies. Have you ever thought of emigrating to Austria, Bunter ? They'd pay you good money there."

" I fear, my lord, that life among a foreign people would not suit me for long."

" Back flies the homing Bunter, like a swallow to its nest. Anyhow, it's my belief that this is just what the murderer did. He stopped his car by that wall, waited till Comstock presented a nice easy target, and then pipped him neatly and drove off. Ha ! " exclaimed Wimsey, " and I wonder if that's why the policeman was on the wrong side of the road. I knew there was something significant in that, if only we could see what it was. Had that possibility occurred to you ? "

" No, my lord. I regret to confess that I had over-looked such an obvious conclusion."

" Don't spoil it, just because I'm one up on you. Be generous, sweet Bunter, and let who will be wiser. They haven't rung up from Winborough, have they ? I'm very much afraid, you know, that when that policeman does recover consciousness, there won't be any Comstock

15

mystery left. If I am right, and the shooting did take place from the road, he probably saw the whole thing. Well, well, we can but wait. Not that it makes any difference to me. I've retired from the case."

" Indeed, my lord ? "

" Yes, I've decided that I don't care who shot Comstock. I'm just rather glad that somebody did."

" I have always understood," said Bunter, " that Lord Comstock was not a very nice gentleman."

At four o'clock in the morning Wimsey was roused from sleep. Standing by the bed, Bunter was shaking him respectfully, but with firmness.

" I beg your pardon, my lord, but the Winborough police-station is on the telephone. Although you gave me to understand that you have retired from the case, I fancied that you would be interested to hear anything they may wish to impart."

" Yes," said Wimsey, struggling with an enormous yawn. " After all, they don't know I've retired, do they ? "

The news from Winborough was interesting. The constable had recovered consciousness and had been able to make a statement.

" I hope I haven't done wrong in calling you up at this time, my lord," said a gruff, but apologetic voice, " but we understood that you wished to be informed at any hour of the day or night, and our orders are to give you every facility."

" Quite right. Has the man got anything useful to say ? "

" I'm afraid nothing helpful regarding the Comstock case, my lord. His story is that he was cycling along the road, and there was a car ahead of him drawn up at the side. He drew out to pass it, but before he could do so the car went on. Before the man could regain his own side of the road, another car came out of the drive at Hursley Lodge, on its wrong side of the road, and passed him."

Hope-Fairweather's, reflected Wimsey, with a prick of professional conscience that he had not thought of asking Sir Charles about the policeman.

" Our man was again about to ride over to his own side of the road, when another car, which we know now was Major Littleton's, came out of the same drive at very great speed and, of course, crashed into him."

" I see," said Wimsey. " No, that doesn't help much, does it ? Did the man notice the car that was drawn up by the side of the road ? " he added casually. " The driver might be able to substantiate part of his story, you see."

" He didn't take a note of the number, my lord. He thinks it was a blue saloon, but he doesn't seem very sure about that. He's only a young chap, and I'm afraid he isn't as observant yet as he might be, in spite of his training."

" And I suppose he didn't notice the driver at all ? "

" It was a saloon car, my lord. I don't think he even saw the driver. But in any case the car was out of sight by the time of the accident, so the driver couldn't help us much either way, could he ? "

" Of course not," said Wimsey.

He went thoughtfully back to bed.

" Nobody seems to know anything about this third pistol," he mused, as he pulled the sheet up round his ear. " I wonder how Brackenthorpe got hold of it."

(VII)

Wimsey sat in Sir Philip Brackenthorpe's room at
the Home Office. Sir Philip sat at his table, facing him.

Wimsey smiled easily. "I've come to tell you, sir, that
I'm retiring from the case."

"Oh?" Sir Philip did not sound very interested.
"You could have sent me a note."

"I'm afraid you're frightfully busy," Wimsey said
apologetically. "Sorry to be takin' up your time, and
all that, but there is one question I wanted to ask, and
I thought it better to put it to you personally."

"Yes?"

"Don't think I'm interferin', but—are you quite sure
it's all right about the pistol? I mean, it won't be traced
to you, and it's safely out of the way now? Sorry to
butt in, but I thought I'd better make sure."

Sir Philip had looked up sharply. "What pistol?"

"Why," said Wimsey innocently, "the pistol that you
shot Comstock with."

Sir Philip drew a piece of paper towards him. He
marked three dots on it, and then very carefully drew
lines from dot to dot. When his triangle was completed
he looked at it for a moment, apparently in deep admiration, and then embarked on a square.

"Do I really understand you to say, Wimsey," he
remarked in a detached voice, "that you imagine that
I shot Comstock?"

"I'm afraid—something like that, you know," said
Wimsey deprecatingly. His narrow face looked more
completely vacuous than one would have believed
possible. He beamed inanely.

"Preposterous!" observed Sir Philip absently, and

tried his hand at a circle round the square. He frowned in a pained manner at the result's lack of circularity.

" My theories often are," said Wimsey, unabashed. " At least, so Parker says. But then, of course, he has the job of disproving the things. That's where the work lies. Anyone can make dashed silly suggestions. Like this one, you know. Do you think I'd better hand it over to Parker to disprove ? I will if you'd rather, Sir Philip."

Sir Philip looked up. " What makes you think such a thing, Wimsey ? "

Wimsey told him.

" But this is just guess-work," was Sir Philip's comment.

" At present. That's all a theory really is, you know. But if it's right, I expect a whole lot of it could be proved. Whereas," said Wimsey brightly, " if it's wrong, I expect it couldn't."

" You haven't even traced the possession to me of one of those pistols."

" No," Wimsey admitted. " That is the snag, of course." His shining face took on an expression of interested inquiry. " How *did* you get hold of it ? "

" We're talking nonsense," said Sir Philip briefly, and made a movement as if to get up.

Wimsey leaned back and beamed at him. " You know, I had my suspicions about you from the beginning."

" From the beginning ? " Sir Philip sat back again, abruptly.

" Yes ; when you called Scotland Yard off and put the amateurs on. That looked dashed fishy to me. But it was a clever move. Scotland Yard won't catch up now. But you shouldn't have given away the fact that you knew Comstock, you know ; it would have come out, no doubt, but you needn't have advertised it ; because to know him, I imagine, was to loathe him. By the way, how *did* you get hold of the pistol ? "

Sir Philip looked at him.

" I'm only asking for your own good," Wimsey said plaintively. " I just want to make sure you haven't done anything silly."

Sir Philip looked at him.

" Am I to hand the theory over to Parker, then ? " asked Wimsey.

" I thought," said Sir Philip slowly, " that you had come here to tell me you had retired from the case."

" I have. The only question now is whether I hand it over to Parker or whether I don't."

There was a long silence. Sir Philip began to draw a most elaborate pattern, based on a rhomboid.

He looked up from it. " The pistol was sent to me, fully loaded, by an anonymous correspondent, with a message inside which ran, if I remember rightly, ' This is just one of a good many that are going to make you wish you'd never been born.' I get a lot of things like that."

" And where is it now ? "

" At the bottom of the sea."

" Does anyone know you had it ? "

" No. It arrived just as I was setting off for Winborough. It was marked ' Private and personal—urgent,' so my butler gave it to me personally instead of handing it over with my other correspondence to my secretary. I opened it actually in the car. Nobody but myself has seen it."

" Then you ought to be all right," said Wimsey cheerfully.

Sir Philip extended one side of the rhomboid to form the base of a would-be isosceles triangle.

" In a way," he remarked, " it wasn't really murder."

" Not at all," Wimsey agreed politely. " It was a legitimate function of your office. A bit unconventional, perhaps, but none the worse for that."

" I'd been wondering on the way down," Sir Philip pursued, " whether I'd stop at Hursley Lodge and have a word with Comstock myself. The man was becoming a public pest. The harm he had done to this country, abroad as well as at home, was already incalculable. For the national good he had to be silenced. I was meditating something in the nature of a personal appeal, backed by threats, before proceeding to sterner measures. I had already made up my mind that if he forced us to do so, we would deal with him on no less a count than high treason. I was anxious, however, that any interview I might have with him should be a complete secret, with no witnesses even as to my own arrival. I therefore stopped my car, as you deduced, by that wall, got out on the running-board, and looked over to see whether the place seemed deserted or not. I saw Comstock standing in a window, quite a short distance away from me. The pistol was in my pocket. I felt very strongly about the man, so strongly that I hardly realized the insane thing I was doing. I took out the pistol and had a shot at him. I can say quite truthfully that I had not the very faintest expectation of hitting him. Indeed, the idea of hitting him hardly occurred to me. I am not merely an indifferent shot with a pistol, I have never even fired one before. The ridiculous idea in my mind, I think, was just to give him a severe fright. But I did hit him ; and if I were a religious man I should sincerely believe that a divine guidance had directed that bullet. I saw him collapse, and continued to watch, in a sort of trance of horror. Then to my astonishment I recognized Littleton bending over the body. That brought me to myself. I got back into my car and drove off. I never saw the policeman you mention."

" You're quite safe from him," said Wimsey. " I don't think anyone will connect that car with Comstock's death for a time yet ; and if they do then, the scent will be too cold."

Sir Philip smiled faintly. " You know, I can't regret it."

" Regret it ? " said Wimsey with indignation. " I should think not. If you don't mind my sayin' so, Sir Philip, it's the best thing you ever did in your life. It's a pity we can't tell the world, so that you can go down in posterity and become a legend. With weepin' and with laughter still is the story told, how well Sir Philip pipped his man in the brave days of old. But, alas! we must keep it under our hats.

" Not," added Wimsey thoughtfully, " that you're in any real danger, because if the worst came to the worst and they did nab you for it, you could always give yourself a reprieve, couldn't you? Or couldn't you? It's a nice legal point. I must remember to put it to Murbles next time I see him."

Best one, and most plausible, so far.

CHAPTER IV

THE CONCLUSIONS OF MR. ROGER SHERINGHAM

Recorded by Dorothy L. Sayers

" It's not a bit of good, Mr. Sheringham, sir," said Chief Inspector Moresby. " I have put you in possession of the facts as notified to me for that purpose, and further than that I cannot go. Indeed," he added, with an air of aggressive virtue, " further than that I am not permitted to go. My instructions being, Mr. Sheringham, that the amateurs are to have a free field, entirely unhampered by the incompetent conjectures of the police."

" Yes, but, dash it," lamented Roger Sheringham, " I don't know how to start on a job like this. It's so in-human—all this grisly great bunch of documents. I've never met any of these birds. You know my methods, Moresby—how can I buzz round and be my bright, inquisitive self among people like the Archbishop of the Midlands and Sir Charles Hope-Fairweather ? "

" You have your authority, sir, same as one of us," the Chief Inspector pointed out austerely.

" That's not the same thing," said Roger.

" Possibly not, Mr. Sheringham, and possibly that may account to some extent for this official blundering that we hear so much about. A great many of our inquiries, when you come to think of it, lie among people who aren't exactly disposed to be chatty and communicative. However, the Home Secretary seems to have made up his mind that a gentleman like yourself, with a public-school education and all that, ought to make a better job at tackling archbishops and such than a common or garden bobby. And no doubt," added Moresby, " he is very right."

" Now you are being bitter, Moresby."

" Not at all, Mr. Sheringham. I only meant that these educational advantages must be good for something or other. Beyond, of course, making it easier to obtain money under false pretences, and write begging letters and so forth. And even then, the judge usually makes some remark about its being a peculiarly bad case, on account of accused having wasted the advantages which ought to have taught him better, and adds a bit on to his sentence for luck, as you might say. Why, only the other day, Mr. Sheringham, we pulled a young fellow in for running a bogus charity. An old Harrovian he was, and been up to Oxford and everything, and he was posing as a clergyman, if you please—said he had been chaplain to the Suffragan Bishop of Balham, and wheedled the money out of the old ladies like——"

" Muggleton-Blood ! " cried Roger triumphantly.

" I beg your pardon, Mr. Sheringham ? " The Chief Inspector, having caught the syllables imperfectly, took them for an expletive, and was mildly astonished.

" I said Muggleton-Blood, meaning that you are right, as you always are. There *are* advantages, and one of them is that I had the honour of being at school with the Rev. Hilary Muggleton-Blood. One of the Shropshire Muggleton-Bloods, Moresby, but quite a decent fellow, for all that."

" And what," inquired Mr. Moresby, " has the Rev. Mr. Muggleton-Blood to do with the case ? "

" He enjoys the responsible but dignified post of chaplain to the Archbishop of the Midlands," replied Roger, " and while His Grace himself is, perhaps, a cut above us, it is not impossible that the Rev. Hilary may be induced to unbend a little, if I approach him arrayed in humility and an old school tie. It is, at any rate, worth trying—though I must admit that, on the occasion of our last personal encounter, he chastised me severely because my person was not meticulously cleansed as to the ears. He was a robust lad at that time and I remember the incident very clearly."

" No doubt you do, sir," said Moresby, with a grin.

Mr. Roger Sheringham found no difficulty in obtaining an interview with the Rev. Hilary Muggleton-Blood. The latter, whom Roger recollected as a brawny youth in the first Rugger XV, had turned into a stout, florid ecclesiastic of vigorous middle-age, with a muscular handshake and a throaty intonation.

" Ha ! " he exclaimed, wringing Roger's fingers in a painful grip, " ha ! Whom have we here ? If it isn't Snotty Sheringham ! This is an unexpected pleasure. And what have you been doing with yourself all this long time, young Snotty ? Sit down, sit down."

" Well, well, well," said Mr. Sheringham, annoyed. He had, until that moment, forgotten his own nickname, but he did distinctly remember that the Lower School had called the Rev. Hilary " Bloody-Mug." With a great effort he refrained from recalling this circumstance aloud ; he felt that it would be hardly politic. All the same, he was hurt that Mr. Muggleton-Blood should require information about his, Roger's, recent activities.

He had thought—but no matter. He modestly mentioned his criminological interests and his connection with the crime at Hursley Lodge.

" It just occurred to me," he said, " that his Grace might have mentioned to you some little point or other which might throw light on the mystery. No doubt he would tell you a great deal more than he would tell the ordinary inquirer."

" Quite so, quite so," agreed the Rev. Hilary. He leaned back in his chair, placed his plump hands finger-tip to finger-tip across his well-rounded clerical waistcoat, and beamed pleasantly at Mr. Sheringham. " What sort of thing exactly did you want to know ? "

" Well, for one thing," said Roger, to whom this point had occurred early in the investigation and proved very puzzling, " how did the old bird come to go down to Hursley Lodge all by his little self ? I thought you never let Archbishops stray about the country unchaperoned."

" Nor do we," replied Mr. Muggleton-Blood, " nor do we. I myself accompanied His Grace as far as Winborough, where I had a small matter of purely diocesan interest to discuss with Canon Pritchard. The Archbishop preferred to go on from there alone, thinking that this might give his visit a less formal and more friendly appearance."

" I see," said Roger. " Then you knew all about this visit beforehand ? "

" Naturally," said Mr. Muggleton-Blood, opening his rather gooseberry eyes very wide. " My good Snotty, you surely do not suppose that an Archbishop can make unexpected and surreptitious excursions without the knowledge of his entourage. His Grace is an extremely busy man—every moment in his time-table is allotted weeks beforehand. It was really with great difficulty that I was able to squeeze in this little expedition, and then only at the cost of putting off a deputation from the United Christian Fellowship for the Preservation of the Rubric. And I must admit," added the chaplain, with a touch of human feeling, " that I heartily wish now that we had preserved the Rubric and given the New Paganism a miss. However, as Dr. Pettifer was extremely earnest in the matter, and I was able to obtain the appointment, and the United Christian Fellowship were prepared to adjourn their deputation till the following week, I felt bound to respect His Grace's wishes."

" What did you say ? " cried Roger. " You made an appointment ? "

" Of course I made an appointment. Dr. Pettifer's time is, as I have explained, very valuable. One would hardly expect him to sacrifice the greater part of the morning merely on the chance of seeing this fellow Comstock."

" But——" gasped Roger. " With whom did you make the appointment ? "

" With the secretary—I forget his name—Pills, or Squills, or something of that kind."

" With Mills ? But Mills says that the Archbishop's arrival was totally unexpected, and that Lord Comstock had given strict injunctions that no visitors were to be admitted."

" Ah ! " said the Rev. Hilary. He smiled, with an expression which was almost sly. " I fear that is not altogether correct. Not altogether. And perhaps I expressed myself a little ambiguously. Yes—I must confess to a slight *suppressio veri*, though it scarcely, I think, amounts to a *suggestio falsi*. I said, I made the appointment with Mr.—ah—Mills ; I made no mention of Lord Comstock. The fact is that, when I rang up Hursley Lodge, the secretary informed me that Lord Comstock was, if I may so express it, in retreat, but would be at home upon the morning in question, and that, if His Grace cared to call, he himself would undertake to bring about a meeting between them. He suggested, however, that it would be better if His Grace's visit appeared to be entirely unpremeditated, and indeed, insisted upon a promise that his obliging interference should not be mentioned to Lord Comstock. His Grace fell in with this suggestion."

" Naughty, naughty ! " said Mr. Sheringham.

" I scarcely think so," replied Mr. Muggleton-Blood. " Dr. Pettifer was not called upon to explain to Lord Comstock the precise mechanism by which his visit had been brought about. Nor would it be desirable, nor indeed would it be Christian, to create unnecessary trouble for this man Mills, when he was acting in the interests of Religion in arranging the interview."

" Well, well, *well*," said Mr. Sheringham. " But why couldn't Mills have told us this ? "

" That I could not say," said Mr. Muggleton-Blood. " I fear, such is the weakness of human nature, he may have preferred to pose as the perfect secretary, rather than as the champion of the Church. By the way, my dear boy, I am extremely remiss. I have offered you no refreshment. Allow me to suggest a glass of old sherry."

Roger accepted the sherry, which was good.

" I am afraid," he said tentatively, " that when the

Archbishop got back to Winborough you must have found him a bit upset by Lord Comstock's reception."

" He was considerably upset, certainly," replied the chaplain, " but chiefly on account of having missed the 12.16. Otherwise "—his green eyes twinkled—" otherwise the interview had passed off quite satisfactorily—considering."

" Satisfactorily ? " Roger felt that his brain was turning. " Dash it all, I don't know what the old gentleman's idea of satisfaction is. Several people overheard them going at one another like hammer and tongs. And when the Archbishop came out, he was in no end of a stew, according to the secretary—too rattled to know what he was doing, and muttering about ' the wages of sin.' "

" Muttering about *what*, my dear fellow ? "

" About ' the wages of sin.' Twice over, he said it—and he was so dazed, he didn't even hear Mills asking if he wanted a taxi till he had repeated the question twice."

Mr. Muggleton-Blood's stout frame began to quiver gently, and a rich chuckle issued from his lips.

" My dear Snotty—my dear old boy ! Have you ever met an archbishop ? Have you ever seen one, except upon the stage ? "

" I have heard the Archbishop of Northumbria preach on the Wireless," said Roger ; " a very fruity discourse."

" No doubt," said the Rev. Hilary. " His Grace of Northumbria is a very eloquent preacher. But whatever makes you imagine, dear boy, that Archbishops in private life go about muttering texts of Scripture ? Nothing, I assure you, could be farther removed from their habits. No, no. Believe me, the man Mills was quite mistaken. If Dr. Pettifer was muttering anything, it was probably something about 'missing the 12.16.' He did, as a matter of fact, miss it, after making a sprint for the station, which was very bad for a man of his weight and years. As I ventured to point out to His Grace, at his age one should know better than to try and cover a mile in seven minutes. But he explained that he hoped to get a lift on the way, whereas to wait while the secretary telephoned for a taxi would certainly have meant missing the train. Personally, I cannot understand why His Grace was not offered Lord Comstock's own car. It seems very remiss, and hardly courteous."

Roger scratched his head.

" I suppose," he said, thoughtfully, " Mills didn't dare suggest using the car, in case Comstock should want it in a hurry. Comstock was that sort of man. The point had not, I admit, occurred to me."

" I asked His Grace why he had not himself thought of asking Lord Comstock for the car. His reply was that, though he had accepted Lord Comstock's offer in the interests of the Church, he did not feel that he could very well ask the man a favour. Nevertheless——"

" Accepted *what* offer ? " yelped Mr. Sheringham lamentably. " What *are* you talking about, Bloody-Mug ? " The name slipped unguardedly from the barrier of his teeth in the anguish of the moment.

" Perhaps," said Mr. Muggleton-Blood, a little stiffly, " I ought not to have spoken so freely. But I gathered —perhaps wrongly—that during this interview, innumerable persons were sitting with their ears glued to the keyhole, and that, in consequence, Lord Comstock's offer to the Archbishop was common property."

" Nothing is known of any offer," said Roger eagerly. He felt that he was at least on the track of something.

Did he walk from the station to the lodge?

Simony, perhaps. He did not know what it was, but believed it to be a crime appropriate to an archbishop. " My dear Muggleton-Blood "—he emphasized the name, in haste to cover up his former indiscretion—" nothing is known of the interview, except that high words passed on both sides and that Lord Comstock used the expression ' clap-trap '; after which he apparently threw a chair at the Archbishop, or the Archbishop at him, and the meeting broke up in confusion. If you can tell me anything further, Muggleton-Blood, I beg you will do so. You really must. You have already said too much not to say more."

Roger thought this last sentence rather a good one. He had found it in a detective story by Morton Harrogate Bradley,[1] and had stored it up for use on some such occasion as this.

" Well," said the Rev. Hilary, " well, my dear Snotty —I do not know that there is any objection to my telling you, particularly as the matter will soon become public property. That is, if the contract holds good, as I suppose it does, in spite of Lord Comstock's decease. The fact is that, after a somewhat heated discussion, Lord Comstock—who, after all (and we must in charity do him that justice) was always ready to put the interests of his newspaper before his private feelings—said to Dr. Pettifer : ' Damn it all, Doctor,'—I repeat his col-

---

[1] The pen-name, as is now pretty generally known, of that charming man, Mr. Percy Robinson. This distinguished writer took an important part in the unravelling of *The Poisoned Chocolate Case*, as will be ascertained on reference to the novel of that name, which work (since I did not write it myself) I have pleasure in recommending to lovers of detection. The author is Mr. Anthony Berkeley, a gentleman for whom I have the utmost esteem.

loquialisms as Dr. Pettifer reported them to me—
' you've got a damned good story there—why waste it
on me ? I'll tell you what I'll do. I'll give you the
leader page of the *Bugle* for it any day you like, and make
it a first-class feature. We're never afraid to let a man
defend himself, and we'll do the thing in style, with
photographs of yourself and your Cathedral and everything handsome about it. Your name would put it over
big—it would be worth five hundred guineas to us—and
that's as much as we pay the world's champion heavy-
weight. What do you say ? We can guarantee you a
circulation of nearly two million, and that's a pretty
fair-sized congregation. How about it ? ' His Grace
was at first somewhat staggered by this proposition—I
confess I thought it a piece of effrontery myself when I
heard about it——"

" Good lord ! " said Roger, " I should think so."

" But he considered that it might be advisable, in these
days, to fight the Mammon of Unrighteousness with their
own weapons—and there's a text for you, if you want
one." Muggleton-Blood chuckled again. " So he agreed
to do it."

" But he didn't take the money, of course ? "

" Now, my dear boy," said Mr. Muggleton-Blood,
" where would have been the sense of refusing the
money ? If you must have a text for everything, I can
refer you to the passage about spoiling the Egyptians.
His Grace accepted the offer, whereupon Lord Comstock
playfully called him a great old bluffer, and in the
excitement of the moment, overturned several volumes
of the Encyclopædia. At this point His Grace recollected
that he had a train to catch, and hurried away."

" But look here, Muggleton-Blood," expostulated

Roger, really shocked, " how did the Archbishop come to fall into so patent a trap? What capital Comstock would have made of it! The Archbishop of the Midlands taking money from Antichrist! Surely, surely——"

" Not a bit of it, my dear fellow, not a bit of it. Lord Comstock's cheque would, of course, have been gratefully acknowledged by the Treasurer of the Church of England Crusade for Combating the New Paganism, of which body His Grace is, naturally, the president. You see, by this means the Church would secure, not only four columns of really unpurchasable advertising space, but also a valuable donation, which, incidentally, would have the effect of very considerably discrediting Lord Comstock in the eyes of his supporters. The Archbishop could not be blind to the advantages of such a proposition."

" Well," said Roger, " I'll be damned! The wily old devil! "

" What you do not appear to grasp, my dear boy," pursued Mr. Muggleton-Blood, " is that a dignitary of the Church is obliged to be, before all things, a statesman. Or rather, a Churchman first and foremost—that goes without saying, but before everything *else*, a statesman. And, since texts appeal to you, there is an expression about the wisdom of the serpent which is singularly apt. So you will appreciate that His Grace is really very much distressed by the sudden demise of Lord Comstock, which may mean the loss of this exceptional opportunity for propaganda."

Roger sat for a moment speechless.

" Look here, Muggleton-Blood," he said, when he had recovered his breath, " can you prove all this? Because it's rather important. I mean it, so to speak, lets the Archbishop out."

" I hardly know what you would call proof," replied the chaplain, " but you might, perhaps, like to see the Archbishop's letter confirming the arrangement. You will treat it, naturally, as a confidential document. I have it here. I was about to seal it for the post when the news of Lord Comstock's death reached us."

He hunted through a sheaf of correspondence, and handed Sheringham a sheet of paper. It was dated on the previous evening, and written from Lambeth Palace, where the Archbishop was being entertained during his stay in London :

" MY DEAR COMSTOCK.—In confirmation of our conversation this afternoon, I write to say that I shall be happy to write a four-column article for *The Daily Bugle* on the subject : ' The Peril of the New Paganism.' The remuneration mentioned by you, viz : five hundred guineas (£525) will be quite satisfactory and will be acknowledged to you from the proper quarter.

" Thanking you for this opportunity of presenting the case for Christianity to the many readers of your publication.—I am, Yours faithfully,

" ANSELM MEDIUM."

Roger was crushed.

" I am really very much obliged to you, Muggleton-Blood," he said humbly.

" Not at all," said the Rev. Hilary. " Very glad to have been of service to you. You must be off ? Another glass of sherry ? No ? Well, good-day, my dear fellow, good-day. It has been delightful to see you again after all these years."

Mr. Roger Sheringham crept away from the presence of Mr. Muggleton-Blood in so unnerved a condition that only after consuming a pint of mild-and-bitter at the Teg and Turnip was he able to sort out the halfpence from the kicks so liberally bestowed upon him. For a short time he dallied with the idea that the Rev. Hilary had been pulling the wool over his eyes—but then, the recollection of that firm and flourishing signature, " Anselm Medium," put all his doubts to flight. An Archbishop might (as he had learnt) suppress an inconvenient truth, but he could not, surely, pledge his wedded and consecrated title to so plump a lie as that letter. And how, reflected Roger, abashed, could he have supposed that one of the Heads of the Establishment could flounder about a rich man's residence in a flurry of religious enthusiasm, mouthing scripture denunciations, and calling upon the wrath of Heaven like a street-preacher ? Oh, shameful and ridiculous mistake !

But, if Dr. Pettifer had never spoken of the wages of sin, how had Mills come to be so precise about it ? Had he really mistaken a vague muttering about the 12.16 for that sinister quotation ? Or had he, supposing (as Roger himself had supposed) that a twentieth-century Archbishop was in the habit of behaving like John the Baptist, put words into the churchman's mouth to suit some hidden purpose of his own ? And if he had—and if Muggleton-Blood spoke truth—this was not the secretary's only lie, for he had himself arranged the visit which, afterwards, he declared to have been wholly unexpected. Something was here for thought.

And then it struck Roger how odd—how almost incredible—it was that no less than three distinguished and improbable people should have chosen, out of all days and hours in the year, precisely the same hour and day to swoop upon Hursley Lodge for the express purpose of quarrelling with Lord Comstock. Could such a thing be chance ? Sir Charles Hope-Fairweather had denied—almost with fury—that he had gone to see Comstock by appointment. If the denial was true, why the fury ? There was something to be investigated here. But how to do it ? One certainly could not ask Hope-Fairweather, for he would assuredly only get a still more furious denial. And, of course, it would be absurd to ask Mills. But how about the lady ? Who was the lady ?

At this point Roger hurriedly drained down the remainder of the mild-and-bitter and became very active. He buzzed about, like a questing bee, from club to club and from pub to pub, until at length, in a hotel bar much frequented by journalists, he discovered one Mr. ffulke Tweedle, a gentleman who specialized in social omniscience, and who was, in fact, gossip-writer to the Comstock weekly organ, the *Sunday Trumpet*.

Mr. ffulke Tweedle had apparently been designed in a moment when nature, having mislaid her ruler, had no instrument handy but a pair of compasses. His head, his eyes and his spectacles were all round and all shining ; his cheeks were round and pink ; his mouth was the up-curving segment of a circle, bounded on the east and west by handsomely-curved parentheses. His form was pleasantly globed in front ; when he stooped, he presented a rear aspect almost perfectly circular, and his voice was rounded and fluting. He encircled Roger's hand with a cushiony clasp, beamed genially upon him and called in mellow accents for refreshments.

" And what can I do for you, my dear Sheringham ? "
Roger explained that he wanted a little information

about the Chief Whip, and had therefore come, as fast as horse-power could convey him, to Mr. Tweedle, " as you know everything about everybody."

" Now, that is very flattering of you, my dear Sheringham," said Mr. Tweedle. " Say when. What is troubling you about dear old Hope-Fairweather ? "

" I expect you can guess," said Roger, " or you will, when I tell you that I am officially investigating the murder of Lord Comstock."

Mr. Tweedle hurriedly depressed the corners of his mouth, and made an inclination of the head as though he had just stepped into church.

" The poor old skipper," he burbled, dropping his flute-notes to bassoon register, " a most melancholy business, Sheringham. I do not know when I have seen the Street so shaken. The fall of a colossus. The blow to me, personally, has been quite shattering. He had his peculiarities, poor old chap, but he was a great man, Sheringham, a really great man. It was a bad day for all of us when Comstock went west. . . ."

He spoke with sincerity ; as why should he not ? The death of a great newspaper proprietor usually means the violent upheaval of his staff, and in these lean days, who does not dread the axe and the sack ?

" Quite so," said Roger, " and that's why I feel pretty sure you'll be ready to help me put his murderer where murderers should be put."

" Certainly," said Mr. Tweedle, " generally speaking ; that is, most certainly. But I must say, my dear Sheringham, that I trust your investigations will be made discreetly. Dear old Hope-Fairweather is a fellow for whom I have a particular regard ; the last time I saw him, we happened to be standing side by side at the reception given to the Bolivian Ambassador, and he remarked to me, ' What a curious thing it is, ffulke, that the——' "

" I quite see your point," interrupted Roger, recognizing that Mr. Tweedle was about to rehearse his next Sunday's gossip-column, " absolutely, of course. I'm not thinking at all of fixing anything on Sir Charles. What could be more ridiculous ? No, but the evidence of a certain lady is very urgently required—and that is where I think you may help me."

Mr. Tweedle looked as portentous as his physical conformation permitted.

" My dear Sheringham—you put me in a difficulty— these matters are a little delicate——"

" I know, I know. But perhaps you haven't got all the facts. If you haven't, they're not for publication, but I know I can rely on your journalistic discretion."

" Of course you may," said Mr. ffulke Tweedle, licking his lips.

Roger gave him a brief outline of Sir Charles Hope-Fairweather's movements at Hursley Lodge.

" Now, you see, Tweedle," he went on, " there can be nothing indiscreet in Sir Charles's relations with the lady, taken by themselves. If there had been, why should she have accompanied him in the first place ? Her presence was not required at the interview with Comstock. And besides, if Mills is telling the truth when he says that Sir Charles wanted a message taken to his car, then it's clear that *at that time*, he wasn't concerned to hide the lady's identity. *Now*, obviously, it's different. He doesn't want her mixed up in it, and he's adopting a very chivalrous and proper attitude. But we needn't—we mustn't—take that attitude. Can you tell us, Tweedle, who the lady may have been—tall, dark, slimmish woman, I'm told, on the more interesting side of thirty— with whom Sir Charles might quite openly and honourably have taken a little motor-run ? "

Mrs. Tweedle's smile was almost semi-circular.

" We—e—ll, my dear Sheringham, I really—no, I really see *no* reason why I should not divulge—in the strictest confidence of course—a little item of social intelligence which will probably be made public before very long. It is whispered among those who know that Sir Charles Hope-Fairweather, who, I need not remind you, lost his charming wife six years ago in the same disastrous aeroplane crash which deprived Society of the witty and genial Major Arthur (' Dart ') Polwheedle and the exquisite Lady ' Bat ' Stukeley, will shortly lead another bride to the altar. The name that is mentioned is that of Lady Phyllis Dalrymple, eldest daughter of the Marquis of Quorn, one of the most brilliant of our Society leaders. His first wife," added Mr. Tweedle, " was, of course, a Pytchley."

" Ah ! " said Roger, wagging his head.

" Mind you," said Mr. Tweedle, " I go no farther than that. I cannot pretend to say whether Phyl Dalrymple is, or is not, the lady you are looking for. But the description—so far as it goes—would apply to her."

" Thanks enormously, Tweedle," said Roger. " I always knew you were the man to come to." He rose from the little table in the corner at which he had isolated his informant and sought for his hat and stick.

" Now, I do hope," cried Mr. Tweedle in some alarm, " that you are not going to do anything precipitate. And above all things, I beg you will not mention me. My discretion is, if I may say so, my livelihood, and——"

" My dear Tweedle," said Roger reassuringly, " wild horses would not drag your name from me. I will be most meticulously careful. And believe me, I am extremely grateful. I'll do as much for you if I get the opportunity. You must lunch with me one day."

" Delighted, delighted ! " said Mr. Tweedle.

" You'll excuse me now, won't you ? " said Roger, and bustled rather importantly away.

His next appearance was at the town residence of the Marquis of Quorn in Berkeley Square. He pranced up the imposing steps and rang the bell with assurance. A footman answered the door.

" Is Lady Phyllis Dalrymple at home ? " demanded Roger, with the air of one who has no doubt of his welcome.

" Not at home," said the footman, as one who had no doubts either.

" Not ? " said Roger, much astonished.

" No, sir," said the footman. " Her ladyship is not at home, sir."

" Dear me," said Roger, " that is very—— Oh, well. You say she isn't at home ? "

" No, sir," said the footman.

" Not to anybody ? " said Roger.

" No, sir ; not to anybody."

(" Aha ! " thought Roger acutely ; " she *is* at home, then.")

" Could I take any message, sir ? "

" Er—well ! " said Roger. He pulled out his pocket-book, extracted a sheet of paper (which happened to be a little statement of account from his dentist), and frowned at it. " This *is* Wednesday, 16th, isn't it ? "

" Excuse me, sir, but was her ladyship expecting you ? "

" I rather thought she was," said Roger mendaciously, " but it doesn't matter."

" Her ladyship, sir, is seriously indisposed, and has cancelled her engagements for to-day. But if you desired to leave a message, sir——"

" N—no," said Roger. " Or, wait—perhaps I might speak to her maid—Mademoiselle—hum, ha."

" Mademoiselle Célie, sir ? "

" Célie, of course."

" I will make inquiries. What name shall I say, sir ? "

" I hardly expect she will remember my name," said Roger, " but you might say that I have come up from Hursley Lodge."

" Very good, sir. Will you step this way ? "

Roger, a little surprised at his own daring and resource, was shown into an elegant and forbidding little room, furnished with three black cubes and four tubular chairs. Here he sat, cooling his heels on a waxed scarlet floor and dazzling his eyesight against four aluminium walls and a prickly nude of the modern French school, until, after an interval of some five or ten minutes, the door opened to admit a very smart and very plain and very Parisian lady's maid.

" Ah ! " said this young person. " You are Monsieur Meelss, yes ? "

For one agonizing and indeterminate second, Roger hesitated whether to be Mr. Mills or not. Then he said, " Yes."

" Ah, bon ! My lady say it is ver' kind of you to come. She quite understand it is all finish' with the death of ce pauvre Lord Comstock. She is sorry that she cannot see you herself, but she has an *atroce* headache and beg you to excuse her."

" Naturally, naturally," said Roger. " Of course, she must be very much upset."

" *Comment?* Upset?"

" By all this," said Roger. " I mean, it must have distressed her very much."

" I do not understand. My lady is indispose—not well."

" I am very sorry to hear it," said Roger hastily, feeling that he had missed a cue somewhere. " I only meant that the murder of Lord Comstock must have given her a shock."

" Oh, that?" Célie appeared to dismiss Lord Comstock. " *Mais, oui,* it was ver' shocking," she amended. " Naturally, to you it is extremely grave."

" Terribly so," said Roger, remembering that he was supposed to be Mr. Mills. " A most frightful blow." It suddenly struck him that the bereaved Mr. Mills ought not to be capering about town in a pale grey suit with a rather lively tie. However, he could not alter that now. " Just so," he added vaguely; " quite. Er—ah! So long as her ladyship——"

" She understand perfectly," Mlle Célie assured him.

Roger only wished that he could say the same, but the worst of assuming somebody else's personality at short notice is that it becomes very difficult to ask questions.

" She weesh me to say," continued Mlle Célie surprisingly, " that it will be quite all right about the little cheque, since, of course, it is not your fault that nossing come of the arrangement."

Roger recovered his breath sufficiently to say that it was very good of her ladyship.

" I did my best," he ventured.

" *Parfaitement, monsieur.* Her ladyship will preserve the greatest discretion, she weesh me to assure you."

Roger said he was very much obliged.

" And she ask me to say again she appreciate the kindness you do in coming, but is it not a little bit risky, *hein* ? "

Roger mumbled something.

" Not so risky, you think, now that he is dead ? *Aha ? Enfin, c'est votre affaire.* But there is a big difference from the 'ush-'ush telephone call on Monday to the big ring at the bell on Wednesday, *quoi* ? After all, if I was to tell the tales out of the school—but I do not do such things, me ! "

Roger gasped, but with admirable presence of mind realized that Mr. Mills was being invited to purchase Mlle Célie's silence about something or the other. And could there be any doubt about what ? Surely not. Even as he reluctantly parted with some Treasury notes, he mentally patted himself on the back. Mr. Mills—oh yes ! his instinct had not led him astray about Mr. Mills.

As he emerged from the house in Berkeley Square, he almost cannoned into a gentleman in a morning coat and a silk hat, who came up full tilt, and apologized to him in smothered accents and with unseeing eyes. Roger, however, had no difficulty in recognizing the bleak, handsome face and impressive stature of the Chief Government Whip. Whatever it was that had caused Lady Phyllis to cancel her engagements, it was evidently not going to keep Sir Charles Hope-Fairweather on the outer side of her door, if that gentleman had any say in the matter.

One more little item of information did Roger yearn for—and it might, he feared, prove difficult to obtain.

Without very much hope, he decided to try the easiest
and most obvious way first. He dashed along to his club,
called for and obtained a copy of Tuesday's *Times*, and
hunted through the fashionable intelligence. As by a
miracle, he found what he was looking for. On the
Monday night, there had been a party at the house of the
Foreign Secretary, and among those present had been
the Lady Phyllis Dalrymple and Sir Charles Hope-
Fairweather.

So, thought Roger, 66.6 per cent. of the incredible
coincidence was practically proved to have been no
coincidence at all. The Archbishop had made an appointment—if not with Lord Comstock, yet with Mr. Mills.
Sir Charles Hope-Fairweather had said he had made no
appointment. Perhaps he had not—but what about the
lady? On Monday, Mr. Mills and Lady Phyllis's maid had
been in telephonic communication, and Lady Phyllis had
known all about it. On that same night, Lady Phyllis
and Sir Charles had met. On the Tuesday morning, Sir
Charles and a lady resembling Lady Phyllis had gone
down to Hursley Lodge together. On the Wednesday,
Mr. Mills was being told to keep the cheque received for
his services, under vows of closest secrecy. "The
arrangement," whatever it might have been, had fallen
through on account of Lord Comstock's death—and the
upshot of the whole affair was that Lady Phyllis was
seriously indisposed and Sir Charles (if one might judge
by his looks) seriously agitated. "The arrangement"
remained a mystery, but Roger scented some kind of
intrigue in which Sir Charles was the puppet whose
strings were pulled from Hursley Lodge and Berkeley
Square. But for Roger one fact stood out clearly.
Mills had lied again. He had known that the Archbishop

was coming; he had known that Sir Charles was coming; he had engineered their appearance on the scene: why?

Roger set this query aside for the moment and asked himself another: Had Mills also arranged the visit of Major Littleton?

The voice of Inner Conviction answered him: Ten to one he had, but it's no use asking them at Scotland Yard.

With a sigh, Roger agreed that Inner Conviction was probably well informed. Well, he must assume this to be the case and go back again to the question: Why did Mr. Teddy Mills engineer this gathering of Lord Comstock's enemies?

The voice of Inner Conviction spoke again, and in authoritative accents: *" Because he meant to kill Comstock and throw the suspicion on the others."*

Well, thought Roger, my Inner Conviction may be perfectly right, but has he, she, or it any reasonable evidence to go on? How about our old friends Means, Motive, and Opportunity, that sinister trinity to whom all good detective writers reverently bow the knee?

Roger always groaned in spirit when faced with Means, Motive, and Opportunity. They had, in time past, made short work of so many pretty fancies. But they had to be tackled. And, after all, he had the comfort of feeling that he was almost certainly working on the right lines. It was not really reasonable to suppose that murders were committed by Archbishops, Chief Whips, or Assistant Commissioners of Scotland Yard; whereas private secretaries, it was well known, would murder their employers as soon as look at them.

and be out of a job

Very well, then : *Means*.

Here, at the very first encounter, Inner Conviction received a nasty jab to the solar plexus. If Mills was to do the murder, then Mills must be provided with a pistol. The firearms expert had said that the bullet extracted from Comstock's head had not been fired from Comstock's pistol, and that seemed to be that. Roger trifled for a few moments with the idea that the marks on the bullet might have been previously faked, but dismissed it as a mystery-writer's dream. Mills did not look the man for that kind of job—his podgy, hairy hands had not the air of being familiar with instruments of precision. Why need one suppose that Comstock was the only man who possessed that particular type of pistol ? One other specimen had turned up : why not two ? Perhaps Comstock himself had had more than one. Perhaps Mills had got a weapon from the same source as Comstock. What source was that, by the way ? Of course, yes : the *Bugle's* crime expert. Roger made a note to interview the crime expert.

But if Mills had had a pistol of his own, where was that pistol now ? And how was he, Roger, to lay hands upon it ? It was all very well, thought Roger, to put investigations into the hands of amateur detectives, but it was hardly fair to expect them to do routine work like searching suspects and combing out houses and gardens for concealed weapons. The whole thing was absurd. Mills and Farrant, and, in fact, the entire household, ought to have been gone over immediately by a body of skilled searchers. Already the criminal had had twenty-four hours in which to get rid of the pistol. What hope was there of finding it now ? Obviously, Roger would have to go down to Hursley Lodge and do his best, but it was all terribly tedious and difficult. Unless, of course, he could get Moresby to help him. But he did not really want Moresby. He felt that if he had to listen to Moresby's self-satisfied voice pointing any more morals, or remarking one single time more that " it wasn't a bit of good, Mr. Sheringham," and that " perhaps he would admit now, Mr. Sheringham," he should scream, or throw something at Moresby. No ; he would stick to deduction and induction to show him where the pistol ought to be, and find it, if possible, himself.

Leaving *Means* in this unsatisfactory condition, Roger passed on to *Motive*.

This looked much more promising. According to Farrant, Mills had been given notice to quit. Of course, Farrant might be lying—if it came to that, everybody might be lying, but, that way, madness would lie, too. He knew now that Mills was a liar : he would assume that he had lied again when he denied Farrant's story. Mills, then, had been given notice, and for a reason which shed a very unfavourable light on Mills's character. Mills was a Judas, a man who could sell his master. Treachery is a crime that Fleet Street never forgives. Undoubtedly, Comstock could have made things extremely unpleasant for Mills ; he could probably have damned him to all eternity as a private secretary ; nobody wants private secretaries who sell information.

And besides these, there might, of course, be other reasons. Who was Mills ? What were his private griefs ? Was there anything in that long and mysterious period of Comstock's earlier life to account for an enmity that should manifest itself, first by betrayal and finally by shooting ? Running over the resources of a mind well stocked with criminological fiction, Roger found that

17

there were a good many possible motives of this kind ;
as, for example :

1. " The Wrong he did my Mo-o-ther ; or, The
   Bastard's Revenge."
2. " Sic Vos non Vobis ; or, The Man who stole the
   Patent."
3. " King's Evidence ; or, Dogged by Dartmoor."
4. " The Catspaw ; or, My Father bore the Blame."
5. " The Girl he Ruined ; or, The Seducer's Warning."

And so on.

An inquiry into Mr. Mills's past seemed to be indicated.
How, Roger wondered, were amateur detectives supposed
to do all these jobs in forty-eight hours ? Obviously, he
would have to tackle Fleet Street again. Weary work.

Finally, came the question of :

Opportunity : and here, Roger realized, his pretty
theory was likely to stand or fall. With a frowning brow
he reviewed the shorthand reports of the available evidence, comparing them with Sir Philip Brackenthorpe's
time-table.

The thing that stood out immediately was that, in this
case, the *terminus a quo* and the *terminus ad quem* were
singularly well defined. At 12 noon or thereabouts,
Major Littleton had arrived and heard Comstock chatting
with Dr. Pettifer. This time had presumably been fixed
by Littleton himself, and therefore did not depend on
Mills's suspected evidence. By 12.22, all the visitors had
departed ; this, to be sure, was Mills's evidence, but,
again, Littleton had apparently not disputed it. At
some moment previous to this, Littleton had discovered
the body of Comstock, with the blood still flowing from

the wound in the head. According to the doctor, death had been practically instantaneous, so that Comstock could not have died more than a minute or two before Littleton's irruption into the study. One must, of course, if one assumed Littleton's innocence, assume him also to be a witness of truth, and, since he was accustomed to police investigation, one must also credit him with powers of accurate observation.

Now, at what precise moment had Littleton entered the study ? And where had Mills been just before that ?

On the first point, the Assistant Commissioner's evidence was more human and less accurate than one might have desired.

On arriving, shortly before noon, he had heard the rumpus in the study and looked about the room " a bit." How big a bit ? Big enough, anyway, to enable him to find the concealed panel. He had then strolled about and looked out of the window. Then he had heard " people moving about in the hall," and after " a bit " everything had become quiet in the study. That no doubt meant that the Archbishop had gone. Here, then, the time-table could be checked. Dr. Pettifer had left himself only seven minutes to catch the 12.16 ; therefore he had departed, on his own evidence, at 12.9 ; therefore, Littleton's two " bits " accounted, between them, for ten or eleven minutes. He had then waited " a bit," opened the door and looked in, and there was Comstock lying dead.

So far, so good. After a brief examination of the body, Littleton had heard Hope-Fairweather's car drive off and had given chase. This, of course, was subsequent to Hope-Fairweather's departure by the front door and before 12.22. For the exact moments occupied by all the intermediate skirmishings in and about the office, one was, unhappily, more or less dependent upon the tainted evidence of Mills, but, if he had been very far out in his statement, Hope-Fairweather would surely have contradicted him. At what time, then, had Mills been able to penetrate, alone, into the study, between 12.9 and 12.22 ?

Here a thought struck Roger. How about that very odd statement by Mills that he had opened the drawing-room door and found the room empty ? Looking over the evidence again, Roger saw that this incident had occurred (according to Mills) *after* Dr. Pettifer's departure and *before* his coming upon Hope-Fairweather in the office. But, during this very period, Littleton, in his own words, had " waited for a bit, expecting that young chap (Mills) to come in and show me in to see Comstock." Now, that meant that if the drawing-room door had really been opened during that time, Littleton must have seen it ; when one is " expecting " someone to come in, one's eyes are usually glued upon the door. Therefore, either Mills or Littleton was lying, and, by Roger's theory, the liar had to be Mills. Very well, then ; had the drawing-room door ever been opened at all ? If it had, it could only have been at one of two moments : either *before* 12.9, when Littleton had been looking for the secret panel and the drawing-room door and had been concealed from view by the jutting of the chimney-breast, or *after* Hope-Fairweather's departure, when Littleton had gone through the secret panel into the study.

Now, then, thought Roger, why the lie ? Why the story of the door's having been opened at all ?

The answer came pat to his mind : In order to suggest

that Littleton entered the study earlier than he actually did and had an interview and a quarrel with Comstock. For Mills had asserted that he had opened the door, found the drawing-room empty, and *heard a crash*. The suggestion surely was that the crash was—not, of course, the pistol-shot, which would only be a faint crack like the snapping of a stick—but the fall of Comstock with the chair on top of him.

Now, then ; what followed ? Mills must, in reality, have seen Dr. Pettifer out at 12.9 and gone immediately to the office—say, at 12.10. There, he had found Hope-Fairweather in difficulties with the table and the tray of correspondence. He had dusted him down and seen him out—say three minutes for that— this brought the time-table to 12.13. According to his own statement he had then again opened the drawing-room door and found the room empty. This would mean that Littleton was already in the study. But that was absurd. One could not allow ten minutes for Littleton to make a cursory examination of the body. What followed ? It followed, as the night the day, that Mills had lied again. Between the departure of Hope-Fairweather and Littleton's entry into the study there had been an interval of something like seven or eight minutes at least, during which Mills could have done anything he chose. He had only to go into his office, take the pistol (that tiresome pistol that had yet to be found) from its hiding-place, softly open the study door and shoot Comstock through the left side of the head as he sat at his desk. What could be simpler ?

Very well ; but now came a complication. Mills had said that immediately after seeing Hope-Fairweather off he had looked into the drawing-room for the second time and found it empty. This was not true ; after getting rid of the Chief Whip he had gone and shot Comstock. But at one point he must have gone into the drawing-room as he said, for he had accurately described the actions of Hope-Fairweather and Littleton as seen from the drawing-room window, and here he must have been speaking the truth, for he had told his tale *before* Littleton and Hope-Fairweather had produced evidence to confirm it. Now, at last, one could make a time-table with some assurance of certainty. Roger, who had been working his problem out over the remains of a bread-and-cheese-and-beer feast in the seclusion of his own abode, pushed his plate to one side, took another pull at the tankard, got pen and notebook and set to work.

12.9 p.m.   Departure of Archbishop.
12.10 ,,   Crash in office ; Mills goes to look.
12.13 ,,   (say) Hope-Fairweather dusted and dismissed. All quiet.
12.15 ,,   Mills shoots Comstock.
12.17 ,,   Littleton enters study.
12.19 ,,   Hope-Fairweather starts up his car.
12.20 ,,   Mills enters drawing-room ; sees Hope-Fairweather departing and Littleton dashing across the lawn.
12.22 ,,   Mills, having got rid of any incriminating traces, such as the pistol, resumes work.

There seemed to be nothing seriously wrong with this, so far as Roger could see. He had allowed six or seven minutes for Hope-Fairweather to regain his car and start up, but in view of the circumstances, this was not at all too much. He had to walk round the wide sweep of the drive. Then, no doubt, he would have had to explain to Lady Phyllis how it was that he had not succeeded in having the interview with Comstock, and that, Roger felt, might indeed have required some explanation; women are very impatient of failure. When he came to think of it, the marvel was that Sir Charles had succeeded in getting away when he did.

Only one point now remained to be considered : why had Mills gone back into the drawing-room ? The answer was fairly obvious. He had gone there intending to get rid of Littleton on some pretext or other. Instead, he had found that the accommodating Littleton had, of his own accord and urged by unseasonable curiosity, jammed his head well and truly into the trap set for him. All Mills had to do was to go quietly away and let the whole lot of them get on with it.

Roger swigged off the remainder of his beer at a draught. He was not ill-pleased with his work. Means might be as yet indiscoverable ; Motive might still remain obscure ; but Opportunity had proved a lala-paloosa.

We next behold Mr. Roger Sheringham at Hursley Lodge.

What the inhabitants of that house of mystery and melodrama thought of Sir Philip Brackenthorpe's inspiration will perhaps never be adequately ascertained or put on record. During the days which followed the shock of Lord Comstock's murder, they were doomed to continual upheaval and interrogation. They could hardly sit down to their meals or snatch a moment to change their shoes or clean their teeth. There had, of course, been first of all, Superintendent Easton and his myrmidons. Next, some people from Scotland Yard had come, only to warn them to expect the worst and go away again. Then at various times there descended upon them in turn a tiresome old female with a screeching laugh and a voice like a church organ ; an urbane gentleman, who looked as though he were connected with the stage ; a chattering man with a monocle and a tame policeman ; and Mr. Roger Sheringham. All these people invaded the study, poked about the drawing-room, camped in the office, snooped round the shrubberies ; raked over the flower-beds, rummaged through the garage, left garden-mould and cigarette-ash all over the house and asked the same idiotic questions. By the time they had finished, Mr. Mills, Farrant, Scotney, the gardener, the housemaid, and the cook could have recited their versions of the affair in their sleep. Mr. Sheringham, breezing cheerfully into the house in the track of all the other investigators, received no very hearty welcome. Ten minutes after his arrival, he asked Farrant, with his customary courtesy, for the loan of a step-ladder.

"Very good, sir," said Farrant, retreating on reverential feet.

Unhappily, he did not quite shut the study door, and the following fragment of conversation was distinctly audible in the hall :

"Emily ! "

"Yes, Mr. Farrant."

"This one wants the step-ladder."

"Ho ! do he ? What next ? Diving-suit, I shouldn't wonder. What's he like, then ? "

"Oh, one of the matey sort. Too bright by half. No class."

"Well, I shouldn't bother about *him*."

Roger was deeply hurt. This came of adopting a

pleasant man-to-man attitude with butlers. When the step-ladder came, he acknowledged it curtly, adding :

" That will do, Farrant. You can go. And, this time, *shut the door.*"

He noted with pleasure a certain uneasiness in Farrant's face.

In searching for the hypothetical pistol, Roger adopted, *faute de mieux*, the line of least resistance. He would search the easy places first, and then the more difficult. It was most probable, of course, that the murderer had taken the weapon away with him and cached it in some unget-at-able spot. But there was just the chance that he had dreaded the idea of being caught with it on his person and had lodged it in a handy place, to be retrieved later.

A long course of training in hunt-the-thimble and other drawing-room sports had taught Roger the truth of the maxim that the best hiding-place was either well above or well below eye-level. He was, for example, well acquainted with the device of the phosphorescent haddock, attached by tin-tacks to the under-side of the dining-room table. He had known this simple ruse to occasion the taking-up of an entire system of house-drainage, whereby three British plumbers and their mates had been given remunerative employment for a week. He had, therefore, spent ten solid minutes on his hands and knees beneath the furniture of the study and adjacent rooms. Failing to discover anything by this means, he had turned his attention to the walls and ceiling. In the drawing-room, there were only a couple of old-fashioned chiffoniers and the top of the chimney-breast above eye-level, the rest of the walls being smooth, except for a narrow picture-rail. The office and waiting-room had only a few low shelves containing files, and were not promising. But the study had bookshelves to within a foot of the rather high ceiling, and each of its three tall doors was embellished with a handsome oak architrave, of pseudo-classical design, surmounted by a floridly-carved frieze and jutting cornice. By standing on tip-toe and stretching his arm to the utmost, Roger could just touch the top shelves and the cornices ; an exceedingly tall man might find it possible to lodge a small object upon them while standing on the floor. Beginning with the wall between the study and the office, Roger planted his step-ladder and searched, being careful to use his eyes only, and not to scrabble with his hands. It was thus that, having laboriously traversed about half the available wall-space, he suddenly found himself gazing, with in-credulous delight, at a small black object perched upon the cornice over the door between the study and the hall. Gingerly grasping his prize in a handkerchief-swathed hand (to preserve possible finger-prints), he nearly fell off the ladder in his excitement at finding that he held a miniature pistol, the dead spit, so far as he could see, of the other two exhibits in the case.

Roger sat down on the top step and gloated. His subtle psychological instinct had not led him astray. He had deduced a third pistol in this place and here the pistol was. Exercising infinite precaution, he broke the weapon and discovered, a little disconcertingly, that it contained, not one, but two empty, discharged shells ; being otherwise fully loaded.

This, however, was a trifle. One other bullet might have been fired at some previous time. Undoubtedly this was the weapon that had shot Comstock. Roger wrapped it up very carefully in the handkerchief, slipped it into his pocket and descended the ladder.

Before confronting Mills with this evidence of his crime, it seemed advisable to get confirmation on a few other points of the story. If Mills had left his finger-prints on the pistol, other confirmation would be scarcely necessary, but it was unlikely that Mills had been so obliging. If only there were some more exact evidence about the time of Hope-Fairweather's departure, it would be exceedingly helpful. Perhaps some of the servants might know. With a stern eye and a peremptory manner, Roger proceeded to examine the household.

It was just at this triumph-peak of achievement that Roger's beautiful card-tower of theory began to crumble and collapse.

Emily the housemaid delivered the first blow.

Yes, she had seen Sir Charles depart. She had been putting away the silver in the dining-room sideboard and had the dining-room door open. She saw Mr. Mills come back from the front door and go into the drawing-room. Yes, into the drawing-room. That would be a little after 12.15. No, certainly not before, because she recollected looking at the kitchen-clock when she brought the silver through, and it said 12.15. It would be about 12.18 when Sir Charles went away. Then she heard some one come running round the house and a gentleman got into the car that was standing under the dining-room window and drove off. Funny, she thought it. She saw the car go, and was just turning round again with the silver in her hands, when she saw Mr. Mills come out of the drawing-room and go straight into the office and shut the door. The kitchen clock could always be trusted ; Mr. Farrant set it every night by wireless. And what was more, she remembered Mr. Scotney coming through just at that very moment when she looked at the clock and comparing it with his watch.

" Scotney ? What was he coming through about ? "

Why, of course, Mr. Scotney always came in at a quarter past twelve, to ask if the car was wanted for the afternoon. Emily, with a toss of the head, seemed to imply that Roger was a poor sort of detective if he didn't know *that*.

Roger experienced a sinking of the heart. If this was all true, then Mills *could* not have shot Comstock. There was no time between Hope-Fairweather's departure and Littleton's entry into the study. He looked hard at Emily. She was a good-looking girl, and Mills was a man with a kind of flashy attraction. Were he and the housemaid in league together ? Perhaps Scotney would be able to give a ruling on the matter.

He went out to the garage, where he found Mr. Scotney occupied in cleaning one of the cars.

" Why, yes, sir," said the chauffeur, " that's right. I came in as usual at 12.15. That was the time, sir."

" Which way did you come ? "

" Through the service-door under the stairs, sir."

" Did you see Mr. Mills ? "

" No, sir ; I heard his voice in the office, sir, talking to a gentleman—to Sir Charles Hope-Fairweather, sir."

" What did you do then ? "

" I went back into the kitchen, sir."

" Was anybody there ? "

" No, sir ; Emily was in the dining-room and cook had just stepped out into the yard. Mr. Farrant was in his pantry, I think, sir."

" I see. How long did you remain in the kitchen ? "

" Well, sir, I waited about five minutes, till I thought Mr. Mills might be disengaged. I heard a car drive off, sir, and presently I saw Mr. Mills come back into the office. Then I stepped across for my orders. Mr. Mills said as the car wouldn't be wanted that afternoon, sir, so I came back to the garage—back here, sir."

Mr. Scotney wiped his hands on some cotton-waste, replaced his grease-gun upon a high shelf, and looked expectantly at Roger.

" Yes, I see," said Roger. " I see. Thank you, Scotney. There's just one thing more. You saw this lady who came with Sir Charles Hope-Fairweather ? "

" Yes, sir."

" Should you know her again ? "

" I think so, sir."

" Is this the lady ? "

Mr. Scotney again wiped his fingers and took the photograph of Lady Phyllis Dalrymple with which Roger had provided himself in town.

" This, sir ? No, sir. Nothing like the lady."

" Not ? "

" No, sir."

" Oh ! " said Roger.

Crash, crash, crash ! The whole pack of cards came tumbling and fluttering about Roger's ears.

Rout followed upon rout.

Mr. Mills, when tackled, was frank and voluble. The Archbishop ? Well, he wouldn't say that he hadn't given a hint—but there ! Mr. Sheringham would understand. The lady of the photograph ? Well, there again, Mr. Sheringham would understand. Lady Phyllis had asked him—absolutely on the Q.T.—to let her have some intimate gossip about Lord Comstock. Her ladyship was apt to get hard up, what with bridge-parties and one thing and another, and, in short, the fact was that she supplied a certain amount of society gossip to the *Morning Star*. Since the *Morning Star* was the *Daily Bugle's* chief rival, Mr. Sheringham would understand that Mr. Mills could not give her any information openly. Lady Phyllis was a very agreeable lady and had behaved generously. Of course, now that Lord Comstock was no more, the arrangement came to an end, but Mr. Mills would be greatly obliged if Roger would say no more about it. Roger, with some disgust, said that he quite understood.

So far, it seemed to be true that Mr. Mills sold information, and it was quite possibly true that he had been given the sack, but looking at the secretary's sly and complacent face, Roger did not feel that a trifle of this sort would work a man like Mills up to the point of murder.

As for " the wrong he did my mother," and all the rest of Roger's alluring motives, they were quickly disposed of. The career of Mr. Mills lay open to the day, and everything he said about himself could be (and subsequently was) confirmed in every detail from independent sources. Mr. Mills was one of four children of a highly respectable chartered accountant in Nottingham. His father and mother were both alive and prosperous. He had been educated in the ordinary way at the local grammar-school and at Nottingham University. He had then taken a course of secretarial training. He had held other posts and could show the highest references. He had entered Lord Comstock's service two years ago—and so forth and so on. Quite a little saga of the " Young Man Who Made Good."

Roger, his head not only bloody but bowed to the earth, thanked Mr. Mills. He scarcely had the strength to put a question about Emily. Mr. Mills showed no sort of embarrassment. Emily was a very steady young woman, engaged to a draper's assistant in Winborough, an excellent match for her in every way. Was there anything further Mr. Mills could do for Mr. Sheringham?

No, thanks (for it hardly seemed worth while, now, to confront Mills with the pistol). Unless—wait! A picture flashed suddenly across Roger's mind of someone he had recently seen, putting an object with ease upon a very high shelf.

" How long has Scotney been with you? "

" Scotney? Oh, about a month."

" Is that all? How do you find him? "

" Quite satisfactory."

" Where did he come from before you had him? "

Mr. Mills obligingly fetched down a file labelled " Household Staff," turned over the contents briskly, and extracted a folder.

" Here you are. Three years. Dr. Slater of Kensington. Perfectly good reference. Sober, diligent, trustworthy, superior. Why? Anything queer about Scotney? "

" Not that I know of," replied Roger, " but one likes to know what all the witnesses are like, in this kind of inquiry. Is that his letter of application? May I look? "

" Certainly."

There was nothing remarkable about the letter, except, perhaps, the handwriting.

" He writes like an educated man, doesn't he? " said Roger.

" Yes; I fancy Scotney's seen better days—like a

great many other people, these times. I sometimes catch him speaking rather above his station, too, poor devil."

" Interesting man," said Roger; " rather an interesting face, too." He scrutinized the photograph attached to the letter of application. " Looks as if he'd been up against it at some time or other. Mind if I keep this letter and photograph for a day or so ? "

" Not a bit. Let me have 'em back some time."

" And I'll just make a note of Dr. Slater's address."

" By all means."

" How did your former man come to leave you, by the way ? "

" Slight accident," replied Mills. " Not his fault in the least. Some fool or other skidded into the car, trying to get round a slippery corner at fifty miles an hour. Unfortunately, Comstock was inside the car at the time."

" Was the chauffeur hurt ? "

" Good lord, no—nobody was hurt. No damage whatever, except half an inch of paint scraped off the offside wing. But Comstock is—was—sacrosanct, you know. When he was there, accidents didn't happen. If they did, then, whether it was your fault or not—the boot for you. One always made that clear when one engaged people."

" I suppose Scotney hasn't had any accident since he came ? "

" Oh no, nothing of that kind. Did you think he might be nursing a grievance ? "

" The idea crossed my mind."

" Then you can cut it out. He has given every satisfaction."

" I see. Well, thanks very much."

On his way back to town, Roger turned his new idea

over in his mind. He could not get away from that picture of the tall chauffeur putting the grease-gun easily away on a shelf far above his, Roger's own reach. He looked once more at the letter of application. Pinned to it was the advertisement in reply to which it had been sent. Roger noticed that, contrary to the more usual custom, the address of the advertiser—Hursley Lodge— was given, instead of a Box number. Everybody in England knew who lived at Hursley Lodge.

It was rather late in the evening when Roger got to Kensington. Dr. Slater had finished his day's work and was, in fact, just sitting down to dinner. He was, however, kind enough to see Mr. Sheringham at once.

" Scotney ? " he said. " Oh, yes. An excellent servant and a most reliable man. I was very sorry to lose him, especially at a moment's notice like that. But the wages were nearly double what I could afford to give him, and I didn't want to stand in his way. I sincerely hope he's not in any trouble."

Roger sincerely hoped that he was, but made a noncommittal reply, to the effect that Scotney's employer had died suddenly, and left him out of a job.

" Can you tell me what he was doing before he came to you ? "

" As a matter of fact," replied the doctor, " I believe he had been some sort of a journalist."

" A journalist ! "

Roger's ears pricked up. Like Job's war-horse, he pawed the ground and said ha ! in the midst of the trumpets.

" He was a patient of mine," went on Dr. Slater. " At that time I had a practice in a rather poor quarter of Islington, and Scotney was on my panel. He had had a

18

very bad illness, poor chap—pneumonia, actually, but chiefly brought on by worry, semi-starvation and lack of clothes, and so on. His wife had died in child-birth just before. A very bad case. I gathered that he had been very badly treated."

Roger uttered a sympathetic croak.

"I don't know if you know anything about Fleet Street," said the doctor, "but if you do, you'll know how it can break a man's strength and heart. It was all right in the old days, I dare say, but now, these great syndicates get hold of a young, promising man, work him till he drops, squeeze his brains dry, and throw him away like a sucked lemon. I've seen it happen scores of times. It doesn't matter to them, they can always get another man. The street's full of these wrecks and ghosts—men who were pulling down their twenty, thirty, fifty pounds a week a year or two ago, and who're thankful now to pick up a few shillings to write another man's column for him. You may think I'm getting too worked up about it, but when I think of one or two good old friends of mine—well, never mind that. I was going to say that, knowing what the fate of a crocked-up journalist was likely to be, I got rather interested in Scotney. There wasn't a lot I could do for him, for I'm not a rich man by any means, but when he said he'd done with journalism and was ready to take any sort of job, I told him that, if he knew how to drive a car, he could come and drive mine. He stayed three years with me, as I told you, and then he got a chance of a job at a much better wage, so I released him at once, naturally."

"Did he tell you whose house he was going to?"

"I don't think he did. He asked me for a reference, of course, and I gave him an open letter—you know—

' to whom it may concern '—that kind. Wait a moment. Somebody rang me up on the 'phone afterwards. Who was it ? Some name like Miller, no, Mills—that was it."

" You didn't know, then, that Scotney had gone to Lord Comstock ? "

" Comstock ? the newspaper man ? No, I certainly didn't. Why, that was the man who——"

The doctor stopped abruptly, as though a hand had been clapped over his mouth.

" Who—— ? " prompted Roger.

" Who has just been murdered, I was going to say."

Roger received the impression that that was not at all what the doctor had been going to say. However, he replied :

" Yes, that's the man."

" Dear, dear," said Dr. Slater. " Poor Scotney's good job didn't last very long, then. I wonder if he would come back to me. Or—I was forgetting—perhaps you have already made your own arrangements with him, Mr.—ah—Sheringham ? "

" I haven't exactly fixed anything up yet," replied Roger, " but I'm very much interested in your account of Scotney. Is Scotney his real name, by the way ? "

Dr. Slater shot a sharp glance at him. " No, it isn't," he said, " but I'm afraid I can't tell you the real one. I only learnt it because I was his doctor, and it would be a breach of professional confidence."

" It doesn't matter," said Roger. " I just wondered, that's all. I suppose he wouldn't care to ' chauff ' under his own name, if it was at all well known."

" Probably that is so," said the doctor in a non-committal tone.

" It's funny, though," said Roger cunningly, " that

he wasn't afraid of Comstock's recognizing him—to say nothing of his old pals on the staff. He would often have to drive Comstock up to the office."

The doctor was not to be caught.

"If," he said evenly, "Scotney's duties ever did take him among his old Fleet Street pals, he would probably rely on the changes brought about by time and sickness, the disguising effect of the uniform, and the fact that people don't expect their old pals to turn up again as chauffeurs."

"No doubt you are right," said Roger. "You advise me to engage Scotney, then?"

"I can only say," replied Dr. Slater, "that I should be only too glad to take him back myself if he was available, and that nobody could wish for a better or more trustworthy servant."

Chief Inspector Moresby had hoped that his day's work was ended. It had been long and tedious. The wretched Little Cadbury case had stretched out a tentacle and drawn him in, and his head ached, and he felt heartily sick of Scotland Yard. So that when Mr. Roger Sheringham was announced at close on eight o'clock, he felt that Heaven had created too many human beings, and that Mr. Roger Sheringham was the one too many.

"Well, Mr. Sheringham," he said, making a great bustle of pulling on an overcoat and taking his bowler hat from the peg, "you've just got here in time. Two minutes more, and I should have been away to my dinner, and high time too. Perhaps you'd do me the favour of stepping along and having a bite with me."

"When you hear what I've got to say, Moresby," said Roger, "you'll forget all about your dinner. Take off that silly overcoat—you don't want one on a night like this—and take a look here."

So saying, Roger proudly pulled out the handkerchief which distended his jacket-pocket, and, unwrapping it, displayed the pistol to Moresby's astonished eyes.

" Dear me, Mr. Sheringham," said Mr. Moresby, " if that isn't yet another of 'em ! And where did you get that, if I might ask ? "

" You'll be surprised when I tell you."

" I shouldn't be surprised if I was, Mr. Sheringham. There's a lot of surprising things about this case. In fact," added Mr. Moresby in a ruminating tone, " the longer I live, the more I find that everything in this world is surprising."

" Yes, isn't it ? " said Roger, who was in no mood for philosophy.   " Is there anybody left in the finger-print department, Moresby ? "

The Chief Inspector summoned a myrmidon and instructed him to take the pistol away and examine it for finger-prints.

" This, too," said Roger, producing the photograph of Lady Phyllis Dalrymple which he had shown to Scotney. " You may find one or two of mine on it, but you needn't bother with those."

" In that case, Mr. Sheringham, you had better let us have a set of your own, for comparison.   If you were to run along with Brunton, now——"

" We'll both go along," said Roger, taking Moresby affectionately by the arm.   The Chief Inspector, seeing his dinner recede from him into a dim and hungry future, uttered a hollow groan, but yielded.

Fortunately, finger-print men are quick workers. Before very long, Roger's prints had been taken, the photograph and the pistol had been dusted with yellow powder, and photographic enlargements of all three results were laid, damp and shining, upon the table.

" H'm ! " said Moresby. " Looks as though somebody had had a shot at wiping the pistol, and not done it very thoroughly."

" That's right," said the finger-print expert. " He's cleaned the stock, but forgotten the barrel. That's a thumb, there, all right, and it isn't Mr. Sheringham's, either. Let's have a look at the lady ; easy to look at, too. Who is she ? "

Chief Inspector Moresby whistled, and darted a sly glance at Roger.

" She's nothing to do with the case," said Roger, airily. " I asked—a certain person to see if he could identify her ; but, of course, he couldn't."

" Well," said Mr. Moresby, " if you took this photograph along for the purpose of getting finger-prints off it, it's a pity you didn't think to clean it first. It's a regular what-you-call."

The photograph was, indeed, a regular palimpsest where finger-prints were concerned, but the expert was not much bothered by it.

" Here's your pistol bloke, all right," he announced, " down here in the bottom corner, quite easy to recognize. Rather an unusual pattern, with a double loop."

" You're sure of that ? " asked Roger. He was swelling with pride and joy.

" Of course I'm sure," said the finger-print man. " Quite unmistakable. Is that all ? Or do you want us to consult the Habitual Criminals' Register ? "

" No," said Roger. " I don't think you'll find him there."

" And who is he, when he's at home ? " inquired Moresby. In spite of everything, he sounded impressed.

" I don't think I'll tell you yet," said Roger. " I still have one or two links of my chain to test. I expect to have these all fixed up by the morning, and then I'll let you know."

" Very good, Mr. Sheringham. As you know, we're always ready to help. And I must say," added the Chief Inspector generously, " you've done remarkably well, sir, in finding this pistol."

" Praise from Sir Hubert is praise indeed," said Roger, much gratified. " By the way, I want to keep the pistol overnight. I'll take care of it and not rub off the evidence."

" It doesn't much matter if you do, sir, now we've got the record. Then I'll see you to-morrow, Mr. Sheringham ? "

" You will," replied Roger patronizingly, " you will. And I think you will admit, Moresby, that amateurs occasionally discover something."

Early the following morning, Roger sought the palatial building which housed the Comstock Press, and on showing his card, was wafted aloft and deposited in the office of one Mr. Blundell Theek, chief crime reporter on the *Daily Bugle*. Mr. Theek was much interested in the pistol.

" Yes," he said, " it's exactly like the one I got from Jimmy the Scrag. Funny the way they seem to keep turning up."

" How long have they been in use ? I understand that the Sussex police captured one a couple of weeks ago at Lewes races."

" Then you may be pretty sure," replied Mr. Theek, with a grin, " that they'd been in the country some time before the police got wise to it. They were about a week behind us, as they usually are, and I don't suppose we exactly took delivery at the ports."

" Say a month or so ? " suggested Roger.

" Oh yes—I dare say there were several knocking about as long ago as that."

" That's what I expected. Now, here's another thing." Roger produced the photograph of Scotney. " Disregarding the chauffeur's uniform and all that, have you ever seen that man before ? I've reason to believe he was knocking around Fleet Street some three or four years ago."

Theek glanced at the photograph, then at Roger, and then back at the photograph.

" Where did you get this ? " he asked in a changed tone.

" Never mind that," said Roger. " I see you do recognize it. Who is he ? "

Mr. Theek rang a bell without replying, and an elderly man came in.

" Dawson," said Mr. Theek, " do you know who this is ? "

" Why, of course I do," replied Dawson. " That's Mr. Hardy. I've often wondered what became of him. He's altered a good bit, but I couldn't possibly mistake him."

" That's what I thought," said Mr. Theek. " All right, Dawson, that's all we want."

" And who is Mr. Hardy ? " demanded Roger, when Dawson had retired.

" Hardy used to be in this department," replied Mr.

Theek. " He was junior crime reporter to the *Bugle* for several years, and a jolly good one, too. I knew him slightly ; I was in the news editor's office then."

" Why did he leave you ? "

" Fell down on a story," said Mr. Theek briefly. " I don't think it was altogether his fault, but there you are. You know what Comstock was. Hardy made a bad gaffe and was fired. He was in a bad state of health at the time, and that put the lid on him, and he went all to pieces. It would be—let me see—four years ago, now. He hung about Fleet Street for six months or so after that, but you know how it is. Once a man gets a name for being unreliable, he's done. Besides, he started to drink too much. Then he disappeared, and I haven't seen him since. He was a nice fellow, and a first-class journalist."

" Was he making much money ? "

" Yes, pretty good, but he spent it all. Everybody does. I'm afraid journalists are like actors—they get a good job and think it's going to last for ever. Still, you know, I always thought, between you and me, that Hardy wasn't too well treated. Northcliffe wouldn't have done it quite like that, but then those days were different. Nowadays it's catch-as-catch-can. Make a mistake and out you go—there are hundreds more ready to snap up your job. I say, Mr. Sheringham, for God's sake don't let anybody know I've said all this. I don't want to go the same way as Hardy."

" Of course not ; but there's just one thing more. Did Hardy feel any personal resentment against Comstock ? "

" It's not for me to say," said Mr. Theek, " but if I had been Comstock, I'd have hated the thought of

meeting Hardy at night, in a dark alley and armed with
a spanner."

" So should I," said Roger, " in his place. And yet,
I've got evidence that he did meet Hardy, time and
again, and showed no particular apprehension——"

" Very likely," said Theek ; " but he mightn't have
known him if he did see him. I doubt if Comstock would
know me, though I've been a good many years on the
staff. The Skipper was a great man, but he hadn't the
royal touch with him. I mean, he didn't make a point
of personally knowing everybody, from the chief sub. to
the office-boy. His slogan was, ' Show me a man's work,
and that's all I want to know about him.' I don't think
it's as good a way as the other, but it has its points and
it certainly saves time and trouble."

" He wasn't perhaps the sort of man who'd take a
friendly interest in his chauffeur, for instance ? "

" I don't suppose he'd ever look at him, unless the
fellow drove him into the ditch and he wanted to tick
him off."

" That explains quite a lot," said Roger.

" So there, Moresby, is my case," said Mr. Sheringham.
" As I see it, it works out like this. This poor devil
Hardy, cherishing his violent grievance against Comstock,
sees an advertisement for a chauffeur at Hursley Lodge.
He applies for the job, and gets it, thanks to Dr. Slater's
recommendation. He'd be interviewed by Mills, who
had certainly never seen him before, and Comstock
wouldn't take very much notice of him one way or
another. Before taking up the post, Hardy gets hold
of this handy little pistol—probably from some crook
or other whom he got to know while he was on the

crime-reporting job. He keeps it about him and bides his time.

"Then, last Tuesday, for some reason, he boiled over; or he saw what he thought was a good opportunity, when all sorts of strangers were sculling round the place. He came into the house, in the ordinary way, at 12.15. He heard Mills and Hope-Fairweather in the office, and knew that Littleton was in the drawing-room."

"How did he know that, Mr. Sheringham?"

"Well, possibly he didn't know it, but he would listen for a moment at the study door and find that all was quiet inside. Then he gently opened the door. If anybody had been there, he could always have apologized and gone away again. But he saw Comstock there alone. Possibly, when he went in, he didn't intend to kill Comstock, but only to have a row with him. But when he saw Comstock sitting there alone at his desk, he saw his opportunity and shot him dead. Then he hurriedly wiped the pistol, pushed it up on to the cornice over the door, and went innocently back to the kitchen. Emily didn't see him; she was putting the forks and spoons away in the sideboard; Mills was occupied with Hope-Fairweather; Littleton, immediately afterwards, came through the concealed door, and found Comstock's body. The whole thing needn't have taken more than a minute. And that," concluded Mr. Sheringham, "is my solution, and the finger-prints are there to prove it."

"Well, Mr. Sheringham, sir," said Chief Inspector Moresby, "that's all extremely ingenious. I think you are very much to be congratulated. It's wonderful, the way you've worked it all out so quick."

" And you think it's the truth, don't you, Moresby ? " A something in the Chief Inspector's tone rang ominously in his ears, and filled him with an odd foreboding.

" Well, Mr. Sheringham," said Chief Inspector Moresby, " as regards its being the truth——"

INTRODUCTION TO PART III

" DEAR JOHN RHODE,

" Do you remember how you propounded a Problem to fit Arthur Barker's title ? Well, here are four solutions—and each of them selects a different Murderer.

" I must say that the Solvers have been more than good-natured. Even if they have introduced a touch or two of parody, they have made their fellow - sleuths extremely ingenious. In fact it seems plain to me that each of the four solutions is the right one.

" It is true that there are some minor inconsistencies— Mr. Mills seems to pop in and out of prison, and there are some contradictory statements here and there—but in the circumstances, since the four Solvers worked on their own, in ignorance of one another's plans, this was no doubt inevitable. I have done practically no editing.

"And now what is the Correct Answer ? You, so I understand, profess not to know. I, on the other hand, dare not say that one of the four solutions is the right one ; nor have I brains enough to produce a fifth solution of my own, incontestably sounder than the others.

" Yet that obviously is my job ; and the only way by which I can do it is by taking to myself an Editorial Liberty to invent facts and to " play unfair." Yes : that is what I must do, and I must hope that our readers, justly feeling that they have been cheated, will realize the merits of the Rules to which my fellow-members of the Detection Club always, and I on all occasions but this, make it a point of honour to adhere. Perhaps they will find consolation in detecting for themselves the breaches of the Rules of which I shall proceed to be deliberately guilty.

" Yours ever,

" MILWARD KENNEDY."

PART III

"IF YOU WANT TO KNOW——"

By Milward Kennedy

MR. ANDERSON frowned at the sound of the buzzer. Slowly, reluctantly, he rose to his feet and walked through the door in the corner of the room into the Home Secretary's presence. People are prone to suppose that the private secretary of a Cabinet Minister is some young man on the threshold of his career in the Civil Service ; some, perhaps, even imagine him a kind of stenographer. They do not stop to consider the differences between a private secretary, an assistant private secretary, a secretary shorthand-typist and a personal secretary. Mr. Anderson in fact was in the early forties ; he was next but one in the department to be promoted to the rank of assistant secretary— which has nothing to do with secretaryship, but implies the control of a considerable section and perhaps a numerous staff. As private secretary, Mr. Anderson drew an allowance which, in days of a falling cost of living index (the corollary being a falling salary), was extremely welcome ; promotion, however, was in his opinion overdue and would be extremely welcome, and, apart from financial considerations, would confer this great benefit that he would no longer spend the day popping up and down, just in the middle of something that called for concentration, to answer a bell like a chambermaid in a crowded hotel.

Besides, Mr. Anderson was tired of Cabinet Ministers. They might be all very well addressing huge crowds on vague political issues—Mr. Anderson could not imagine himself making a speech—but in office they were more trouble than they were worth. If they ignored the department's advice, they got themselves and everything into a mess ; if they took it—well, they could claim very little credit. In fact, they wasted a great deal of time in wondering whether or not to take it, and in discussing the problem with their private secretaries.

Brackenthorpe was all right in his way ; quite a good sort, and up at Oxford with Anderson's eldest brother. But as an administrator—well, he simply could not get it into his head that the Home Department did things in certain ways, because those ways were best. . . .

" I thought as much," said Anderson to himself, observing that the Home Secretary had before him the file dealing with the Comstock affair. Now there was a case in point : fancy taking the whole thing out of the hands of Scotland Yard just because an Assistant Commissioner had been more or less on the scene when the thing happened.

" We don't seem much forrarder with this inquiry, Anderson," said the Home Secretary.

" We ! " thought Anderson. He made no reply.

" I—er—don't you think we ought to get the views of—er—the departments concerned ? "

" I understood it was rather urgent," said Anderson. (" What on earth is he getting at ? " he asked himself. " Only one department is concerned, and that's the

C.I.D., and that he has ruled out." He almost smiled as he wondered what the Chief Inspector of Factories would say if asked to express his views on the Comstock Inquiry.)

The Home Secretary cleared his throat and glanced at the clock on his table.

" Let's see. There's a Cabinet at eleven, isn't there ? I must be off. I tell you what, Anderson. You'd better look through this file and—er—let me know what you make of it."

" Very well, Sir Philip."

The Home Secretary cleared his throat again.

" You'll find on the file," he said, " a memorandum which I dictated. Don't—er—pay too much attention to its conclusion, which may be described as a little *jeu d'esprit*. But don't forget that it's all—er—rather— h'm—urgent."

Mr. Anderson knew perfectly well what the file contained ; he had long since read through the Home Secretary's " memorandum." He knew, too, that the Home Secretary had been on the point of reminding him that the papers were secret, and only just in time had remembered that no one was better able than the private secretary both to judge whether a paper was secret and to treat it appropriately (which does not always mean secretly) if it was.

The Home Secretary knew all this, too, and it annoyed him.

" There's been too much delay already. Much too much. These—h'm—experts ought all to have got to work at once. I gave 'em forty-eight hours——"

" But not collectively," Anderson remonstrated, in a gentle tone. " They would have fallen over one another,

19

and perhaps there would have been a couple more murders. Besides, I understood you to say ' forty-eight hours each.' "

The Home Secretary particularly disliked the reference to the possibility of further murders ; for Anderson at the beginning had protested against the " expert " idea. Mrs. Bradley, he argued, was possibly a murderess already ; Mr. Sheringham was almost certainly an accomplice after the fact ; Sir John Saumarez ("not that that is his real name ") was married to a lady who had been found guilty of murder ; and the Sunday papers had more than once linked the name of Lord Peter Wimsey . . . and, after all, his brother the Duke. . . .

" Well, it's high time——" Sir Philip began, about to repeat his complaint of delay in the inquiry.

" Yes," said Anderson, glancing at the clock and instantly assuming that the reference was to the meeting of the Cabinet ; and in a minute or two Sir Philip, escorted by his assistant private secretary, was on his way to Downing Street.

When Gambrell, the Assistant Private Secretary, returned, he found Anderson frowning over the Comstock file.

" Look here, Gambrell," he said, " he wants us to look into this. Why, God knows. It's no concern of ours. However, we've both read the papers, and I suggest that we have a bit of a conference on them. We can take his room for the rest of the morning. Miss Head can hold the fort here."

Gambrell was only an Assistant Principal, but he had some ten years' service to his credit, and was almost as well versed as Anderson in the problems of administration ; but on this occasion he was puzzled.

"How do we start?" he inquired, when the couple had adjourned to the comfort and seclusion of the adjoining room.

They sat face to face across a table at the far end of the lofty room. Anderson was tall and dark, lean-faced, with one eyebrow more uptilted than the other and consequently a permanent air of polite scepticism ; he wore a double-breasted black coat and smartly striped trousers, and outside the office might easily have been thought to belong to the staff of the Foreign Office. Gambrell, in contrast, was short and chubby, with big round spectacles ; he met the world with a stare of innocent wonder, and his rather shabby tweed suit completed the illusion that he was an overgrown schoolboy up in London for the day.

At Gambrell's remark, Anderson's eyebrows twitched into a slight frown.

"I suppose we'd better treat this just like any other file—consider the action proposed, consider whether it is warranted by the facts—and, of course, whether the facts are all stated—and then consider what the results of taking the action would probably be."

Gambrell did not dissent, though he had some doubt whether this procedure would answer very well in this particular case.

"Well?" said Anderson, discerning the doubt.

"By all means," Gambrell agreed, "only there seem to be some—well, some preliminary observations to make."

"Fire away!" said Anderson, pulling a pipe from his pocket, and looking very much more human.

"It struck me," Gambrell began, "that the experts weren't too anxious to report their findings to us."

" I should not call that an over-statement," was Anderson's comment. " If we hadn't managed to pinch Mrs. Bradley's diary, we should certainly have got nothing out of her. Lord Peter Wimsey—well, we know about him. Sir John Saumarez omitted to invite any of our people to his *séance*, and if we hadn't sent in a man in plain clothes——"

" Mr. Sheringham——" Gambrell interrupted.

" Yes, he was different. Anxious to explain his final opinions, but I gather the Yard man—yes, Moresby— had a job to get out of him all his earlier views *and* his facts."

" It really looks as if the C.I.D. have a case to go to the Treasury for extra staff for liaison duties with distinguished amateurs," Gambrell observed, smiling. But Anderson, removing his pipe from his mouth and fingering the file, recalled him to serious affairs.

" They seem between 'em to have unearthed a good many facts," said Anderson. " But as I see it none of 'em proposes action based upon all the facts. Mrs. Bradley, for instance—she comes first in the file. The chief point in her case—her real case—is that there were only two revolvers. But thanks to Mr. Sheringham we know there were three."

" Yes, but——"

" I know. The third didn't fire the shot that killed Comstock either. We know that, from the police report that came in this morning. To that extent Mrs. Bradley's theory still holds good. But if there were three, why not four ? "

" Incidentally, the police report on the third revolver seems to do in Sheringham's theory. They say it was two months or so since it was last fired—quite apart from the fact that this particular bullet wasn't fired by it."

" Let's stick to Mrs. Bradley, shall we ? " Anderson demanded. Gambrell shrugged his shoulders.

" I think we shall have to take things out of the order in which they happen to be in the file," he protested stubbornly.

" As you like," said Anderson, obviously convinced that the concession was foolish ; but then the whole business had been so irregularly handled.

" Why not consider first who's cleared by the various inquiries, and who is not ? " Gambrell boldly proposed. " And begin with the Home Secretary—in theory he seems to have confessed to the murder."

" Plainly ridiculous," Anderson said severely. " First of all, this business about the pistol being sent through the post, loaded——"

" There *are* people who break the rules of the Post Office," Gambrell mildly suggested.

" Idiot ! I didn't mean that. But who ever heard of a butler handing a parcel to the Home Secretary in person just because it was marked Personal and Private and Urgent and all the rest ? Aren't those precisely the parcels which are always opened by a third party ? "

Gambrell nodded.

" The fact is, the public imagine that a Cabinet Minister has to keep his own secrets," the Principal Private Secretary was off upon his favourite hobby-horse. His Assistant was hard put to it to unseat him, mainly by referring to the obvious ease with which criminals could dispose of Home Secretaries if Home Secretaries and their butlers really behaved like that.

" Quite so. And in the next place there's this business

about a single-handed trip to a by-election. Appar
ently some extraordinary kind of lunch-hour gathering,
too. *We* know, my dear Gambrell, that Brackenthorpe
didn't go off by himself like that, and never does. The
chauffeur took queer, and all that nonsense. Really, the
public. . . ."

" The less said about motor-cars the better, in these
days of economy," said Gambrell. " If the Press got
to hear about the carryings-on of the Cabinet, they'd
shout louder than ever for *us* to have our pay docked!"

" Anyhow," Anderson went on, resuming his pipe,
" we know that the Home Secretary's story is absurd."
He struck a match. " And all that that implies," he
added softly. " Accordingly, we wash out the Home
Secretary. Who's next, in order of precedence ? "

" The Archbishop should have come first, I fancy ? "
Gambrell answered.

" The Archbishop is obviously cleared," Anderson
pronounced, " Wimsey does that—all that stuff about
the bleeding. Mills saw the Archbishop off, then came
back and found Hope-Fairweather polishing the parquet ;
then Hope-Fairweather went—and about the same time
Littleton found the blood still running. The Archbishop
is indubitably innocent."

Gambrell agreed that that was so. " But all the same,"
he demanded, " why that story he—or his chaplain—
told Sheringham ? "

" Isn't that pretty plain ? "

" Is it ? That lie about business with Canon Pritchard,
when the Canon wasn't in Winborough at all at the time."

" Don't you see, my dear Gambrell ? The Archbishop
knew he was in a bit of a fix, or thought he was. As we
know from the servants' evidence, he did have the hell

of a row with Comstock. And then Sir John Saumarez
fairly picked on him—professional jealousy, if you ask me.
And after that *séance*—mind you, Sir John produced no
real evidence, but I daresay he reconstructed the interview up to a point——"

"You mean that Anselm Medium went home and got
his chaplain to fake up a good story ? "

"Yes. And it *was* a good story—all that about the
signed article. Just the kind of thing the Archbishop
would have liked to pull off."

Anderson laughed, and Gambrell followed suit.

"Pretty cool, wasn't it ? To produce a letter which
you haven't posted as proof that you're telling the truth
about an interview to which the letter refers ? That was
what made me wonder. . . . But I agree with you,
Anderson. Wimsey has cleared the Church."

Anderson awaited the next candidate for clearance.

"Littleton," Gambrell announced.

"Pity we've washed out the Home Secretary," said
Anderson, knocking out his pipe crossly into the waste-
paper basket, and then stooping to prevent a con-
flagration. "His evidence cleared Littleton."

"Incidentally, that was another weak point in his
story," Gambrell observed. "He said he stood there
staring at the window, and though he saw Littleton, he
never saw Hope-Fairweather. Yet Hope-Fairweather
must have been in full view when he came to the drawer
of the desk. Look at the plan."

"Besides which, is it credible that Brackenthorpe
continued to stare for a long enough time for Hope-
Fairweather and Littleton to go and get their cars and
drive out of the grounds ? But don't let us waste time.
We've washed out the Home Secretary."

His tone suggested satisfaction at the performance.

" By the way, about this plan of Hursley Lodge,"
Gambrell pursued another side track. " There's no
scale, but according to Wimsey, it's only thirty feet
from the window to the wall."

" Well ? Pretty small, I know, but——"

" It's true there's no scale——" Gambrell went on.

" And yet the Home Secretary preferred to rely upon
the local police, who produced the plan," the other
interrupted.

" Yes. But—well, I think Wimsey guessed at the
distance from the size of the room. What he *ought* to
have done, if he hadn't time to measure, was to judge
by the garage. Ten foot wide, at least ; which adds
ten foot to the distance from window to garden
wall."

Anderson fidgetted impatiently with the file.

" I was only going to say," Gambrell persevered,
" that I don't believe that a bullet fired from one of those
little pistols would still be rising at forty feet, which
further disproves the Home Secretary's story."

" One theory at a time," Anderson requested, " or
since you prefer it so, one person at a time. Littleton's
next, I think."

" I must admit," said Gambrell slowly, " that I don't
quite see how to clear him conclusively. We'd better
look into the various time-tables——"

" No, no. Not yet. Put him on a list of Judgment
Suspended."

" Mills, too, in that case."

" If you like. It seems most improbable that he did
the trick. I mean to say, to choose a time when the
house was crawling with people——"

" You don't think that may have been the very reason ? "

Anderson frowned.

" Gambrell, you've been reading detective stories. You can't put down Mills, because Wimsey surely has cleared him. Yes ; here we are. Either Littleton or Mills is cleared. If Littleton's story is true, that the blood was still flowing when he went into the study, then Mills can't possibly be guilty of Comstock's murder. On the other hand, if Littleton is lying—but I don't see what possible motive he can have unless he's guilty himself."

" In either case, then, Mills is innocent," Gambrell said, but he did not look altogether satisfied. " I suppose Wimsey is right about Mills ? "

" It's a matter of time-table," Anderson replied. " A good many of the details which are down on one list or another are more or less irrelevant—at this stage. I assume twelve-sixteen, as per Wimsey, for the time when Littleton found the bleeding corpse—that seems to be about right, whichever way you look at it. Now there's a brief space of time, twelve-eleven to twelve-twelve, or say twelve-twelve and a half, when Mills was alone. But if he'd done the shooting then, the wound would not have been bleeding at twelve-sixteen. I wonder, though. If we assume another half-minute error in Wimsey's time-table and put Littleton's entry at twelve-fifteen and a half—that's three minutes. I wonder whether the blood would flow as long as that ? "

" Matter for the experts ? " Gambrell suggested.

" Yes. But assuming it to be possible, it seems to me more likely that Hope-Fairweather than Mills did the shooting."

" I don't see that."

" It's just that Mills knew that Littleton ought to be
in the drawing-room. If he really looked in and didn't
see him, it seems to me incredible that he would have
then and there risked everything—with an Assistant
Commissioner of Police loose somewhere, but Mills
wouldn't have known where, on the premises."

" If he's lying—if he did see Littleton in the drawing-
room ? "

" In that case, would he have gone, the second after
he'd shot Comstock, to interview Hope-Fairweather ?
One unwelcome visitor had already walked in un-
announced into the study that morning—and that really
is the strongest argument of all, it seems to me, for
Mills's innocence."

Gambrell still looked a little uncertain.

" Well, if you still aren't convinced, put down Mills
with Littleton on your ' Still Suspected ' list ; but I
insist that you put an asterisk against his name, to
indicate ' Highly Improbable.' Now who's next ? "

" I suppose it ought to be Hope-Fairweather. But
after what you've just said—about the time-table
ruling him out unless there's a fairly substantial error
in it——"

" I don't deny that there may be. It's pretty difficult
to estimate to a second how long it took Mills to see the
Archbishop off, for example."

" Still, before we tackle him, how about the unknown
lady ? "

" Mrs. Arbuthnot, you mean. Well ? "

" There's this much to be said against her, Anderson,
that the easiest way to have shot Comstock was from
outside."

" Nonsense," said Anderson. " Shot in the *left* temple
—the ' inside ' one, so to call it ! "

" Yes, but obviously if a lady appeared at the window,
Comstock would have turned towards her. . . . Re-
member the marks of a lady's shoes outside the window ?
Mrs. Bradley found them, or Mrs. Bradley's girl friend."

Anderson laughed, all " man-of-the-world-with-more-
experience-than-you-my-young-friend."

" Quite a number of ladies walked on Comstock's
grass from time to time," he said. " But that's only
one point. The other is about the temple. When I
read that someone has been struck on the temple, *I* always
mean right on the side of the head. You know, ' going
grey on the temples,' and so on. I dare say that technic-
ally the temple includes the forehead above the eye ;
but at all events I made inquiries in this case—the bullet
entered the side of the head, from the side. That clear ?
Very well : then whoever shot Comstock wasn't standing
face to face with him. And I really don't see him making
a point of presenting his profile to a lady who appeared
from nowhere outside his window."

" *All* right," Gambrell agreed hurriedly. " All the
same, there's some funny stuff about Hope-Fairweather
and his lady friends. All this about Lady Phyllis
and——"

" I don't see it, Gambrell. The story which Sheringham put together may very well be true. I imagine
that Hope-Fairweather dined with his niece by marriage
before he went on to the party where he met Lady
Phyllis. I imagine that Mr. Mills was ' acting a lie '
when he let Mrs. Bradley assume that his affair—oh,
perhaps only an affair of business—had been with a
typist. And I can quite understand that Lady Phyllis

was thoroughly upset when she heard that her dear Sir Charles was mixed up in the Hursley Lodge business—either because he'd been there with an unknown female *or* because Mills obviously wasn't above a bit of quiet blackmail."

"That's all very well," Gambrell objected, "but remember that Hope-Fairweather's companion was only his deceased wife's niece. To suggest that Lady Phyllis would have been jealous——"

"It's not an important point," Anderson admitted, refilling his pipe. "But it's pretty plain that Hope-Fairweather's journey—or its purpose—was a thing he would want to keep quiet from Lady Phyllis. Mrs. Arbuthnot, *qua* Pytchley, may be a desirable relative, but if Comstock was blackmailing her . . . On the other hand, the news that Hope-Fairweather had been to Hursley Lodge and *might* have heard something from Mills would upset Lady Phyllis pretty thoroughly. It seems to me that both of 'em had good reason for being a bit secretive."

"I see that," said Gambrell slowly. "You think it's certain, then, that Mrs. Arbuthnot didn't do the shooting?"

"No, I won't go so far as that—yet. In my opinion, we can't consider her without considering Hope-Fairweather's story. And the Home Secretary's."

"What, again?"

"I'm afraid so," Anderson answered; his smile was not so much apologetic as self-satisfied. "Let's consider Hope-Fairweather's story. But before we do that, tell me what is the outstanding quality in a good Chief Whip?"

Gambrell considered the riddle for a few seconds.

" Tact," he ventured.

" Right ! " said the more experienced Anderson, " Without a doubt. Tact. Ability to handle awkward people and awkward situations without having a row."

" I don't see——"

" No need to see. Just keep it in mind. Now for Hope-Fairweather's story. Short and sharp, wasn't it ? He burst into the study. Comstock staring out of the window. ' Hullo ! ' says Comstock, civilly enough, to a man he hardly knows. And more or less next second he falls down, all over his chair, and somehow gets himself underneath it. Hope-Fairweather doesn't give him a thought or a glance. Just pinches the papers and hops it. That a fair summary ? "

" I think so," Gambrell said, with a nod.

" To my mind it was a devilish risky story to tell— or thing to do."

" You mean you think Hope-Fairweather did the shooting, and this story was the best he could think of, to try to clear himself ? "

" No, I don't think that. I'm inclined to think either that Hope-Fairweather never went into the room at all, or that he was actually there, as he says, when Comstock was shot."

Gambrell looked at Anderson with a puzzled expression.

" Aren't you contradicting yourself just as Wimsey did ? You know, the time-table was supposed to show that if Littleton is telling the truth about the flowing blood, then Sir Charles can't have done the shooting."

" Ah, but I'm prepared to show a margin of error in the time-table. In fact, I don't see any way out of that— unless you're prepared to believe either that Hope-Fairweather hasn't got back the documents, whatever they were, or that some kind friend sent them back to him afterwards. I don't see Mills doing that—and I don't see who else could have done."

" Farrant," Gambrell suggested.

Anderson shrugged his shoulders.

" Possibly, but extremely doubtful. He would have had to do it immediately after he discovered that Comstock was dead, and before he gave the alarm. It isn't likely that his first thought would have been for Mrs. Arbuthnot's papers, whatever they were. Of course, if Farrant is the murderer—but we'll come to that later. Let's get back to Hope-Fairweather."

" I must say," said Gambrell, " that if Hope-Fairweather's story isn't true—or rather, if he isn't the murderer—I don't see why he should have told the story. It would be going out of his way to implicate himself."

" Mightn't he have a motive for that ? "

" Don't ask me," said Gambrell. " I'm arguing on the other side."

" My dear Gambrell, you can't have thought things out. To begin with, remember that Hope-Fairweather did not produce his story when first he was summoned by our Chief to his august presence. At that time he had no idea where he stood, or what the police knew, or even what had happened. But after that things began to get awkward. Sir John had a go at Miss Hope-Fairweather ; and Lord Peter Wimsey made a set at Sir Charles himself—but in doing so made it clear that he had at least half an eye upon the Lady in the Car."

" Well ? "

Anderson did not answer at once ; he was having trouble with his pipe.

"My dear fellow," he resumed, at length, "just think of Hope-Fairweather's story. He gets in, unannounced. Comstock is standing by the window. He's supposed to say 'Hullo,' and be quite nice—which seems improbable. In any case he obviously would turn and face the newcomer. Hope-Fairweather might walk straight towards him or he might go towards the desk; I'm sure he wouldn't walk towards the wall by the window."

"Sorry, Anderson, I don't see——"

"You must. If Comstock was facing the door to the office when he was shot, he was facing pretty well northwest. In which case the shot was fired from the southwest—from some way to the right of where the word 'wall' appears on the plan."

"Very well. But still I don't see——"

"Just keep it in mind. In the second place, don't you think it a bit unconvincing, the way Comstock is supposed to have just 'slithered to the floor,' yet managed to knock over the chair and get himself more or less underneath it? And thirdly" (Anderson went on hurriedly, since Gambrell manifested a tendency to mutter "I don't see"), "d'you think that Hope-Fairweather, or anyone else, *could* watch even Comstock fall in a heap and make *no* attempt to see what was the matter?"

"Perhaps he *did*——" Gambrell began.

"So I think. And when he realized that Comstock had been *shot* he decided not to give the alarm. . . . *That's* just the difference—you might or might not call for help, but you certainly would not, so to speak, ignore the fellow's collapse."

"Yes, but I don't——"

" Oh, for the Lord's sake don't say that again. Just listen to me. What happened, I suggest, was this. Hope-Fairweather went down with Mrs. Arbuthnot to try to get back the papers, whatever they were. He proposed to exercise his celebrated tact ; Mrs. Arbuthnot made it plain enough that she didn't think tact would do the trick. Very well : Hope-Fairweather was a bit uneasy about her—insisted on stopping the car out of sight of the house and on leaving her in it. He's shown into the waiting-room, and waits there—hears the Archbishop's departure, hesitates, and finally decides to enter unannounced. The decision takes him a minute or two, and when he *does* go in, or perhaps even as he's opening the door, Comstock's shot."

Gambrell gave signs of a desire to interrupt ; Anderson frustrated his objection.

" Hope-Fairweather hadn't seen who did the shooting, but he made sure Comstock was dead and he pinched the papers, as he admitted, and he cleared out as quickly as he could. Tact again—tact for his own career. He found Mrs. Arbuthnot back in the car, and off he drove, with nothing said on either side, so to speak. The next thing is, he's asked to come over to the Home Office. He tells his ' I-know-nothing ' story—only to come up against the fact that the police know he had a lady with him. Obviously, he wonders how they know that— guesses that the fair Betty did *not* stay in the car all the time. After the interview he tackles Brackenthorpe— in the House, most likely—and extracts another fact or two—the slightly upward course of the bullet, for instance. On the other hand, Brackenthorpe suggests that the lady did the shooting, and sees that Hope-Fairweather has his doubts about her.

"No doubt they both agree that the less said the better, but at the same time they fix up more or less between them the story which Hope-Fairweather is to tell *if* by any chance there's a serious likelihood of a charge being brought against Mrs. Arbuthnot. Its chief and subtle point is this—that if Comstock was standing up when he was shot, then Mrs. Arbuthnot, from the garden, a much lower level, couldn't possibly have done the shooting. That's the essential point of the story. Its other implication was, I should think, not intended— I mean that to fire the shot at the suitable angle, laterally, Mrs. Arbuthnot would have had to walk right past the study window, towards the kitchen garden——"

Gambrell pondered this theory.

"Hope-Fairweather was taking a risk, on his own account, all the same," he persisted, "if he invented the story about being in the room when Comstock was shot."

"Not particularly." Anderson spoke in his most matter-of-fact tone. "Not if the Home Secretary promised him that he would make sure that it would be all right. And when Wimsey came along, the Home Secretary was as good as his word. He produced a story which satisfied Wimsey."

Anderson paused and laughed.

"I dare say that what inspired our gallant chief," he went on, "was Wimsey's suggestion that the calling-in of the experts was the Home Secretary's way of bottling the whole thing up. It suggested, don't you see, that Wimsey was quite prepared to be bottled up himself. In fact, he made it pretty obvious to Hope-Fairweather— who obviously rang up Brackenthorpe immediately after Wimsey's visit—and later to Brackenthorpe, too, that

20

his sympathies were wholly with the man—or woman—
who shot Comstock."

"That seems to hold together. But what about the
lateral angle from which the shot was fired, if Hope-
Fairweather's story was true ? "

"Oh, that. Yes. Don't you see, Gambrell, that that
is yet another argument against Brackenthorpe's story
being true ? He said he had a sudden idea of calling on
Comstock on his way to Winborough. The angle of the
bullet's flight, according to Hope-Fairweather, means
that Brackenthorpe's car should have stopped almost at
the far end of Comstock's property, pretty well behind
the trees there, and not square with the window. He'd
surely have pulled up before that ; and so, according to
the policeman's story, he did. By the way, don't forget
that he had had this plan to study—I'm sure he's never
in his life been to Comstock's house at all."

"Very well," Gambrell said, as the other paused and
relit his pipe. "Wash out Hope-Fairweather *and* Mrs.
Arbuthnot—no, wait. If Hope-Fairweather's lying, she
may have done it after all."

"Shot Comstock while her uncle, so far as she knew,
was practising his famous tact in the self-same room, and
strolled away past the gardener and into the car, all by
the time her uncle got back ? No, I don't see it. Much
more likely she began to go to the study window, out
of restless curiosity, saw Littleton in the drawing-room,
and thought better of it. In any case, how could she get
hold of a peculiar revolver ? The fourth in the case,
that would be. No, I say, cross her off and consider the
next possible suspect."

"Scotney's clear—though there *are* his finger-prints
on the third revolver."

" Weeks since it was fired."

" I know. But how the devil—or why—did the revolver come to be where Sheringham found it ? "

" Well," said Anderson slowly, " here's a theory—no more than that. Suppose Hardy, alias Scotney, came into the house at twelve-fifteen, as he says, and suppose he tells the truth up to, say, a bit after twelve-twenty."

" More time-tables," Gambrell groaned.

" I know. I start now with the assumption that Lord Peter correctly decided the time of the Archbishop's departure, and that Comstock was shot at about—well, I put it at about twelve-fifteen and a half just now. In any case, the time was virtually *before* Scotney came into the house—there's Emily's evidence to that. I suggest that Scotney went into the study at about twelve-twenty, with his pistol in his pocket ; he may always carry it— bandits and that—or he may have got all worked up to finish off Comstock. Most likely the latter ; and then he finds Comstock dead, and he loses his head a bit. I gather he's a nervous sort of chap—his life-history shows that. He feels he must get rid of the pistol at once, so he gives it a hasty wipe over and pushes it up into the cornice-affair, and then he just steps quietly out again. Emily had finished putting away the silver by twelve-twenty, by the way. Anyhow, Scotney goes to Mills for his orders, Mills being back in his office by, say, twelve-twenty-two, and then gets on with his job in the ordinary way."

" And Scotney never recovers the revolver ? "

" No. On my theory he knew Comstock was dead. He didn't give the alarm—naturally enough, if he had meant to kill him himself. He'd slip away and lie low—

as soon as he'd seen Mills—hoping that the weapon wouldn't be found, or that he'd get a chance, before it was found, to get rid of it. But of course the place was full of police as soon as the murder was reported—he's never had a really safe chance."

" And, as you say, there are his nerves. Yes, I think that is fully endorsed. I suppose you'd argue that as an ex-crime expert of the Comstock Press it's not astonishing that he had one of those revolvers."

" Comstock, I imagine, got his specimen through his undischarged expert, so why shouldn't a discharged expert get one ? "

" I'll give you Scotney," said Gambrell generously. " And that brings us—let's see—to Farrant the butler— Briggs the gardener—Emily—and the cook was about the place too, I fancy."

" No," Anderson pronounced, " you must give me all of them."

" Expound."

" Why, even if Farrant and the cook and Emily were all in a sort of gunpowder plot, none of them could conceivably have risked crossing the passage with Mills showing out the Archbishop, and with the knowledge that at any moment another visitor might be shown into the study. As for Briggs—no, that's almost as unbelievable. Remember, he saw a lady wandering about the garden."

" Why not suspect the servants, in spite of the crowd on the premises ? You're prepared to suspect Littleton, and what applies to Farrant applies to him——"

" Psychology, my dear Watson. An Assistant Commissioner of Police knows that he isn't a suspicious character, just because he's Assistant Commissioner of Police.

The same can't be said of a butler. Especially a butler who's already left one bullet in the study wall."

There was a short silence.

" Then it comes to this," said Gambrell, " that there's only Littleton left on our List of Possibles."

Anderson shrugged his shoulders.

" I didn't say so," he said. " I'm quite prepared to believe that Comstock was shot from outside, and that he was sitting down when he was shot. Sitting in his chair and facing just about south-west——"

" With his back to the writing-desk," Gambrell remarked scornfully. " What earthly reason——"

" Keep calm," Anderson begged. " If only you had allowed me to go through the file in the regular way, you wouldn't have lost sight of several essential facts."

" What are they ? "

" You've forgotten the thing which Mills forgot. And you've not observed that by proving the Home Secretary a liar, we've proved that one of his subordinates is, too."

" Oh, hell ! I told you that Littleton——" Gambrell began ; at which moment the door opened and Miss Head half entered.

" Sir Philip's just rung up," she said. " He wants you to go round at once, Mr. Gambrell——"

Gambrell swore again, and hurried from the room. Anderson took up the telephone and requested the Exchange to get him on to Major Littleton, at his house.

.   .   .   .

" So you've been into it, have you, Anderson ? " the Home Secretary asked. He had had a good morning— the Cabinet had shown itself readier to listen to him than to the President of the Board of Trade, and on top of that he had had an excellent lunch. " And you have come to the conclusion that I ought to see Major Littleton ? "

" Yes," said Mr. Anderson.

" H'm. And you say that he wants to see me ? "

" Yes," said Mr. Anderson again.

Sir Philip found a space on his blotter which was comparatively free from geometrical design. He frowned at his rhomboid, wishing that his private secretary would be a little more forthcoming, without having to have his opinions dragged out of him. But what could one expect of a Civil Servant ?

" You said something about self-contradictory statements made by the police, didn't you, just now, Anderson ? I think you had better tell me rather more of what you have in mind."

" I said the authorities," Anderson corrected him.

The Home Secretary looked up quickly, and half fancied (but it seemed incredible) that he had caught Anderson smiling to himself at his remark.

" Go on," Sir Philip told him testily.

" I am unable to accept, sir, the statements made by or attributed to the police-constable who was knocked down by Major Littleton's car and who is still in hospital."

" Oh ! "

Sir Philip's pencil stopped abruptly in mid-tracery.

" I don't so much mean his first alleged statement. You may recollect " (he fancied that Sir Philip would do nothing of the kind; he never read a file carefully) " that he is supposed to have said to his wife, " I was on my right side."

" Well ? Go on."

" If he was bicycling *towards* Winborough, then he certainly was on his right side—but was he ? "

" I really don't know."

The Home Secretary sounded impatient. His secretary no longer concealed his smile.

" You ought to, Sir Philip. The man is also alleged to have said that he rode past your car. Now you, sir— this, of course, is pure theory—stopped your car and stood on the running-board and looked over the wall at Lord Comstock."

" That's the idea—but as I told you, you needn't take the *whole* of my—er—confession seriously."

" I don't, Sir Philip, any of it " (at which Sir Philip raised his eyebrows), " but if you *had* done what you say in your memorandum, you, being also bound for Winborough, would have stopped on—as it were—your wrong side of the road ; on the right-hand side, the way you were going."

" Obviously."

" The constable's second story is—or is alleged to be —that he drew out to pass your car and just then you drove on ; and before he could get back to his proper side, out of Lord Comstock's drive came first one and then another car, each on its wrong side, and so he never got back to his own side of the road."

" Well ? "

" I could perhaps swallow that if you hadn't been going in the opposite direction to the constable. But since he wasn't really ' passing ' you but meeting you, obviously he had time and space to get back to his proper side. For that matter," Anderson added thoughtfully, " I should have expected you to go outside him, over to your left."

Anderson paused, but the Home Secretary made no comment. He seemed to be absorbed again by his blotter-drawings.

"I would add two comments, Sir Philip. First of all, in so far as your and Sir Charles's stories fit together, they suggest that your car was standing well out towards the end of the Hursley Lodge grounds, and not bang opposite the study window ; so that the story of the two cars dashing out on the wrong side of the road wears very thin. In the second place——" he hesitated.

"Go on," Sir Philip's voice sounded sorrowful, rather than angry.

"We know you weren't there at all," Anderson continued, "and therefore the policeman's story won't do at all."

"Unless there was another car, not mine, and another man, not me, peering over. . . ."

Anderson shook his head.

"No ? " said Sir Philip.

"No, sir. I don't think so. You see, this second statement of the constable's wasn't heard of till after Lord Peter Wimsey had been to see Sir Charles Hope-Fairweather. Of course, it might be difficult to trace the telephone call from Sir Charles's house to yours, but there would be no such difficulty over your toll call to the Winborough police-station."

The point of Sir Philip's pencil broke. Anderson was satisfied that he need not in fact request the London Telephone Service to give details of the call; he was sure now that it had been made, and that was enough.

"A career of crime requires a great deal of planning," said Anderson. The Home Secretary smiled, remembering how he had battered the President of the Board of Trade, the ceaseless advocate of National Plans.

"I was a little hasty," he admitted, "but I could not resist the temptation of arranging an interruption of Wimsey's slumbers, in exchange for the bad night he had given Hope-Fairweather and me."

"Very well then," Anderson resumed briskly. "We now know that the constable's second story wasn't his story at all, but a fake."

"Which leaves us with the first story, that he was on his right side—on the left of the road—and going towards Winborough."

"Not necessarily, sir. It is quite a common thing for people to pronounce the ' y ' in ' my ' like—er—like the ' i ' in ' this.' Consequently ' my right ' and ' the right ' frequently sound very much alike. And in this case the words are supposed to have been the constable's first utterance on his recovery of consciousness."

"Please go on, Anderson. This philology is most interesting, but——"

"The man *was* bicycling from Winborough, not to it, and he *was* on the wrong side of the road when Major Littleton crashed into him ; Major Littleton being on his proper side, and at the same time no blame attaching to the policeman."

"But if he was on the wrong side——"

"He was there in the execution of his duty."

"Major Littleton is here," said Gambrell, poking his head round the door in the corner.

. . . .

"Certainly, Sir Philip," said Major Littleton. "It was obvious to me from the start that the all-important witness was the constable. I hadn't actually got the

Green Bicycle Case in mind, but, of course, the two affairs are almost exactly similar. In this case, the peculiar feature was, I think, that the ground rises inside the hedge of the property opposite Hursley Lodge, so that the lad who was fooling about with his air-rifle, calibre ·15, happened to have a clear field of fire right over the road, into Comstock's study.

" Of course the constable didn't realize what the effect of the shot had been ; he merely warned the boy—in other words, gave him a telling-off—for loosing off across a public highway. But, in fact, he actually saw the shot fired which polished off Comstock."

There was an uncomfortable silence. The Home Secretary felt that an apology was expected of him, but he did not feel in the mood to give it. After all, Littleton had been behaving most indiscreetly when the accident happened, and no one would have expected Comstock to be shot by accident, by a boy of fourteen, home from school, convalescent from mumps, and fooling about with an air-rifle that was anything but a toy.

" I don't know why I wasn't told——"

" You hardly gave me—or the C.I.D. as a whole—much opportunity."

Sir Philip was not finally defeated yet.

" I suppose you refer to my handing over the inquiries to other persons. In that connection, haven't my instructions been disregarded ? You say it has been established that the bullet was fired from this air-rifle. . . ."

" As to that, I would remind you that the C.I.D. were only—suspended—while the amateurs had their forty-eight hours. And I may add that the instructions to the local police to take the constable's statement, now that he is able to talk properly and freely, and subsequently to examine the bullet and the air-rifle came direct from the Home Office. From Anderson, I believe."

There was another pause. Major Littleton felt that his last remarks had sufficiently recognized that if it had not been for Anderson he himself would never have realized how intelligent as well as humane he had been to take such care of the injured constable.

" If I may say so," he went on, determined to get a little of his, and the C.I.D.'s, own back, " Anderson was extremely wise to realize that in a matter of this kind, it is usually advisable—well, to ask a policeman."

.   .   .   .

" Not a doubt about it," Anderson was telling Gambrell. "Of course I didn't know what the policeman would say. I merely came to the conclusion that very likely the shot had been fired from outside, but not by Briggs, or Betty, or Brackenthorpe, and from a rather greater distance—which, of course, implied a different sort of weapon. Then I saw that there was a bank the other side of the road, and a point more or less level with the study window where there were no trees between the study and the bank. And then I saw that the place where the policeman was knocked over wasn't far off that line—and it struck me that it might do no harm to find out what the policeman really had to say about it. In a way it was a forlorn hope, for if he'd seen anything sensational he'd surely have reported it when he came to, and was fully himself again ; and then it struck me that he might not realize what a sensational thing he had seen. At all events it seemed to me to be —to put it mildly—worth while passing on the hint to

Littleton. . . . After all, that was the *regular* thing to do." Gambrell sighed.

" I very nearly spotted it this morning," he said. " I was just getting there when you put me off by saying that there was something which both Mills and I forgot."

" Put you off ? That ought to have helped you. Just think again of the order of events, with the times, accurate or approximate, omitted. Exit Archbishop. Pause. Enter Hope-Fairweather—and at that moment Comstock swings round, away from the Chief Whip, in his revolving chair. Never even sees Hope-Fairweather, I fancy. And at that very second—over he goes, chair and all."

" But the noise—there were only two crashes, and the second was Hope-Fairweather's tray of papers."

" Who says there were only two ? Mills was at the front door when Comstock was shot. Littleton apparently never heard the first crash ; why should he hear the second ? Or if he heard it, he thought nothing of it. The butler and cook had moved on, after the Archbishop's departure. Only Hope-Fairweather heard it."

" According to the time-table——"

" Yes, but I'm pretty sure the intervals given on the famous time-table are too long. Hope-Fairweather was in the hell of a hurry—Comstock was dead, he had got his precious papers, dear Betty was outside in the car— he didn't spend three minutes murmuring polite nothings to a fellow like Mills."

Gambrell grunted.

" And what did I forget ? " he asked.

" The reason why Comstock's left temple was just nicely placed for the bullet."

" Obviously he was swinging round towards the office door."

"Obviously not. He'd have swung to his left, and if the bullet had hit him it would have been somewhere in the back of his head. No, I'm sure he never saw or heard the office door open—or just thought it was Mills, and paid no attention."

"Give it up," said Gambrell.

"What would Comstock naturally do after the Archbishop had gone? After they had had a furious row, in which Comstock had refused to give up his Antichurch stunt? Why, ring up his blessed newspaper, of course, and tell 'em to go for the Church harder than ever, say how he had handled the Archbishop. . . ."

There was a pause.

"Farrant corrected Mills, because he said he had touched nothing in the study. Farrant pointed out that he had stood by the window telephoning. . . . The private telephone, to the Comstock Press, stood on the window ledge behind Comstock's chair, and Comstock was swinging round, to his right, to pick it up. . . ."

Mr. Anderson frowned at the sound of the buzzer. Slowly, reluctantly, he rose to his feet, and walked, through the door in the corner of the room, into the Home Secretary's presence. . . .

Mr. Gambrell remained seated at his desk, a humbler variety of Mr. Anderson's, and stared through his big, round, steel spectacles, at the fireplace. He wore a worried air.

"All very nice," he thought to himself, "and there's no reason why it shouldn't be true. But there's only one thing that *makes* it true, and that's the fact that the markings on the bullet show that it came from that air-gun. Apart from that—no, there's really nothing. I imagine that the injured constable has told the truth, and that he did see the boy fire the rifle—it doesn't follow that the bullet hit Comstock; the constable doesn't assert that, either.

"Wait a minute, though. Is there no reason to disbelieve Anderson's story? The essential, final proof is a thing about which we have to take the expert's word. Might not the expert—in the public interest and all the rest of it—make a deliberate mistake about the bullet markings if the alternative was to put the police generally—and the Assistant Commissioner in particular —in a very awkward position?

"And after all *if* Hope-Fairweather did actually see Comstock shot, and if Littleton only went into the study when Anderson and the rest say he did, it seems to be a toss-up whether the wound could still have been bleeding then.

"If it wasn't the boy with the air-rifle, who could it be but Littleton—with a fourth revolver in his possession of which no one knew but himself? How simple, to reveal the one which did *not* fire the shot, and to get rid of the other; simpler than Mrs. Bradley's ingenious ' faking ' of the barrel and hammer—though even that was surely something more than a ' detective-story notion,' for, after all, an Assistant Commissioner of Police has a specialized knowledge. . . ."

Gambrell's gaze, still worried and unhappy, left the mantelpiece and travelled to his own desk. What was the use of his spectacles? Thank goodness, it was no concern of his. Anderson had certainly been right when he insisted upon handing the inquiry back to the police at the earliest opportunity. If you couldn't go to the police in a case like this, well, where were you? When in doubt, whatever you want to know—and in this instance it was certain that the police *did* know, though whether they would tell. . . .

Gambrell's eye lit up. His sorrow vanished. He had caught sight of a bulky file, on the top of his ' in ' tray. He seized it and opened it. Yes, there was the paper which he had been trying to collect for the past week, and which it was so important that the Home Secretary should see at once. With no further thought for the tragedy at Hursley Lodge he plunged into a topic which concerned and therefore interested him—the Department's proposals as to the attitude to be adopted by His Majesty's Government towards certain proposals for the provision of rest and alternation of shifts in automatic glass works where work is continuous.

The buzzer sounded twice. Mr. Gambrell frowned, and slowly and reluctantly rose to his feet. . . .

FINAL NOTE

I SHOULD like to testify that all my collaborators not only have been most indulgent towards me, but have been scrupulously fair, and have not wanted to know too much. Miss Sayers has been something more than indulgent, inasmuch as she agreed, at my urgent request, that Roger Sheringham should not show much interest in the police-constable who alone, as I became convinced, could rescue me from my difficulties. This explains why that ingenious gentleman overlooked a point which did not escape Lord Peter Wimsey.

MILWARD KENNEDY.